Jak felt the earth ripple beneath him

"Ryan..."

"I feel it," the one-eyed man gritted, helping Mildred through the gap. "It's about to go!"

"John's hurt and he's still back there," the woman cried.

Suddenly it was as if someone had jerked the cave to one side. The rock around them pulsed and moved as if it were living matter. The dirt floor rose as they were flung down. The wave surge had them, the friends not knowing if they were carried forward or backward, up or down.

The pain and the force of crashing against rocks was overwhelming. Each person suffered alone, no longer knowing where the others were.

And then total darkness engulfed them as the force of the wave was too much to take.

A black curtain dropped—oblivion.

**Other titles in the
Deathlands saga:**

JAMES AXLER

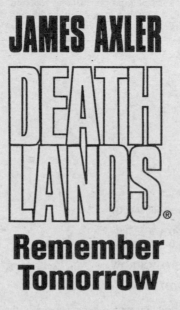

DEATH LANDS®

Remember
Tomorrow

A GOLD EAGLE BOOK FROM
WORLDWIDE®

TORONTO • NEW YORK • LONDON
AMSTERDAM • PARIS • SYDNEY • HAMBURG
STOCKHOLM • ATHENS • TOKYO • MILAN
MADRID • WARSAW • BUDAPEST • AUCKLAND

First edition September 2007

ISBN-13: 978-0-373-62589-5
ISBN-10: 0-373-62589-8

REMEMBER TOMORROW

Mankind, by the perverse depravity of their nature, esteem that which they have most desired as of no value the moment it is possessed, and torment themselves with fruitless wishes for that which is beyond their reach.

—François de Salignac de la Mothe Fénelon
1651–1715

THE DEATHLANDS SAGA

This world is their legacy, a world born in the violent nuclear spasm of 2001 that was the bitter outcome of a struggle for global dominance.

There is no real escape from this shockscape where life always hangs in the balance, vulnerable to newly demonic nature, barbarism, lawlessness.

But they are the warrior survivalists, and they endure—in the way of the lion, the hawk and the tiger, true to nature's heart despite its ruination.

Ryan Cawdor: The privileged son of an East Coast baron. Acquainted with betrayal from a tender age, he is a master of the hard realities.

Krysty Wroth: Harmony ville's own Titian-haired beauty, a woman with the strength of tempered steel. Her premonitions and Gaia powers have been fostered by her Mother Sonja.

J. B. Dix, the Armorer: Weapons master and Ryan's close ally, he, too, honed his skills traversing the Deathlands with the legendary Trader.

Doctor Theophilus Tanner: Torn from his family and a gentler life in 1896, Doc has been thrown into a future he couldn't have imagined.

Dr. Mildred Wyeth: Her father was killed by the Ku Klux Klan, but her fate is not much lighter. Restored from predark cryogenic suspension, she brings twentieth-century healing skills to a nightmare.

Jak Lauren: A true child of the wastelands, reared on adversity, loss and danger, the albino teenager is a fierce fighter and loyal friend.

Dean Cawdor: Ryan's young son by Sharona accepts the only world he knows, and yet he is the seedling bearing the promise of tomorrow.

In a world where all was lost, they are humanity's last hope....

Chapter One

"Whoever they were, they sure didn't believe in house-keeping," Mildred Wyeth said dryly as she surveyed the smoke-blackened walls and the piles of trash that littered the floor of the redoubt room. Once an office, the comp terminals had been ripped from the walls, the desks had been broken up for firewood. The garbage spread across the room had the look of something long dead, a fire extinguished by the smoke-triggered sprinkler system.

Doc Tanner stood in the doorway behind Mildred Wyeth, shaking his head sadly and making tsking noises through his teeth. "Truly, this is a sad sign of the madness that descended on people when the fires rained from the heavens. Consider it, my dear doctor. From the condition of the wreckage, and the perfect stillness that seems to surround us, I would be not in the least surprised to learn that this was perpetrated some decades ago. Possibly almost a full century."

"Your point being?" The black woman sighed. She knew where Doc was going with this, but wanted him to take the shortcut rather than the scenic route: she was tired, ached all over and had very little patience for Doc's long-winded perorations.

"Simply this, my dear doctor. This small piece of

carnage must have been perpetrated within a few years of what the whitecoats lovingly termed 'nuclear winter,' that age of madness.... As if giving it a natural and seemingly innocuous name would, in some way, atone for the foul—forgive me, I'm moving away from my theme," he added, catching himself, "I merely meant to make the point that within a few years, people seemed to bo reduced to the level of unthinking savages. The knowledge of old tech would not be wiped out that quickly.'

"Yeah, I know what you mean, Doc, but it isn't always that simple, is it?" Mildred replied. "Panic sets in, rad sickness maybe.... Who's to know the psychological state of anyone who managed to somehow drag themselves here through what was happening outside. Who's to know, even, the psychological state of whoever was inside?"

"Myself, perhaps," Doc uttered, his mouth set grim as memories of his time at the hands of scientists fluttered at the edges of his consciousness while he fought them back from a full remembrance that would drive him into madness once more. He shook his head, half dismissing the memories, half sorrowful at what conclusions he could draw. "If they were military men gone mad, then they were no more than the next in a long, long line," he said softly. "Pray let us leave this as a memorial to their insanity."

"I won't disagree with you on that one, Doc." Mildred turned on her heel and followed the old man into the corridor of the redoubt.

They had jumped into this place a few hours previously and their bodies were still recovering from the rigors of the mat-trans unit. To be broken down into molecules and transported across vast distances in the blink of an eye before being reassembled was hardly the ideal way to travel. The stresses placed on the psyche— let alone the human frame—were incalculable. Doc was one of those who found it hardest to recover and his mind always seemed to lag a little behind his body. Mildred was inclined to let him ramble at these times, especially if there was no immediate danger. And it did seem as though the redoubt had been invaded, looted and long-since abandoned.

The companions had split into three groups. Usually, Mildred would go with J.B., while Ryan and Krysty recced together, and Doc would accompany Jak. The sharp skills and instincts of the wiry albino teen would cover for Doc's occasional frailties of mind and body. But after a mat-trans jump, Jak was always one of the last to fully recover. Something about his body makeup responded poorly to having itself ripped apart and re- constituted, and he was always weak for a while after, needing more time to recover. Chances were he was sharp, as Ryan always allowed them time to get it together, but chances were something the one-eyed man never took, so J.B. would ride shotgun for Jak until the redoubt was secured.

Secured—that would imply that there was anything left in the empty military base to be secured. As Mildred could see, the place had been gutted. Either a fleeing army presence or invaders who had in some way been able to gain access and had taken anything with them that wasn't nailed down and could be of any use.

The situation worried the woman. They were short

on supplies and the kitchens, sick bays and armories of these bases had come in useful in the past. It was especially reassuring when you had no idea which part of the continent you were currently walking under. Until they found a reliable map source or actually surfaced, they had no idea where they were geographically.

Mildred suddenly stopped and rubbed her eyes. She had to be more tired than she had realized, starting to let her thoughts stray in such a manner. She was aware of Doc at her elbow.

"Mildred, are you feeling quite yourself?" he asked solicitously.

"No, I don't think I am, to tell you the truth," she replied.

Doc's next comment disarmed her totally. Shaking his head sadly, he said, "Madam, I fear you now know how I feel most of my life. Come, let us secure the area and report back," he added, moving off and leaving her to gape at his bony frame receding down the corridor ahead of her.

They finished their recce, finding nothing to show any signs of life, and then returned to the anteroom adjoining the mat-trans chamber, where they were due to rendezvous.

The others were already waiting for them when they arrived. From their relaxed body posture and the fact there had been no audible signs of action, Doc and Mildred knew that theirs hadn't been the only fruitless search. Briefly, she filled them in on what she had Doc had found.

"Guess we can rest up here for now—still daylight up top, though," J.B. added, checking his wrist chron.

"We're too exhausted to go into unknown territory right now," Ryan said, shaking his head. His shaggy black mane came down over his forehead, almost but not quite obscuring the beginnings of the jagged scar that ran into his eye, continuing along his cheek beneath the eye patch that covered the empty socket. It only served to accentuate the penetrating ice-blue of his remaining orb, always focused on the task ahead. "Break out some of the self-heats we've got, then find one of the dorms that isn't trashed and get some rest. We'll have a watch rotation, even though this seems safe."

"I figure the only thing that would chill us in here is the boredom," Krysty added, "Which, come to think of it, wouldn't be such a bad way to go."

"Mebbe, but not yet," Jak interjected.

The mood had lightened a little. Although the redoubt had yielded nothing, it seemed a safe place for one night's rest, and rest was all they really wanted after the jump.

Moving from the antechamber to one of the dorms on another level, Mildred began to get a fuller picture of the redoubt, which seemed to be built on a smaller scale than some of the others in which they had landed. There were no levels with bays for transport beyond a few small wags and the levels seemed to be less spread out, with fewer rooms before they ascended. Mildred mentioned that and Ryan grinned.

"Yeah, well, I didn't bring you this way just for fun," he ventured. "Take a look in this room up here." He led them into what had once been an office, indicating a room plan on the wall facing the door. It showed the full layout of the redoubt, with all the storage and habitation areas clearly marked. "It doesn't look like this carried much in the way of heavy-duty equipment," he remarked. "Mebbe it was just a kind of way station between two larger posts, carrying a few supplies and acting as some kind of lookout. Not many sec here and not many pickings for whoever got in here…unless it was them trying to get out."

"I wondered about that we both did," Mildred added, catching Doc's look. "If it was someone from outside coming in—"

"Don't worry about that, Millie," J.B. cut in. "Me and Jak took the top level. The main sec door is secured and we couldn't find much in the way of damage to account for entry. No one can just hack their way in unless there's been some kind of earth movement or they knew the sec code. And there's only a few stress cracks in the tunnel walls near the top. If they knew the code, they haven't been back for a long time. And if they were on their way out, they thought to close the door behind them."

It was as close as the taciturn Armorer ever came to a joke and one of the longest speeches anyone had heard him make for some time. If nothing else, it signaled how relaxed he felt with the situation.

"So it's okay for us to rest up here for a while before moving out," Ryan stated. "But I wouldn't want to hang around too long."

"Why not?" Krysty asked. Her hair formed a titian-red halo around her head, even the cold blandness of the overhead neon was transformed into a warm glow of fire as it reflected the aura around her head. The curls and waves cascaded over her shoulders, running wild and free. This helped explain her question: the mutie genes running through her veins made her hair sensitive, and prehensile, responding to imminent danger by curling up protectively around her. The fact that it was so loose and free bespoke the complete lack of threat in the redoubt.

That hadn't escaped the one-eyed man's notice. "There might not be anyone around to harm us, but there are still some things I don't trust."

"I'm with you on that, boss man," Mildred muttered, running her finger along the surface of the room plan and examining the gray residue that gathered on her fingertips. "Look at the dust on here," she added.

Doc furrowed his brow. "Your logic escapes me, my dear woman. This has been uninhabited for a long while, I would guess. Naturally, there would be some kind of dust gathering."

Krysty kissed her teeth, annoyed with herself at having missed the obvious. "Yeah, but this isn't natural, is it, Doc? These redoubts have air conditioning and temperature and humidity control. They have some kind of weird antistatic device that keeps dust out of the atmosphere. So if there is dust, then it means that the air-filtration system isn't working properly."

"Exactly," Ryan added. "If that part of it is down, then how do we know that our air is being recycled efficiently. How long will it last? Long enough, hopefully, to get some rest," he continued, answering himself. "Mebbe it's fine. I just don't want to take chances."

"Once more, I defer to your powers of observation," Doc bowed. "Where we would be without you, I dread to think."

"I could say the same about you," Ryan answered with a grin. "So let's eat, get rested and get moving."

The companions left the room, taking another look at the one clear streak illuminating the plastic covering of the room plan beneath its tawdry layer of dust as they did so. Once they had ascended to a higher level in the redoubt and found a dorm that was relatively unscathed, they stripped down the equipment and bags that they carried, those things that were their lives and survival.

"Pity it has to be this shit again, but at least it keeps us going," Krysty said sadly as she handed out the self-heats. The packages—cans or foil containers—contained within them all the nutrients they needed, heated by a mechanism within the packaging that was instigated by the act of opening. Unfortunately, the contents were tasteless and bland, the only traces of any flavor being colored by the chemicals that were used to preserve the contents. They were a last resort when there was nothing else to be found, but they did their job: they kept the companions alive and nourished.

The friends ate in silence, trying to keep their food down. It wasn't easy. When they finished, Ryan was the first to his feet.

"I'm going to see if the showers are still working on this level. Mebbe it'll wash away the taste of those fire-blasted self-heats."

Shower rooms were attached to each of the dorms and it took only a few moments for the one-eyed man to ascertain that the hot water systems and pumps were still in a roughly working order—roughly, because the temperature of the water fluctuated, despite the setting, and a couple of times the man had to be sharp enough to dodge red-hot or icy blasts of water as the old pumps faltered. Nonetheless, he felt refreshed when he emerged. Warning the others, he searched for fresh underwear in the dorm, hoping that whoever had looted the redoubt would have been looking for blasters and food, not clean clothing. They were lucky; there was enough for all of them.

It was a relaxed time; something they needed after the jump and before heading out into the unknown. They'd found one map in the redoubt, and perhaps they would find others if they looked in the morning, maps that might tell them where they had landed. But now, the only thing that mattered was to rest.

"I'll take first watch," Ryan announced. "Then we work it in shifts, alphabetical order," he continued.

"Pray tell, friend Ryan, do I count as *D* for Doc, or *T* for Theophilus?" Doc questioned with a mischievous grin.

"Hell, I can't remember the last time anyone called you anything but Doc," Ryan laughed.

It answered the question and emphasized the relaxed mood. It was to prove an uneventful night, the only disturbance the changeover of watches. J.B. succeeded Jak, noticing that the albino youth seemed loathe to leave his post.

"Best to get some rest, Jak," he said softly as he sought to relieve him.

"If can rest with nightmares," Jak replied. "Always bad after jump. Not able to really rest until on outside, when need to be triple red." Jak shrugged as he walked away and left J.B. to his post. Not for the first time, one of the companions found themselves wondering what really went on behind Jak's impassive exterior.

Krysty snuggled in next to Ryan, feeling the warmth of his hard, muscular body. It was a rare occasion when they got to be this close, with this much security around them. He responded to her touch and moved in to fit closer to her. They didn't talk as they joined together. They had a closeness that Ryan had never known with anyone else. Love was a word that had little value in the world in which they lived, but if there was anything between them, it was love.

Across the dorm, the same thing was happening for Mildred and J.B. For Millie it was a difficult thing. She had known the predark world and had some inclination of what the word love had come to mean. J.B. was from a different world—one into which she had fitted rather than buy the farm, but still one that was alien to all she had learned in her formative years. It wasn't often that there arose the opportunity to stop and think about it— only occasions such as this. As she lay with J.B. nestling against her, she did stop to think about it. It was just as well that there was so little time, as any amount spent pondering on this would be enough to drive her insane. Mebbe she was insane. How else could you get by in this world?

It wasn't a pleasant thought on which to drift into a— mercifully dreamless—sleep. If only the same could be said for Doc, who murmured and muttered to himself, twisting and turning beneath the sheets as his mind replayed incidents from his past, confusing the three centuries into which the man had been mercilessly born, dragged and thrown. Images and people, half-memories blended into fictions, wild dreams from the edges of reason: all these assailed him as he slept.

And so they passed the night, each in their own cocoon of silence.

"TIME TO GET TO IT, people," Ryan said as he rose from his bed. He left the dorm to find Mildred, who had taken last watch and had been glad of the wakefulness to keep her darkest thoughts at bay.

"Five o'clock and all's well," she said with a grin as Ryan came into view.

The one-eyed man looked at his wrist chron. "It's past eight," he replied in a puzzled tone.

Mildred shook her head, rubbing her eyes as she did. "Forget it Ryan, it was just some old joke that would have been funny if you were as old as me. What's the agenda?" she added, without giving him time to respond to her previous comment.

"Eat—if we can face more self-heats—then try and find something that'll tell us where we are when we hit the surface. Mebbe even take another chance with that shower system. Last chance we may get to stay clean for some time."

"Y'know, even the thought of a self-heat and getting scalded is good right now," Mildred answered with another shake of the head. "I can't believe I just said that."

Ryan laughed. It wasn't often that the one-eyed man had the opportunity to do that. Far, far too often there was nothing whatsoever to give him cause for laughter. But these snatched few moments, underground and secure, gave them all time to relax momentarily, just enough to stop their minds snapping with the tension of living outside.

After breakfast Ryan and J.B. mounted their own small recce of the office units in the redoubt, leaving the others to shower and get ready to leave. Neither man knew if he would find what he were looking for, and both would have been grateful for just a sign.

"Ryan, back here," J.B. called after a short while, sticking his head through the doorway of an office unit where Ryan was breaking open a filing cabinet. The comp terminal stood useless on the desk, long since fused and failed. "I've got a comp that works and is tied in to what Mildred calls the mainframe."

Ryan left his task and followed his comrade along the corridor to the office in which he had been scavenging. Finding remnants of what had been before was always a problem: much of the information in all the redoubts had been stored on computer, but these were erratic now, prone to either break down, be broken, or be inaccessible to people a century or more on who don't have a password. There was some paper information, but then it is a matter of hoping that it could be found or that it hadn't been destroyed by looters or by the original inhabitants before they bought the farm.

To find a comp terminal working anywhere other than a low-level, sealed chamber was rare; one that was still connected to the redoubt's mainframe comp was even more rare.

Maybe they were about to get lucky for once.

The two men hunched over the desk, the terminal casting a glow over their faces, shadows and light accentuating the crags of Ryan's weathered face and the lines of worry and battle that etched the Armorer's visage. Their mouths were set in grim concentration. There was nothing to be happy about until they actually found some useful information.

"Got it," J.B. declared in triumph as he managed to

call up an outline map of the area surrounding the redoubt. A couple more keys punched and the map pulled back to reveal the larger area.

From the outline, they could see that they were in the middle of what had been Arkansas before the nuke-caust. There was a large town within a day's walking distance to the northwest of the redoubt.

"Worth checking it out?" J.B. queried.

"Old villes like that are never totally deserted. Usually some kind of life attaches itself. We just have to be triple red until we find out what kind it is." Ryan paused, his brow furrowed in concentration. Eventually, he added, "Arkansas—that name's familiar. We ever come this way with Trader?"

J.B. blew threw his pursed lips as he racked his memory. "Think we might have at one time. Weird land up there, part dust and part sand. Gets real dry and then they have monsoons that sweep everything away. Yeah," he said suddenly, snapping his fingers, "there was that time when one of the wags got driven off the road in a mudslide after one of the rains. We had to chain War Wag One to it and pull the bastard back onto the blacktop. Trader cursed all the while about the fuel it was taking, then cursed about losing the wag when we said he should just leave it if he felt like that."

Ryan smiled wryly. "Came out with some shit about a rock and a hard place."

"Yeah, and you told him that he wouldn't be having this trouble if there had been some rocks and a hard place 'stead of all that mud."

Both men laughed at the memory. J.B. shook his

head. "I thought the old buzzard was gonna blow you away where you stood, he looked that mad. 'Stead, he just started laughing."

"Crazy man and a wise man," Ryan said softly, remembering the wily old man who had taught them so many of the things that were still keeping them alive. Then something clicked in his brain. "Got it!" he exclaimed. "Listen, I think I remember something. If this is where I think, then there's a ville near here on one of the surviving blacktops. It was about one day away from where that fireblasted wag hit the mud. Mebbe about two days from the remains of the old ville—About here," he added, pointing to an area on the screen that was to the west of the predark conurbation.

"That's good. It's somewhere to aim for." J.B. nodded. "Only one thing, though…"

"What's that?" Ryan asked.

J.B. grinned. "I hope it ain't mud season. I just had another shower this morning."

The two men left the office and returned to the rest of the companions. They were in the dorm, preparing for the trip outside. Ryan and J.B. outlined their position and destination, giving everyone—including themselves—a half hour in which to be ready to leave. By their wrist chrons, they could see that it was light outside and without knowing how hot the sun got during its peak, Ryan wanted them to make some distance and scout out any shade or shelter should it be necessary.

Such was their efficiency and experience in getting ready to move out that long before the half hour had elapsed, the companions were making their way to the upper level and the sec door that exited onto the outside world. As J.B. had said, the walls, floor and ceiling of the tunnel leading to the highest level had taken the brunt of whatever earth movements had occurred during and immediately after the nukecaust. Cracks ran along the concrete that constituted the tunnel and, despite the concrete's thickness, some were large and deep enough for moisture to have seeped through over the decades. Spoors of mold and fungus peppered the areas around these cracks, small pools of stagnant water gathered on the floor.

"Can't have been too bad, as the walls are still pretty sound," J.B. commented. "Figure the door should work okay. The mechanism on all the others has, so it's only gonna be a warp that jams the bastard."

"Let's hope not," Krysty added, almost to herself. Some of the upper level sec doors had been shut when J.B. had recced the day before, but had responded when he had punched in the sec codes scratched on the metal plates above the keypads. One of the plates had "Help me" scratched on it, and another "Next stop hel." The sec man had either been interrupted or he couldn't spell. Not that it mattered. J.B. wasn't much of a reader and it was too long ago for him to care. All he was worried about was whether or not the doors would respond. Fortunately, whatever damage the earth movement had caused, the electrics on the doors were still working. So the only thing that could prevent the exit door rising was if the earth movements had buckled the frame, jamming the door.

All this went through Krysty's head and the anticipation of potential danger made her hair start to move

gently, the flowing curls tightening almost imperceptibly.

Almost, but not quite. Ryan caught sight of her. "Everything okay?"

She smiled ruefully. "Yeah, everything's fine, lover.
It's me getting nervous, not any immediate danger."

Ryan didn't answer; it wasn't like Krysty to get
nervous, but if she was sure there was no intimation of
danger— No, he wouldn't take chances.

"Okay, J.B. When you hit the lever, I want everyone
back in a defensive position. Can't be too safe, right?"

The others followed his command without question.
Too many times they had walked straight into danger.
They knew the wisdom of the one-eyed man's words.
The tunnel was supported by a series of buttresses that
formed a semicircular arch from floor to floor, arcing
over the ceiling. Some of these housed sec doors, others
stood alone. The companions drew back so that they
took cover by these arches, blasters ready if there was
a need to fire. J.B. stood alone by the final sec-door
panel. Ryan stayed nearest and gave the bespectacled
Armorer the nod when J.B. cast him a questioning
glance.

J.B. blew on his fingers, tapped in the code, pressed
the lever and brought his Uzi up to waist height.

The outside atmosphere had obviously had some
effect on the outer door, as it rose far more slowly than
the interior doors. There was a grinding in the mechanism and the shriek of metal scraping against protesting
concrete as it began to move. The earth movements had
caused the frame to warp a little. The redoubt had been
looted. At some point, someone had to have got in

through the outer door. The question was, had the earth shifted any more since then?

The light of midmorning was intensely bright as it began to show itself under the shuddering, slowly moving sec door. Compared to the bland fluorescent light that lit the redoubt corridor, it was incandescent. More than one of the companions cursed as the brightness made them squint, unable to see any dangers that lay beyond.

By the time that the sec door had fully opened, they had adjusted to the light and could see that the entrance to the redoubt lay in the side of a shallow valley, with a dirt track running up around the edge and over into the land beyond. The earth in front of them was dry, sandy soil, littered with small rocks and pebbles. Whatever else, they could see that it wasn't rainy season and it looked like it had been a long time since it had been.

The area looked deserted. Ryan signaled them to wait, listening intently for any movement beyond, stretching the tension to a point where he hoped that any waiting enemy would lose their nerve and force an attack, showing their hand.

There was nothing. Ryan looked back at Jak and at Krysty. The red-haired woman shook her head, her hair now flowing free. If there was any danger out there, she would sense it. Jak also shook his head, his white, stringy hair framing his impassive face, red eyes glittering in the new light. Although he had no mutie capabilities, he was a natural hunter whose abilities had been honed to an almost preternatural degree. If someone was out there waiting, he could sniff them out.

Ryan gestured for his people to move out, still keeping their defensive formation. The one-eyed warrior himself was in the lead, with Jak, Krysty and Mildred fanning out to scan the area surrounding the narrow valley. Doc came out before J.B., who kept to the rear and guarded their backs.

They would have felt faintly absurd, if not for the fact that they had seen people buy the farm for less caution over the years. Absurd because the area was deserted, with no signs of life beyond a few lizards and scrub plants that struggled to survive in the harsh environment.

Ryan gestured to J.B. that it was clear and the Armorer tapped in the sec code, the door grinding ponderously shut behind them. He followed the others until they were gathered on the highest ridge of the valley. It was only about eight feet above the valley floor, but it still afforded them a decent vantage of the land surrounding.

"Dark night, it's bleak," J.B. said with admirable understatement as he joined them, casting his eyes over the terrain. The valley walls had to have been higher at some time, but the nuclear winter and the harsh climate changes over the past century had beaten them down to the dry husks of hillocks that they now were. The topsoil and any grasslands had long since blown away, only the hardiest of scrub remaining, shallowly rooted in the powdery dirt. The land had been flattened by the intemperate climate, leaving nothing but a flat, despairing landscape that tried and failed to support life.

"Sure as heck won't be many folks trying to eke a living round here," Mildred commented. "And not much shelter from the elements for us, either."

"I figure that ville me and J.B. were talking about must be north-northwest from here, so if we head in that direction…" Ryan looked to J.B., but the Armorer was ahead of him. Taking the highest point of the land and using the sun and the mini-sextant he always carried with him, J.B. was sighting their position and plotting their direction. "It might be a couple of days hike from here," Ryan stated, "so we need to keep a sharp eye for water and shelter." He looked up—clear skies with nothing to shield the sun as it beat down. "I don't like skies this clear when there's land this dry. It gives me a bad feeling."

"My dear Ryan, it would give me the perfect opportunity to top up my tan. I feel all this living underground is giving me somewhat of an unhealthy pallor," Doc remarked with a crooked grin, the irony of his words emphasized by him removing his hat to mop his already sweating brow.

Direction defined, they set off on the long march. Strung out in a line with J.B. now on point, they kept their heads down, avoiding the glare of the sun as it grew brighter in the sky, and remained silent. What was there to say? They were hiking through a desolate landscape with nothing to remark upon and wasted words would just use energy, making them thirsty when they needed to conserve water.

Apart from scrub and the occasional lizard, there was little sign of life. In the distance they occasionally glimpsed a solitary bird of prey or the intimation that there were flocks of smaller birds—a misty cloud moving in the blue that could be a wisp of cumulus or a flock on the wing. Nothing closer. Any mammals that scratched some kind of a living from the land were safely burrowed away, the occasional hole in the ground being all that betrayed their presence.

The companions trudged on, measuring the tedium of time only by the achingly slow movement of the sun across the sky. At least it wasn't quite as hot as they feared. They had been through worse. In fact, there were even a few breezes that gently crossed the empty land, relieving the beat of the heat.

Breezes that slowly, almost unnoticeably, grew stronger.

It was Mildred who first noticed it. Quite by chance, she looked to her left to relieve the boredom of looking at the ground in front of her.

"Oh shit… Ryan," she said softly.

Lost in some reverie of his own, Ryan snapped back to attention when he heard her voice. He looked back at her and followed the direction in which she was pointing. All the companions followed the direction of her finger.

"By the Three Kennedys," Doc breathed. "It was Montana, 1878, when I was last privy to such a sight."

"Yeah? And this might be the last time you see it unless we can find some cover," J.B. murmured.

What had caught their attention was awesome and beautiful, but almost certainly deadly. In the distance, gaining ground rapidly on them, a zephyr was whipping the earth into a turmoil. Clouds of dust and dirt were flying at strange trajectories as the currents of air flung them from their path. Now they understood why the breezes had become more insistent. The outlying currents had stirred the air for some miles around, and were increasing with every second. In fact, at the speed the zephyr was moving, it would reach them very shortly.

The storm surrounding the air currents was violent, ripping up great chunks of earth, hurling rock and stone about at vicious speeds.

"Cover," Ryan yelled, already aware that the noise of the approaching storm was growing, drowning him. He cast about for some kind of shelter, something that would cover them until the zephyr passed over. That wouldn't take long, the speed at which it was moving, but long enough to injure or chill them.

"There," Jak yelled, indicating a cave that seemed to disappear down into the ground. It wasn't set into a hill of any kind, but seemed to be the only indication that there had once been raised land. It was more like a pothole. But it was shelter.

"Okay, let's go," Ryan yelled, running toward it, tracking back to one side to help Doc, who was slower than the others. Mildred, Krysty and Jak gained the entrance, with J.B.—who had been farthest back— catching up to Ryan and Doc, grabbing the old man's arm and helping Ryan to speed him along. Dirt and stones rained on their backs; wind plucked at their clothes.

The zephyr was almost on them as they dived for the entrance to the cave.

Chapter Two

The sudden darkness was engulfing and all Ryan, J.B. and Doc could feel was the scouring dirt whipping against their backs, rocks and stones thudding into them and the dry, powdered earth forming a choking mist that swirled around them, clogging their mouths, noses and lungs.

Lights exploded all around behind closed eyes, coughing spasms racked their bodies and the hard rock of the cave floor, covered with the thinnest layer of dirt, was hard against their bodies as they landed flat and awkward, unable to see where they were going.

"Grab them, get them back in," Krysty yelled, taking Ryan by one arm and hauling him farther back into the darkness of the caves. J.B. felt two hands on his body, searching for a hold. As he felt himself dragged in one direction he dug his boot heels into the cave floor, pushing with his calves to aid his rescuer by propelling himself as hard as he could. It was more than Mildred expected and she nearly stumbled and fell, the sudden momentum taking her by surprise.

"Don't, John, it'll be okay," she whispered.

He marveled that he could hear her above the noise of the storm, then realized that it had lessened. Was that because they had moved into the caves or because the speed of the zephyr was taking it past them already? He had always thought that zephyrs were supposed to be complex but quite harmless combinations of air currents. Someone should tell that to the motherfucker outside. He knew his thoughts were rambling; he had to have hit his head when he fell. It would be good to stop pushing and just relax. He felt himself go loose.

Jak took hold of Doc. The old man had fallen well and wasn't too hurt. He was coughing and retching, strings of bile and dirt splattering the floor around him, but he was conscious and aware of Jak's hands upon him.

"Heavens, sir, I can manage myself. I'm not that decrepit that I—" He failed to finish as another spasm racked him, the effort of speaking dragging more dirt from his chest. He wretched once more.

"Talk later, walk now," Jak murmured, taking Doc beneath the arms and lifting him into a semi-upright position. "You walk okay? Just nod," he added, not wanting Doc to succumb to more spasms. When Doc assented, Jak spoke just once more. "Keep head low— not high in here." Jak's red eyes were better suited to the darkness than anyone else's in the group, but even he was having trouble adjusting to the almost total darkness.

Stumbling, crashing into the jagged rock walls and trying to avoid cracking their skulls on the low roof of the cave, the companions made their way back. As the air cleared of dust and Ryan and J.B. were able to breathe more easily, their senses began to return. They hawked and spit the dirt from their lungs; the strength began to flow back into their limbs. Doc, despite the rigors of puking so frequently, found himself able to breathe a little better and, after what had seemed an age but had only been a couple of minutes, the dust storm caused by the zephyr was far behind them.

"Fireblast, it's darker than a coldheart's soul in here," Ryan uttered. "I can't see where the hell we're headed."

"None of us can," Krysty added. "Not even Jak, I'd reckon."

"Too dark," the albino replied. "Better stop. Bad feeling about this."

"Sounds like a good idea," Ryan stated. "Find out where the hell we are before we lose the way back. Besides which, I don't like this smell."

"It is like a charnel house, but not one which has been well maintained," Doc interjected, his voice high and strained, cracking from the dust that had caught in his lungs despite his body's attempts to expel it. His frail physique was showing the strain. Doc's body, stressed in unimaginable ways by the hardships of his previous life, was sometimes apt to react in ways that baffled the others. He had been less buffeted by the storm than Ryan and J.B., but was taking longer to recover.

But there was nothing wrong with his sense of smell. The dark caves, riddled with a dank, damp aura now that they had obviously been traveling downward, were filled with the sickly sweet odors of flesh in varying stages of decay. Come to that, their heavy combat boots had already crunched underfoot what may have been wood, but which may also have been old bone. They had sheltered in caves on numerous occasions, and had come to discover that caves could be the homes of some triple-dangerous creatures.

About their persons, among the supplies that were spread evenly between them, they carried flashlights that had been scavenged from redoubts. These were battery operated, the batteries being the harder part to obtain. As each of them found their flash, they hoped that theirs would still be working. Almost simultaneously, they switched them on.

Two were still giving a strong beam. Ryan's was weak, but illuminated a small area in front of him. He moved it around and could see that Mildred and Krysty had the working flashes. J.B.'s, Jak's and Doc's were all dead.

"Better than nothing." He shrugged, turning his weakened beam onto the floor of the cave. "Shit, look at that."

The stronger beams cast their light over the area of the cave floor surrounding the companions. Scraps of fur and skin were littered between jagged edges of bone that covered the floor, almost like a carpet. The earth was stained dark. Some of the bones still had rotting meat attached to them, but others were old and dry. The smell didn't come from anything that remained, but rather was the result of no circulating air. The odor of decay and death had stayed in the enclosed space until it had become embedded in the walls.

Jak hunkered down, running his hands over the forest of bones, lifting a few to examine. "Small animal, all of them," he said, looking up at Ryan, his eyes glittering in the beam. "Whatever did this couldn't find big prey. Mebbe not too much danger. But mebbe a lot of them," he added with a shrug.

"Yeah, but what?" Mildred queried. "I thought it

was only small stuff could live in this. What's down here and where did it come from?"

"Madam, the second part of your query is irrelevant," Doc husked, his voice still tight and painful. "Much more pertinent would be to ask what did this and is it still here?"

"Right, Doc," Ryan agreed. He noted that the old man had looooned his LeMat percussion pistol in its resting place, ready to draw and fire when danger threatened. "Triple red, people, but triple careful with blasters," he added pointedly. "It's a confined space down here and we could end up chilling ourselves from ricochets."

Doc allowed himself a small smile. "A point well made." He eased the LeMat back into place and took his sword stick from its sheath. The blade, finely honed and made of Toledo steel, glittered in the beams of the flashlights.

"The thing is, if whatever it is knows we're here, why isn't it attacking us and defending its territory?" Mildred mused.

"Sizing us up," Krysty answered with a shudder. Her hair had begun to coil protectively around her head and neck.

"Watching…waiting," Jak added simply. In each hand, one of his razor-honed, leaf-bladed knives was poised and balanced, waiting for the first sign of attack.

Using the flashlights that still had strong beams, the companions surveyed the area around them as far as the light penetrated the blackness. The tunnel system formed by the caves honeycombed off in several directions. Straight ahead of them the system plunged on into the darkness, gradually descending into the depths of the earth. To their rear, in the direction from which they had traveled, it seemed to go up…but had they arrived in a straight line? In their hurry to get away from the storm and in the confusion of carrying those incapacitated by the storm's sudden violence, none could say if they had arrived at this point from a straight line or if they had veered into this area from one of the tunnels leading off what appeared to be the central corridor. Whatever, it seemed that all the tunnels in the cave led into darkness with no outside light source to guide them. Yet they couldn't be that deep or have come that far.

Another problem was the height of the cave. Nowhere had they been in a position where they could stand straight. At some point, Jak had been able to avoid stooping but even he was now inclined forward. And as he was just under five feet in height, it gave them some idea of how low the caves were. Bent forward, calf and thigh muscles aching under the strain, all were aware that they were in the worst position to defend themselves from attack. Whatever lived in these caves and had left these remains, they could be pretty sure it was on all fours.

"Why won't it show itself?" Doc whispered.

"Mebbe there's only one of it and it knows it's outnumbered here. Mebbe it doesn't want to fight in the place it keeps its kill. Mebbe a lot of things. The only thing I know for sure is this is too confined a space to fight and we should get the hell out without disturbing it, if possible."

"Too late for that," Jak said with a shake of his white

mane, ghostly in the beam of the flash. "Can hear something move…" He paused, furrowing his brow as he tried to listen. The others didn't dare breathe. Jak chewed on his scarred lip. "Too many cave, too many tunnels. Sound getting messed up." He looked Ryan in the eye. "More than one, though."

"We move now," Ryan snapped. "Keep going straight back, keep close, go single file."

"Ryan, we got a problem," J.B. said softly. The Armorer had been quiet since they had stopped and only spoke now because he had to. "I'm still fucked by that crack on the skull. I don't trust myself to cover your asses."

Ryan's jaw set. Without J.B. at the back, there was a chance that an attack from behind could take them out. His best option was to put Jak there, but he had wanted the albino at the front, using his keen senses to detect any danger that may be ahead.

"Jak, take the back for me. J.B., go in the middle in case you need help. I'll take the front. Someone give me one of the strong flashlights." Krysty didn't hesitate to hand over hers.

Proceeding with caution, Ryan began to lead them back—hopefully—the way they had come. He scanned the floor of the cave for any sign of footprints, but the earth was too thin, too easily disturbed to keep much shape. Their progress was slowed, too, by the necessity of checking every branching tunnel leading off their path. The darkness could hide any number of secrets and he used the flash to either illuminate the enemy or scare it away.

The sounds that Jak had been able to pick up faintly

were now growing. The honeycomb effect of the caves meant that it was impossible to detect direction in the overlapping acoustics that threw echoes around them. The only thing for sure was that the creatures were getting closer—for that amount of sound could only be put down to more than one creature.

"Triple red, people," Ryan breathed, drawing his panga from its sheath on his thigh. He had that familiar churning of the gut, that instinct that told him the enemy was about to attack. The only problem was from where…?

Behind him, Doc had his sword blade ready, and J.B.—despite his unsteadiness—had unsheathed his Tekna knife. The only blasters were those held by Krysty and Mildred, who didn't carry blades.

At the rear, Jak was ready with his knives, casting glances behind him. He had taken Mildred's flashlight to illuminate the rear, leaving her with Ryan's dimmed flash to aid them in the middle of the group. He was sure that the flash was catching something as they turned corners—the sudden gleam of a watching eye, but always just out of reach.

He killed the light and counted five, listening to the lowing cries of whatever tracked them. He could smell them now and smell their readiness for attack.

Suddenly, he hit the switch on the flash, and the tunnel behind them was illuminated. This time there was no mistaking what was at their rear.

"Ryan!" Jak yelled.

The one-eyed warrior whirled in the enclosed space and as he did so his flashlight caught more of the creatures coming at them from one of the side tunnels. The pack had been smart enough to split into two to attack. He hoped that they wouldn't be any smarter than that in battle.

The only good thing about the attack happening at this moment was that they were between cave branches. There had been a tunnel ahead of Ryan, and a couple of tunnels some thirty yards to their rear, but at each side was solid rock. They had to deal with attackers coming from only two directions, but the downside was that they were now trapped in a pincer movement.

"What are they?" Mildred breathed. It was a rhetorical question and she knew that no one would have the time to answer. It was nothing more than an exclamation of surprise.

For the creatures that attacked them from two directions were nothing more than dogs, animals whose ancestors had been domestic pets and had perhaps strayed from villes nearby and become lost in the wastelands above, seeking shelter beneath. Part of her brain—that part not switched automatically into combat mode—could see that the pack was a mongrel mix. All looked rabid, sores and welts littering their bodies. They had suffered from pack inbreeding and being rad-blasted, some of them had only one eye, some bulbous growths on their heads, others moving fast but with an awkward, almost lame gait.

One thing they all had in common was their teeth: jaws that were strong with sharp teeth that glinted yellow. Their low cries increased in pitch and volume to excited howls of anticipation for the battle and fresh meat.

Given that they were moving in packs from two directions, a load from J.B.'s M-4000 and the shot chamber of the LeMat would have decimated their ranks and made the fight easier. But the dogs moved too fast, closed too quickly. How many of them there were it was difficult to tell, but they closed with a speed that meant there was no time to draw and fire.

The dogs were on them in a blur of fur and muscle, flashing teeth and tearing cloth. The carious breath of the creatures was enough to make any of the companions want to vomit, but they had to choke it down: heaving would have been effort wasted, would have given the creatures that fraction of a second needed to get the first snap of the jaws, tearing at their flesh and scenting blood, spreading disease into any wounds.

The flashlights hit the floor, the beams low and casting shadows up the rock wall, making it dark above a height of three feet and difficult for the companions to see what was happening. They would have to fight according to touch, smell and hearing alone. It wasn't the first time they'd been in a situation like this.

Jak's knives moved in a whirl as he ducked the snapping creatures, the razor-sharp metal tearing through fur and flesh into muscle, jarring against bone. Whimpers and squeals of pain mixed in with the frenzied howling as some of the dogs went down, injured or dying. The scent of blood filled the air, driving the surviving dogs on. But some turned on the injured and vulnerable, their feeding frenzy enough to make them turn on their own.

Ryan's panga sliced through the air, one pass of the blade hitting a dog in an artery, the hot blood spraying across his face, making his eye sting as it hit, filling his mouth and nose so that he had to spit it out, spluttering as it blocked his breath. But he didn't stop cleaving the air.

Some dogs were getting through between the two point men. Doc thrust at them with the blade, the tightness of their confined space stopping him from using the blade as he would have wished; a sweep of the blade was as likely to strike Mildred or Krysty as it was a dog. At Doc's back, J.B. was shaking his rugged head to clear it, using the Tekna knife to slice at the attacking creatures with short jabs and thrusts, keeping them at bay.

Which left Mildred and Krysty to pick their targets with care. The men had tried to protect the two women, as they had no blades. Blasterfire was something that all of the companions wished to avoid. There was the danger of missing the target and hitting one of your own; the danger of ricochet and also the danger of any instability in the tunnels themselves. The honeycombs of rock had seemed secure enough, but there had been earth movements at one time. If the caves were in any way unstable...

Using their blasters was the last thing either woman wanted, but the dogs had swept over the companions with such force that, no matter how hard the men worked with their blades, they needed assistance. Claws and teeth were causing scratches to skin, tears to clothing. How long before a set of jaws sunk into flesh? If one went down, how long before the others? Without knowing how big the pack was, there was no way of knowing if they were ahead of the game or falling behind.

"Pick one of the bastards and chill it. We've got to," Mildred yelled.

"Better get it right first time," Krysty yelled back.

Almost simultaneously their blasters exploded, the sound filling the caves and echoing around, drowning the howls of their attackers.

Only two shots, but they were enough to rebound and reverberate around the cave system, unsettling the delicate balance weight that kept the caves' roofs from hurtling down. A few pebbles and small rocks dislodged, the sheets of stone, slate and rock that constituted the cave system moaning, those few small stones enough to start a chain reaction that would cause the whole of the system to move.

Not that the companions knew anything of that. Temporarily deafened by the noise of the blasterfire and still battling against the almost total darkness above waist height that handicapped them against the ravenous pack, they were fighting what was beginning to feel like a losing battle. The fur and muscle came hurtling from all angles. The slavering jaws and fetid breath, the snap of the teeth as they grasped thin air or snagged cloth and the growls that were low in the throat, infused with the bloodlust unleashed by the cuts and bruises on the companions as well as the wounds of their own injured: these were all that could be discerned.

Krysty yelped in pain as she was cut by the sweep of Doc's sword stick, slicing through more rabid canine flesh in the attempt to drive it back.

"A thousand pardons—would that I could see clearly in this pit of hell," Doc yelled with what, for him, was a remarkable brevity. Krysty didn't reply; her attention was taken up by the sudden onslaught of mad dog from another position.

Jak could feel the blood of his enemies cover him. Yet as one creature fell back, another seemed to take its place, unheeding of the leaf-bladed knives as they sliced as cleanly through the dogs as they cut through the surrounding air. Paws with sharp claws, honed on the rocks of the caves, cut at his camo jacket. The sharpened pieces of metal and glass that were sewn into the jacket, making it so heavy, served their purpose as they cut the pads on the dogs feet, making them yelp and pull back. The sounds and smells of combat, the hot blood that splashed across his face, drove him on. Jak switched from being Jak Lauren to being a predatory animal that sought to eliminate its prey before it became the prey.

Mildred, already bent double in the confined space, felt one of the creatures thud into her as it leaped against her chest, driving her back against the wall of the cave, the jagged rocks cutting into her spine and driving the air out of her body. Her back muscles twisted and spasmed. The yellow teeth and bloodshot eyes of the dog suddenly loomed into view with a clarity that was hideous, even in the near dark of the tunnel. She raised her ZKR, her hand pinned to her side, twisting her wrist against the body mass of the dog, even as she felt the ligaments tearing with the effort. She felt her hand against the warm, matted fur of the creature, could feel the barrel of the pistol against the ridge of muscle along the dog's rib cage.

She squeezed the trigger and felt the impact shudder up her arm as the shell ruptured the creature's muscle and bone, shattering and spreading damage internally.

She only hoped that the creature would have enough muscle and bone bulk to deflect and trap the shell, lest it burst out the other side of the creature and take her out in some way. Thankfully, the sudden impact for which she had braced herself didn't come and she felt the creature lose all life, falling away from her. She eased herself away from the wall, her back protesting as the released pressure allowed her muscles and ligaments to ache freely. But there was no time to pay heed to them, as another blaster shot went off beside her already ringing ears and started a low rumble that grew in volume around them.

Krysty, off balance from Doc's sword blow, had been driven even more so by two dogs that sensed her sudden vulnerability and attacked. She lashed out at one dark shape with her foot; the pointed silver toe of her cowboy boot, with all the power of her calf and thigh muscles behind it, connected with the point of the dog's jaw by chance and rendered it senseless. The other dog managed to evade her defenses and jumped for her throat. She raised a defensive arm and brought up her .38 Smith & Wesson blaster to fire. But her timing was awry and as the blaster exploded in her grasp she knew that she had missed the dog. She felt its jaws close on her arm, only the thickness of her bearskin coat stopping it from driving its sharp teeth into her flesh. She clubbed underneath its body with the butt of the blaster, catching it in the balls and making it yelp in sudden agony and surprise, its jaws loosening enough for her to pry her arm free.

But the real damage had already been done. The stray shot ricocheted around the rocks of the cave, taking out chunks and causing fissures to open along weaknesses in the tunnel walls. The tunnels trembled. The ripple effects of the fissures spread and the walls and floor began to move, rock dust powdering from the ceiling of the cave.

"Dark night, it's coming down," J.B. breathed, shaking his head to try to clear it, the sudden adrenaline burst of this added danger dragging him back from the brink of blacking out.

The dogs yelped in panic, forgetting their prey, intent only on escaping the danger they now felt was more imminent. They melted into the tunnels, leaving only the dead creatures, the floor slick with their blood. They dissolved into the darkness so quickly that it was hard to believe that the tunnel had been thick with them just a few seconds ago.

But the companions now had more pressing matters than the flight of the dogs occupying them.

Ryan scooped up the flashlight at his feet, miraculously untrampled and still working. It was the only one that was still casting light. He threw the beam in an arc across the cave as far it would stretch. The cracks and falling dust seemed localized.

"This way," he yelled, gesturing them toward an area in front of him. They scrambled forward in the darkness. If not to safety, at least heading to a place that seemed a little more stable. J.B. stumbled and Millie held back to assist him. Jak was already past them, helping Doc gain ground on Ryan and Krysty, who were about ten yards ahead, visible by the flashlight beam. The rock around them groaned, great fissures opening into gaping maws that presaged chunks of stone falling at their feet and on their heads. Jak had Doc's arm, but the old man slipped on a slick patch of bloodied earth, losing his footing and stumbling, his arm wrenched out of Jak's grasp by the downward momentum.

Jak turned on his heel as he ran, trying to reach back for Doc....

The tunnel's roof fell, slabs of rock coming between them, the impact making the ground shake under Jak's feet, a falling shard glancing against his temple and nearly knocking him out. In the darkness and the sudden disorientation of the fall, he lost sight of Doc and lost his balance.

It may only have been a second or it may have been an hour. Jak didn't know, but he was snapped back into consciousness by the sounds of rock being moved around him. Not the random noise of a fall, but the methodical sounds of digging.

On the other side of the fall, Ryan and Krysty pulled at the rocks with grim determination. They had no idea how far behind them the others were, but they knew that the way ahead was clear. Although the tunnel looked stable enough for the moment, they knew there wasn't a second to waste in getting to their companions.

Jak, in a hole barely big enough to move around in, began to dig toward the sounds as much as possible. To his relief, there was only an inch or two of rockfall between them and he was soon able to make a hole, squinting against the light as Ryan shone the flash through.

"Jak," Ryan said in an urgent whisper, "where are the others?"

"Doc just behind—fall as rocks come down. J.B. and Mildred?" Jak shrugged. He, too, whispered, aware that too much noise could bring a further fall upon them.

"Let's try and get through to Doc next," Krysty said softly. "If he was just behind Jak, there might only be a few inches of rock there, too."

"We'd better hope so," Ryan answered, casting his eye over the tunnel behind them. "I don't reckon we've got that much time."

Some distance away, unable to hear the others, both Mildred and J.B. were painfully regaining consciousness—Mildred considerably sooner than the still-dazed armorer.

"John?" She groped around in the darkness, guided by the small moans that accompanied his labored breathing. Her fingers brushed against him in the darkness. "John, are you okay?"

"Dunno—" he gasped. "Feel heavy in the legs, like I'm pinned—"

Groping blindly, it took her a few seconds to determine that the Armorer's feet were trapped in the rockfall. She was lucky. Although confined, her limbs were free and nothing felt broken, although every muscle and tendon ached and she had a nasty suspicion that she had sprained her right wrist: touching anything with it sent a sharp pain through her arm that made her stomach lurch.

"Listen, John, I can help you move the rocks, but I've only got one good hand— John?" she added in a more urgent tone when he failed to respond, "John, listen to me—try to stay awake."

"Uh-huh," he returned in a vacant grunt.

Mildred cursed to herself and started slowly, painfully moving the rocks from his feet, careful not to disturb the surroundings. Only when she had safely done this could she even afford to think about making progress to where the others might be.

A few feet ahead of her, Jak was making progress toward Doc, passing the rocks and stones out to Ryan and Krysty. They worked in a chain; it was quicker in the enclosed space afforded them and also quieter.

The sweat dripped off Jak's stringy mop of hair, falling into his red eyes and making them sting so that he had to blink heavily to keep focused on what was in front of him. He was able to blank it out, having experienced far worse. Besides, the flash cast some light on what lay ahead, despite the fact that his own body bulk blocked most of the beam as Ryan shone it from behind him. However, he could see a dark patch emerging through the rocks, a dark patch with a gnarled hand at the end of it. Doc's sleeve.

"See him," Jak croaked to the duo at his rear, redoubling his efforts. He cleared enough space around Doc to free the old man. Doc's breathing was labored and harsh, rattling in his chest. He raised his head as the weak light illuminated him.

"Glad as I always am to see your face, friend Jak—" he stopped to cough "—never as glad as I am now."

Jak grinned. "Talk later, move now."

Gently, the albino teen cleared more space around Doc and pulled him clear of the rocks. The old man had been lucky: a long slab had fallen across him, preventing the smaller pieces from weighing down and crushing his back. It had made him easier to move, a few stones rattling to the cave floor behind his feet.

"John, I can hear something!" Mildred exclaimed softly, starting to pull at the rocks, testing for those which she could move without too much risk of bringing others down upon her. She began to make a path, hearing the movements of rock caused by Jak moving Doc, and figuring that they weren't too far away.

Meanwhile, Jak had managed to pull Doc out of the pileup and while Ryan cast an anxious glance at the area beyond, Krysty checked the old man. His breathing was shallow and fast, taking in little air.

"How is he?" Ryan queried.

"Not so good. We need to get him out of here as soon as possible. All the dust and shit from the cave-in has given him some kind of respiratory problem."

"Soon as we find Mildred and J.B.," Ryan stated, watching the point where Jak's body was disappearing into the rocks as he tunneled toward the missing companions.

Mildred could hear him coming nearer as she, too, cleared rocks from her path. "John, hang in there," she whispered over her shoulder. "We're nearly there."

Like Doc, she had never been so glad to see Jak's face as when he removed the last piece of rock that separated them. He grinned, but said nothing, moving back to allow her to wriggle through the small hole he had made.

"John?" She waited until John muttered an acknowledgment before she continued. "John, we're through—just follow me."

J.B. heard her words as though they traveled through a long tunnel.

Jak was helping Mildred to squeeze through the gap he had made when he first felt a ripple in the rocks beneath them, a trembling that foretold of a wave to come.

"Ryan—"

"I feel it," he replied, rushing to help Jak pull Mildred through the gap. "It's about to go."

"John's hurt and he's still back there," Mildred said urgently, turning back to see if the Armorer was following her. There was no sign of him.

She was about to speak again when it hit, like someone had taken hold of the cave and tugged it. The ripple was the forerunner of a wave that had built deep within the cave system, as though the initial rockfall had traveled down and come back on itself, magnified tenfold.

The rock around them pulsed and moved as if it were living matter. The dirt floor rose up to meet them as they were flung down. They were carried on the wave, but felt as though they were going nowhere. The bulb broke in the flash and the companions were plunged into darkness. They didn't know if they were moving forward or backward, up or down; all they knew was that they were being buffeted. Each one felt the pain and force of being flung against rocks. Each was alone, no longer knowing where the others were…and then there was total darkness as the force of the wave, the pummeling of the rocks, was too much to take. A black curtain dropped over all of them.

Oblivion.

Chapter Three

Strange and haunting visions filled Ryan Cawdor's head. Trader loomed large, laughing at him, spittle running down his chin, eyes wild and fiery, calling him all kinds of a stupe for getting them into this position. Then Trader mutated into his dead brother Harvey, who was dripping blood and falling over as Ryan pummeled him with blows, screaming, "You as well?" Ryan's twisted nephew Jabez laughed in the background before coming forward with a long sword grasped in his hands. Ryan was astounded to find that he had no weapons with which to defend himself.

Jabez yelled triumphantly, charging toward him, swinging the blade. Was that Dean in the background saying "It'll soon be over, Dad"?

With a rebel yell, Jabez brought the blade down onto Ryan…

The one-eyed man sat bolt upright, yelling into the darkness. There were several things that made him aware it had been nothing but a nightmare: it was now dark and cold when moments ago it had been warm; he ached all over, feeling as though he had taken a trip down whitewater rapids without a boat; all the blood he could feel on his body was now dried, cracking on his skin as he moved; his head felt as though someone had been using it as a hammer.

Then it hit him. He was sitting upright, but not in a cave under tons of rock. He was breathing and still alive, and although it was dark all around him, as his eyes adjusted he could see that it was actually the dark of a moonless night, a few stars visible through a cloudy sky. It was also fireblasted cold, as he was suddenly aware of his breath misting in front of him.

Tentatively, testing for any breaks or sprains as he got to his feet and disentangled himself from the few rocks and the mounds of soil that were covering him, Ryan rose and took a long look around, trying to get his bearings. In this darkness, in a landscape that had been ground down into featureless blandness over the decades, it was a thankless task. Even though his eye had now adjusted to the gloom, he could see nothing that would mark out the territory as anything familiar.

As he looked around, he found it hard to work out how, exactly, he had ended up at this point. He could remember trying to dig out Mildred and J.B., and then some kind of quake in the caves. Somehow they had been caught on an earth-movement like a wave, thrown out of the cave system when it crested at the surface. At least, he had. What about the others?

Moving slowly, still testing the range of movement he had, sharp pains reminding him of the violence his body had encountered, Ryan began to look around. He was moving more easily with each step; aching limbs that were cramped as much as bruised started to respond; his circulation pumped stronger as he exerted himself.

Ryan tried to keep down the anxiety that was rising within him. As he circled the debris, he began to feel that he was alone and that the others were lost to him. The thought that fate could have separated them after all they had fought against was something too cruel to contemplate.

He heard a groan. Whirling, trying to locate where it emanated from, he saw a pile of rocks and debris begin to move, accompanied by more moans. Moving as swiftly as his still pain-deadened and cramping limbs would let him, Ryan half ran, half dragged himself to where the moans and movement were. Falling to his knees, he began to dig around the source of the moaning. He scooped away piles of earth and small stones, picking out larger lumps of rock. He had no idea who was underneath, or what part of them he was uncovering, until a foot came into view—a foot shod in a cowboy boot that glittered, even in this fallow light, at the toe.

"Krysty," he whispered, relief flooding him. He burrowed frantically, uncovering her prone body. She moved against him as he reached her torso, feebly batting at him with weak arms, as though trying to ward off an attacker. It was simple to deflect these movements and keep uncovering her.

By the time he was able to take hold of her, she was semiconscious, muttering to herself. As Ryan tried to lift her free, he stumbled, his legs and arms giving way under the weight. It was all he could do not to drop back onto the rocks. Sweat spangling his brow and running in rivulets down his face, he braced himself, taking the faltering steps necessary to bring them beyond the area of rock debris.

As he placed her on softer earth, she opened her

eyes. But they were still unseeing and she mumbled incoherently.

"Wait, wait here," Ryan said hoarsely, the effort of uncovering and then carrying her having drained him. "I'm going to look for the others."

Leaving her, he stumbled back toward the area of debris. Now, as the sun began to rise and cast the first pallid glow across the land, he could see that they had been forced out through the mouth of a pothole that was almost flat to the earth. It was a little like the one they had dived into when the storm had hit, and Ryan scanned the area, hoping that he would be able to recognize the landscape now there was some light.

It still seemed alien and unidentifiable.

No matter. The important thing now was to try to find the others—if they had been as lucky as Krysty and himself. He didn't feel lucky as pain lanced through him, and his head felt as though it had swollen to several times its normal size. But at least he was alive. What of the others?

He began to plan a methodical search, using the light to finally ascertain the extent of the debris thrown up from the pothole. It extended in a radius of several hundred yards and, looking to where he had dragged himself out and where he had found Krysty, he could see that they had been flung some ways. The question was, where would the others have been thrown?

As the area lightened with the rising sun and he was able to get a clear view, Ryan felt both positive and depressed at the same time. Krysty and himself were alive, so chances were that the others also survived. The area proscribed by the arc of debris gave him a definite area in which to make a search. That was the positive part. By the same token, it would soon start to get hot, making searching hard. Krysty was still laid out and he wasn't exactly triple fit right now. And why hadn't the others made any sound to indicate they were still alive? Mebbe they were somewhere in the debris…but mebbe they'd bought the farm along the way.

He heard movement behind him and turned slowly to see Krysty hobbling toward him. Which was just as well, as his slow turn was supposed to have been quick, but his protesting muscles and tendons were failing to respond to his demands.

"Hey," she said in a small voice almost as bruised as her body, "found anyone else yet?"

He shook his head. "Where to start?" he added, gesturing at the debris.

"Two pairs of hands are better than one, right? I'll start over there—" she gestured a few hundred yards away "—and you start here. We'll work around until we reach the other's start point. Okay?"

"Good as any other plan." He shrugged, watching her limp toward the point where she wanted to start digging, and realizing that she'd chosen a far-flung point to give her the time to psyche herself up for the search, pushing her tired and aching body as she walked.

Letting her go, Ryan bent his back toward his own task.

With two of them, the task seemed that much easier, despite the increment of heat that would make it impossible in a few hours. Heads down, not wanting to waste time looking up unless they heard a shout from the other, they both went about their task.

It was slow and tedious, but it did yield a result. Ryan heard Krysty call, her voice small but triumphant. He couldn't make out the words, but he looked up to find her waving at him, gesturing urgently to the rubble at her feet.

Ryan began to move toward her, stumbling over the debris, his aching legs not as feeble as before, but still not carrying him as fast as he would wish. He careered over the rocks and soil until he reached the point where Krysty was now down on her haunches, slowly but purposefully moving earth and rock. Ryan could hear Krysty mumbling and he could hear another voice trying to answer, moaning in pain.

Falling to his knees, the one-eyed man began to dig around the voice, around the area where Krysty was already burrowing. Ignoring the sun beating down on his back, he moved earth, stone and rock until a form became discernible.

Within five minutes, Krysty and Ryan had managed to uncover Mildred. She was coated in a layer of dust and her clothes were ripped, with some signs of bleeding on her left leg, but otherwise it seemed to be shock more than anything that was keeping her down. They gave her water and she choked some of it down. Looking around with unfocused eyes, she tried to take in what had happened, squinting against the bright light, unable to discern at first that it was Ryan and Krysty who had uncovered her.

Stumbling between them, they carried her free of the debris and left her, imploring her to rest up as they resumed their search. But it was too much for Mildred to see them return to their digging while she was simply lying there. Forcing herself to her feet, she staggered over and joined Krysty as soon as she was able to keep her balance.

The sun moved farther into the sky, the Arkansas dust bowl getting hotter and more oppressive. All three of them sweated heavily, the salts in their dehydrated muscles cramping as they sifted their way through the rubble, working out from the center and clockwise. Finding Mildred so quickly had been an incredible stroke of luck, and one not readily repeated. It was a hard slog.

They had been digging for almost two hours, by the progress of the sun, when they made their next discovery. Or, rather, when they became aware of something stirring....

Mildred heard it first. Unable to waste breath on speaking, she tugged at Krysty's arm. The titian-haired beauty ceased her own excavations as Mildred indicated where she had heard the noise. In the sudden silence, Krysty was able to divine that the noise was coming from only a short way away. It sounded like someone trying to burrow their way out. The two women exchanged glances, then made their way over to the source of the sound.

Coming upon the site, they could see that there was someone beneath the rubble who was struggling for release.

"Ryan!" Krysty yelled, her voice cracking from dehydration and tiredness. "Over here!"

Ryan looked up to see Krysty and Mildred standing over a pile of rubble that seemed to be moving of its own accord. He rushed across the rubble, his limbs stronger, feeling renewed with each step now that they had found another one of their company.

Krysty and Mildred were digging when Ryan arrived, moving rubble from on top of the moving body, desperately trying to free it. They scrabbled away the soil and rocks until a mane of white hair became visible, followed by a white, scarred face that was bruised and covered in blood and dust.

"Jak!" Ryan exclaimed, pulling the youth clear of the debris.

"Shit, thought was buying farm," Jak muttered, coming to his feet. Despite the fact that he had been unconscious for some time and covered in rocks, the albino's remarkable powers of recovery showed themselves as he shook himself. Despite the fact that he was aching all over, he still held himself upright and seemed less affected by their strange journey than those who had been moving around for some time.

"What happened? Where Doc and J.B.?" Jak asked tentatively, moving all his limbs, testing his muscles. Ryan filled him in briefly on both what he knew and what he had supposed.

"Start looking for others," Jak said simply when Ryan had finished.

The albino joined Ryan on the far side of the ruins, while Krysty and Mildred resumed looking around the area where Jak had stirred.

The search continued for some time, with no further success. The sun grew high, the heat beat down and the search became harder because of the conditions, because of their weariness, and because it seemed to be so fruitless. The area of debris that was unturned grew smaller, and still no sign of anyone.

"Here!" Jak yelled suddenly. He beckoned the others toward him. Ryan was closest and as the others struggled toward Jak, Ryan could see something poking up from the rubble where the albino was standing. As he got nearer, he could see that it was the end of a black cane.

Doc's sword stick.

As Ryan reached the spot, Jak was already on his knees, clearing away the debris on the body. Ryan fell to his knees when he was close enough and started to move the rubble, shifting soil and rocks methodically. When Mildred and Krysty reached them, they, too, fell to their knees and began to dig.

Doc wasn't moving under the rubble—come to that, they had no way of knowing if he was actually under there or if it was merely his sword stick.

Clearing the rubble around the end of the stick, Mildred heaved a sigh of relief when she found that Doc's fist was wrapped stubbornly around the silver lion's-head. More rubble found his arm uncovered, while Jak had managed to unearth his head and shoulders. It took some time to clear all of the debris from around and over him, but eventually Doc was completely clear.

Mildred examined him as thoroughly as she could. He was breathing shallowly but regularly, and there seemed to be no bones broken. But he was unconscious. Opting to move him clear of the area, Ryan and Jak took him between them and carried him clear of the area. The movement stirred him and he began to speak…almost inaudibly, with no real coherence.

"…when shall we three meet…parting is such sweet—such sweet what, do I wonder? My dear, you look so sweet tonight…. I thought I would never see you again, sweet Lori…. Or is it Emily? Did either of you really exist, I wonder, or were you little more than the fevered imagining of those sweet, immortal moments before death finally claims its own? Can it be immortal if measured against death, I wonder? Ah, what a dilemma for any philosopher…a problem so simple a five-year-old could solve it. Someone, pray go and get me a five-year-old child before it drives me mad."

Ryan was glad when they were able to put Doc down on the flat earth and he was able to return, with Jak, to the rubble and his search for J.B. Mildred and Krysty remained with Doc, trying to nurse him back to full consciousness.

"Ryan, think Doc okay?" Jak asked as they returned to their search.

Ryan shrugged. "Mebbe."

Jak looked at Ryan's grim visage, the fire in his ice-blue eye, and he knew that Ryan wouldn't rest until the Armorer was found: Jak agreed with that, but was also worried about how long they could keep going out in this heat, with little in the way of water and supplies.

Jak looked up to the sky, squinting at the sun. "Past noon—soon be too hot work. Dust bowl keeps heat. No good to J.B. if wipe us out."

Ryan drew a deep breath. "Yeah, you're right. We'll take the next two hundred yards, roughly, of debris, then rest up for a while. We'll also need to work out what water and food we've got, see how long we can do this, though if we're lucky we won't have to hang around too long."

"Yeah, mebbe," Jak mused, noting that there was a note of doubt in the big man's voice. Like Jak, Ryan was wondering if they would be able to find J.B. And like Jak, he was loathe to voice this doubt.

So they kept digging....

By the end of the day, as the darkness fell, there had still been no signs of the missing Armorer. There was still a vast area of uncovered debris to be raked, but they were sore and weary, muscles and bones protesting at the strain. Doc had been resting, his breathing still shallow and difficult from his problems prior to the cave-in, but the others had all bent their backs to the task. Using whatever scrub they could find, they built a fire and sat silently around it, eating from self-heats without once complaining about the taste. There was a gloomy, depressed aura around them.

"Think find him?" Jak said after a long silence, voicing the thought that the others had dared not.

Ryan looked across at the young man, the fire catching a reflection in his good eye, seeming to emphasize his mood. "We've got to. Can't stop trying," was all he said.

They mounted a watch through the night, taking it in turns to guard while the others caught some much-needed rest. Sleep came easily, as their bodies tried to recover from the rigors of the day. It was hard to rouse each other at the turn of the watch. But the violence of the earth movement had scared away any predators and there were no signs of the mutie dog pack that had caused them so many problems. Even the snufflings and shufflings of the small mammals that tried to eke a living out of this inhospitable terrain were few and far between.

Morning came, but the rising of the sun offered no release from their mood. Acknowledging how exhausted they all were, and that going full-tilt would benefit no one, Ryan organized a rota where they would divide up the remaining area. They would search in pairs, one on while the other rested. He excluded Doc, much to the old man's initial annoyance. Although Doc's breathing had improved, a turn in the sun would likely cause the old man severe problems as searching through of the rubble only stirred up more dust and dirt in the air.

And so the search continued. Grim, bitter, monotonous and depressing. The sun rose higher in the sky, burned down on their backs as they searched. There was no real shade, only that which they could construct with their coats and a few sticks taken from the surrounding scrub. The air was stifling. They were dehydrated, barely keeping their water levels up, striving to conserve the water they had left. On his off-time, Jak tried to search for any water holes that may be around for the wildlife. There had to be some sources of water for them to live in this harsh environment. But he drew a blank. Whatever source they had for their water was deep in the burrows, down where the water table existed, coming nowhere near the surface.

By the fall of the day, they were all beginning to give up hope. There was only a small area of the debris that hadn't been combed; they had little in the way of supplies; and another day or two under the harsh Arkansas sun would fry them.

"We can't stop," Ryan said simply. "He's got to be here somewhere. We were all pitched out here, so he must have been, too. We just haven't found him."

"But what are the chances of finding him alive now?" Mildred asked. "God alone knows I don't want to think about this, Ryan, you know that. But it's been two days. If he's been buried and unconscious that long, under this sun…." She shrugged.

"We can't give up now," Ryan muttered tersely.

"I'm not saying we do. Just that we need to face the fact that we might not find him. And if we carry on looking too long, we'll buy the farm ourselves," Mildred countered.

Ryan's face was grim. "You think I don't know that? One more day, going through the last of the rocks. If he's chilled, then we give him a decent burial, right?"

None could argue with that statement.

With the rising sun the next morning, they began again. Working once more in shifts, they searched the last area of debris. It was empty.

"Fireblast! What the fuck happened to him?" Ryan seethed with impotent rage. "He can't have just vanished. Mebbe…mebbe he was thrown beyond us."

"How could that have happened?" Krysty queried. "For Gaia's sake, Ryan, look around you. Where else could he have been? There is nowhere else."

Ryan slowly turned 360 degrees. Beyond the circumference of the debris there was nothing except flat dust bowl earth. Nowhere that the Armorer could be hidden, chilled or alive. The flat, dusty landscape seemed to mock him with its bland openness, hiding nothing and revealing nothing about where J.B. had gone.

"We're here. All of us," Ryan reiterated. "We got thrown out. J.B. must have been, too. He can't have been left in there."

"Ryan," Krysty said softly, "it was a maze down there. It's incredible that we all ended up in the same place. We could have been swept down any number of tunnels that didn't immediately cave in. J.B. might still be down there."

"I can't leave it at that," Ryan said with an irritated shake of his head. "We've got to search around here, just mebbe…I dunno, just mebbe…"

They divided into two parties, Doc joining Mildred and Jak, and they started to search the immediate area, moving out in a spiral to cover as much ground as possible.

It was a short, bitter search, fraught with frustration. All the while they walked under the burning sun, they knew it was useless. But it was something they had to do. They couldn't rest until at least the token had been made. No matter how exhausted, no matter how dehydrated.

No matter how hopeless.

Eventually, they could search no more. They were low on supplies and water and they had to move on. Ryan acknowledged this when they came back together.

"J.B.'s gone," he said simply. "Bought the farm. I guess we have to say that, now. We could stick around and keep looking, but where? As far as I can see, this fireblasted flatland is giving us nothing. It's kept him down there, in a rock grave."

No one else spoke. There was nothing to say. Ryan continued.

"Seems real weird having no body to bury, nothing to speak over, but I guess that shouldn't stop me saying something. If he's gone, then he deserves a send-off.

I've known J.B. a long, long time. He seemed a strange kind of man when I first met him. I'd never met anyone who knew so much about the one thing and who was so intense about it. When I joined Trader, people talked about J.B. in a funny way. He didn't have many enemies, but didn't have many friends, either. He was a difficult man to get to know, but I did get to know him. And a better man I've yet to meet. Always at your back, always by your side. I'll never meet anyone like him. That's all…."

Ryan turned away. Strong emotions other than anger and fury were things that you didn't let show. You couldn't afford them, at least not outside of some kind of privacy. But losing J.B. was a time when he could let it show, just for a moment. Truth was, Ryan Cawdor had just lost a part of himself, a friend and an ally. And it pained him.

His back still to them, Ryan heard them all say something about the Armorer. Krysty and Jak were to the point: a good comrade lost. Mildred had a little more to say. J.B. had been the closest person to her since her revival from cryogenic suspension and to lose him was devastating. She whispered a few words, and then Doc had his turn. He, predictably, rambled on. He had good things to say, but a way of making them last forever. Ryan wanted to stop him, say they had to start moving on right now. But he owed the old man his right to say goodbye.

Finally, Doc petered out and Ryan turned to them.

"Okay. We've done what we had to do. Now we need to get the hell out of here. There's nothing for us around here and it's been a while, so I figure we should give this up as lost and head back to the redoubt. Mebbe we can jump to somewhere better than this."

Mildred furrowed her brow, eyeing him up. "You sure about this, Ryan? We haven't rested well since we were thrown out of the caves and we're dehydrated. Are you sure we should jump?"

"The chances of finding a ville quickly are slim, Mildred," Ryan replied. "And we can get some water at the redoubt. The water recycling was working okay a few day ago, right? We've jumped in worse states than this. It's our best option."

"You're the boss," Mildred replied cautiously. She wasn't too sure of the wisdom involved. They had left the redoubt partly because they were worried about the air system, which cut out the alternative of resting up a night before jumping. How would Doc and Jak take a jump, given that they were the ones who suffered the most afterward?

Having said that, they had no idea how long it would take them to get to the nearest ville and it was obvious that Ryan was determined to leave the dust bowl behind. He had no intention of staying in the place that had claimed the life of his best friend. And she couldn't, in all truth, disagree with that notion.

And so, taking their position from the time and placement of the sun, they struck out for the redoubt.

It was another grim day. The heat was oppressive. Each step seemed like an effort and in many ways it didn't seem to matter if they ever reached their goal. They had lost one of their number and things would never be the same. Others had come and gone, but J.B. was different. And on a practical level, it meant that they had lost their ammo supplies, grens and plas ex. It didn't matter right now, but it may wherever they landed.

The light was failing when they reached the area housing the redoubt. The fact that it had taken them so little time to reach the entrance was an indication of how far the earth wave in the tunnel had carried them.

It was quiet around the area and there was no sign of any life at all. It seemed somehow appropriate. Ryan found the hidden keypad, still recessed despite the rigors that had stripped the landscape, and tapped in the access code. The door groaned open.

They wearily entered the redoubt and made their way down the tunnel. There was nothing to make them keep alert. It was empty, just like when they arrived. Deserted for decades and likely to be deserted for an equal length of time once they were gone.

Which was why it struck Jak so hard. Something just out of the corner of his eye didn't seem right. He looked again.

"Ryan, wait," he said sharply. "Look."

Ryan's eye followed the direction Jak indicated. There, on the floor and partially up the wall, was a smear of blood with a small pool gathered beneath.

It was still wet.

"Shit! Someone else?" Ryan spun. There had been no sign of anyone approaching the redoubt from the outside and the smear was too fresh to have been left by the companions a few days before—even assuming that they had forgotten about it.

Ryan slipped the Steyr from his shoulder, gripping it in one hand while he drew the Sig Sauer and checked its status: fully loaded.

"Triple red, people," he breathed. "We've got company."

The others didn't need telling. Already, they had blasters in hand and had snapped out of their torpor. It was a mystery how someone else came to be in the redoubt, but a mystery that was completely unimportant right now. All that mattered was locating the enemy before the enemy located them.

"Keep together—line out and stay hard," Ryan whispered.

Stringing out in a line, with Jak taking J.B.'s usual point position, they began to make their way down into the lower levels of the redoubt. There was no sound to indicate where the intruders might be and no other signs of their presence. They cleared each room lining the corridor before progressing onward.

It was only when they reached a junction that things went haywire.

Ryan was first across, checking the corridor on the left. He got no further than the junction before blaster-fire exploded out of nowhere. His momentum was carrying him forward into the firing range and it took all his strength to reverse his center of balance and pull back, large-caliber rounds pitting the walls of the corridor.

Mildred returned fire with a few shots squeezed from her ZKR.

"Incoming," Jak yelled, snapping off a couple of shells from his .357 Magnum Colt Python as rifle fire started to pepper them from behind.

"How the fuck—" Ryan began, before realizing he was wasting breath. How had they managed to get behind the companions when they had checked all the rooms along the way? The only way would have been if they used the air-con shafts, which meant that whoever they were up against had a working knowledge of the redoubt.

Those firing on them from behind were keeping well in cover and return fire was pointless. They couldn't turn left or right, in case they walked into a hail of fire. Their only chance was to head straight across and reach the end of the corridor, where it doglegged to the right. It was about fifty yards and they'd have to do it in shifts.

Jak kept the rear covered, while Ryan and Doc took the first run. On a count of three they flung themselves across the junction, Ryan firing to his left with the Sig Sauer while Doc was ready to pepper any fire from the right with the shot chamber on his LeMat. There was none, but to take that corridor, which ran for over a hundred yards exposed, would have left them open to fire from the rear.

When Ryan and Doc were over, Mildred and Krysty followed, with Jak between them, moving backward rapidly.

Once across, Ryan headed rapidly for the dogleg while the others covered the rear from follow-up attacks. The one-eyed man skidded to a halt as the corridor turned and recced around the corner, using the Steyr to draw any fire before risking a glance.

It was clear. He beckoned to the others and they followed.

They ran down the dogleg to the next level of the redoubt, only to find that their way was blocked by a closed sec door.

"Fuck it, they must know the codes to get that down," Ryan breathed. "This door was up when we left."

"Who the hell are these people?" Mildred asked, not really expecting an answer.

"People who know what they're doing, my good woman," Doc murmured. "You do realize that, with a minimum of firing and without showing themselves at all, they've forced us into a corner. And too damned easily."

"You're right, Doc. We've been triple stupe and let them run the play," Ryan agreed. "Minds too busy elsewhere to get it together."

"No time for recriminations, lover," Krysty told him. "We've got to get ourselves out of this before we have the luxury to do that."

"Yeah, but how? We don't know how many of them there are or where they're coming from. We've got our backs to a wall that could lift at any moment and we can't lift it unless we want to expose ourselves."

Ryan thought fast. There were two rooms on this leg of the corridor, both open and empty. To put themselves in one would give them cover on three sides, but would also imprison them.

Right now, cover was important. Even though he had a suspicion that this was what the enemy—whoever it was—had been directing him to, he still indicated that they should enter one of the rooms.

Jak kept watch while they built a barricade. His instincts were sharp, and were needed more than ever.

"I don't get it," Krysty said as they worked, the imminent danger echoed in the way her hair clung to her head and shoulders. "Why didn't they take us out when they had the chance? Why are they driving us into this?"

"Perhaps, my dear, they wish to take us alive," Doc mused. "This would be the best way. Force us here and then sit it out until we cannot go on."

"But why wouldn't they figure we'd come out blasting? Don't they think we'd risk buying the farm?"

Doc allowed himself a sad smile. "We might, but that doesn't increase their risk, does it? If we get chilled, we get chilled. This is, however, their best way of taking us alive with a minimum risk to themselves."

"They're here," Jak said simply, pulling back into cover.

The companions took cover, blasters ready. Shapes flitted past the doorway to take positions on the far side and the companions fired. The roar of blasterfire and the stench of cordite was broken only by the screams of those they hit. From around the door, fire rained in on them. The barricade began to crumble.

"Have to take them head on," Ryan yelled. "Otherwise we'll be chilled meat anyway."

They reloaded, ignoring the hail of fire around them as it ripped at their makeshift barricade and pit the walls with gaping holes of gouged-out concrete. They readied themselves for the attack. It was an almost suicidal charge, but they didn't have the stomach to sit it out and wait to buy the farm.

"Ready?" Ryan asked. He was answered by gestures of assent.

One way or the other, it looked as though they were ready to join J.B., wherever the hell he may be.

Chapter Four

Nothing made much sense to J.B. as he lay in a pool of water, a stream gently trickling around him. Nothing except the pain he felt, as though every muscle in his body had been torn, every bone fractured, every ligament wrenched. Even the pumping of his blood sent liquid pain coursing through his veins. If he could see through the agony enough to think with any kind of rationality, he would be surprised that the levels of pain hadn't made him black out. But everything was too painful, the world too red and full of pulsing lights for that: he had no idea where he was and only a few vague memories of how he'd gotten there.

His head—that had been the thing that hurt most to begin with. He had been in a tunnel and he vaguely recalled something to do with dogs attacking him. Then the walls have caved in on him and he remembered the crushing pain of being under their weight. And then...

And then it went really crazy. It seemed like the whole pile of rocks around him had just been picked up and flicked over, like some force had turned the world upside down. He could remember the strangest sensation, in the blackness, of feeling an immense wave of motion wash over him, pushing him forward and then sideways as he hit a solid barrier that drove the breath from his body. He was tossed around like a branch in a dust storm, hitting the sides of the tunnel that was crumbling around him as he felt himself fall. He'd hit his head again and had the idea that he was blacking out and coming to, blacking out and coming to. How many times he had no idea. All he knew was that he had kept falling down until finally he hit water.

It wasn't deep and it wasn't moving fast, but he still hit it so hard that it felt like falling against another wall of rock. But this one gave under him and he found himself struggling not to breath, not to drag water down into his lungs as his descent slowed until he hit the floor of the river. Some part of his brain that was working despite himself wondered about the river. He'd figured there had to be a water table at some point, but not that it would be so deep. Stupe, how the brain does this when he should be thinking about staying alive.

The wave that had propelled him this far reached the water and the sluggish stream began to move faster, taking him with it. He had no idea which direction he was going in, only that he had to try to keep his head up and breathe in only when he could suck air into his lungs. Which would have been hard at the best of times, but he kept nodding in and out of consciousness from the blows to his skull.

The water seemed to fill the tunnel as it churned harder and faster, the force of it slamming against his body almost as hard as the rocks he'd been pelted with a short while before. There was less air, fewer pockets for him to gasp in quickly when he had the chance. The lights in his head began to glow more brightly, to move around in strange, dancing patterns. There was a humming in his ears, growing louder by the second, almost deafening. His lungs felt as though someone had tossed a torch of napalm into them. They were going to burst soon if he didn't take another breath, yet he could feel he was still underwater.

So this was how it ended? He felt unimaginably weary and a lassitude descended on him. He didn't care if he took in a lungful of water and drowned. Anything would be better than the awful burning in his chest.

J.B. relaxed and prepared to buy the farm. He exhaled and slipped blissfully out of consciousness.

He woke up with a head that felt like someone was pounding rocks on it and incredible pain everywhere else.

At least he was still alive.

He wanted to open his eyes, but was afraid of increasing the pain. He felt around him, slowly, with his fingertips. It was a muddy soil, slimy and slippery with a layer of water about two inches deep all around him. He could feel the water moving slowly past him in a trickle. It had to be dark where he was, as no great source of light penetrated his eyelids. And the water was flowing in a direction that took it from his legs up past his head. His legs felt particularly leaden. He flexed his calf and thigh muscles, which screamed protest at him. He stopped immediately, grateful for the sudden cessation. Then, steeling himself, he tried again.

From the resistance, he could tell that his legs were trapped from midthigh down and from the give, he knew that it wasn't rock containing him, but mud. How the hell could he have gone through head and shoulders first and end up with his legs stuck so firmly? Trying to figure it out made his head spin and didn't matter anyway. The fact was that he was stuck. Yeah, he had to have dislodged something as he came through the hole, and it fell around him, trapping him. Stupe thing was that he felt better for that, despite the fact that it did him no good.

Dark night, he needed to get the hell out of here before the water started to rush again, either sweeping him away or sweeping over him and drowning him once and for all. But he was so tired and it hurt so much.

J.B. sank back into unconsciousness once more.

"FUCK'S SAKES, Sim, I don't see what the problem is, here. Dammit, can't Silborg or Denning see to their own damn problems?"

"Calm down, you're starting to really bug the shit out of me." The tall, broad-shouldered man called Sim cuffed his companion against the ear. It wasn't hard enough to be meant with any malice, but despite his advancing years and graying beard and ponytail, Sim was still a strong man. The blow stung, making his companion wince.

"Fuck's sakes, watch what you're doing," grumbled Hafler, who was smaller, skinnier and younger. He had a sharp, pointed face and his hair was cropped back apart from a thin Mahican stripe along the top of his skull. Both men were dressed in coarse linen trousers, plaid woolen shirts and heavy working boots. They were covered in splashes of mud, some old and dry, some more recent. Both had spent the day in their own sector, repairing and unblocking wells that had been damaged in the recent quake. The tremor had been felt all over their ville and while some were repairing houses and huts, they were part of the teams that had been sent to repair wells in the northern sector.

Only now, as a favor to Denning and Silborg, who had more damage in their sector to the south than the other three areas put together, Hafler and Sim were attending to the last well that was failing to bleed precious water into the storage tanks. It was hard enough keeping the ville watered as it was—they'd had to dig deep to find any water at all—without the wells blocking up from earth shifts.

This well was the most isolated and, as it was closest to the quake, the most likely to be badly damaged. Hafler was sure that this was why Silborg had asked them to take it on—that man would do anything to avoid work. Sim figured that someone had to do it, and as they'd finished their work, why not them? Besides, he had a similar opinion of Silborg and knew that he wouldn't bother to do the job properly. Hafler was a born whiner, but at least he always did a good job.

The two men could see the well from several hundred yards away. Its lip was built up to a height of four feet from old brick and concrete built into a round wall, augmented by wattle and daub and some cement that they had managed to dredge up from a scavenger hunt to the prenuke villes nearby. Could have traded for it, but it was difficult to come by in a usable state and they didn't want to skimp when building a wall around a well. Water was a precious commodity, the one thing in which they couldn't trade.

The wall kept out any small mammals, stopping them from falling down and blocking the well. But the one thing they could do nothing about were the quakes. There had always been a few as the land was unstable, but never anything like yesterday's. The damage had been widespread, if not too serious to repair quickly.

"You want to go down, give me a report?" Sim asked as they neared the lip.

Hafler sneered. "What're you asking me for, Sim? You know an old fuck like you ain't going down there when you can get someone younger—like me—to do it."

Sim gave him a mirthless smile. "How did you guess?" he said, dripping with sarcasm.

"Yeah, real funny," Hafler moaned. As they approached the lip of the well, he began to climb up, sitting astride the top. He held out his hand and Sim handed him a rope that he tied around his waist. Then he held out his hand again and the big man handed him a flashlight. Still without a word, Hafler solemnly tested it.

"Jeez!" Sim exclaimed. "It was okay half an hour ago."

"Yeah, I know," Hafler replied. "But who knows when these batteries will fuck up. And you're not the one who'll beat the end of the rope when they do."

Sim sighed. "Just get your ass down there, will you?" he murmured, tying the rope around his own waist and bracing himself.

"Okay, just don't even pretend that you're letting me fall, right?"

"Would I do that?" Sim was the picture of injured innocence.

"You said that last time," Hafler said as he disappeared from view.

Stooping, the big man picked up the excess coils of rope, paying them out as the thin man descended down the well. If there were repairs to be done, then they would have to go and get a wag with materials. If it was a blockage, then he would pitch the rope and join Hafler at the bottom, clearing the obstruction. Strictly speaking, someone should always stay up top, but it was quicker if they took a few risks. As long as Xander never found out.

Inside the well, Hafler descended at an even speed, clutching the rope with one hand and using the other to play the flash beam around the walls. This was one of the deepest wells and he started to feel closed in as the circle of sky above him grew smaller. His boots dug into the walls of the well, earth reinforced by stanchions and wattle and daub. It didn't strike him as the best way to keep a well open, but given the scarcity of other materials, there wasn't much of an option. Even so, the sweat spangled his top lip and ran down his brow as he tried not to think about the walls collapsing on him.

The beam of the flash swept lower as he descended. No sign of any collapse or instability yet. In fact, it seemed as though this well had stood up to the quake much better than any of the others they had attended to this day. In which case, what the hell could be blocking it?

For the closer he got to the bottom, the more he was sure that there actually was a problem with this well. He knew the sounds of water in the wells during different seasons and this should sound like a healthy stream. Instead, it sounded like a trickle. Something was stopping the water from flowing. He cursed to himself. It was too deep to spend too much time down here moving mud and unstable earth with any kind of comfort.

Hafler played the torch toward the base of the well, expecting to see a pile of mud and rock that needed digging out. The last thing he expected was to a see a man, covered in mud, blood and bruises, laying across the channel, his legs embedded in a small mudslide.

Hafler tugged the rope urgently. Sim put his head over the top, causing the rope to give and Hafler to jerk downward.

"What's the problem? Kinda scary in the dark, is it?"

"Don't fuck me around," Hafler snapped. "Look at this." He played the beam down again until it shone across the prone form of J. B. Dix.

"Shit," Sim breathed. "How the hell did he get there? Come to that, who is he? Don't look familiar to me."

"Y'know what? I don't care if he's your fucking cousin. He's the block in the well and we need to get him out."

"Sure we can't just leave him there?"

"Yeah, right—and have Xander ask us why the water's dried up or why it's diseased when this fucker rots?"

Sim sniffed. "Yeah, guess so. Tell you what, I'll let you down, then you tie the rope round him and clear that mud jam around his legs while I pull him up."

"Great plan," Hafler muttered sarcastically, though in truth it was the only thing that could be done.

Sim lowered Hafler down until the small man was standing in the shallow stream. There was barely room to stand beside the prone body and it was hard for him to untie the rope, squat and tie it around the limp body in the confined space. But he did find out one thing…

"Take him up," he yelled, tugging on the rope when it was secured around the prone man. "And guess what—the fucker's alive," he added, giving the unconscious J.B. a savage kick in the ribs to vent his anger at having to move him. The impact made the Armorer stir. "Yeah, and there'll be more of that, you awkward fuck," Hafler muttered.

He flattened himself to the side of the well while the body, jerking, was tugged past him. He had the flash fixed into his belt, shining downward, and the light from above was blocked by the prone figure, which kept bumping into the walls. Scatterings of earth and pebbles fell from the construction, dislodged from the body's upward journey.

"Careful, you old fuck, or you'll bring it down on me," Hafler muttered to himself before turning his attention to the floor of the well. The water was now running more freely, although uncovering the Armorer's legs had brought down a little more mud. The depth was up to the tops of his workboots and his wet feet told him that the boots weren't in the good condition he'd thought they were. Ignoring this, Hafler set to work clearing the obstruction and shoring it up with the slabs of rock—dislodged by the arrival of J.B.—that had been used to form a channel in and out of the well, the smaller channel being on the outward flow, acting as a dam to build the water level. While he worked, he tried not to think about the fact that he was at the bottom of the well, without any lifeline to the land above.

Up top, Sim was straining, face reddened and veins

popping on his neck, as he hauled J.B. toward the surface. He was older and less fit than he cared to imagine and was having problems getting the deadweight to the surface. As the body reached the top of the wall, it caught on the uneven surface, and Sim had to strain with every ounce, bracing his feet in the dusty soil that provided little grip, to get him over the lip.

The unconscious form flopped over the wall around the well and crashed to the ground, raising a cloud of dust as it hit the earth hard, feet and arms bouncing upward with the impact. A grunt escaped from the Armorer but as he was still comatose, it was a question of air being expelled rather than acknowledgment of pain. Sim drew several deep breaths, feeling his heart pound like a hammer as he tried to return to normal. Finally, he trusted his strength enough to walk over to the prone body and bend to retrieve the rope. He lifted J.B.'s head, looking at the battered and bloody face.

"Bastard," he hissed, slamming the body's head back down. "More trouble than you're worth. Let's see what Xander has to say 'bout you."

He poked his head over the lip of the well, staring down at the point of light below. "How you doing?" he yelled down.

"Nearly finished. Where's that fucking rope?" Hafler shouted in reply.

Sim let an evil grin cross his face. "Can't get that fucking knot you tied around that other bastard out," he yelled. "Can't get the rope down—you'll have to climb up without it." He chuckled as he listened to the stream of abuse that came up from the bottom of the well.

"That'll teach you," he said to himself before tossing the end of the rope down the well.

When Hafler had pulled himself up, they stood over the body looking down on it.

"Reckon we should just chill the fucker now?" Hafler asked. "It'd save us a lot of trouble."

Sim hoicked up and spit on the Armorer. "Nah. Let's see if he comes around first. Take him back and see what Xander says. I reckon he'll be interested to know just how this fucker ended up down there."

"Shit," Hafler cursed, kicking J.B. again. "I know you're right, but that means we've got to carry this son of a bitch back to the ville."

Between them, the two men picked up the Armorer's body and began the long haul back to the ville. The sun was still high, although beginning the long journey into night and the heat beat down on them. J.B. was out cold, a motionless deadweight. Hafler had hold of his legs while Sim had hold of his shoulders. The thin, rat-faced man cursed without pause, railing at the fate that had led him to be assigned to Sim, to have to cover someone else's ass on the south sector, to find this motherfucker stupe at the bottom of a well and for him to actually have the audacity to be alive.

"That's it, that's enough," Sim said, unceremoniously dropping the body onto the dirt and turning to face his companion. "I've had enough of you moaning all the fucking time, boy. You want this guy chilled, so we don't have to drag him back? Okay, you chill him." The big man took an old Colt .44 six-shot blaster from the back of his waistband. The blaster was vintage, but highly polished and well maintained. It was obviously more than just a weapon to Sim, it was an object of some pride. This was clear from the way he checked that it was fully loaded and handed it carefully to Hafler.

Hafler had his own blaster, but he knew what this piece of hardware meant to his companion and he took it almost nervously, a slight tremor in his hand.

"Don't do that, boy, it might go off in the wrong direction." Sim murmured in a calm voice.

"Nah...nah, I'm not using this," Hafler said, shaking his head violently and handing back the blaster with something that approached urgency.

Sim took it, shrugged and pointed the barrel at the Armorer's skull. "Whatever you say, boy. But you moan anymore and I'll take him out right now. And you'll have to explain to Xander why we didn't bring him back for interrogation if he ever gets to find out."

Hafler sucked in his breath. "Don't be stupe. You know I wouldn't want that... Okay, okay, I'll keep it shut, right?" He managed a pathetic attempt at a smile.

Sim's own grimace of a smile was broader: round one to him. "Good. Then just pick the fucker up and let's get rolling."

The two men picked up the Armorer as before and resumed their trek. Hafler couldn't stop the muttering under his breath that came as second nature, but made sure it was low enough not to annoy Sim.

Gradually, the landscape changed a little. The scrub became a little denser as they hit the remains of an old, predark woodland. A few hardy specimens had survived and they provided what little cover there was for the small, reinforced sec post, dug down into a trench and reinforced to two feet above ground level.

"Hey, what you two assholes got there?" yelled the sec man in the trench, his head alone visible above the reinforcements.

"They got something?" a second voice queried, his head also appearing above the reinforcement. Whereas the first sec man had a lean face framed by long, greasy black hair, the second had a bullet head on which the hair was savagely cropped. He also had what looked like a cigar clamped in his jaws, billowing a foul smoke.

"How d'you know it was us, Deke?" Hafler whined.

"The man Upton here says *assholes,* can only mean you two," Deke replied with a beatific grin.

"Fuck you," Hafler grumbled, which only made Deke laugh harder.

Upton, who was as tall and rangy as the shape of his face suggested, scrambled out of the sec dugout to examine what the two men were carrying. He prodded the Armorer's inert body with the end of the remade Sharps rifle he was carrying. "So where you find this one?" he asked mildly.

"Weirdest thing. We covered this well in south—"

"Silborg and Denning—lazy fucks," Upton interjected, nodding wisely.

"Exactly," Sim continued. "One of the wells was blocked and when we looked down it, what did we find but laughing boy, here. Fuck knows how he got there, but there he was, blocking the water flow."

"Never seen him before and he don't look like one of the scum," Upton mused. "So not a mutie and not on convoy. A real little mystery."

"Only until the bastard wakes up. Xander'll get it out of him."

"Yeah, but we'll probably never get to know," murmured Deke, who had clambered out of the dugout to join them and had his Lee-Enfield .303 slung casually over his shoulder. Out on this post, the men eschewed SMGs in favor of rifles with which they could pick off any threat at distance.

Sim shrugged. "Xander's baron. Guess it's his right to know and his right to tell us or not."

"Mebbe…but I'm curious."

"Curious chilled the cougar," Hafler said solemnly. They all looked at him. "Something my mama used to say," he added weakly.

"Really?" Deke asked innocently. "All she used to say to me was 'more, more…harder, harder.'"

Three of the four men laughed hard. Hafler managed a weak smile. Because, unlike Upton and Sim, he knew that Deke was only being truthful.

"Fuck it, can't stand around here all day. We've got meat to deliver before it goes off," Sim said, gesturing to Hafler to pick up the Armorer's feet. Bidding their farewells, they left the two sec men to return to their post in the dugout and carried on toward their ville.

Another half mile brought them to the outer defenses of the ville. Their path across the scrub crossed a couple of dirt tracks and then finally met up with an old two-lane blacktop that was scarred, pitted and twisted by the quakes and ravages of the nuclear winter, but was still basically traversable. It was used regularly by the convoys of traders that came in and out of their ville, both as a stop-off to rest awhile and as a trading post. When they came to the blacktop, they turned right and headed toward the ville, clearly visible now.

It was a squat ville, with buildings no bigger than two stories high, all either the remnants of the predark suburban development or constructions that had been erected around the existing buildings, cobbled together from whatever materials could be found or traded. It gave the ville a lopsided, nightmarish look. A settlement filled with strange angles, abutments were used to shore up buildings that otherwise may have collapsed. Everything was either brown or gray. Color faded quickly in the heat and dust, and even black soon washed out. A pall of smoke hung over the whole area, coming up from the businesses and homes beneath. Even this far out, a buzz of noise could be heard. It was never quiet.

Encircling the ville, broken only on the blacktop by two heavily reinforced steel and concrete bunker houses that acted as sec posts, was a barrier of old barbed wire. Sharp fragments of steel and metal glittered here and there up to a height of eight feet. It had taken a long time to erect the fence. Sim still shivered at the memories of being on the construction crews. Some of the men had fallen onto the wire while putting it together, and were either sliced to ribbons by the metal and glass and bought the farm through blood loss, or died slowly and painfully from the poisons carried on the old barbed wire.

They approached the sec posts, grim and forbidding. You couldn't see if they were occupied or by how many men, but anyone inside could see you coming from a distance of several miles.

Sim and Hafler were only about a half mile away and they were known to the sec crews. So, as with the earlier sec post, they were greeted by sec men who came out to meet them. All three sec men were dressed in dusty combat fatigues, carrying AK-47s. All walked in the same way, as though they were still wary, even though they knew the approaching duo. The only differences were their heights and builds.

"Who's that?" asked one of them, shorter and rounder than the others. "I don't recognize him."

"You wouldn't," Sim began, the weariness evident in his voice as he told the story once again. They were waved through the sec post and they gratefully entered the boundaries of the ville, marked by a banner that hung limp in the still air, strung between the two sec posts. Its lettering was faded against the bleached-out cloth, but still readable.

Duma.

Sim and Hafler had seen it so many times they didn't even acknowledge it as they passed under, continuing their trudge toward the heart of the ville.

The noise grew from a buzz to a clamor as they entered the area of population. The ville was built around a system of tracks and roads hacked into the dust bowl, radiating either side of the blacktop, which cut through the ville. From one end of Duma you could see clearly the sec posts guarding the road leading out on the other end. Dwellings and businesses were one and the same, with everyone trying to hustle something from where they lived and slept. Most had signs outside selling goods and commodities of all kinds, some were bars and some were gaudy houses. There was no division between the trade area and the living area, and children ran wild among the streets, trying to steal trinkets and dried fruits and meats from their displays. Adults chased them and beat them if they caught them.

Only two areas differed from the rest of the ville. A cleared space on either side of the blacktop, fenced in and guarded, offered parking for the wags of the trading convoys. The ville's baron figured that the convoys would spend more jack in the ville if they could leave their wags protected by his force—for a small consideration, of course.

The other area lay to the right of the blacktop from the direction they had entered. The fenced-off area, with three old buildings inside, represented the baron's personal dwelling and trading space. It was the only place where people weren't allowed to walk freely. A trickle came in and out to conduct business of one kind or another, but they were regulated by the two sec men who stood, in dusty fatigues, at the only gate in the fence.

This was where Sim and Hafler headed, carrying their prize. J.B. was still unconscious, had remained so throughout the journey. Somewhere deep in his subconscious he knew that he was on the move, but his pain and injuries were so great that his body had shut down to recover from the trauma.

Sim and Hafler wondered if the bastard had chilled on them before they had a chance to get him back to the baron.

"What the fuck is that?" one of the sec men on the gate asked as they came into view, gesturing at J.B. with his AK-47.

Sim sighed and went through the story one more time, adding that they had brought the man to the baron as soon as possible.

The sec man scratched his head. "Shit, that's a weird

one. Guess the baron'll reward you for this," he added, waving them through.

Not to incur his wrath for bringing their find back chilled would suit them. Both fervently hoped that their charge was still breathing, as they hadn't checked for some time.

The compound in which Xander, baron of Duma, lived was heavily guarded. Sec men walked around inside and outside the buildings, dissuading any of the ville dwellers from stealing and pilfering while they were inside the compound fence. The buildings that housed his home and headquarters were three old predark houses, all of them redecorated on the inside. Walls had been ripped out to form long halls and rich hangings and ornaments traded with the convoys adorned them. Heavy furniture reflected the dark tastes of the man who ran Duma, and also of his father, who had founded the ville.

Sim knew that at this time of the day Xander would be in the building he reserved both for meeting the incoming traders and for dealing with any complaints or requests from the residents. Xander had a reputation among traders of driving hard but fair deals, which was how he had built up the ville founded by his father. But once the convoy left the compound, they would trade with the rest of the ville's residents.

The two workmen carried the Armorer through the entrance to the building, where the sec man on door duty just gave them a puzzled glance. Sim struck out at a marching pace toward the dais where Xander was seated on a heavy wooden throne, listening to a linen dealer from Duma outline a way of extracting more material for less jack from the convoys. It was the sixteenth request in a row for permission to rob slyly and he no longer wanted to hear details—he just granted his permission to get the boring little man out of sight.

Two workmen carrying a filthy and unconscious body piqued his interest. "Well, well, what have you got for me here?" he asked, dismissing the linen dealer with a wave of the hand.

Sim and Hafler unceremoniously dumped J.B.'s body in front of the baron and Sim unreeled his story once more, this time, making sure he didn't sound so bored in the telling, in case the baron detected this and think it a slight against him. When he had finished, Xander sat back and steepled his fingers, suppressing a smile.

"Now that is something to make life a little more interesting. Take him to the security block and get a healer to have a look at him. I want him to live, so I can find out what the fuck brought him here. You did well, boys, and I won't forget it."

He dismissed them with another gesture, and they picked up the Armorer's inert form, carrying him off. Hafler was pissed off, having expected some kind of reward, but Sim was just glad to be getting out in one piece. Xander had an unpredictable temper and you never quite knew when you were doing the right thing for him.

Now escorted by a couple of sec men the baron ordered to accompany them, Sim and Hafler carried J.B. out of the building and back into the throng beyond the gate. With the sec men clearing a way through those who were either curious enough to try to get a look, or those who were just in the way because they were conducting business and couldn't be bothered with a sick man, Sim and Hafler made quick time to the secure block. This was a heavily guarded building with barred windows, built to house jolt- or brew-crazed convoy crew who ran amok while spending—or being fleeced of—their jack.

The rooms of the building were windowless barren cells containing plain plank beds and sputtering overhead lights that were fed by a generator on the outside of the building. The two workmen placed J.B. on a plank bed and waited awkwardly while one of the sec men went to fetch a healer.

"You need us here?" Sim asked finally, noticing how Hafler was shuffling from foot to foot. The sec man shrugged, but said nothing. So they waited.

Eventually, the second sec man returned with a healer. Grant was a man in his fifties with a shock of white hair and a limp acquired in a fight thirty years before. He had been a sec man then, and had trained as a healer rather than be put onto menial tasks such as sewage clearance, his limp making him unfit for sec or work-party duty. Despite the passing years, he still had the mien of a sec man and struck fear in both Sim and Hafler. He knew both men: work duty was hard and every worker had passed through his hands at some point.

"Boys," he said, indicating J.B., "tell me where and when."

Sim told his story over once more, stopping to clarify when Grant questioned him on certain points about where J.B. had been in the well and what it had looked like around him. Sim had to get Hafler to answer these questions, and the younger man was visibly rattled talking to the grim-faced healer. Finally, Grant was satisfied.

"Okay, you boys can go…for now," he added. They were only too pleased to hurry out, leaving the healer and the sec men alone with the outlander.

Grant examined the Armorer. To his surprise, there were no broken bones, although the man had several contusions and swelling around the back of his skull, down to the base, which suggested he had been hit several times. There were some animal bites, multiple bruises and contusions around the body, but nothing major that he could see. There were no swellings or lumps to suggest internal hemorrhaging.

Grant rose to his feet. "We'll just have to wait for him to come around, see what he says. The man's dehydrated, so we'll need water nearby and someone to try to wet him from time to time. I'll send a servant. What really interests me," Grant continued, reaching down and flicking through the canvas bags that were still attached to J.B.'s body, "is where he got all these blasters and grens. Funny things to be carrying around for no reason in the middle of a quake. Tell you boys what. He's going to have a hell of a headache when he wakes up and an even bigger one when he has to answer all the questions Xander'll put to him…."

Chapter Five

"Dark night, where the fuck…" J.B. opened swollen eyelids. The overhead light pinpricked through the skin in red dots and he caught the glare full in pupils that had been accustomed only to darkness for the past few days. The sudden flare of light made his head spin and he closed his eyes again.

He could vaguely recall the last time he had been awake and how much he had been hurting. He could still feel aches and pains all over, but now it was nowhere near so intense. It was, at least, bearable.

He heard someone cross the room and his head was lifted, water spilling from a cup down his chin and onto his chest. It reminded him how thirsty he was, and he gulped deeply, his parched and sore throat responding to the cool liquid.

J.B. opened his eyes to see that a gaunt, aging man with a shock of white hair was holding the cup to his mouth. He didn't recognize him and momentarily wondered why he was being so good to him, especially as his grim visage and the old scars around his neck suggested that he had a past specialized in being less than reasonable.

Grant let J.B.'s head back onto the pillow that had been provided. The Armorer had been stripped and washed down while he was unconscious and the plain plank bed now boasted a thin mattress, a blanket and a linen sheet. The rest of the room was still as Spartan and unwelcoming as it had been before.

"About time," Grant began without ceremony. "They told me you were starting to stir a couple hours back and I came straight over. You've kept me waiting, all right."

"I'll try to remember that, next time," J.B. replied, struggling to move and support himself on one arm, taking a good look at his surroundings.

"Funnyman," Grant stated flatly. "Let's see how funny you are when you've got some questions to answer."

"Got a few of my own," J.B. murmured. "Why am I here? Looks like a cell."

"That's because it is a cell," Grant cut in. "Secure unit, make sure you can't escape."

"Now you're the one being funny," J.B. replied, feeling the weakness course through his system side by side with the pain.

Grant shrugged. "Didn't know what kind of a mutie you might be until you woke. Could have been strong enough to cause some damage in an ordinary healing room."

"I'm a mutie," J.B. snapped. "And it hurts too much to even think about escaping. Shit, I must have been fucked up if I've been out... How many hours?"

"Hours?" Grant barked with a harsh laugh. "They brought you in three days ago. You were out then and you've been out ever since."

The Armorer furrowed his brow. His brain—still be-fuddled from the blackout—was struggling to take the information in. He'd been unconscious for three days? He tried to think back, but all he had were a few garbled images and impressions. Mostly he just remembered the water and the pain. Another question surfaced, a more immediately important query.

"Why have you been keeping me alive, tending to me? Three days is a lot of time to spend on…an outlander." As he said it, it occurred to J.B. that he had never seen the man in front of him before; and yet, he couldn't clearly remember seeing anyone before. Of course he knew what people looked like, how they acted, but he couldn't recall anyone he'd ever known.

Grant leaned forward, studying the Armorer like he was some kind of insect. "Why d'you say that?" he asked quietly. "You say it like you think you know me."

J.B. shook his head, instantly regretting it as the world began to spin. His stomach turned over and he thought he was going to throw up. He gulped down the bile, took a deep breath, then answered as best he could.

"It's just that…just that as I said it, I realized I didn't know if I knew you."

"But how can you know me? You've never been here before."

J.B. screwed his eyes tight, trying to focus his thoughts. It was a simple sentence, but thinking was still cloudy, the throb of his pain cutting through. "I didn't say that I thought I knew you, only that I wasn't sure," he answered eventually, "like when you see someone you don't know, you know that… Like you know when you see someone you do. But I didn't know if I did or didn't…"

"So you're telling me you've lost your memory?"

Grant queried. He was now standing over J.B., almost looming. If it was meant to be intimidating, it was working, especially while J.B. felt so weak. But why the hell should he be scared? They'd kept him alive this far, so they had to have a reason.

"Look," J.B. uttered wearily, "I can't explain why I feel like I do, I just…don't know."

Grant stood looking down, saying nothing. He seemed to be assessing what the Armorer had said. Finally, he nodded, and went to the other side of the room where he sat on a wooden chair; it was the only other piece of furniture in the room and it had been brought in especially for him. J.B. noticed his limp as he made his way to the chair and figured that the man had earned it the hard way, to judge from the look of him.

Grant sat down, looked at the ceiling. "How did you get to be at the bottom of a well?" he asked suddenly.

"What?"

"You were found at the bottom of a well, blocking the flow of water. How did you get to be there?"

J.B. leaned back on the bed and closed his eyes. He could remember being in the water, swept along by a tidal-strength wave that threw him against rocks, battered him and tried to drive the air from his lungs. He remembered those lungs burning like fire as he kept what little air he had down; darkness and the occasional surfacing to gasp in more before being dragged under once again; the darkness before, when he had the weight of rock on him, holding him down; before that the animals, teeth, fang and claw; and always that it was dark.

He spoke these impressions as they came to him and Grant listened. He was more than just a medic. Because of his early years in sec, he also conducted interrogations of enemy or dissident forces. There was nothing he hadn't seen over the past twenty to thirty years and he had a nose for when he was being told truth.

He knew that J.B. was telling him the truth, as far as it went. The man could remember very little. Certainly, that tallied with the injuries to his skull. If anything, it was incredible that it hadn't been fractured from the blows it had taken.

But this truth wasn't enough.

"Very well," he said finally, in the same flat tone as before. "I'll tell you what I think, shall I?"

"Does it matter?" J.B. queried.

"It does, because it determines whether you live a little longer or whether we dispose of you now," Grant stated in a matter-of-fact tone.

"I'll tell you what I think," he repeated. "You were found at the bottom of a well, as I said. This was following a quake in the area, where we expected some damage to be done. What we didn't expect was you. I think that you were in a cave system and that during the quake you were thrown into the deep river that we tap with the well and forced through the river's channels until you arrived up here."

"I had kinda figured that myself," J.B. muttered.

"Quite, but we didn't know this, did we? And now we do. And I also believe you when you say that you can't remember—at least, not right now—what you were doing underground in the first place. You don't look like one of the scum, that's for sure."

J.B. shot him a questioning, puzzled glance.

Grant shrugged. "We have a little problem with a mutie community around these parts. Mostly they keep to themselves, but they do like to do a little scavenging."

"Which is why you thought I might be a mutie, right?"

"Exactly. We also considered how much of a threat you may be, seeing as you were carrying enough grens and plas ex to blow up half the ville, ammo for several blasters, and—"

"Mini-Uzi, Smith & Wesson M-4000 and a Tekna hunting knife," J.B. finished for him. The words were reassuring; they reminded him of a part of himself that was buried under the memory loss and something came back. He felt an assurance that he was comfortable with these things.

"Interesting," Grant murmured. "And do you remember what you were doing with all that ordnance?"

J.B. didn't answer immediately. He considered that. There was something that was struggling to get out from under the blanket that covered his past, but it just couldn't force its way through.

"It's what I do," he said simply. That was all that was clear to him.

"I see." Grant rose to his feet and went to the door. He tapped, waited for it to be opened. Beyond him, J.B. could see a heavyset man in fatigues, an AK-47 slung over his shoulder. "We'll want to talk to you some more, but rest for a while," Grant said.

"Who's 'we'? You keep saying 'we,' but there's only one of you."

"I'm not acting alone," Grant replied. "All these

questions are on behalf of Xander and I'll be reporting to him shortly. He'll no doubt want to see you himself in due course. I would hope that more of your memory may have returned by then."

J.B. was about to ask who Xander was, but was forestalled by Grant's abrupt departure. The man left the room and barred the door with a swiftness that was surprising in one so lame.

The Armorer lay back on his bed. There was a lot to consider here, almost too much for someone who had only recently regained consciousness. Who was this Xander and what did he want from him? With his memory shot, what could he tell Xander that he hadn't already told the gaunt man? What had they done with his weapons and the bags containing the ammo, grens and plas ex?

The canvas bag… Carrying it came back as the briefest flash of memory, something he knew that Grant hadn't told him.

Would they give him his clothes back? At least give him some dignity? And what would Xander do if he couldn't remember…or if he did and it wasn't what Xander wanted to hear?

More importantly, who the hell was he?

That would be a start.

THE DAY PASSED SLOWLY for J.B. After a short interval, he was brought some food by a person who also checked his wounds. The young woman was less than five feet, with long dark hair knotted into a ponytail. She had delicate hands, and a slim figure that was visible beneath the linen shift she wore. Her hands felt good to him as they wandered over his body, checking the bruises and changing the few remaining dressings on deeper cuts. She ran her left hand over his groin.

She was accompanied in the room by the heavy-set sec man, who was holding his AK-47 at port arms, ready to step in if the Armorer offered him any trouble.

J.B. may have been in trouble, but it wasn't the kind that needed sec interference.

Under the sheets, the woman's hand began to move up and down him, slowly and teasingly. Although the rest of him was still aching from his ordeal, this part of him ached for a different reason. The sec man to her rear could see what was she doing and turned his head, trying not to laugh.

J.B. wanted to stop her because he felt he was being used as some part of a game, but at the same time he wanted her to continue because, if nothing else, it made him forget the pain in the rest of his body.

She suddenly stopped, took her hand away and stepped back, adjusting the sheets.

"There, that'll do for now," she said ingenuously.

The sec man laughed as the woman turned away. "You're an evil bitch, Maggie," he told her.

She smiled at him and her hand cupped his groin. "You'll find out how evil later…if you're lucky," she replied.

They left the room, the sec man shooting J.B. a pitying glance as he closed the door behind them.

Left to himself, the feeling in his groin now starting to subside, J.B. eased himself out from under the sheet, reaching down for the tray she had left on the floor. The food was basic: a stew of some indeterminate meat with a few vegetables thrown in. It looked as though it had been simmering for days to soften the coarse-fibered meat and it tasted salty, with just a hint of something hot to try to hide the lack of flavor. It didn't work. The stew was almost inedible, but it was the first solid meal he had eaten in days, so he devoured it quickly, before taking great gulps of water to counteract the salt.

When he had finished, he didn't feel better for it. He felt bloated and as though he was about to throw it all back up. He sat back on the bed and closed his eyes. Gradually his stomach eased.

J.B. began to concentrate on the rest of his body, on those parts of him still hurting the most. Left elbow was weak; okay when still, but trying to bend it was difficult as it was stiff and painful. His right shin was sore and still had some kind of cut or bite on it which needed dressing. His spine was a little stiff, but not that painful. His head still felt like someone had taken a hammer to it and he could feel that it was still swollen and sore, with contusions and cuts around the back of his skull. He thought it was a miracle that he had managed to live through whatever the hell he had actually been through.

Adding things up, it didn't look too good at the moment. He couldn't remember who he was or how he had got here. Xander—who he assumed was sec chief, if not baron—wanted answers from him that he probably couldn't give, and wouldn't be best pleased with that fact. He may resort to torture, or just decide to have it done with and execute him. And, frankly, he was in no state to fight his way out. He had no weapons—dammit, he didn't even have any clothes right now.

The future looked bleak. Somehow, he had escaped buying the farm only to end up here. Thinking about it was driving him mad but that was all he could do. There was nothing else to occupy his mind.

And so he waited, huddled under his blankets, for whatever might happen next. He just hoped it wouldn't be too long in coming, though it seemed to be just that.

In the cell, with no windows and the overhead light on permanently, he had no way of telling if it was day or night, or of measuring the passing of time by the movement of the sun.

Drifting in and out of sleep, dreaming of random faces and events that may have been people he had known or may have been something from his imagination, J.B. would suddenly jolt awake to the harsh light of the Spartan cell. He may have been asleep for seconds, or hours; the time between rests may have been minutes or hours. Time had no meaning. The only thing he knew for sure was that it was always the same thing that snapped him back. He would be beaten down by rocks, then sucked into a long tunnel of water, where he found it hard to breathe. Everything came back to that and it was so strong that he found it hard to imagine that he even had a life before.

How long would he have to wait?

He could hear movement outside in the corridor, muted voices and footsteps. There were at least three men and he heard the sec man who had laughed at him earlier speak. The door to the cell was thrown back and Grant limped in, carrying a bundle of clothes that he threw at J.B. The Armorer separated them and recognized that they were his old clothes, although he couldn't grasp why he should know that when he could recall little else. They had been washed. There was a battered fedora hat with them and it struck a chord somewhere in him.

"Get dressed. Quickly," Grant snapped.

"What about the rest of it?" J.B. asked. "Where is my bag?"

Grant allowed himself a twisted grin. "Please don't think we're stupe. That won't help matters," was all he said by way of replying before leaving the room.

J.B. could still hear voices outside. They were waiting for him to get dressed. It could be a good sign. On the other hand...

Slowly, sparing his aching limbs, J.B. dressed, then sat back on the bed and waited for the next move. Feeling in the breast pocket of his shirt, he found a pair of wire-rimmed spectacles. He put them on and his vision was suddenly sharper, clearer. That was a relief. He'd put the fog through which he'd seen down to the concussion he had to have suffered. Although how his glasses had managed to survive what he'd been through was something he didn't even want to consider.

Outside, through a spy-hole in the door, Xander watched the Armorer as he sat back. The baron frowned and asked Grant, "Could it really be him?"

Grant shrugged. "You know the stories better than I do. But it sounds like everything you ever told me."

Xander chewed his lip. The chances were too great. But if it were, then why was he alone?

Only one way for the baron to find this out.

Xander threw back the door and strode into the room, his imposing physique seeming to take up much of the light and space in the room. He was a big man, just over six feet, and stockily built although now running to fat. He had wiry reddish-brown hair streaked with gray and a beard to match. His clothes were of the finest silk and satin. Altogether, he was an imposing presence in such a place.

J.B. sat on the bed, unmoving, not even staring. Xander could see that it would take a lot to intimidate this man. The baron was aware that Grant had followed him into the room and was standing as respectfully far back as the lack of space would allow.

"I'm Xander, baron of this ville," he began.

"I kinda gathered that," J.B. drawled. He was determined not to be fazed by this man and wasn't even bothered by the fact that Xander could hold the key to his living or buying the farm. The way he saw it, there was little he could do to affect the decision and he'd been through too much lately to bother about it.

Xander smiled. The man had the icy cool of the stories he had heard. "Perceptive. This ville, by the way, I don't know if Grant has told you—" he gestured to the healer behind him "—is called Duma. It was started by my father, who found a small ville already here and took advantage of his contacts to make it something bigger, richer. He was a trader and he wanted to settle in one place. He made this the main rest spot for convoys around here and a good place to do some trading while they were getting drunk and screwing gaudy sluts. I've tried to keep up my daddy's good work."

"Great for you, but what does that mean to me?" J.B. shrugged.

Xander examined him closely. "Could mean the difference between you staying here and having a good life or being a problem that we have to deal with accordingly."

J.B. didn't like the sound of that *accordingly,* but let it slide. The baron was enjoying the sound of his own voice and he might yet say something interesting.

Xander continued. "Grant here tells me that you've got very little knowledge of how you came to be at the bottom of one of my wells. And, more importantly, he tells me that what you went through has knocked your memory out of you." He paused, waiting for the Armorer to confirm this, which he did with a brief inclination of his head. "So you've got no idea who you are. Grant figures that you're telling the truth, and he's real good at spotting bullshit," Xander added.

"That's good to know—wouldn't want you to think I was lying," J.B. said, straight-faced. So much so that Xander truly couldn't tell if he was being sarcastic.

"Well, I tell you, my friend, I think I know who you may be," Xander said, leaning in slightly to judge J.B.'s reaction. The Armorer remained impassive. Xander, still not knowing what to make of his captive, continued. "Many years ago, my father, when he was alive, used to tell me stories of a man they called simply Trader. He was the best—the smartest, hardest, fastest and the best nose for jack in the game. He was the number-one man until he disappeared. And they used to tell stories about two of the men he rode with. A one-eyed man with a heart of steel who used to ride shotgun." Xander looked, but there wasn't even a flicker of recognition from J.B. "Man's name was Ryan Cawdor. And he had someone who they say traveled on

with him, a guy with glasses and a battered old hat—
like we found on you."

Still nothing.

"Guy was an expert on weapons. No one knew
blasters like this guy. They say it was his life, that he
was obsessed and that he had a gift for it. He could
figure out what blasters people used just by the sound.
He could strip and rebuild blindfolded, mebbe even
with one hand behind his back. Always carried a lot of
shit around with him. That's kinda like you."

J.B. felt uneasy, but his impassive face let nothing
show. Behind the mask, however, something was stirring. The way in which he'd reeled off a list of weapons
without even thinking about it earlier…and, come to
think of it, he did know a lot about ordnance. This much
he knew without even really thinking about it. And he
was really pissed off at the way they refused to return
his canvas bag. But, for all that, he could dig nothing
else out of his memory that gave him clues to his life
before a few days ago. All that Xander had told him
sparked nothing in the way of memory, only the uneasy
feeling that this man knew who he was more than he
did himself.

Xander could determine none of that, so he used the
last throw of the dice. "I can tell you that man's name.
It was Dix, John Barrymore Dix, called J.B."

The baron paused, waiting for it to sink in. J.B.
looked at him and shook his head.

"You figure that's me, right?"

"Is that what you think?"

J.B. paused and considered his answer. If he said no,
then the baron may take him at face value; he may be

in line for a chilling. On the other hand, if he said yes, then he may be in line for a chilling anyway, depending on what this J. B. Dix had done. The truth of the matter was that he had no idea if he was this man Dix or not. Yeah, there sounded to be some similarities, but so what?

"What I think," J.B. said slowly, "is that you reckon I'm this Dix guy. And mebbe I am. I know that I know a lot about hardware and the glasses and hat thing fits. But that ain't a whole lot to go on and I don't know shit about Dix. I don't know shit about anything before I woke up in this room."

Xander glanced behind him toward Grant. J.B. saw the gaunt, gray-haired man nod, almost imperceptibly. Xander turned back to J.B.

"I think you could be. So does Grant. And we also figure that you're being straight when you say you don't know. So what I'm gonna do is give you a little test. Follow me."

Xander turned and left the cell. Grant beckoned J.B. to follow and the Armorer rose from his bed, wincing at the stiffness and aching in his body as he began to walk.

He followed Xander into the corridor, with Grant falling in behind. Once beyond the door to his cell, J.B. could see that there were two sec men accompanying the baron, one of whom he recognized as the sec man on watch. The other had to be the baron's personal bodyguard. He, like the heavyset sec man, was wearing fatigues and carrying an AK-47.

They walked along the corridor of the secure block. The walls were painted a dull white and reflected the overhead light dimly. There seemed to be eight rooms in the block, all leading off the one corridor, which terminated to the rear in a solid wall. J.B. glanced back over his shoulder to check and was ushered on by Grant; but not before confirming his suspicions.

One thing for sure, even though he had been brought in unconscious and given medical treatment, they hadn't wanted to risk his escaping. It was a windowless hellhole and made him wonder why Xander found such a block necessary.

He had the feeling he would have to tread very carefully.

The sec man in front of Xander led them out into the light. J.B. was surprised. For no reason he could explain, he had assumed it had to be some time during the day, but as they walked out into the air, it was cool. Dusk was falling and there was a glow of ambient light starting to come from the surrounding ville. The blocks he could see were similar to the one he had just left, apart from the fact that they had windows. Duma looked dull and functional. And although the air was cool, it wasn't sweet. Smoke from fires, the smell of smelting and of old chemicals being mixed with natural oils and herbs, the stink of hot, sweaty people fueled on brew, jolt and sex—it all seemed to hit him in one.

As did the noise. The secure building, fenced in by wire, had been soundproofed by the thickness of its walls and its lack of windows. But beyond its borders, the hum of people and machinery, the sounds of an overcrowded and busy ville, seemed to close in on him.

J.B. slowed, trying to take it in. A sharp push from Grant reminded him to move quickly.

Xander strode ahead, flanked by both sec men, leaving Grant in sole charge of the Armorer. They either felt that he was no threat or that Grant could handle him. In truth, J.B. was too sore to fight, and where could he go?

He followed dutifully, trying to take in as much of the ville as possible. He wanted to get some kind of idea of the place he had landed in. So far, it just seemed to be thriving—beyond that, he couldn't tell. And he wasn't about to get the chance to find out. Xander had already turned into another building, this one guarded by two more sec men, dressed similarly despite their wildly differing builds. Both shouldered AK-47s and from some distant part of his mind, J.B. found himself wondering how Xander had managed to gather so many of those blasters in one ville. He had to have traded for a bulk order…for a moment, something nearly came back to J.B. Something about trading, blasters and grens…

"Move," Grant grated, prodding J.B. once again. The Armorer had slowed as he had tried to gather his thoughts and Grant's intervention had distracted him.

J.B. moved, following Xander into the building, which was larger than the secure block and had windows that were protected by iron and steel bars driven into metal and concrete frames. This building was a bleached-out brownish red, and was two stories high. J.B. looked up at the ceiling as he walked into the building, past the sec men on duty. It was lit by artificial light once again and not by oil lamp or naked flame. Whatever else, Xander had to have found himself a good source of fuel to power generators.

Inside, the building was divided into rooms leading off the main hall, which was open to a staircase leading to the upper story. Two sec men patrolled along the mezzanine, with another one seated on a wooden chair in the hall. He sprang to his feet when Xander entered. Unlike most of the sec men J.B. had seen so far, who were either Caucasian or black, this one looked Hispanic, which struck J.B. as odd. He wasn't sure why, but he had a vague idea that he'd traveled around a lot, and rarely seen someone Hispanic in this central part of the Deathlands. Then another strange thing hit him. How did he know where he was? Xander and Grant hadn't mentioned the geography of Duma to him; perhaps things were starting to seep back into his empty memory.

"Esquivel, where's Budd?" Xander snapped.

"Sir, he's just out back, sir," the sec man snapped back, but with more respect in his voice than he'd been shown.

"Dammit, why isn't that old bastard here when I want him," Xander growled.

"'Cause it don't matter who you are, when nature calls you gotta answer. You want me to shit on your lovely clean floors?" grumbled a grizzled old man, with a halo of black and gray hair surrounding a tanned pate that bled down to a leathery, weather-beaten face. He was skinny and still pulling his belt tight as he entered the hallway from the rear of the building.

Xander laughed, short and explosive. "You old bastard, always trying to wind me up."

"What d'you mean, 'trying'?" the old man replied. "Anyway, I'm here now." He stopped short when he saw

J.B. He examined him with a quizzical eye. "So this is him, is it?" he queried softly.

"Could be," Xander replied in equally soft tones. "Let's see what he's got."

J.B. was angered by the way they talked about him as though he were a pack horse, as though he wasn't even there. But he kept it caged up. There was nothing he could do at this stage except keep calm and see what they expected of him.

Budd beckoned to the Armorer. "This way," he said simply.

Casting a glance at Xander, Grant and their accompanying sec men, J.B. followed the old man as he opened the double doors leading into one side of the building.

J.B. let out a low whistle. It was the only sign he gave of being impressed, but it was enough. And there was certainly something to be impressed by. This was the main blaster armory for the ville, presumably to arm the sec force. There were crates of AK-47s—confirming J.B.'s suspicions—and also racks of SMGs, mostly Uzi and Heckler & Kochs, as well as a variety of automatic and semiautomatic pistols, old revolvers that were both Colt and Smith & Wesson of twentieth- or even nineteenth-century vintage. There were crates of ammo for all of them and there were even quantities of less-common weapons, such as Thompson SMGs—J.B. could recall learning somewhere that these had an early twentieth-century vogue—and derringer pistols of an earlier vintage. There was also a small crate of Vortak precision pistols, which ran on a gas system and struck some kind of memory in the Armorer that he couldn't pin down.

J.B. walked around, naming each blaster as he handled it, checking the condition and rooting through the ammo.

"What else you got?" he asked. He'd figured it out. If he was this J. B. Dix guy they assumed him to be, then he would know all this shit. And to his surprise, he did. Seeing the weapons triggered memories and familiar feelings, and he found that he knew about everything he saw. Dark night, mebbe he actually was who they said.

Budd led J.B. from the room and across the hall. While Xander and Grant watched, J.B. checked the heavier antipersonnel and antitank rocket launchers, mortars and bazookas that Xander's Armorer had amassed. He figured that this old guy Budd knew his business, as they were a good selection and were well-maintained. There was enough ordnance here to knock out a ville twice the size of Duma.

And the old man wasn't finished yet. He led J.B. up to the second story. Up here were supplies of plas ex, old gelignite kept in stabilizing conditions and grens of all kinds: shrapnel, concussion and gas. J.B. detailed all their effects, now aware that he was being tested in some way. It came back to him easily.

He and Budd walked back down to the hall, where Xander and Grant were waiting.

"Tell you something," the old man said, before Xander even had a chance to ask, "if he isn't the man your father used to speak of, then he sure as hell has spent a long time learning how to copy him. The looks fit and he told me a couple of things about some of these blasters that even I didn't know."

"So you are J. B. Dix," Xander said simply.

"Guess I must be, if you all reckon. Still can't remember much about what happened to me before a few days back, but then again I didn't know I remembered that much about ordnance until I was faced with it. So I guess I'll say, yeah, I am."

Xander nodded slowly. "Okay, but if you are J. B. Dix, you and Ryan Cawdor—the one-eyed man—were virtually joined at the hip. When you left Trader, you were both together. He'd be as much of an asset to me as you are."

J.B. wasn't sure he liked the sound of that, but knew he was in no position to call the shots. "Look," he said slowly, "I don't know when I last saw this Ryan Cawdor. In fact, I don't remember him at all right now. I may have been with him when this happened or I may not have seen him for years. Hell, he could have bought the farm, for all I know." He shrugged. "It's not my problem, is it?"

Xander eyed him, trying to work out if he was holding back. "Listen," the baron said finally, "I'll cut you a deal. I cut deals, that's what I do. They're hard, but I always abide by them. And I expect the other side to do the same, right?"

J.B. nodded.

Xander continued. "I want Duma to be the biggest ville in these lands. I get the best convoys through here and we have good things, make a lot of jack. That's good for me and it's good for everyone here. And that's also good for me, right? The happier everyone is, the easier it is to be baron and the less I have some chickenshit after my ass. But to keep that steady, I need the best sec force and the best armory. Budd is good, but he's getting old and this is a big place. It takes more than one to run it and I want you to take over from him, run it with him till he chills—" the baron didn't see, or ignored, the expression of anger and outrage on the old man's face "—then run it yourself with your own, hand-picked underlings. It's good jack, but you do it right or I'll have you hung out to dry."

J.B. paused. It was an offer he couldn't turn down. It sounded good and he knew he wasn't likely to fuck up and bring down Xander's wrath on himself. But he still had an underlying feeling that he'd like to have seen more of Duma before blindly accepting. All he knew was the secure block, the armory and what Grant and Xander had told him. How much of that was true?

Shit, what else could he do?

"Okay, I'll take it."

Chapter Six

Ryan Cawdor felt the slug burn as it ripped through the scant protection offered by his jacket and shirt. The burn was like ice, cold and numbing rather than hot as the metal pierced the upper layers of skin. It was only in that split second after, when the nerve endings were severed by the brutal trajectory, that he felt the pain begin to bite.

It hurt. But his adrenaline was pumping hard and the one-eyed warrior was focused on staying alive. There would be time to worry about the wound to his upper arm later…or else it would be too late to care, as he would have been chilled in battle. All that mattered now was forging forward, driving the enemy back. He didn't even feel the blood as it trickled down his sleeve, soaking the cloth and dripping onto the hand that clutched the Sig Sauer, slippery in his palm.

Instead, Ryan yelled defiance and kept firing, running forward, driving the enemy back.

The companions had no idea who had been able to gain entry to the redoubt or where they had come from. They only knew that in their weariness and their grieving for the lost J.B., they had allowed themselves to be run like rats in a maze, pushed into this corner where they had nothing to do except come out fighting or curl up and wait to be chilled.

No way that was going to happen.

The barricade they had built for themselves in the redoubt office was flimsy and wouldn't last long against any kind of concerted attack. They knew that they had enemies on either side of the doorway, waiting for them to put their heads above the battlements and pick them off.

Or mebbe—just mebbe—whoever had run them to ground here wanted to keep them alive. Otherwise why not pick them off when they were exposed in the corridor? Why pen them in if not as a prelude to an offer of surrender?

If there was to be any hesitancy about chilling them, then it gave them a slender advantage. Because they didn't care who bought the farm if they got in the way.

Without J.B., the companions had little in the way of spare ammo apart from what they carried with them and no plas ex or grens of their own to augment their blasters. They would have to blast their way out rather then prepare the way by using explosives. They could sit and wait, but how long would that give them? They had few supplies and they couldn't afford to rest. Time was a precious commodity at best; now, it was at a premium.

Tactics were simple because there was no alternative. They had to do the unexpected. Instead of sitting there and waiting for the end, they had to come out firing. The hope was to take the enemy off guard, to hit them when they were least expecting it.

It was a risky stratagem, to say the least, but the only one that was open to the companions.

Knowing that there were groups of the enemy on

each side of the doorway and that they were shooting occasionally into the room, the companions timed the frequency of the shots. They were desultory, designed to pin down rather than to damage. There was at least half a minute between each shot. In this enclosed and confined space, a half minute was a long time.

To the right of the door, the enemy group would be back up against the closed sec door. The companions hadn't heard it open, so it made that group a sitting target with nowhere to run. To the left, the enemy would be able to flee up the corridor and around the dogleg bend. This made the group on the right the more dangerous, backed into a corner and literally fighting for their lives.

Ryan whispered his plans to the others, Jak chipping in ideas. It was simple in essence and relied on speed and the ability to keep going, even if caught by blasterfire. The first they could guarantee, the second was down to the fates.

The only thing to do would be to break cover between the containing fire laid down by the enemy. They would then have a few seconds to make the space between the barricade and the doorway, coming out firing. Ryan would opt for his Sig Sauer, as this was a battle for handblasters.

Ryan and Jak would make the initial break. They were faster than any of the others and Ryan felt compelled to lead by example. Jak would veer to the right of the doorway, taking out the enemy backed against the sec door, while Ryan sought to drive back those who could escape up the corridor. Doc would be third out, using the shot chamber of the LeMat to deal with the group gathered by the sec door, while Mildred and Krysty would join Ryan. If not for the fact that his erratic pace couldn't be relied upon, Doc would have been in the vanguard with Ryan. There would be no time for the enemy to tap in the sec-door code and at such close quarters the spread of the shot would be just enough to ensure maximum damage to the group, no matter how many it constituted.

Plan set, it was left only to count down to action. When they were primed, Ryan and Jak waited for a shot from the doorway, then counted to five together. Their eyes met, and they launched themselves from behind the barricade.

It took six or seven seconds to reach the door from the barricade. Enough time for another shot to be loosed from the doorway, catching the one-eyed warrior on the inside of the arm, and enough time for an anxious shout to be given from the startled shooter.

A sudden barrage of shots echoed loudly in the corridor, the space within the enclosed room suddenly alive with hot lead and steel as the slugs whined in the air. Ryan and Jak ignored them and attained the doorway. It was too narrow for both to jump through at once, and Jak was there with an edge of speed. He propelled himself through, firing from his Colt Python as he jackknifed in the air, unthinking of any danger. He saw one man's startled face as the powerful blaster ripped a hole in his chest cavity, the bone splinters spreading through his internal organs, joining the waves of pressure caused by the slug pulping his insides. He was chilled long before he fell.

As Jak took the airspace, Ryan opted for the floor.

Throwing himself across the concrete, ignoring the jarring pain in his shoulder as he hit, ignoring even more the friction that ripped his clothes and took off the top layer of skin as he slid sideways. He remained focused, the adrenaline pumping through him seeming to slow down time, allowing him to think clearly and concisely, picking his targets.

There were four men and one woman, all with rifles. They had been sent to snipe and contain, obviously. They weren't close-quarters fighters. Two of them stood openmouthed, momentarily frozen in shock by the sudden appearance of the two companions. Two of them had already begun to turn tail and run. But the woman raised her rifle, pulling back the bolt on the ancient blaster, ready to drill another—perhaps more lethal— hole in Ryan.

She was first. Had to be. Ryan sighted her with the Sig Sauer, aiming high to get her chest or face. A gut shot wouldn't stop her firing, whereas the chest or face would take her out immediately. But bumping across the corridor floor, there was no guarantee that the shot would be true. He had to rely on his instincts and just hope. He squeezed the trigger rapidly, feeling the recoil of the blaster drive his already aching shoulder into the concrete just a little harder.

His instinct was true as was his aim. As she raised the rifle to her right eye to sight in, a neat red hole was drilled in the center of her forehead, causing her to look surprised. She dropped the rifle before crumpling neatly to the floor.

Ryan saw this as he skidded into the far wall of the corridor, cursing as the impact on his already damaged shoulder temporarily numbed his fingers, causing the Sig Sauer to slip and leaving him temporarily defenseless.

He had no need to worry. Mildred and Krysty were already out into the corridor, Mildred snapping off shots from her Czech-made ZKR that took down the two runners, catching one in the lower back and the other in the right thigh. Meanwhile, Krysty let loose with her Smith & Wesson, picking off two startled marksmen who were slowly starting to react and raise their rifles. Too slowly. One was driven off his feet by a short-range shot that hit him in the chest, while the other found that the pain of having his groin and lower abdomen pierced by a .38 caliber shell was too distracting to allow him to sight and fire. He screamed in a high-pitched, wailing tone as the rifle clattered to the floor and he sank to his knees, his hands clutching uselessly, trying to staunch the flow of blood.

Neither woman gave much thought to guarding their backs. They knew they didn't have to worry.

Jak had taken out one of the enemy, but that left others. And the manner in which the albino cannoned against the far wall meant that he was momentarily out of the game. He was, in theory, defenseless: but only in theory, for he knew that Doc would be on his tail, cleaning up after the initial assault.

Doc had been physically more frail than usual since the rockfall in the tunnels had caused him respiratory problems, and the subsequent search for J.B. had given him little time to recover. He was an old man in many ways and needed more time for recovery than the others. That was something circumstances had refused to allow him. But Doc had something else, an inner strength that was greater than many realized. The physical and psychological traumas he had experienced in his life could only have been borne by someone who had vast reserves of inner steel. It was something that he drew on now, when it was most needed.

Pushing his limbs even though they ached, even though his lungs felt they were about to explode and his blood pressure seemed set to pump his lifeblood so hard that it would burst through his skin, Doc was on the tail of Ryan and Jak like a terrier after a rabbit. He was totally focused on his task and nothing would deflect him from it.

As Jak sailed through the air, taking the enemy by surprise and taking out one of them, Doc was at his heels. The old man crossed the floor in seconds and stepped out into the corridor, wheeling round to face the sec door and bracing himself as he did so. There was a matter of yards between himself and the four people gathered by the barrier. One of them had been hit by Jak's shot and was collapsing into a heap of blood and ruptured flesh on the floor. The other three were stunned. Then one of them—a woman dressed in rags—whirled to tap a code into the sec door. Who knew what lay on the other side—more marksmen or just a means of escape?

It didn't matter. They could not be allowed to trigger the sec door or to recover enough to fire on Jak, who was now sliding down the far corridor wall, already rolling to come up in a combat stance.

Doc leveled the LeMat, shifting his aim so that it was on a line bisecting the two stunned marksmen and the moving woman.

The shot charge from the ancient percussion pistol was so loud within the confined space as to almost create a cone of silence as the sound spread out. Smoke filled the air, catching on the breath and searing the lungs.

The three marksmen had no chance. The shot spread out over a couple of yards, lethal pellets of hot metal propelled at enormous force, flaying at anything soft that may be in its path. Something soft such as human flesh.

The three enemy marksmen were cut down before they had a chance to react, the pellets puckering at their skin before tearing into flesh and shattering bone, gouging into eyes and causing the balls to pop, spilling mucous liquid down faces already smeared in gore.

It was over in a second. By the time Jak was in combat stance, ready to fire again, the three remaining enemy were neutralized with extreme prejudice.

Both Doc and Jak took this in within a fraction of a second and turned to face the retreating enemy on the other side.

The two runners cut down by Mildred were still alive. The man with the thigh wound was dragging himself toward the dogleg, while the man hit in the spine was mewing pitifully on the concrete floor, trying to pull himself forward. It would almost have been kinder to chill him with a second shot, but Mildred and Krysty were occupied by another problem.

Now that all the companions were out in the corridor, there was little cover for them—a few tunnel buttresses to cover behind, but that was all—and they were open to attack.

Around the bend of the corridor, enemy shooters were beginning to fire. Any thoughts they may have had about trying to take the companions alive were now dismissed as they saw their compatriots cut down. And they had more than ancient rifles with which to fight.

The snipers had been sent in purely to contain. These fighters had no such restraints. There was more than one, perhaps as many as half a dozen; it was impossible to tell. All that was known for sure was that they were armed with SMGs and were using them to strike back. The harsh, guttural chatter of a Heckler & Koch MP-5 was punctuated by the high-pitched chop of an Uzi. Bullets hit the walls and ceiling of the corridor. Chips of concrete and little clouds of dust were flung out by the impacts, ricocheting around the companions. The enemy blasters were firing blind, but there was a very good chance, with that volume of fire, that they would score some decisive hits.

"Cover, don't return unless you get a good sight," Ryan yelled, diving for the scant cover of a tunnel buttress, ignoring the protest of his skinned and aching shoulder and the burning in his arm. He wiped the blood from his palm, slicking it down the leg of his pants. His hand was still slippery, so he holstered the Sig Sauer and unslung the Steyr from his good shoulder. He sighted on the bend, hoping to get a good look at the enemy.

If they were anything like the ones they had chilled, the enemy were an inbred-looking bunch, ugly bastards with an attitude to match, but not too quick on the uptake. Scant consolation when they had rapid-fire SMGs as blasters, unknown amounts of ammo and better cover. The companions had made some progress, but not enough. In fact, they may have done nothing more than dig themselves a deeper hole.

Two enemy gunners stepped out of cover, keeping low and firing indiscriminately at the area where the companions had been standing. It didn't matter. All five of them were sheltering behind buttresses. Ryan was the farthest up, while on the other side Mildred and Krysty shared shelter. Jak was on the right of the tunnel, like Ryan, while Doc was one buttress removed from Mildred and Krysty. This left Ryan and Jak in better cover, but with a worse angle of fire.

The two enemy gunners cut loose, while another two—with their blasters slung over their shoulders—ran out, crouching low, to try to take their compatriots back into cover. For the man headed for the runner with the punctured thigh, it was an easy task. He grabbed his man and hauled him back while the hail of SMG fire kept the companions pinned back behind their scant cover. But for the runner headed for the spine hit, it was much more difficult. His objective was closer to the companions and less able to move.

The runner looked terrified, but he kept moving, stooping even lower to grab his target and try to haul him to safety. He cursed loudly and incomprehensibly as he took the outstretched hand of the stricken marksman, who was beginning to fade from this world.

His target's lack of energy and his own panic were to cost both of them dear. Ryan sighted the stricken man. To take him out would be a mercy, as a cripple couldn't survive long in the Deathlands. One shot from the Steyr drilled a hole in his back, puncturing his lungs and drowning him in his own blood. It was a marginally better fate than chilling slowly from his spine wound.

The impact made his attempted rescuer curse louder and step back in shock, straightening. This brought him into the line of fire of the blasters that had previously been covering him, firing over his head. The hail of fire caught him in the head and shoulders, fine sprays of blood, bone and brain matter raining out of his disintegrating skull as his torso was jerked like a spastic puppet by the multiple impacts. The momentum kept him upright long after he had bought the farm and he only slumped to the concrete when the firing ceased.

Above the deafening noise of the SMGs, Ryan could hear an incoherent voice yelling. The blasterfire died quickly and the corpse slumped to the floor.

There was a pause that seemed to lengthen out into an eternity as both sides held their fire. For the companions, there was nothing for them to target, the enemy forces were concealed around the end of the dogleg bend. But the enemy didn't appear to be too keen on firing at the companions either. The silence settled into a blanket that seemed to settle uncomfortably over the scene.

Ryan looked across to Jak. The albino gave a brief nod and then, as Ryan kept him covered, he dropped to the ground and quickly slithered across the floor to come up again next to his leader. It took a matter of seconds and if there were any enemies watching, they weren't quick enough to snap off any fire.

"What think?" Jak whispered.

"Too damn quiet for my liking," Ryan replied. "What the fuck are they doing around there? No sign of an attack, for all we know they could have pulled back."

Jak shook his head. "Would have heard. Sitting waiting."

"Yeah, but for what?" Ryan wondered. "If we stay here, they can just sit us out like before. But without any grens to hit the bend, we're risking running into a hail of fire."

"Could open sec door," Jak murmured, looking back over his shoulder to the closed door that provided them with a dead end.

"They could have men waiting for us on the other side. We'd be exposed."

"Mebbe, but why not use it to hit us now?"

Ryan considered what Jak suggested. If the enemy had men stationed behind the sec door, then the right time to hit them would have been while they were being assaulted from the front.

Although they spoke quietly, Doc was close enough to catch what was being said. He drifted out from cover, moving quickly from buttress to buttress, until he was opposite Ryan and Jak. There was no way that the buttresses could cover three people, but standing directly opposite allowed him to speak without too great a chance of the enemy—some three hundred yards away, around a bend—overhearing.

"A word, my dear Ryan," Doc stated. "It occurs to me that our enemy has a great knowledge of the redoubt. Perhaps one handed down for many years."

"Great, Doc, could work that out myself," Ryan answered, a little puzzled.

"I fear that you may, perhaps, be missing my point," Doc mused.

"Then mebbe you should get to it, and quick," Ryan informed him.

"A fair point," Doc agreed. "I shall, without any further ado. My point is simply this—if these people have had what they consider a unique access to the redoubt, then they would not have countenanced the notion that someone else may also have such knowledge. To wit, they may not consider that anyone else may have a knowledge of the codes used to operate the sec doors. And thus, they may have reasoned that simply to close the corridor off would be enough to both deter and stay us. Therefore, they may not have stationed anyone on the other side of the door for the simple reason that they would not have need. To contain us here and then pick us off would be all the strategy they needed."

"If that was simple, I hope to hell that you never have to go into detail," Ryan muttered. "But you're right. That would explain why they haven't used the sec door to hit us from behind."

"Ryan, if cover, then I hit code. We need to put up heavy fire when opens, they be on us," Jak said quickly.

Ryan agreed. To get past the sec door would give them a get out from this closed situation. But the enemy would hear the door opening and would hit them hard. They'd have no choice. The companions would have to move quickly and make every shot count. Without J.B.'s Uzi and the spare ammo he carried, they could only fight for so long against such heavy SMG use.

"Jak, tell Mildred and Krysty on your way back,

then hit the code when I give you the signal. We all have to be ready to move." His mind racing, he could think of only one way to buy the necessary space. He looked across to Doc. "Wait until they start to come into view— they'll have to when the door opens—and hit them right in the middle with everything you've got," he said, indicating the LeMat.

Doc cradled the ancient pistol to him, his hand resting on the barrel that delivered the shot charge. In this relatively enclosed space, the hot metal dispersing in the air would be the best weapon they could call to hand.

"I shall endeavor to do my best," Doc solemnly intoned.

Ryan tapped Jak on the back. "Go."

Keeping low and moving in an irregular zigzagging pattern, Jak moved back, taking as much cover as possible, toward the sec door, pausing only to deliver instructions to Mildred and Krysty, who had remained just out of earshot. He reached the next support buttress to the sec-door arch. There was a ten-foot gap and to cross it and tap in the code would leave him with his back exposed for a vital second or two.

Ryan saw Jak take up his position. He checked the Steyr and the Sig Sauer. For ease of movement he would swap the rifle for the handblaster as they retreated, but he wanted to make sure that he had both primed and ready for a firefight. Next, Ryan looked back at his people. Jak, impassive as ever, was poised and ready, seemingly at ease and ready to move with the speed and accuracy of a snake. Mildred and Krysty were behind their cover. Both had their blasters ready and their balance poised to make a break for the sec door as it opened. Finally, he looked across at Doc. The old man would be the slowest out of the blocks, but the firepower of the LeMat dictated that he should stay at the front with Ryan. The old man stood rigid and firm, jaw set grimly, a light in his eyes that showed him to be somewhere else in his mind, about to fight yet another old battle. He met Ryan's eye and indicated his readiness with an inclination of the head.

Ryan looked back at Jak and nodded. Now.

Jak darted to the sec-door panel and punched in the code. The door began to move, the whirring of the predark machinery seeming somehow louder than usual in the encompassing silence. Mildred and Krysty raised their blasters and began to track backward, leaving cover and moving toward the door. Ryan and Doc faced the dogleg bend, waiting for the first signs of advance.

There was an incoherent cry from beyond the corner of the tunnel. The enemy had been content to sit back and wait rather than incur losses and hadn't even bothered to mount a watch on what the companions were doing.

Yelling and cursing, a group of enemy came around the bend, firing indiscriminately, peppering the corridor with blasterfire. Doc and Ryan stood firm, despite the ricochets and lumps of concrete that flew around them. They didn't dare look back to see how their companions were doing. Ryan was too busy trying to pick off runners with the Sig Sauer, while Doc waited, patient and yet anxious, trying to pick the optimum moment to fire.

Mildred, Krysty and Jak ignored the mayhem around

them. If they were hit, there was nothing they could do about it. Right then, they had to trust luck to get through the sec door and into cover on the other side. If they were really lucky, Doc and Ryan could pull back and they could keep the enemy at bay while they closed the door. That would buy them a few seconds in their flight, and seconds were the most precious thing they could wish for. Meantime, as they stood in the open, they snapped off shots at the oncoming gunners, hoping to at least make the least brave of the enemy dive for cover, even if they didn't chill or injure a few.

The enemy was gaining ground. It was a matter of getting the right distance for a spread of shot with the right distance for power. Doc couldn't think about it, only consider that tightening in his gut that told him it was now or never.

Doc calmly stepped out from behind the buttress, raised the LeMat and fired into the middle of the enemy fighters. The roar was deafening and he remained upright and unyielding, even though his face was cut and bleeding from concrete chips. He felt shells pluck at his clothes, tearing material and snicking at his flesh, creasing the skin and drawing blood. One hit him full in the shoulder, driving him right back, the impact making him grunt. But the hardy old man had so much adrenaline pumping through his body that the wound hardly registered.

The others, scrambling under the sec door, were also hit by the debris of ricochets; stray shells hit around them and even nicked them. Most were ricochets with the real sting taken out by the time they hit. But what was left was more than enough. Agonizing, flaming pain was something that became the only way to prove you were still alive, as the blood flowed from skin tears. Not enough to slow them, but enough to hurt like hell and drive them on.

Doc was immobile. It seemed as though he had stood firm for hours, but in truth it could not have been more than a moment. Ryan grabbed him and hauled him back, firing as he raced backward towards the sec door. Doc, jolted out of his stunned reverie, followed, loosing the ball charge from the LeMat, howling like some primeval beast in a combination of bloodlust, anger and agony.

The shot charge from the LeMat had done its work. The front ranks of the enemy fighters were down, many chilled instantly, others in intense pain and buying the farm from the injuries to their heads and bodies inflicted by the spray of hot metal. The floor of the tunnel was slick with blood and gore, making it hard for the fighters behind to keep their footing as they tried to pick their way around the corpses and the barely alive, firing all the while.

Not thinking about the air around him, alive with potentially lethal hot metal, Ryan took a flying dive at the sec door. Mildred and Krysty were on their knees from positions of cover, firing around Ryan and Doc, while Jak began to tap in the code to close the door.

Ryan's hand was securely clamped on Doc's coat collar, and as he launched himself he brought the old man with him. Doc hit the floor and skidded along with a thud that knocked the air out of his lungs and stopped his screaming.

They slid between the doors as SMG fire impotently

peppered the thick metal doors, buzzing like angry insects as it deflected harmlessly away. The companions were up and moving out of range, Ryan and Doc having scrambled to their feet. Mildred dropped back to support Doc, who had been pulled upright by Ryan. The one-eyed man was having problems of his own. The wound in his arm had opened up a little more and his sleeve was now heavy with blood. There was no time to staunch the flow.

The same could be said for Doc, who was now losing blood quickly. Almost on the run, swearing heavily, Mildred searched her med bag for something with which to pad the wound until she could tend to it properly. Doc was pale and drawn, only his immense will keeping him from blacking out.

"Leave me," he said through gritted teeth. "I'm holding you back."

"Like hell we will," Ryan snapped. "We don't even know where we're going or if we'll get there."

"Head for the mat-trans. No fit state, but at least a jump'll get us away," Krysty breathed heavily.

Ryan nodded and they headed for the gateway level, none wanting to waste valuable breath on words. But they shared the same thoughts—these people knew the layouts of the redoubts, so even if they hadn't guessed where the companions were headed, they at least knew all the corridors. That meant that rather than chase them, they were likely to send out scouts, so the companions could be met at any junction by enemy fighters.

It was useless just to watch their backs as they would in any other comparable situation. They had to watch everything.

Coming to junctions slowed their progress, as Ryan

and Krysty went ahead, checking before they crossed, with Jak and Mildred supporting Doc. Ashen-faced, breathing only with the greatest difficulty, Doc was almost out on his feet and needed rest.

But there was no rest. They came to within two corridors of the mat-trans unit when it all fell apart.

Krysty and Ryan gestured the others back as another junction came into view. It was a T-junction with a corridor leading off to the left and it should have been simple. Krysty dived across the open space while Ryan swung the Steyr around the corner. She was almost across when one shot, coming out of nowhere, hit her on the foot. The silver decorations on her cowboy boots saved her The slug hit the metal at the base of her heel, denting the silver but being deflected rather than penetrating into her foot. However, the force was enough to throw her off balance and twist her ankle. She yelped at the sudden stab of pain, but rolled with the momentum and came up into a crouch on the other side.

Ryan snapped off a shot from the Steyr and was rewarded by a hail of blasterfire that pitted the expanse of wall running between Krysty and the rest of the companions. Behind the firing, they could hear the sounds of several fighters moving into position.

"Fireblast!" Ryan cursed, realizing that Krysty was now cut off from them. There was no chance of getting across the divide with the manpower and firepower between them.

Too late—perhaps weary, perhaps the injuries beginning to dull instinct—Ryan saw a lone runner moving toward Krysty, using the buttresses as cover. But she'd seen this and snapped off a couple of shots.

Her aim wasn't good enough. Unharmed, the enemy runner hit the sec door and closed off one end of the corridor.

Ryan realized that the enemy's knowledge of the redoubt and superior numbers was about to win the day, and there was nothing they could do about it. Covered on two flanks, they could only go back the way they had come if they left Krysty behind.

"Ryan," Jak called.

Ryan turned to see another batch of enemy fighters appear at the end of the corridor. A quick head count took in a dozen. They were withholding their fire, but advancing with their blasters ready.

Ryan looked at his companions: Krysty, isolated and crouching awkwardly to protect her ankle; Mildred, eyeing the oncoming enemy anxiously while trying to tend to Doc, who was now slumped against the wall, sinking toward the floor; Jak, ready, like Ryan, to fight to the last, but with only two of them?

Why wasn't the enemy firing?

Ryan and Jak exchanged glances. If they were going to be chilled, make it quick rather than tortuous and take some of the bastards with you. Both men raised their blasters....

Chapter Seven

The enemy stood about fifty yards away. They were a bunch of misshapen men and a few women, dressed in a bizarre combination of rags and better clothes, as though they had placed their new acquisitions on top of their old rags, rather than discard them. They showed signs of mutation and inbreeding, with slack faces, deformities and some lameness among them. But they were all well armed.

The moment seemed to stretch to infinity. Ryan and Jak could feel the blood pumping through their veins, their muscles and tendons tense, their fingers tight on their triggers, the pressure building as the yielding metal began to move.

Krysty had her own Smith & Wesson up and ready. If they mowed down the others, she would have at least a degree of shelter, a moment of time on the other side of the corridor, shielded by their bodies and the greater distance, to perhaps take out a couple more of the enemy before she, too, was claimed.

Mildred glanced from Doc to the enemy fighters and to Ryan and Jak. Doc was almost delirious as he grew weak from blood loss, from weariness, from the lack of oxygen getting into his bloodstream via his still-weakened lung capacity. He was hollow-cheeked, looked like a man ready to take the last train west.

But still the enemy didn't fire. Their blasters were raised and they should have cut down the companions with no compunction.

A harsh voice shouted guttural commands that seemed to Ryan to be in a language he had never heard. It was the same voice he had heard barking incomprehensible commands at their first firefight. The enemy fighters dropped their blasters to a forty-five-degree angle. They could still raise and fire within a fraction of a second, but it was a gesture intended to convey that they would not immediately chill.

The voice continued. Barking, harsh, speaking something that sounded like English. Ryan looked across to Jak. The albino's face was as impassive as ever as he returned Ryan's gaze. Whatever was in those ruby eyes was completely unreadable. But he did raise a scarred eyebrow. Without having to swap words, both men eased the pressure on their trigger fingers without lowering their blasters.

The ranks of enemy fighters parted and a squat, fat man with a lame right leg hobbled through. He was speaking, but the words were still mangled. Now Ryan could understand why. The man had a cleft palate, which distorted his speech. He also spoke as though his throat was permanently full of phlegm, an impression reinforced by the way he suddenly stopped midsentence and hoicked a phlegmball across the floor. He finished his sentence and looked questioningly at Ryan, who shook his head; partly to clear it, partly to indicate that he didn't understand.

The man began to speak again. This time he was

slower, making an obvious attempt to be understood. By the same token, Ryan tried to concentrate, even though there was blackness closing in at the edge of his vision. Trying to concentrate on the cleft palate was helping to keep the blackness of unconsciousness at bay. The one-eyed man blinked heavily, listening intensely to what the fat man had to say. Gradually, it began to take shape.

"Think you must be triple stupe if'n you can't even understand what the fuck I'm saying. Guess that should be your problem, if not for the fact that we've got you cornered and could just blast the shit out of you…. Fact is, we could make you nothing more than shit stains on the walls. Ha! Kinda funny, that is. Anyways, I'm guessing by that fucked-up look on your face that you're starting to understand what I'm saying. Shit, fucker, just nod your head if you do…"

Ryan nodded. The man's voice was thick, deep and the affliction to his mouth made his words heavy. But once you got the cadence and the weird rolling rhythm of his speech, it did actually start to make sense.

"Good, 'cause I got somethin' to say. We been running around after you and you took out some of my people—not stupe fighters, but real good marksmen. Made 'em look like triple-stupe mad dogs before you cut 'em down. Now I guess I should be kinda pissed about that and mebbe I am. But fuck it, we came after you first and it ain't our fault—nor yours—if you happen to be better fighters than us. But you're less fighters than us—a whole lot less. And we coulda taken you apart if'n we wanted. Right now, one word and you're history, like the rest of this pesthole planet. We's just living out the end-times, but if'n it's us or you, then you don't have to be some kinda clever shit to work it out, right? I said, right?"

Ryan nodded once more. He felt tired, weak and he wondered where the rambling diatribe was going. The only good thing was that they hadn't been chilled yet. That gave them a crumb of hope for getting out of this and that was enough to keep him clinging tenaciously to consciousness for the moment.

"Okay, so you're still paying attention. See, I figure you must know somethin' about this place, 'cause you ain't running blind. Now that kinda puzzles me, 'cause far as I knows, we's the only ones around here that knows about here. Those horsefuckers in Duma don't know about it, do they?"

The squat man looked from Ryan to Jak and then at the others, trying to see if the name meant anything to them. His eyes were screwed up, his pendulous nose almost dangling onto his deformed lip, which no amount of stubble could disguise. He looked grotesque and absurd; this, the man who held their fate in his hands.

"Guess y'all ain't from there, after all," he said slowly. "Kinda figured not. And you ain't from no convoy, 'cause there ain't been wags out around here for ages. Saw you before the storm and waited. Figured you'd come back if'n you wasn't chilled."

Mildred stood up, leaving Doc, who had lapsed into unconsciousness, and stepped forward.

"Will you just tell us whatever the fuck you've got to say before you kill us and then get on with it? If I'm going to die, I want it to be because I'm filled with lead, not because some asshole bores me to the grave."

The fat man looked at her, amazed. "Chill you, stupe bastards? What have I just been saying? We coulda chilled you a whole shitload a'times if'n we really wanted to—but that ain't what we want. We wanted to take y'all prisoner, mebbe see if you could be of some use. Always use good fighters, and you need a place to rest. 'Sides, we need more fighters for our next raid. Shit's running low and this place got cleared out long ago. We want you to join us."

Ryan could barely believe it. This fat idiot had wanted to form an alliance, so he had chased them through the redoubt wasting his own men and inflicting damage on them. What kind of a triple-stupe moron was he?

"Why the fireblasted hell didn't you just say—" Ryan managed to croak out before the blackness engulfed him.

"Shit, guess you better pick up old One-eye, there," the fat man said as he watched Ryan crash to the ground.

THERE WERE STILL A LOT of questions that remained unanswered and a lot of things that didn't add up, but the companions were in no fit state to argue right now. For whatever reasons he and his people might have had, the fat man had offered them an alliance—respite and shelter—at a time when they could fight no more.

The companions holstered their blasters, allowing some of the opposing forces to come forward. Slinging their SMGs over their backs, two men took hold of Doc, lifting him gently and supporting him between them. Mildred had to look away when she saw that one of the men had no nose, merely a pustulating hole dripping mucous where his nose should have been, his breath whistling heavily in the large, open space.

Three came forward to claim Ryan: two men and a woman. Although there was little to tell between them, as all were short and fat, shuffling rather than walking, with upturned bits of noses, tiny, unblinking eyes and warts spread across their features. All three could have been from the same family.

Come to that, many of them looked as though they came from the same small gene pool. Mildred looked at them and also at the party that came from the side corridor. They were all either small, fat and piglike or tall and thin with facial distortions. The man with no nose was very like the fighter who now opened the sec door that had cordoned them off, joining his fellows.

As they turned and began to trek back along the corridors, talking softly among themselves, giggling and looking at the companions as they walked among them, Mildred could also see that facial deformities were just one aspect. A lot of the people, particularly the men, had trouble walking. They shuffled, dragging one lame foot, like their chief. Taking as close a look as she dared without arousing suspicion, Mildred could also see that a number of them had hand or arm deformities. These seemed to be mostly among the women.

The fat man had mentioned the name of a ville, somewhere he thought they had come from. Wherever it was, it obviously wasn't as isolated as the place where these people lived. Too many generations with only their families to interbreed. That may explain the bizarre behavior, the physical problems of inbreeding usually being matched by mental instability.

This didn't reassure her. They were being marched out of a redoubt—Ryan and Doc both unconscious from blood loss—by a group of inbreds who were probably mentally unstable, heading toward who knew what fate?

Krysty had been having similar thoughts and she had decided to try to find out a little more. Ignoring the men and women who tried to touch her hair as they walked, laughing as the prehensile curls recoiled from their touch, she addressed the fat man who was in the lead.

"Listen, where are you taking us? And what were you doing down here?"

"You ask a lot of questions 'sidering I could ask the same, well, the last one, any rate. See, we's on a scavenging hunt. No food or shit left down here. That cleaned out a whole long time ago. 'Fore I was borned, or most of them here. But mebbe there was something we could take out that was left, use to trade with the convoys. Not that the fuckers stop for us—just want Duma. But mebbe we stop them and trade. Chill the fuckers if'n they don't. But I's a fair man, see?"

It was an answer that, perhaps, left more questions than it answered. But as Mildred and Krysty exchanged glances, one thing was certain. Whoever these people were, their ancestors had known the secrets of the redoubt and had plundered it long ago. Which explained how they got in. The sec code had to have been handed down. Perhaps at one time their ancestors had wanted them to use the redoubt as a safe place—perhaps they had even known something about the mat-trans—though that must have all been lost and garbled long ago.

The fat man continued. "See, we was looking for things to use in trade and I guess you were, too…or at least, you was looking for some kinda supplies. You look all beat and I figure that storm couldn't have done much for you. Specially as you came back with one less than you went with. So we all looking for something here, and it figures that it'd do us good to work together. We can always do with outsiders to help us, so I figure this is good for all of us, right?"

He gave them a smile that looked more like a hideous leer. Both Mildred and Krysty felt that the alliance was something to which Ryan had given tacit agreement by not opening fire when he and Jak had the chance. Some chance of getting out was better than none. But all the same, there was something about this tribe that stank to high heavens, more than a three-day-chill stickie laid out in the sun.

Krysty looked across at Jak. The albino was unreadable. There was no way that any of them could ever tell what was going on in his head. He gave her some indication by a very slight, almost imperceptible shrug. And he was right—what could they do? At least they were still alive. It was a question of playing percentages, something that Ryan would always do if he had the option. The one-eyed man may be laid out at the moment, unaware of what was going on around him, but his style of leadership had impressed itself enough for the others to follow what would have been his lead.

The party of inbreds, with the companions uneasy among them, reached the outer sec doors and one of their number punched in the sec code. The door opened to reveal that it was now dusk outside.

"Hey, looks like it's nearly night," the fat man enthused. "Mebbe we'll find us some critters come out in the dark that we can chill on the way home. Mebbe give us the chance to get some fresh meat in the pot." He cackled, and some of the others joined in with him. It made the companions wonder what the hell they would get to eat when they arrived wherever the hell it was they were headed.

Because right now, it looked like another march lay ahead of them. They'd had no indication of a ville on their previous journey through the territory surrounding the redoubt and nothing to show that there were any wags hidden away on their way back.

Then again, there had been no signs of any tracks to alert them as they approached. Maybe these people weren't quite as stupe and mad as they feared.

"How far have we got to go— What do I call you?" Mildred asked, adding, "I don't know how much more Doc can take. Ryan should be okay, but Doc's lost a lot of blood."

The fat man sniffed as he led them out of the shallow valley and around to the rear of the redoubt entrance. The soil had been scoured so thin by the elements that the concrete lining the redoubt tunnel was visible, like bone, through parts of the incline.

"You can call me Boss...Boss Buckley. The Buckleys been the mainstay of Nagasaki since before the nukecaust. We's the ones kept the whole fucker going, in more ways than one. Yes, indeed." He started to laugh, petering out to a cough that presaged another glob of phlegm that spattered on the soil, staining it.

Krysty frowned, looked across at Mildred. The name was familiar to her: Nagasaki was something she had heard of back in Harmony. Something to do with the times before the nukecaust and when the nukes first began. It had some kind of symbolic meaning that she couldn't recall right now. But how did it get to be the name of some pesthole ville full of inbreds?

Mildred returned the glance with a shrug. She remembered only too well the dark shadow of nuclear warfare under which her generation had been raised and which they had helped reach fruition. The pictures and old news footage she had seen back before she was frozen flickered through her memory. It was a dark heritage, but how did it lend its name to where these people came from?

Both women were lost in their thoughts and didn't notice that Buckley had stopped by a small gathering of scrub. Jak, however, had seen why. He marveled at the ingenuity of the camouflage, even though the logic to it was a little askew.

Under Buckley's direction, some of the inbreds moved the scrub. It formed a screen over a pit about four feet in depth, some twenty feet in length, and about twelve feet in breadth. Within this were two wags, each hitched to two sickly and weak-looking mules. Two of the inbreds coaxed the mules up out of the pit with whispered words and clicking tongues.

"We'll never all fit into that!" Mildred exclaimed.

"Don't have to," Buckley grunted. "Always hide our mules and wags like this, so's any passing convoy don't get wind of the special place. Couldn't dig that deep and wide without it looking strange. Not that much scrub around here. But we take it in turns—some walk, others ride, then we change around. Ain't perfect, but what is now? Least ways all of us get to rest up some on the way back."

With the mules and wags now on the flat, Doc and Ryan were loaded on one, with Mildred, Krysty and Jak on the other. They were given first chance to rest, while some of the inbreds mounted around them. The others walked by the side of the wags.

They headed to the south. Mildred and Krysty found themselves falling into intermittent sleep, disturbed only by the occasional blastershot as someone took a potshot at a passing small mammal or lizard. Only Jak remained alert, not trusting to fall asleep while the others also dozed.

The journey took all night. The sun was rising and the companions were now walking beside the wags, when Buckley hailed them and pointed ahead.

"Nagasaki," he said simply.

Mildred looked ahead at the low gathering of ramshackle huts and ruined buildings that constituted the ville and she despaired of being able to tend to Ryan and Doc in such circumstances. Even from this distance, it seemed to be a pesthole and as the wags trundled nearer, her worst impressions were confirmed.

Most of the population of Nagasaki seemed to have followed Buckley on the trip to the redoubt, for there were only a few older people coming from the dirty collapsing buildings to greet them. Mildred guessed, from the condition of most of the war party and from a look at their ville, that old age wasn't a viable option in Nagasaki and most of the people would buy the farm relatively young, either from injuries incurred in battle or simply because their inbred state would pass on illnesses and weaknesses that would pick them off when still young.

There were a few animals—a couple of pigs, some chickens and something that may have been a goat of some kind—wandering through the dust and mud that constituted the streets of the ville. In truth, ville was too grand a description for this collection of ruins. It was more like a series of huts that had been built around a couple of old predark ranch houses. Mildred guessed that before the nuclear winter, it had probably been a viable ranch and farm.

The straggling dwellers came out to the war party and the companions could see that they were as badly deformed as the others, merely younger or older. Even the animals with them looked inbred.

The wags pulled up in the middle of the cluster of dwellings. To the rear of the main ranch house, Mildred could see that an old barn had been rebuilt. More, in fact: it looked as though the old structure, which stood apart from the rest of the dwellings, had been reinforced and made secure. She wasn't sure—it was too far and too obscured by the other dwellings to tell—but it looked as though a dry moat had been dug around it, with a footbridge connecting the barn to the rest of the surrounding ville.

She looked across at Krysty and then at Jak. Both had also seen the barn and although Krysty looked concerned, Jak gave a small shake of his head. The time to worry about it would be later. It gave the place a sinister air, but there were more pressing concerns.

Such as attending to Ryan and Doc.

Buckley hopped down from one of the wags and gestured to some of his people, barking guttural, almost unintelligible commands at them. They lifted the prone figures of Doc and Ryan off the wags. Doc had briefly recovered consciousness, but was now out once more; Ryan was conscious but weak.

Buckley turned to the others. He seemed to be making an attempt to regulate his speech, realizing that they were still having trouble understanding him. "I'm giving you the best that we got, so's you can get your two men up and running again. You're coming in with me—I gets to live in the best 'cause I's the leader and that's the way it's always been. So you follow me, and we'll all meet up later and talk about what we do, yeah?"

With a curt nod and not waiting for a reply, he turned and limped away into the old ranch house, followed by the men and women who carried Doc and Ryan. The remaining three companions followed, using the few seconds in the open to try to get a better look at Nagasaki.

Mud, dirt and slack jaws: that seemed to sum up the ville. The huts and the two ranch houses were covered in filth and looked as though they hadn't been cleaned for several generations. The streets were caked with filth, sewage seeming to flow into the mud and dirt at random. It was amazing that the dwellers hadn't perished from disease—although it did occur to Mildred that their inbred and possibly mutated genetics, over a period of generations, may have built in an immunity to the crap around them. The dwellers who watched them go into the ranch house could all be divided into the tall and thin, and the short and fat, obviously the two dominant families in the original settlement. The two things both groups shared were a vacant stare and a slack, openmouthed look of confusion; their brains scrambled by the small genetic pool. But the companions had fought against them and wouldn't take that as a reason to underestimate their capacity for savagery.

Inside the ranch house, the furnishings were all from the predark era and were battered and filthy. Tables that had chunks splintered from them, sofas and chairs that were almost bereft of stuffing, their linen and leather covers in rags and strips. There were still some paintings on the walls, but time and the environment around had eroded them so that whatever they may have once portrayed was lost forever. The carpets underfoot were nothing more than loose colorless fibers that flapped over stone flags that were grimy with neglect.

"You get settled in here, sort out your wounded, and we'll meet later," Buckley said, directing them into a room that was shuttered from the ville outside. It was as filthy as the other rooms, but had three beds that were at least covered with rags that had once been blankets and mattresses that may, at one time, have been stuffed. It could have been worse, but not by much.

"Jesus, what a dump," Mildred muttered as the door closed on them. "How the hell can I treat Ryan and Doc in conditions like this?"

Jak checked the shuttered windows and the door before indicating that it was all right to talk. There were no spies.

"What the hell have we gotten into?" Krysty questioned. "These people are really fucked. One thing's for sure, Buckley's got nothing good in store for us."

"Second that," Jak agreed. "But now we need get Doc, Ryan, up, fighting. May need every hand."

"Yeah, but I wish I just had better conditions to work in. It's not exactly sanitary in here," Mildred muttered.

Ryan had been listening, drifting in and out of sleep. He felt as helpless and weak as a child. He told Mildred as much when she tended to his wound, wincing as she stripped the material from the congealed blood around the arm wound and cleaned it with old antiseptic that she took from the supplies she kept in her med bag. Fortunately, it was only a flesh wound and the bullet had passed directly through. She applied a dressing.

"I wish we'd had time to see if there were any medical supplies left in the redoubt or we'd found a ville with decent facilities. Dammit, there's not even anything here we could use for a dressing, let alone…" she tailed off, then took a deep breath before continuing. "You've lost a lot of blood because we couldn't staunch the flow early. There's no major damage, but you're not going to be back to full strength for a couple of days."

Ryan cursed. "Whatever this Buckley's got in mind for us and whatever we're going to have to do, that's the last thing I wanted to hear."

"Could be worse, could be Doc," Jak said quietly.

"Yeah, what about Doc?" Ryan queried.

"He's in a mess," Krysty replied. While Mildred had been attending to Ryan, the red-haired woman had been making a start on preparing Doc for treatment. She had stripped him of his coat and cut away the arm of his shirt, peeling back the matted and congealed cloth to reveal the wound in his shoulder.

The SMG shell had ripped through the flesh just above the bone, exposing the whiteness but, fortunately, not splintering it. It was a deep gouge, and would have been enough to have knocked him off his feet in ordinary circumstances. The adrenaline rush of combat had kept him upright, but the wound had been deep and long enough to cause a vast amount of bleeding. As well, despite his toughness and willpower, Doc wasn't as strong as the others. It meant that he was now weakened considerably. He would have benefited from blood or plasma, had any been available.

Mildred cursed repeatedly to herself as she painstakingly cleaned the wound and tried to dress it, aided by Krysty. Doc was beginning to regain consciousness, flinching and moaning as the wound was cleaned.

Mildred dressed the wound as best she could, but Doc was a real cause for concern. He would be unable to defend himself adequately for some time and his shoulder may never quite be the same again. She couldn't be sure with these facilities, but some of the tendon and muscle around the shoulder joint might have been damaged. The size of the wound also meant that, despite her attempts to clean it as best as possible, Doc was open to infection.

"Shit, shit, shit," she cursed as she finished dressing the wound. "I just hope the awkward old buzzard can get through this."

Doc opened one eye and said weakly, "My dear doctor, I am alive. This, at least, puts me ahead of the game, I would say."

After attending to the minor abrasions and cuts on herself and the others and cursing the aches and pains from muscle pulls and grazes that nothing could be done to alleviate, Mildred sat back. She could do no more.

Now they had to wait until Buckley came back for them, and they found out just what exactly the ville chief had in store for them.

"You think we'll get some food, even some water?" Krysty asked with a cynical edge to her tone.

"Looks to me like they have enough trouble even feeding themselves. Did you see any farming or live-stock?" Mildred wondered.

"Only those weird, mutie-looking creatures—I'd have to be triple starving to go near them," Krysty replied.

"Then how do they eat?" Jak queried. It wasn't something they cared to think about too closely right now and the conversation petered out.

In the semidarkness of the shuttered room, time passed slowly. They tried to rest, but some noise filtered in from outside. Arguments and fights among the dwellers and the sounds of mundane tasks being carried out, the yelping of small animals and the cries and im-precations of workers.

Just another day. Except that it wasn't for the five who sat or lay in the darkened room, waiting for their fate.

Eventually, Buckley came to them. The room was now almost dark, the light seeping through the shutters down to nothing as night began to fall. Jak sat up as he heard footsteps approach: three people, two of whom were lame.

"Buckley," he whispered to the others.

As the chief of the small pesthole ville threw back the door, the companions might have seemed at first glance to be relaxed, but all were poised. The fact that Buckley hadn't stripped them of their weapons suggested that he meant no harm—but a person could never be certain, particularly in this inbred settlement where insanity might be second nature.

"Hey, how you all feeling now?" he asked cheerily as the door banged against the wall. "You're feeling better? 'Cause we's gonna eat and talk about getting some convoy stuff. See, I figure you're gonna be a lot of help."

"Even with two of us operating injured?" Ryan asked, heaving himself off the bed with some effort. Doc was sitting up, but anything other than gradual movement was still difficult, even though the rest had allowed him to regain some strength.

"Hell, yeah. Don't you worry 'bout that." Buckley grinned—not a pleasant sight—before adding, "But first we got introduce you properly to everyone. See, we don't have many strangers and it helps to let everyone know who you are and what you're doing here."

To each and every one of the companions, this stank of bullshit. But they had no option but to go along with it and see what the ville chief had in store for them.

They followed Buckley and his two guards along the corridor into the main room of the ranch house. There was food on the table—a stewpot covered in the crusted remains of previous meals, filled with something indistinguishable—and pitchers of water that looked less than clean. It was waiting for them, but despite their hunger and thirst there was no great enthusiasm stirring among them.

Before they reached the entrance, Ryan asked, "The others have told me that this is called Nagasaki. It's a strange and unusual name for a ville around here." Unconscious on the approach to the settlement, Ryan had been told by Mildred and Krysty, who had also relayed to him what they knew of the original, predark Nagasaki. Ryan had seen something in old vids and books, and he, too, was curious.

Buckley looked at Ryan suspiciously. "Didn't know you knew 'bout 'round here, but you're right—is an unusual name. Given to us by those who came before. They knew, see."

"Knew what?" Ryan prodded.

"'Bout what was going down," Buckley replied obscurely. "Look, see if this don't tell you." Beckoning them, he changed direction and led them back into the ranch house. They followed him down a side passage until they reached a closed and locked door. He took a key from a leather pouch around his neck.

"This is real important," he breathed, with an air of awe in his voice. "I get to keep the key 'cause I'm the leader and it's handed down. See, the ones who came before started this place 'cause they knew what was coming. Not many get to see in here very often and it's a real treat, I tell you."

This much was obvious to the companions, as the two men with Buckley were breathing heavily, drooling with excitement. One of them was making small yelping noises in the back of his throat, as though he had to choke down his excitement.

What the hell could be behind the door?

With great reverence, Buckley unlocked and opened the door. Inside the room, which smelled musty and close, as though all the doors and windows were always shut, there was an oil lamp that he lit, the growing light throwing shadows across the room and revealing the secrets that were held within.

"Sweet mother," Mildred breathed. Doc choked back the bile that rose in his throat. The others stood frozen in bemusement.

The walls were plastered with photographs—some prints, some taken from newspapers and magazines, yellowing and fraying—that showed victims of the first atomic bombs at Nagasaki and Hiroshima. The burns, the flayed flesh, the devastation: all was writ large, repeated over and over across the walls. A banner hung over a desk in the far corner of the room, proclaiming this to be the head office of Nagasaki, the first church of the bomb. Mildred walked over to the desk and read a scroll that was pinned to the wall beneath the banner. It told of the commune's belief in the power of the bomb, evinced by the photographs, and how it would clean the world like the fires of the Lord when it hit once more.

"Sick mother," Mildred whispered to Krysty. "I heard about people like this. They figured a bomb was coming, tried to build sanctuaries, worshiped it like it was going to be a cleansing fire. Usually it meant it'd get rid of anyone not like them. Guess they found out the hard way that it fucked anyone."

Buckley turned away from the shrine. "C'mon, people. Let's get you introduced to the others."

Chapter Eight

Buckley led the companions back out of the squalid ranch house and into the more squalid patch of earth that passed for the ville's square. In truth, it was little more than an area of mud that hadn't been covered with a shack. He was still flanked by the two ville dwellers, both of whom were in state of excitement following their exposure to the display in the locked room. Ryan noted that Buckley had been careful to lock the door once more as they left, and it was obvious that the contents of the room—as exciting as they were to these people—were only to be gazed upon at certain times.

As they followed Buckley and his two men, aware that none were bothering to guard them, each wondered what may lay in store. In Nagasaki, with far superior numbers, and the fact that two of the five companions were still weak from their injuries, Buckley was obviously at ease with letting them walk unguarded. He saw them as no threat on his own turf, even though they still had their weapons.

The problem was, he was right in this assumption. Jak looked back at Ryan, who was moving slowly although clearly stronger than a few hours earlier, and then at Doc, who was being assisted by Mildred. Both men were in no fit state to fight and as the other three wouldn't leave them—and even a stupe inbred like Buckley could see this—then they were effectively trapped here until recovery. To fight would serve no purpose other than to buy the farm.

Still, as Jak shot a glance at Krysty, he could see that his own instincts were correct. The woman was trying not to show it, but she felt great danger. She carried herself with what seemed to be her usual confidence, but her hair was clinging close to her head and shoulders, the ends flicking nervously, like defensive serpents. It confirmed the dull ache Jak had in his gut, the rush that usually told him when the hunter had become the hunted and it was time to be ready for combat. Years of staying alive had honed this to an almost preternatural level and as they left the house and squelched out into the mud, he knew that he wasn't wrong.

In the fading light, with oil lamps and sputtering torches, flames flicking and hissing from the pitch that fueled them, the group of people who constituted the ville of Nagasaki seemed even more sinister and deformed than in the light. The lengthening shadows picked out every deformity on their faces as though they were features on a sculpture, using them to throw shadows and leave pools of light that did little to improve their resemblance to anything human. Their eyes glittered and glowed in the light, the drool on their chins sparkled like diamonds in the reflective glow.

Mildred suppressed a shudder as they left the entrance to the ranch house and stepped out in front of the ville dwellers.

Ryan, assuming a more practical attitude, noted that all of the people were still armed. There seemed to be no sec force as such in this pesthole ville. Everyone seemed to act as sec when necessary. Was this because they were united, or because they didn't trust one another? Even more bizarre, could it be both? Whatever, the important thing was that they knew for sure that every man was an enemy. Every man because they were all armed. Enemies because they wanted the companions for some reason of their own, and there was no way that Ryan wanted his people to stay. Casting his eye quickly over them, he could see that he would get no argument on this score. It was just a matter of when they could escape, not if.

A ripple of excitement spread through the crowd as the companions appeared. Buckley held up his arms to silence the gathering. From a quick head count, it seemed that everyone in the ville was out to hear what their leader had to say.

"So I guess you all know why I's called you here right now," he began. "These—for those's who wasn't 'round earlier—are the new friends we found today."

There was something sinister about the way he said *friends* that sent a shiver down Krysty's spine. Looking at the others, she saw that she wasn't alone.

"And they's gonna help us in getting some good new shit from the convoy as it's coming through in the next day or two. We know which way and we know kinda when. But what we need is someone who won't stand out like we does—which is where you come into things," Buckley added, turning to the companions.

Facing back to his people, he went on. "What we's gonna do is give y'all a chance to help look after these folks. Equal shares for all in all things is what I says.

But if'n you do'm any damage and they can't help us on the morrows, then ya'll gonna pay big time. Am I right?"

This didn't sound good. The companions would be split up and at the mercy of whoever they were billeted with, unable to fight if needs be, because they had to worry about what would happen to the others if they did. And the use of the word *damage* suggested that things could get a little dangerous.

"Chief, we can stick together, be less of a problem to you that way," Ryan began, trying to reason with Buckley in what was a awkward situation.

Buckley turned to face him, an evil leer splitting his face. "Aw no, One-eye, it ain't that easy. We ain't had anyone from outside with us for a long time now. Guess'n we gotta have our fun, too. We ain't gonna hurt you," he added in a tone that suggested that hurt was exactly what was on offer.

The ville chief turned back to his people and dismissed them before leading the companions back inside. All they could do was exchange glances. Even with their weapons, attack would have been futile at this point. They were in the center of enemy territory, outnumbered—although not in the ranch house—and were in a weakened state.

They just had to roll with it.

"Get eatin'. You'll need to build your strength for what we'll be doing," Buckley said abruptly, gesturing to the table where the rancid stew lay cooling.

None of them felt that hungry when faced with this slop, but they hadn't eaten for some time and if only to keep their bellies filled and their reserves of stamina topped up for the struggle ahead, they slopped some of it onto the small boards that passed for plates. At one time, whoever started the community had some decent silverware that was probably used only on special occasions. Now it was debased, had no value, and was treated with offhand disdain. Which was exactly the way these people now seemed to treat life.

Which meant that Buckley would have no problem in chilling them if they didn't go along with him for now.

The food was nearly inedible—greasy, fatty lumps of indeterminate meat floating in a thin gruel thickened with something that may have been maize, with a few tough, fibrous, unidentifiable vegetables thrown in. Chunks of the crust that had gathered around the lip of the pot broke off and fell in, hard, cold and fatty.

As they ate, trying hard not to taste the rancid meat, washing it down the filthy water, Mildred wondered idly what the chances were of some intestinal or gastric bug laying them low before Buckley and his people had the chance to do likewise.

They ate in silence, which was broken only by the slurping and snorting of Buckley and his personal guard. When they had finished, Buckley sat back and belched heavily, making the guards laugh and splutter food across the table and into the stewpot. Mildred had to try very hard to keep her meal down, feeling it press at the back of her throat with burning bile.

"Well, what d'y'all think of it?" Buckley asked.

Doc sat back and, despite his still-weakened state, intoned in a booming voice, "That was inedible muck and there wasn't enough of it."

Buckley looked at him strangely. "Shit, you really

are strange fuckers, ain't y'all?" He pushed himself back from the table and stood up, his vast girth wobbling. He broke wind noisily, imitated by the two guards, who giggled moronically. "Guess it's time that we got y'all farmed out for the night. Remember, y'all can hit back if you have ta—I's won't hold it against y'all if you do. It can get a bit hot at night."

The fat chief stomped off, followed by his guards, leaving the companions to follow.

Outside, in the cool night air, they shivered, but not just because of the sudden chill stepping from the ranch house. It was a shiver of apprehension for what was to come and what the fat man had implied by his words.

Already, there were screams and wild laughter coming from some of the huts. They passed one that had no covers on the open window. Looking in, they had a vision of hell that was no more or less frightening than the photographs in the locked room. Inside the hut, lit by the flickering of an oil lamp, were three people. One was a woman, two were men. All of them looked alike: short, fat, faces covered in warts. As all three were now naked, it was clear that it wasn't just their faces that were covered in warts and carbuncles. Their bodies, with their vast folds of flesh, were peppered with these growths, too.

As the companions passed the window with Buckley and his boys, the chief chuckled. "I do like folk as know how to enjoy themselves," he said.

It was an ominous sign.

As they walked through the small center of the ville, the companions were aware of rutting sounds coming from other huts and houses. There was also a gathering of about a dozen people near the dry-moated barn. They had formed a circle and were carrying torches of flaming pitch.

"Shit, you never told me there was a fight," Buckley said, cuffing one of his guards. It seemed a strange comment, as none of the companions could actually recall either of the guards uttering a coherent word. Indeed, even now the man just held his head and gibbered.

"C'mon, this should be good," Buckley urged, hurrying to join the small circle. His guards hurried after him, leaving the companions behind.

"What the hell is going on here?" Krysty whispered. "Are they all stupe or just mad?"

"Too much inbreeding," Mildred murmured. "Face it, they're all related several times over and insanity is an everyday norm to them. We're in big trouble, people, as there's no way we can tell how they're going to act."

"Keep ready and blaster to hand," Jak whispered. His body language confirmed this, as he stood in a manner that suggested he was wired for attack. It was a defensive posture, ready to respond to any noise. It wasn't even conscious. His honed senses were keeping him on the razor's edge.

Ryan shook his head. "We can't take them all on— we're one missing, two wounded. I dunno about Doc, but I'm still not on top of the game."

"My dear Ryan, I feel like I'm on the bottom being trampled," Doc murmured.

"Okay. We don't have any choice but to go along with Buckley. You heard what he said—if they get a little feisty, we can defend ourselves."

"Yeah, he says that now. But what if it actually comes to the test?" Mildred queried.

Ryan didn't get a chance to form an answer, as Buckley yelled back over his shoulder. "Get your asses over here—y'all missin' the fun!"

Buckley's idea of fun might prove to be a little different to theirs, but they were all acutely aware of the fact that they had to play along with him. Besides, it'd take them nearer to the dry-moated barn and Jak and Mildred had both been wondering for some time why it was partitioned off in such a way.

As the companions got nearer, the circle parted slightly to allow them a view of what was going on.

"They's playin' crow," Buckley breathed, his words slurring and becoming more indistinct in his excitement. He beckoned the companions to join him in the circle. "Watch this," he said, spittle running down his chin.

In the middle of circle, warily padding around each other, were a man and a woman. The woman was short and fat, with warts and carbuncles. If not the fact that her hair was black as opposed to the gray of the woman they had seen earlier, the companions could have assumed it was the same person, swapping sex for combat. This woman had her hair tied back and was carrying a leather cat-o'-nine-tails.

Her opponent was tall and thin and carried a length of wood with nails banged through it. He was breathing hard, his flattened nose making it difficult for him breathe easily. He had one eye, his right socket being a mess of scarred flesh, but with no hole where an eyeball could possibly have sat. The scar also puckered the corner of his mouth into what looked like a sardonic smile. Mildred wasn't sure, but she thought she also caught sight of a vestigial third nipple in the middle of his chest.

It was difficult to tell as, like the woman, he was slicked with a film of sweat and blood. They had obviously been fighting for some while and the cat had scored his flesh, raising ugly red weals that spurted beads of blood, weeping sores opened on his back where old wounds had been restruck. The beads had spilled and mixed with his sweat—the heat of combat and also of the pitch torches being intense in the circle—forming a sheen that made him shine in the flickering light.

The woman was also covered. She had landed more blows than her opponent, but he had still managed to land some of his own. Her stomach and back were raked with deep cuts from the dragging nails, the blood flowing freely. Already, it was starting to clot, suggesting a few lucky blows at the beginning of the fight. From his defensive stance and her aggressive passes with the cat as they circled, it was clear who was now taking the initiative.

She flicked her wrist and sidestepped a swinging blow from the man, surprisingly agile considering her size, and as he stumbled past her the knotted leather thongs of the cat scored into the skin on his back. He screamed in pain, a high, keening wail that rendered the air, overscored by the crack of leather on flesh. He stumbled and fell in the mud, rolling to come up on his feet and parry another blow from the cat with his stick. The leather thongs wrapped around the stick, and with a tug she pulled it out of his hand. It flew out of the circle, over the heads of those gathered. But the few moments it took the thongs to unravel from the nailed wood gave him the time he needed to attack. He launched himself at the woman while her stance was open, her torso exposed as the momentum of the cat flung her arm back. He had to get in his attack before she could pull back her arm and become defensive.

Head down, with an agonized roar that summoned up all the pain and effort he forced into the move, the tall man lowered his head and launched himself at her. It was a matter of a couple of yards and a few steps, but it was enough for him to use as a springboard, his feet leaving the ground as he turned himself into a human missile, his skull a hard object propelled at speed that cannoned into her exposed and vulnerable breast.

The woman's considerable bulk trembled as she absorbed the impact, which threw her backward, stumbling a few steps before finally losing her balance and sprawling in the dirt. The man was now on top of her and pinned her arms back over her head. With a roar, she raised her head sharply and butted him in the area where his nose should have been, were he not one of the dwellers to have a shapeless mass instead of that organ. He screamed, blood streaming down his face, and reared back.

She used this opportunity to buck her hips beneath him, the immense power in them throwing him off her, his balance disturbed enough to give her the advantage. He fell sideways into the dirt.

As he lay on his back, the woman scrambled to her feet and stood over him. Their weapons were now forgotten. As, indeed, was the idea of fighting. Despite the pain he had to be suffering, the man had sprouted an erection while he straddled her and this showed no signs of drooping. Her eyes fixed on it, and before he had the chance to move, she had positioned herself over him, squatting down on her haunches suddenly so that his prick was impaled in her. She began to ride him enthusiastically while the surrounding crowd cheered her on. The blood and sweat on their bodies mixed into a kind of war paint that glowed and glistened as they moved in the torchlight.

It was a bizarre, savage spectacle, yet one from which the companions could not—dare not, given the rapt interest of the man whose hands held their fate— tear their eyes.

"I recall reading, it seems so long ago, about rites and ceremonies that involved such fornication and savagery among what we laughingly termed primitive peoples. But to witness it, it seems truly to be the more things change—"

"—The more they stay the same," Mildred finished. "I kind of know what you mean, Doc."

"Shit, don't know 'bout any that—just that these be harder fuckers than look if have fight again," Jak murmured.

"Yeah, and we're not in the way of being ready," Ryan added, only too aware of his own still-aching injuries and the weakness that hadn't yet passed.

"We may have to be," Krysty whispered. She felt uneasy with the savagery that they had just witnessed. Although there were many awful sights she had seen in her life, there was something twisted about what was happening that ranked with the worst. Usually, they had some idea of the mentality with which they were dealing, but this was moving out into the unknown.

Buckley turned to them. "Hell, this gets your blood a'fire, don't it just. This'll mean that we's ready when the time comes."

"What time is that?" Ryan asked. "You keep talking about a convoy, but what—"

Buckley cut him off. "That ain't your problem, One-eye. First y'all gotta get some rest so's to be ready, right? And that's what I'm sorting for y'all now." The ville chief turned back to the group around the rutting couple and yelled something incomprehensible. He was now talking fast, not making the effort to be understood by the outlanders, and the ville dwellers switched their attention to him, listening while he pointed at individuals, rattling out orders. Behind the crowd, the fat woman and the tall man finished their rut and she pulled herself up from him, leaving him lying limp and exhausted while she waddled over to the others. Buckley directed a comment at her and she gazed straight at Ryan, a hideous grin splitting her wart-covered face.

Buckley turned himself to the companions. "Guess'n that's settled that. One-eye, you'll be staying with Mags—she'll look after you," he added with a wink.

"Blackie, you'll be with Si, Dee and Mal," he told Mildred, indicating the three they had earlier glimpsed through a window, who had now wandered out to join the crowd.

Great, Mildred thought, this was going to be a hell of a night to try to get some rest. The way they were looking at her made her skin crawl. Meanwhile, Doc and Jak had been assigned to their own billets and the chief saved the best for last.

Turning to Krysty, he said, "As for you, Red, ya'll be safe with me." A leering wink and the spittle running down his chin told a story that was at odds with his assertion.

The companions exchanged glances. There was nothing they could do to stop their being separated, as Buckley held all the cards. They were weakened, outnumbered and had to play along until they had a chance to recoup and run.

But would they get that chance? The hungry and curious looks on the faces of the crowd around them spoke of a hard night ahead. Unconsciously, all the companions fingered their blasters. But they were surrounded in unknown territory and the chances of blasting their way out were minimal. The only choice that gave them some kind of option for maneuver was to go along with Buckley, split up and try to make it until sunup.

It wasn't an option any of them could openly embrace.

The crowd dispersed and they were led off to their billets. The fat woman, Mags, took Ryan by the arm. She was smiling at him, but it was the smile of a predator. She was still slick with sweat and the smell coming from her was rank. She was rushing, barely able to contain herself. In a heightened state of arousal, she felt sure this was going to be a good night for her.

Her shack was toward the back end of the ville and she pulled Ryan so hard that the still-weakened man nearly fell a few times. She helped him to stay upright, burbling at him in rapid-fire tones that he couldn't understand—although the meaning was clear enough not to need words.

Stumbling through the mud, she reached her shack and threw the door open, almost pushing him through the narrow gap. Ryan stumbled and fell in the darkness, landing face-first with a jolt on a pile of thin sacking that stank so badly it made him wretch. He rolled over as she lit the oil lamp that was the shack's sole illumination. The place was strewed with stinking, rancid clothes and bits of rotting, discarded food. The only thing that seemed to be maintained in any way were the blasters and knives that stood in one carefully swept corner. The blades of the unsheathed knives glittered cruelly in the flickering light and Ryan noticed her eyes flicker to them.

She advanced on him. Ryan, still weak, tried to move out of her way, but she was fast and she was on him in seconds, pinning him down with her bulk. Her hands were everywhere, seeming at once to hold him still and search his body. Her fingers found his crotch and felt for his prick. Despite his own revulsion, she was surprisingly light and dexterous and he found his body responding.

Ryan felt incredibly weak, with little physical strength to resist, even though every other part of him wanted to fight. Summoning all his strength, he flipped her away from him. It took her by surprise and she yelped as she skittered across the room, unable to prevent herself from falling.

She reached out, grabbing one of the knives, and got to her feet in a combat stance. Ryan had maneuvered himself so that he was seated with his back against the far wall of the shack. His unsheathed the panga, and the curved blade took her attention.

"Yeah, try it bitch and I'll cut your fucking throat before you can do anything," he hissed in a low, cracked voice.

Her face writ large with frustration, she settled opposite him on her haunches, the knife still in her hand. They fixed each other with a glare.

It was going to be a long night.

WHICH WAS EXACTLY what Doc was considering as he sat on the floor of the shack in which he was billeted. He was with two men, one fat and warty, the other thin, with a cleft palate and eyes so close together that they seemed to blur into one by the fading light of the tallow candles that lit the shack. Both men had so far spoken to him only to tell him their names and to indicate where he should sleep. Otherwise they had ignored him. But Doc had an intuitive feeling that, as soon as he fell into sleep, they would attack him in some way. And yet it was so hard to stay awake. He was carrying the worst injuries of all the companions and had the greatest need to rest. Yet he knew that there was no way that he would.

Try as he might, Doc's eyes began to droop, his mind wandered and his weary body let sleep begin to claim him. He felt himself drift and it was only the sudden sharp pains that made him jolt awake.

The two men, giggling, were using knives to strip his clothing from him. One of them was using the point of his knife to inscribe a design on Doc's bare chest. Wild-eyed and confused, Doc reached for his LeMat, only to find that it had been taken from him.

But the two men didn't realize the secrets of his walking stick. With a cry that was half-anger, half-fear, Doc struggled free, grasping the stick with both hands and unsheathing the blade of finest Toledo steel. As he unsheathed, the arc he proscribed sliced into one of the men—the fat one—who screamed in a high-pitched, frightened tone as his chest and face were scored by the blade.

The two men scuttled away and Doc fixed them with a glare. "One step and I swear I shall cleave you in twain," he uttered, not caring whether or not his words made sense. The tone was enough.

The pain from his cuts was fresh enough to ensure that he would be able to stay awake this time.

JAK HAD NO SUCH TROUBLE. The albino was fitter than the others, had less injury and strain to carry, and was less concerned with whether or not they should pick the right time to move. He only knew that right now, he had to establish control over the situation. He was with a man and a woman, both tall and lanky, both with hideously deformed faces, who towered over him. It was obvious they were looking to enjoy their captive.

Jak let his body posture seem submissive until they were in the hut and then whirled before the couple had a chance to light their lamps. In the darkness, his sensitive eyes were better attuned than theirs, and he could see them look surprised, as though they didn't know how to respond. Jak reached into his jacket and took out a couple of leaf-bladed throwing knives, keeping them light in each palm. He advanced and skipped around the pair, cutting at them and forcing them into a corner, where they cowered, whimpering in shock and pain.

Jak settled himself in the opposite corner. "You move, I cut you. Chill you slow. Understand?"

He saw them nod, gibbering softly. For Jak, it was going to be an easier night than for some of the others.

MILDRED WAS FARING LESS WELL. A sense of dread filled her as she was led back to the hovel shared by Si, Dee and Mal. She neither knew nor cared which was which, only that she couldn't get the vision of what she had seen a few hours earlier out of her head. When they closed the door of the shack, and she was faced by all three of them in the faltering lamplight, a shiver crept down her spine.

One of the men spoke to the other two. She couldn't make out what he was saying at first, his voice was so deep and guttural, but gradually, the words began to make sense.

"...so is it any diff'rent or is it the same?"

"Guess we got all night to find out," the woman said with a malicious cackle. "Could be kinda fun."

The second man said nothing, just giggled softly to himself.

Mildred backed into a corner. She hadn't caught all of it, but she had a pretty good idea what they were talking about.

"Hey, no need to be scared," said the first man. "This could be real good—y'might even like it."

Mildred doubted that very much, but was in no position to argue. She just had to defend herself.

The woman sprang forward with shocking speed, a

knife appearing in her hand from seemingly nowhere. She was on Mildred before she had a chance to move, pushing her back against the wall, pinning her arms, the knife slicing into her clothes and pricking her skin, drawing blood.

"Hell, her blood's same color's ours," the first man said with amazement in his voice. "Wonder if'n she's same color as you down there," he added, gesturing to his crotch.

The woman and the second man howled with laughter. Before she had a chance to brace herself, Mildred found all three of them on her, tearing at her clothes, trying to get her naked. If she let them trap her in the rags and get her defenseless... She didn't even want to contemplate what could happen.

Struggling, she managed to free her ZKR pistol. Angling the barrel as much as she could against the body bulk on her—she didn't know which of them it was—she snapped off a shot that echoed through the night. As did the howl of pain as the second man—who had done no more so far than giggle—fell back, clutching at his midriff, blood flowing through his clenched fingers.

"What do you do that for?" the woman wailed before her features contorted into rage. "I'll teach you—" She launched herself at Mildred. With the first man doing likewise, Mildred found herself fighting, almost blindly, for her life as the two fat people crashed onto her.

The shot had echoed around the ville and had probably saved Krysty from an equally awkward situation. For Buckley had taken her back to his ranch house and then sent away his two guards before producing an old plastic container with a noxious homemade brew in it, which he had persuaded her to share. His capacity for the alcohol was less than he thought. Either that or Krysty had a strong constitution, as the ville chief was soon drunk, reeling around the rooms of the ranch house, talking to Krysty in a thick, guttural voice that she had trouble understanding. The gist of it was that he had something to show her.

Didn't she just reckon. Torn between playing along for group safety and stopping things right now, the woman allowed Buckley to take her hand and lead her to the locked room. He fumbled with the key and led her inside. Krysty stood by him, not quite sure what course of action to take, shuddering when he took her hand and placed it on him.

"No, you've got that wrong," she said softly, trying to humor him and keep him calm as she let him drop from her hand.

"Wha'? Wha'? You stayin', you does what I's say," he mumbled, grasping her by the arm. It was a tight, hard grip, his fingers biting into her flesh. She flexed her muscles and drew back her free arm to punch him. That was when the blastershot rendered the air.

Buckley seemed to snap out of the alcohol- and lust-fueled trance that he had been in and lumbered from the room, leaving Krysty behind him. Whatever happened of a night in Nagasaki, blasterfire was still obviously unusual.

Krysty ran after him, to find half of the ville had gathered outside the hut. The rest of the companions were there and Buckley had already pushed his way in by the time that Krysty arrived. Over the wailing of the wounded man, and the shouting of the other two ville dwellers, she could hear Mildred try to explain what had occurred.

Oddly, she noticed that none of the ville dwellers were ready to take arms against the outlanders, which she would have expected. From the looks of the other companions, she could see that they, too, found that strange.

Buckley shut up the yelling fat couple by striking both of them so hard that they fell to the earth.

"Dammit, you was told to be good, not to fuck them over. We's needing them—y'all knows that." He turned to the crowd, searching with his eyes for the companions. "One-eye," he yelled, "you and your people come stay in the big house, where y'all and us can't do any more damage. The rest of you keep the fuck quiet. We's got some huntin' to do," he added cryptically.

The rest of the ville stood and watched as the companions detached themselves and followed the ville chief. It was uncanny the way the ville dwellers just stood silently. Mebbe the sinister import of his words was the reason.

We's needing them... Whatever he had meant, it had ensured their safety.

But perhaps only temporarily.

Chapter Nine

After Xander and Grant had departed, J.B. stood in the entrance hall of the armory, waiting for old man Budd to make the next move. He had seemed to be okay with the idea of J.B. working with him when the baron had been present, but the Armorer could feel the air grow frosty as soon as the double doors to the outside closed.

"Guess you'd better get yourself a room. Mebbe go into the ville and get some more clothes and shit—you didn't bring much with you," Budd rasped, his tone cutting beneath the words.

"I had things with me. Mebbe Grant can get them to me," J.B. said, trying to remain neutral.

"Mebbe... Esquivel!" the old man yelled, turning away and calling for the sec man. After a few seconds, the Hispanic guard wandered into the hall.

"Yeah?" he muttered, taking the opportunity to cast a closer eye over the Armorer.

"You wanna take this guy and get him some shit, 'cause he's only got the clothes he stands up in," Budd said. It was an order rather than a request.

"Yeah, sure," the sec man replied laconically. He beckoned to J.B., and together the two men left Budd standing in the hall, glowering after the departing Armorer.

They walked out into the early evening, the air still humid and stinking. They quickly moved past the enclosure that surrounded the building and into the main body of Duma.

J.B. was glad to be back among people going about their everyday business. There had been an atmosphere inside the armory that he was sure he had felt before, but not being able to remember much of anything made it difficult for him to pin down what had been going on. Here, outside, he felt much more at ease. The ville was packed with people buying and selling, arguing and fighting. Scuffles erupted on every corner, quelled by the distinctively dressed sec force. It was an edgy, hustling ville, but it reminded him obliquely of so many others he had seen, even if they were barely remembered.

"So what do you need?" Esquivel asked, interrupting J.B.'s train of thought.

"More clothes, I guess. Another pair of boots. I dunno what was in the bags that Grant still has."

"You don't know?" Esquivel eyed him suspiciously. The Armorer had assumed that everyone at the armory knew how he had come to Duma, so he filled Esquivel in on the details as they walked the streets, dodging wags and running children. As he talked, J.B. was aware of a few stares thrown at him, some hostile and others merely curious.

"News travels fast, even if you didn't catch it," he finished, indicating the latest passerby to stare curiously at him. "You're a trading ville, they certainly ain't looking at me 'cause they're not used to outlanders."

"Yeah, guess there were a few loose mouths from the

secure unit," Esquivel murmured by way of reply, adding cryptically. "Just hope they don't get known to Grant."

"So what's the problem, then?" J.B. prodded. Adding, when Esquivel looked blank, "Why am I so fucking important or weird that people are staring?"

"It's not every day that someone turns up at the bottom of a well," the sec man replied. But the tone of his voice and the way he wouldn't meet J.B.'s eyes suggested that it wasn't the whole story. It seemed to the Armorer that he would have to watch his back.

The two men entered a trading post that was little more than an old house with the front windows knocked out and replaced by a sheet of old Plexiglas, cemented into place. Inside was dingy and dirty, and smelled of old rubber and leather, along with tobacco and alcohol. It was more like a bar than anything else. A small, gnome of a man of indeterminate age was bent over a counter, meticulously sewing the upper of a work boot to a new sole cut from an old tire.

"Yo, Boney, heads up—you got a customer," Esquivel said as they entered.

"Go fuck yourself, asshole," Boney replied in a tone that underscored the insult with good humor. The sec man laughed and gestured to J.B. to look around at the merchandise on offer.

The Armorer pored over footwear, looking for something hard-wearing but still supple enough to leave his feet in one piece if he had to march long distances. He paused for a moment. Why had he made that stipulation to himself? It was like another isolated piece of the puzzle, with nothing to fit around it.

Esquivel watched him with interest while he searched. J.B. only noticed after he'd found a suitable pair of boots and looked up to see the sec man studying him.

"Something I can do for you?" J.B. queried, keeping his tone flat.

The sec man shook his head. "Just wondering how much you really remember, I guess. Not every day we get such an enigma."

Boney looked up from his work, no longer ignoring them. "E-what? Shit, you just make that up, Es?"

The sec man smiled. "Just something I picked up from those old predark books Budd's got. It gets kinda boring sitting around there all day, otherwise," he added almost apologetically. "Means a mystery, something you can't quite fathom out."

The man behind the counter looked at J.B. for the first time. "Don't look much of that to me. Just some poor dude got caught in a rockfall and got lucky, came out alive. Lucky the only thing you lost was memory— and mebbe that was a good thing. After all, you don't know what you might have done before," he added.

J.B. slammed the boots onto the counter. "I'll take these," he snapped, bringing the conversation to an end.

"How you gonna pay for them?" Boney asked. "Way I figure it, you ain't got no jack and I don't give credit."

"Here," Esquivel murmured, pushing forward a handful of jack. "Budd'll take it out of what the dude gets paid."

"So he's working in the armory, then?" Boney grinned, having established what he really wanted to know. "The rumors are true?"

"Depends what the rumors are," Esquivel drawled,

"but ain't no rumor about the way Xander treats shit that gets out of hand."

It was an obvious warning and J.B. was intrigued to see the way that the relationship between the two men, which had previously been that of long-established friends or acquaintances, suddenly changed.

"Whatever you say, Es," Boney muttered coldly, taking the jack. He returned to his work without another word and the two men turned to leave the shop. They were stayed by a woman who flung the door open and barged past them to the counter, slamming down a pair of damaged boots, heels and soles coming away.

"Listen shithead, I had to work two nights to pay for these, with a piss-poor lamp, trying to work out why the crankshaft on Xander's personal wag was fucked. Probably some asshole like you who fucks it up in the desert," she flung a look over her shoulder at Esquivel. "Last thing I want is to blow hard-earned jack on shit that falls apart in a week," she added, gesturing to the boots.

"Honey, you could earn some jack making me hard and then blowing it," Boney said with a sleazy grin. "And then you'd have all the boots you want, without having to get on your back. Ah, I dunno, though…" He looked across to J.B. and Esquivel, winking to bring them in on his little joke.

It didn't work on the woman. Without warning, she hit him with a right jab that knocked him backward. He stumbled and fell into the shadows at the back of his store.

"Don't try that shit on me, asshole. I ain't got a price, 'cept for putting back together the pieces of old tech that you assholes can't work properly."

Boney lifted himself to his feet—J.B. could now see that he was only about five feet in height—and rubbed his jaw ruefully.

"No need for that, Ella-Mae," he said sadly. "I'll replace the goods. But the offer still stands."

"I ain't for sale," she hissed.

"Shit, babe, everyone's for sale one way or the other. I sell myself for boots and shoes so's to get by. You sell yourself for fixing stuff—"

"But I ain't selling my pussy," she interrupted.

"You be the only one who ain't," he answered, but without any rancor or judgment. "It's a seller's market and there's always men who want pussy. You could do a whole lot better—"

"Mebbe my idea of better ain't the same as yours," she snapped. "This is over. Just give me the boots."

Boney took another pair and placed them on the counter. She turned and made to leave without casting another glance at him. But she did come face-to-face with J.B. and Esquivel, who were still standing by the door.

"Yeah, and your problem is?" she rapped, as they were slow to move out of the way.

"No problem, just curious," J.B. said softly.

"'Bout what?" she snarled.

"'Bout why you're so pissed at everyone. And mebbe about a few other things."

"Yeah? And mebbe I'm more than a little curious about you—a man who comes out of nowhere, claims to have no memory and just mebbe is some kind of legend to the likes of Xander. That's a bit convenient for you, isn't it?"

J.B. shrugged. "Mebbe. But I'm not making it that way. That's other people."

"Tell 'em that when it blows up in your face," she said in a softer tone. "Mebbe they won't see it that way."

J.B. paused, then nodded. "It's a fair point, Ella-Mae."

She smiled. "Yeah, and if you want to discuss it some more, then come and see me sometime. Laughing boy here knows where I am," she added, gesturing to Esquivel before leaving the store.

All three watched her go, then Esquivel indicated to J.B. that they, too, had to leave. As they departed, Boney was still rubbing his jaw thoughtfully.

Out on the sidewalk, Ella-Mae had disappeared into the crowds. J.B. looked out for her dark, curly hair tied up on her head and the oil-stained jeans and cotton shirt that she had been wearing. But she was only about five-four and easily vanished among the people crowding the streets.

"She'll be around, dude," Esquivel said. "She's always around." When J.B. shot him a questioning stare, he continued. "See, in some ways this place ain't run like other villes. Trade is what we're all about and anything that can be traded is. I mean everything. And everyone."

"So what Boney was saying about pussy?"

"Is about right," Esquivel told him as they walked on to a store that sold linens and cottons, where J.B. could pick up a change of clothes. "See, I don't actually come from here. I was in a convoy, fell out with the trader running it and figured that I'd do a little sec work until

I could find another convoy. Mebbe I never will. Been here a long time now and it's hard to get out. There's a lot of good things here, but…I dunno, gaudy sluts are gaudy sluts and other women don't wanna do that or don't have to or whatever. Most guys wouldn't want their old lady to be one. But here, it's like who can get the most jack any way possible and every woman will sell it—her old man may even sell it for her. That was kinda weird at first. Everyone doing it. Thing is, Xander actually expects it and if you don't get your old lady to sell her pussy to any passing convoy, he gets kinda pissed at the way you're turning up the chance to make jack, specially as he gets a cut."

J.B. shook his head. "Can't say it seems familiar to me. But Ella-Mae doesn't sell herself?"

Esquivel shook his head.

J.B. added, "Then how the fuck does she get away with that?"

"What you heard her say about the wags? She's the best mechanic I've ever seen. She's got an affinity for old tech in the same way that you—if you're who Xander thinks you are—have an affinity for blasters and shit. Girl's a natural and that's bought her ticket out of doing what she don't want."

"Must have been a gamble telling Xander that," J.B. mused.

"Yeah, well, ain't many who can cross the big man and come out of it in one piece, y'know?" Esquivel said with a wry grin. "Listen, we better stop this. Mebbe too many ears to hear this kind of shit, y'know what I'm saying?"

J.B. looked around at the passing residents of Duma, going about their business, and the passing traders from convoys, looking for some action during their downtime. There was a certain sharpness, wariness about the place, something J.B. felt certain he'd have to tune into if he was going to survive in Duma.

They picked up a change of clothes, Esquivel paying in the jack that was Duma's currency, and headed back to the armory.

"You'll be eating with Budd tonight and I'll tell him how much the clothes and boots amounted to. He's gonna have fun with that," Esquivel smirked.

"Yeah, what's going on?" J.B. asked after a moment's pause. "Soon as Xander left, the old man seemed to change."

"You'll find out soon enough, dude, without me telling you," was all the sec man would tell him.

Back in the armory, J.B. found where he would be sleeping. It was an airy, well-lit room at the back, on the upper floor. While he had been out, Grant had seen to the delivery of the Armorer's bag and as he checked it he felt sure that none of the ammo or grens had been taken from him. His own blasters—the Smith & Wesson M-4000 and the Uzi—had been returned, as had his Tekna knife. Oddly, though, he noted that he had supplies of ammo for other blasters. Did this mean that he hadn't been traveling alone? If so, what had happened to the people he had been traveling with? Come to that, who were they? And if he had been alone, did that mean that he had carried other blasters with him that had been lost along the way?

He also found a mini-sextant in among his belongings, and just holding the thing in his hand felt right. It also sparked a feeling of unease within him. It held within it a secret about who he was and what he had been doing. It was such a familiar object and yet even though he thought long and hard about it, he couldn't recall anything about how he had obtained it or the last time he might have used it.

Frustrated, he packed the instrument away, along with his change of clothes. Looking around the room he had been given, he could see a table, a chair and a bed with a good mattress, clean sheets and blankets. Inside, he knew that this stirred some kind of memory, but as with everything else, it was just that fraction out of reach. One thing he did know: to find such luxuries was rare for him and he was loathe to think about being without them again. And yet he had the feeling that circumstances may be working against him to pitch him out before he had a chance to settle and gain some new memories to replace the blank spaces in his head.

Putting these thoughts to one side, he decided to go down and join Budd. He was hungry and he also wanted to work out why the old man's attitude had changed so rapidly. It was obvious that he had feigned his enthusiasm for J.B. so as not to piss off the baron. But the big question was why he didn't want him around.

J.B. found that the old armorer ate with the sec men in the kitchen at the back of the house. It was warmer there than anywhere else, with a middle-aged woman, glistening with sweat, working over a log-fueled stove. Several sec men, including Esquivel, were sitting around a long wooden table that showed signs of heavy age and use. Budd was with them. As soon as J.B. entered the room, the hum of conversation died.

"So you've joined us," Budd stated flatly.

"If you've got no objections," J.B. countered.

Budd shrugged. "Not my call. Sit down and eat with us. You know Esquivel," he added. "These others are Drury, Caine and Easy." He pointed to each in turn and they acknowledged J.B. "They're on duty here tonight. Xander works a rotation system on the sec around here—Xander wants Esquivel to stay here on permanent duty and keep an eye on you," the old man added with relish.

J.B. wasn't surprised that the baron wanted to put a guard on him. Caution wasn't a bad thing, despite the fact that the baron was convinced of his identity. Duma had enough of an armory to make that an imperative. But he was damn sure that Budd wasn't supposed to let this slip—something confirmed by the look Esquivel shot him. The air suddenly grew frosty once more, despite the heat of the kitchen.

J.B. sat and the woman put a plate in front of him, with fatback bacon, beans and cornbread. "Yeah, and I'm Liza, though that ignorant old fart thinks I don't count, seeing as I'm only a woman," she said.

The sec men laughed and J.B. was glad for her breaking the tension that had suddenly sprung up. But he still wanted to know why Budd was hostile. And seeing as Esquivel had evaded the subject, he'd just have to find out for himself.

They ate in silence for a while, none willing to risk the old man's rancor and ruin the meal. But something had to break the uneasy quiet. It came in an unexpected manner.

Just as they were finishing, J.B. heard something behind him. Someone else entered the kitchen, and as he looked up and caught the expression on Budd's face, he could tell that it was someone the old man was pleased to see.

"Hey, wonderin' where you were, boy," Budd said with undisguised warmth. "Y'nearly missed the eats."

"I was just trying to work out why that MP-5 wasn't working—I can't find a damn thing wrong with it."

The voice was soft and firm: a youth, but one who was old beyond his years. J.B. shifted in his seat to get a look at the newcomer, who was also eyeing him with curiosity. The lad was only about eighteen, with light brown skin and long dreadlocked hair that was tied up behind his head. He was about five-eight, and only a hundred or so pounds. Despite the obvious lack of bulk, he carried himself in a manner that suggested a wiry strength. For a moment, it reminded the Armorer of someone—maybe more than one person. The long hair, but plaited... And yet a flash of something pale and milky white. It was there and gone before he had a chance to focus on it.

Their eyes locked for several seconds, each trying to assess the other. J.B. knew instinctively that the young man was the reason for Budd's hostility toward him, but couldn't quite work out the reason.

Esquivel broke the silence. "Olly, guess you didn't get to meet the infamous J. B. Dix earlier. And J.B., this is Olly, Budd's son."

Dark night, now it became clear. The old man had been training his son to succeed him. And from the comments the lad had made about the MP-5, he was a keen student. But now Xander had installed J.B. and ruined the old man's plans.

J.B. didn't blame him at all for being hostile. But, at the same time, he found himself with no say in the situation.

"So you're the one that rode with Trader," Olly said slowly, looking J.B. up and down as though merely looking could divine his secrets.

"That's what they say. I can't remember a fucking thing, and like I keep telling your father," he added pointedly, "it's not me who's making these claims."

"Same effect, though," Budd grumbled.

"Leave it, Dad," Olly murmured, seating himself. "It's too late tonight, but first light tomorrow we'll see if he's as good as they say."

Esquivel shot a wry grin at J.B. The sec man was aware of J.B.'s earlier encounter with Budd and the impressive results. But let the boy find out for himself.

There was tension in the air now and J.B. felt that he didn't need to be around this shit. He got up and made to leave the room.

"Till tomorrow, then," he shot back over his shoulder. He walked out without looking back and was halfway to his room when he heard footsteps behind him. Instinct kicking in, he whirled and went into a defensive crouch, moving toward his tracker. Engaging the enemy in an arm hold, he flipped him onto his back and had the point of the Tekna at his throat before he realized it was Esquivel.

"You've been here too long," J.B. murmured, "I could have had your throat out before you reacted."

"Mebbe, mebbe not," Esquivel replied calmly. "I could have taken you out, but Xander wouldn't like it.

I had to risk you'd look before striking. 'Sides which, you're a little jumpy."

"Yeah," J.B. replied ruefully, coming to his feet and resheathing his blade. He held out his hand in placatory gesture and Esquivel took it, allowing the Armorer to assist him to his feet. "I figure that must mean I've had to be lately."

"Yeah, well, just watch yourself in here. Any more stunts like that with another sec, or better still with Budd, and they may just use it an excuse to buy you the farm."

"What about the boy?"

Esquivel shrugged. "He's okay—a nice kid with a real gift for this. If you take over, I figure you'll keep him. It's just that his father wanted to hand it over totally to him. You're a problem he didn't need."

"Y'know, the stupe thing is I understand that," J.B. mused. "I didn't want this any more than he did. But he'd better not try to fuck me over."

Esquivel shook his head. "He's too scared of Xander to do anything—unless he could pass it off as accident or your fault, which is why you need to get off the wire. As for Olly, he wouldn't do anything 'cause it'd come back on his dad. Besides which, if you really know your stuff, he'll get too interested to hold any grudge against you."

J.B. looked shrewdly at the sec man. "Guess Xander knew what he was doing when he put you on my back."

Esquivel shrugged again. "Listen, I know why you wanted out of the kitchen and I figure you haven't had some fun for a while. So, seeing as you've got the rest of the night and fuck all to do, why don't we hit a few bars and you can see a little more of Duma and what it's like."

"You got the jack," J.B. said.

Esquivel grinned. "Yeah, but Budd'll enjoy taking it out of your pay."

NIGHT IN DUMA WAS different to day only in the amount of light that was artificially generated. Oil, generator-powered incandescents and old salvaged neon lights cast a series of conflicting glows and shadows across the sidewalks and roads of the ville. Unlike the farming-oriented villes or those that had to be careful of their resources, Baron Xander had built Duma into a ville that was possibly one of the richest across the Deathlands. By attracting convoys and making it a meeting and trading point for them, and by schooling his subjects in the art of draining every last drop of jack from the convoy teams while they were in the ville, Xander had found a way of keeping the wealth of the convoys within the boundaries of his fiefdom.

And the best way to get jack from a convoy team was by offering brew, jolt and pussy—mebbe not in that order.

Along the crisscrossing main streets of the ville, which were broken only by the blacktop that ran through the center, virtually every building offered all three—at a high price. There was no cost-cutting or free enterprise in Duma, no bargains to attract the customers. They would come anyway and Xander set the prices, which weren't to be tampered with.

The teeming streets were full of drunk and high people, the women competing to take in patrons. The drunker the better. That way they could get them in and out quickly, making way for the next paying "guest."

The noise, smoke and stink of sweating, drunken humanity was almost overwhelming. But if this was to be his new home, then J.B. figured he'd better get used to it.

By that time of night, he was also getting less attention than he had earlier in the day, as the people around were too drunk and too absorbed in their own interests to care. The Armorer and the sec man slipped into a bar.

"Best drink around here. Icepick don't mix too much shit in with the brew, try to make the alcohol last longer. And he does the best moonshine in the whole of Duma. Swears it was something that was in his family way before the nukecaust. 'Course, he's also full of shit, so I wouldn't trust that part. Drink will blow your head off, though." Esquivel grinned as they settled themselves at the bar.

"Sounds good to me," J.B. agreed, as the sec man ordered for them.

When the glasses, filled with a grayish brown spirit, were in front of them, J.B. picked his up and turned around to cast an eye over the bar. It was full, most of the patrons either standing by the bar or sitting around a handful of tables that were scattered across the small floor. Chairs backed into one another and it was easy to see that the later it got and the drunker and more stoned the patrons became, the more likely it was for fights to break out. Most of the trade seemed to know one another and were clustered into small groups around the tables, arguing and laughing loudly by turn. The women with them were gaudies, some not even bothering to look anything but bored, who were hired for later in the evening.

Music was provided by a black guy who sat in the corner, playing a guitar and picking, singing an old song about giving love a bad name. J.B. had another flash of memory, someone once telling him that music was a universal certainty that survived all and had common themes. Songs survived where people didn't. A flash of someone who talked in a long-winded, odd fashion that wasn't always understandable...but was somehow familiar.

A few cheers and a smattering of applause made him realize that the musician had finished. He was replaced by a white guy with a set of drums, who stared to beat out a series of slow rhythms.

"This is worth watching," Esquivel murmured in his ear, ordering another two shots of the spirit. Its coarse, woody taste wasn't exactly pleasant, but J.B. appreciated the warm glow it left as it slipped down his gullet.

As the drummer continued, a woman came into the room from the back of the bar. Moving to the drumbeat, she began to strip slowly. With his attention half-focused on the audience, J.B. found it hard to get into what she was doing. The effect she had on the crowd was fascinating, as quiet spread over them, their concentration rapt.

"Enjoying your first night in Duma?" someone whispered in J.B.'s ear. And unless he had changed sex, it wasn't his sec escort. The Armorer turned to find Ella-Mae at his elbow, a grin on her face and a glass of the liquor in her hand.

"Guess you might say that—though I'll wait and see what happens next before I really make up my mind," J.B. replied, indicating the area where the woman held court.

"Would have thought you could guess that," she said. "Or at least guessed why Es bought you here…likes his jollies a certain way." With which she indicated the stage, where the woman was pleasuring herself.

"Dark night," J.B. whispered as he turned to watch the woman.

The drunk and stoned patrons whooped and hollered, but J.B. found it all a little strange. He had the vague notion that he'd seen some weird sights over the years—even if most of them were lost to him now—but this was one of the strangest simply because he'd never seen it done in a bar.

"Not doing much for you?" Ella-Mae whispered in his ear.

"Can't say it does," J.B. replied mildly. "But then, I didn't know this was going down. You, on the other hand… Well, mebbe it does it for you."

"Okay, that makes us even," she replied with a grin. "You gotta drink somewhere and most places have something going on. As it happens, Jessie there is a nice girl when she isn't onstage. But then, everyone's got to earn jack."

"There must be other ways," J.B. mused.

"Not under Xander," she answered, unable to keep the edge of bitterness out of her voice. "I'm lucky and I don't forget it. I can't forget it."

J.B. looked at her. There was a fire in her eyes that was appealing. Ella-Mae obviously took no shit from anyone and was hurt for those she knew who had no other options. She was a deep woman and he found that fascinating. Certainly, if he could trust her, she'd be a good ally in this ville.

The roars coming from the performance area suddenly alerted him to the fact that something was going on. Turning, he could see that a drunk had his pants around his knees and was trying to get his flaccid member to respond enough to join the woman's performance. He was so drunk that the woman was able to scramble around and get to her feet. The drummer had stopped and had dropped his drums, pulling a length of metal pipe from down the front of his pants. He held it like he knew how to use it.

J.B. looked around. The situation was still fairly good-natured. The men just wanted to have fun and weren't about to let a drunk spoil things. Besides, who wanted to use blasters in an enclosed space like this? Chances were that you'd buy the farm accidentally by your own hand. Esquivel was talking to two sec men who had dropped by the bar on patrol. None of them looked particularly concerned.

But Jessie was about to change all that. Looking down at the drunk, still on his knees, she stood with her hands on her hips, and spit, "Shit, boy, it'd take three of you to make me happy."

J.B. winced. What was about to happen was obvious. Next to him, he heard Ella-Mae suck in her breath. "Get ready to fight," she murmured to him.

With a roar, the drunk rose from the floor, nearly tripping over his pants, and flung himself toward the nearly naked woman, lust now replaced by rage and humiliation. The drummer stepped between them and swung the metal pipe, connecting with the side of the drunk's head and knocking him sideways, blood splattering from the cut on his temple.

The drunk's compadres flung over their table, making for the drummer. But the room was so crowded that in doing that they clattered into surrounding parties of drunk and stoned customers, who also responded in kind.

Within thirty seconds, the bar was a heaving mass of fighting humanity. Backed up against the bar, J.B. could only dodge as glasses and a chair flew over his head. Roaring incoherently, one of the customers aimed a punch at the side of J.B.'s head. The Armorer parried with his left arm, blocking the blow, and chopped at the man's windpipe, knocking him back. That left him unable to defend himself as one of the man's friends tried to swipe at him with a broken chair leg. Before it could reach the Armorer's skull, Ella-Mae swung a haymaker that hit the assailant on the point of the jaw, driving him backward.

"Head for the door—cover our backs," J.B. yelled above the fracas, receiving a cursory nod from the dark-haired mechanic. He looked around, but there was no sign of Esquivel or the other sec men. But in the heaving, brawling mass, anything was possible.

Side-by-side, the two began to fight their way out, using their fists and feet to carve a path. A couple of times, one or the other had to yell a warning as pieces of table or broken chair flew about the room. But they had the drop on the majority of the crowd, as they were still relatively sober. Attacks were easily blocked and they formed a formidable duo, each hitting home on their targets with controlled force.

They managed to reach the door with only a few glancing blows and spilled out onto the sidewalk with a few drunks who fell in their wake.

"Fuck it, you know how to show a girl a good time, dontcha?" she gasped, leaning over and trying to catch her breath. Her shirt was ripped and she had a couple of bruises on her cheek and above her left eye, but was otherwise unmarked. The Armorer could feel an ache in his still-mending ribs and a small cut was opened under one eye, but otherwise any bruises were lost on his still-healing face. He couldn't feel anything fresh.

He laughed.

"Where did you learn to fight like that?" he asked between breaths.

"Told you, I'm no one's gaudy and some don't like the word *no*," she explained. Pulling herself upright, she pointed over J.B.'s shoulder. "Here's your bodyguard, late as usual. Es was probably around the back waiting for me to get you out. I'll see you around," she added enigmatically, blowing him a kiss before turning and melting into the crowd.

J.B. watched her, then felt a clap on his shoulder. He turned to see more sec men pouring into the bar behind the Hispanic's shoulder. Esquivel was bruised, with a deep cut over his forehead, staunched by the torn-off sleeve of his shirt. He had a wild gleam in his eyes.

"Hey, J.B., man," he roared, barely containing his amusement. "Welcome to Duma!"

Chapter Ten

"Man, look at the state of you this morning." Esquivel laughed as J.B. entered the kitchen. The Armorer sat down at the table and Liza put a plate of food in front of him.

"Don't you ever want your pretty face to heal up and give us the benefit of your good looks?" she added, so much to Esquivel's amusement that he almost choked on his coffee.

"Yeah, ha-ha, very funny," J.B. muttered. "You don't look so great yourself," he directed at Esquivel, who had a bandage tied around his forehead and a swollen eye that was a vivid red and purple.

"Ain't me you got to worry about, it's Budd and Olly. The old guy ain't gonna be happy with you late and looking so suave," the sec man countered.

J.B. ate in silence, pondering this. It was important that he bond with Olly if he was going to work here. The old man would be unbudgeable and stolid, but his son may have more flexibility. After he had finished, he and his sec shadow went to the grens room, where the old man and his son were at work, transferring a new load of gas grens from the wooden crates in which they'd arrived into the specially built metal cabinets in which Budd stored them.

"Well, well, glad you could be bothered to join us," the old man said, stopping work and applauding sarcastically as J.B. entered. "I'm sorry a little work detracts from your time fighting and womanizing."

"Think what you like," J.B. said in as noncommittal a tone as he could muster. He noticed that Olly said nothing as he walked over to the crate and picked up one of the grens. It was of a type he'd seen before, a U.S. Army issue from the mid-twentieth century. Except these were in the worst condition he had ever seen. Some of them were unstable, with the metal pins corroding—partly from exposure to moisture and partly from where the constituents of the gas within were breaking down and eroding through the casing.

"Where did these come from?" he asked.

"Trader called Simms sold them to Xander. Claims he got them from a ville down in the swamps. Guess that would account for the way in which the outer's got a little rust and damage," the old man replied.

"Tell Xander he's been had. And if I was you, I'd get the jack back and get this shit out of here now. The pins are metal, but the casing is a kind of polycarbon. That erosion is where the gas inside is eating it away. Listen, you keep these here and one of them could go at any time, take the whole place with it if it starts a chain."

"The hell it will," the old man bristled.

Olly had taken the gren from J.B. and was examining it. "I figure he might be right," the youth said softly. "I told you that wasn't any metal. What do you say we put these back very carefully, then you send Es over to ask the baron where Simms is right now?"

Budd was breathing heavily, pissed that his son had

sided with the outlander he saw as a threat, yet realizing that Olly was right. Still, he couldn't admit to J.B. being correct.

When the old man refused to speak, J.B. turned to his shadow. "Olly's right—I reckon Xander'll want his jack and an explanation. And get a couple of sec men up here to carry these cases—ones with safe hands, okay?"

As Esquivel left the room, Olly carefully placed the gren back in the box. "Guess we'd better be triple safe getting the others out of the store," he said to J.B., adding, "Then, I was wondering if you'd give me a little help with something."

Budd left them, refusing to speak, the anger almost visibly coming off him. Neither J.B. nor Olly mentioned that, but packed the grens carefully. When four sec men appeared, J.B. directed them on handling the cases, then joined the youth in the lower-level blaster room.

As he entered, Olly was already holding a Heckler & Koch MP-5. "This is the blaster I mentioned last night, though you might have forgotten after a night out with Es," he added with a grin. "There's something fucked about the firing mechanism, but I can't work out why it jams. Mebbe you could take a look at it."

It was a piece of bridge-building that the Armorer appreciated, and he took the blaster from the youth. Examining it, he was able to identify a fault in the MP-5, where a small piece of the mechanism had been dented in combat, causing it to catch and jam. The two men stripped the blaster and J.B. showed Olly how to effect a running repair on such a fault. Again, J.B. had to have known that through experience, but how he had acquired the knowledge was still a blank.

From there, Olly took J.B. through the stock that Xander had acquired in this section of the armory. Budd had already shown him this, but the youth was making a gesture.

They were in the middle of stripping and reassembling a mini-Uzi, with J.B. showing Olly how to increase the rapidity of assembly, when Esquivel appeared.

"Pigs in shit, boys, pigs in shit." He grinned. Olly made an obscene gesture at the sec man, but was laughing as he did so. Then Esquivel's mood sobered. "J.B., my man, you're about to learn what justice means in Duma. Xander's sent some of the boys out to find the scum who sold him the grens. Fool's still in the ville, they reckon, and there's another little matter that he wants you to see attended to."

J.B. looked from Esquivel to Olly and back again. The youth looked a little sick. "I'd forgotten it was today," he said in a small, low voice.

"Dude, I know Chino was your bud, but he overstepped. Everyone's got jack here and they can always get a little more. But Xander has to have his part of the action, you know that."

Olly said nothing, just managed to nod slightly. "We'd better get going," he said to J.B., leaving the Uzi half-assembled.

J.B. shot a questioning glance at his shadow as Olly departed. Esquivel shrugged and said softly, "Olly used to play with this guy when he was a kid. See, you know what I was saying about jack being everything here?

Mebbe sometimes it can be harsh. We live well, better than any other ville I've seen, but that has its price as well."

J.B. followed Esquivel, philosopher and sec man.... Well, maybe you needed to be, to get by in Duma.

As they left the Armory compound, J.B. could see that the streets were as full as ever, but this time everyone was headed in the same direction, toward the blacktop that bisected the ville. Thinking about what the sec man had said to him, J.B. took note of the people around him.

It was easy to differentiate between the ville dwellers and those who were serving on trading convoys. The latter were dirtier, more disheveled and even at this time of the morning were showing signs of hard drinking. Whereas the ville dwellers were conspicuous in their better clothes, their healthier look. Things that came from a higher level of living, with more jack to buy goods and more goods to use and then sell on as surplus.

The way in which the two-lane blacktop bisected the ville now began to make a lot of sense. Xander—and his father before him—had taken this ville and built it up, choosing the blacktop and this part of the dust bowl deliberately, realizing the potential of having weary convoys traversing the wastelands and needing a little rest and recreation.

It had made everyone who lived there rich. But to keep that safe, it required a strong and noticeable sec force. Hence the fact that every sec man J.B. had seen was dressed the same way and carried the same kind of blaster. Looking out for them, he lost count of how many after a while. It took a lot of jack to keep so many men and get so much matching equipment to make them so conspicuous. Then again, it needed to be spent if Duma was to cling on to what it made and remain secure to any degree from an outside attack.

J.B. realized that Xander was showing him a lot of faith because he had heard stories of J. B. Dix that made him out to be the best in the whole of the Deathlands. If he was Dix—and he had no reason to doubt this, even though he could never swear to it—then he would have a good life if he lived up to expectation. But he was suddenly aware of what it took to keep Duma this rich, the part he would have to play in this and the potential cost to himself if he stepped—or even appeared to step—out of line in any way.

"Hey man, you're quiet. What's the problem?" Esquivel asked as they approached the blacktop.

"No problem. I just think I'm realizing something," J.B. replied.

"I did try to tell you," Esquivel said simply. "But I figured you might need to see it up close."

The crowds gathered around the blacktop were densely packed and it was difficult to make out exactly what going on at the head. As the Armorer and his shadow pressed through, the crowd parted for the sec man and whispered and pointed at J.B. He heard a few of the muttered comments and gathered from them that working in something like the armory was an exalted position, one of those jobs that didn't give you the shitty end of the stick, something that the workers of Duma aspired toward. For J.B. to be carried into town a wreck from the bottom of a well and then appointed heir-in-chief to Budd was something that caused resentment in some quarters. He'd have to be careful of this: but not now. This would be a different lesson entirely.

As the two men pushed their way to the front of the crowd, it became clearer what was going on. A wag stood in the middle of the blacktop, detached from the enclosures of wags that stood on either side of the ribbon. It was battered and scarred, an old predark truck that had been reinforced with metal sheeting on either side and now stood silent by the side of the blacktop. It was a simple transporter to be loaded and unloaded, not a sec wag. Two men stood beside it, one a sec man, recognizable by his uniform. J.B. thought it may be one of those he had eaten with the previous evening, but he couldn't be sure. The other man was tall and thin, with long, straggling brown hair that blew across his face. He was unshaved, dressed in a denim shirt that was open to the waist, combat pants that were dusty and stained, and unlaced combat boots. He had a number of pendants hanging around his neck and metal bracelets jangled on each wrist. He looked like he'd spent too long on the road. He also looked like he had fouled himself with fear.

"That's Simms. He's part two of the, uh, entertainment," Esquivel whispered.

"That all it is?" J.B. snapped back.

"I think you know the answer to that, dude," Esquivel answered. "Like all good entertainments, this can teach you something. And hey, mebbe that's the real point. After all, why else would a piece of fun be compulsory?"

J.B. looked along the line of the crowd, the front

rows of spectators held by a line of sec guards, who stood facing them. There was a general murmur of anticipation. Along the way, J.B. could see Olly. Unlike the others around him, the youth looked pale and drawn, as though he would puke at any moment. He seemed detached from the crowd, somehow on his own.

J.B. kind of knew how he felt.

On the far side of the blacktop, the crowd parted in a wave, moving from the back. As the movement rippled nearer the front, J.B. could see that it was Xander, flanked by Grant. The baron cut an impressive figure, but the sinister aspect that the gaunt, lame man at his side gave to the procession was a portent. Behind them, hands bound behind his back and attached to a chain by a collar around his neck, was a young man of about Olly's age. He was shorter, with olive skin and slicked back black hair. His torso was exposed and was covered with weals, open wounds and bruises. He'd taken a hell of a battering and he looked only half-conscious as he stumbled after the baron and Grant, the chain held from behind by one of a pair of sec men, the other of whom was using the barrel of his AK-47 to spur the man on.

He had to be Chino.

The babble of the crowd faded to silence as the baron strode purposefully across the ribbon until he was dead center.

"Simms, I want you to see this," he declaimed in a strident voice, beckoning to the trader and his guard. Simms seemed unwilling to move, but the sec man with him gave him a less than friendly prod with his blaster. Reluctantly, he moved around to face the baron. Behind Xander, Chino had stumbled onto the blacktop, his appearance causing a ripple of discussion from the crowd. The noise died down again as Xander held up both hands, arms aloft.

"People," he began in a loud, clear, piercing voice. "You know why you are here. This young man has been stupe—triple stupe. We stand together and we prosper, we try to go alone and we fall. That was the principle on which my father founded Duma and it's the principle on which it has prospered. I ask you, do you want to go back on that?"

There was a roar from each side, as the crowd gave voice. Xander waited until it had died down to continue.

"Chino tried to skim jack off the top of his takings before giving me what is Duma's due. Duma's people, not mine. Yours. You are Duma and Duma is you. He skims what should come to the ville and we all suffer. One does it, all do it and we fall apart. So he has to be punished. I don't do this for myself, I do it for you. As I would do it to any one of you if you try. As it should be done to me if I do."

J.B. felt like turning away in disgust. Although there was an element to the words that contained some truth, this was swamped beneath the baron's hypocrisy. At the end of the day, the young man had tried to cheat Xander out of his share—his share for doing nothing—and was being punished for trying to keep hold of his own hard-earned jack. This was the baron's noble cause.

He caught Esquivel's eye: his face was impassive, but his eyes read J.B., and the Armorer could read him. They each knew the score.

Chino, still dazed from his injuries, was beginning to realize what was happening. Try as he might, he couldn't hold back the tears that started to fall as he burbled through split and swollen lips, pleading for his life. Neither could he hold back the stream of urine that trickled in fear down his leg, staining and dampening his combat pants.

"This is what happens to those who try to cheat Duma, who try to go against the whole," Xander yelled, taking a blaster from inside the rich robe he was wearing. Even at this distance, J.B. could see that it was a Luger—a big, heavy handblaster that carried a 9 mm shell and could do some serious damage at such a short distance. He hoped that Xander would make it quick for the young man, who had now sunk to his knees. Quick, as much for the ashen-faced Olly as for Chino himself.

Xander had no such intention. This was for display, to make a point to the assembled crowd. It was never going to be quick.

Xander beckoned to Grant, who kicked Chino in the back, sending him sprawling to the dusty asphalt. The gaunt healer then grabbed the young man by the chain attached to his collar and hauled him to his feet, holding him at arm's length, the chain wrapped around his fist, pulled taut.

Xander held the muzzle of the blaster a few feet away from the young man's face. It had to have filled his fuzzy, tear-filled vision and Chino yelled incoherently.

He'd paid for that the moment he tried to skim the baron.

Xander lowered the muzzle, so that it was at an angle of less than forty-five degrees. Then he fired twice, shifting his aim to the left a few degrees between squeezing the trigger. The two shots sounded almost as one, loud and echoing over the hush of the assembled crowd, matched only by the tortured and agonized screams of their target.

It seemed to the assembled crowd as though Chino's legs bent back in an unnatural way. The close proximity of the blasterfire and the diffused force of the slugs as they hit the solid bone of his kneecaps pushed his legs back at an angle that looked impossible. A spray of blood, bone and flesh scattered on the asphalt and splashed on both Xander and Grant. Deprived of the hinge mechanism that kept his legs rigid, Chino collapsed onto the asphalt, screaming in a long, endless wail, punctuated by sobs of indrawn breath. His upper body thrashed, his neck still pulled up taut by Grant's grip. His legs, below the knees, were still—useless sticks pointing at strange angles.

Xander stepped up to the wailing man and two more shots echoed in the still air. One in each shoulder, pinning the man back to the asphalt, rendering his arms useless appendages that flopped on the asphalt surface of the blacktop. Chino stopped wailing, his screams deadened by the shock of the second assault. He lay back on the road, gasping for breath, eyes wide but unseeing. His head was at a painful angle, still constricted by the collar. His life dripped onto the asphalt and even though there was no way that J.B. could see from where he was standing, he was sure that the young man's eyes had begun to cloud over from shock and blood loss.

The crowd was silent, almost as though it was scared to break the baron's concentration and the spell he was weaving on the asphalt ribbon. It would have been like interrupting a teacher during a vital lesson. The Armorer looked for Olly in the crowd. The youth was still standing at the front, eyes wide with horror and pity, swaying slightly as he watched his friend slowly buy the farm.

Xander looked up at the crowd gathered on each side of the blacktop, and spoke in a loud, clear voice. "This man went against us all. This is how anyone who dares to cheat the people shall end their life. First the suffering, the punishment. But I am not a cruel and unreasonable man. There shall be a swift relief from such pain."

With which, the baron stepped up to Chino's quivering body and put the blaster against his forehead, squeezing the trigger. The explosion sounded around the ville, the young man's head drilled with a neat hole at the front, the back exploding. Xander stepped back.

"Take him away," he ordered the sec men who had been standing by, waiting for his word. Grant dropped the chain and stepped away to allow the sec men to drag the body off the ribbon and into the crowd on the far side of the road, who parted with alacrity and then quickly reformed so that the Armorer couldn't see what happened to the corpse. He looked along the line of the crowd, and could see that Olly was unable to tear his eyes away from the bloodstains on the asphalt.

"Where you going?" Esquivel murmured as J.B. began to edge sideways.

"Something that's gotta be done," J.B. replied cryptically.

As the two men made their way to the shocked youth, Esquivel following on J.B.'s heels, Xander turned his attention to the trader Simms, who had been watching the execution, openmouthed, from the side. It was obvious from the man's hanging jaw and staring eyes that he expected the same thing to happen to him.

"Bring him around," Xander commanded the sec man guarding the trader. Nudging him with the butt of his AK-47, the sec man prodded the thin, pale trader into life. Simms seemed to jolt from a trance and looked wildly around him as he moved to face the baron. The bracelets on his wrists jangled as he used one hand to push the long, stringy hair from his eyes; eyes that stared bloodshot and scared at the surrounding crowd, focusing finally once more on the blood and brain that stained the ribbon. He was visibly trembling.

In the crowd, J.B. had reached Olly, Esquivel on his heels.

"You okay, kid?" J.B. whispered.

"What do you think?" Olly countered in a husky, barely audible tone. "I've just seen—"

"You've just seen what happens when you cross Xander, that's all. He was your friend, I know, but he knew the risks he was taking. It was a gamble and he lost. End of story. Don't end up like him. Mourn losing him, yeah, but learn. Stay frosty for this and then let it out in private. You've got a good future—don't fuck it up because he was stupe. You need time to think about this, right?"

The Armorer delivered this speech rapidly, in an urgent whisper. He didn't want anyone around to catch any more than was necessary and he didn't want Olly to endanger his position in the ville by coming to the attention of Xander when he was like this.

"Dude's right, kid," Esquivel agreed. "Later, howl your heart, boy, but don't let anyone see."

Olly looked at them both and nodded slowly before turning back to the ribbon, eyes seeing nothing, shutting it out until later.

J.B. felt a nudge at his elbow. Turning, he found Ella-Mae standing there. "Kid okay?" she asked. When he nodded, she added, "He's a good kid. You ain't so bad yourself. I'll be seeing you later."

She melted into the crowd, leaving J.B. to wonder just exactly what she meant. Meanwhile, Xander had begun to speak and the Armorer turned his attention to the baron.

"You people may be wondering why this man is here. Traders, too. This is just by way of a lesson to you all. See, this man sold me some hardware that turned out to be faulty. It could have taken out some of my own people, blown up my armory. I paid him a good price in good faith. Those of you who trade with me regularly know that I'm fair with you."

Casting a quick glance around, J.B. could see that this wasn't quite the way the outside traders and convoy members saw it. But they elected to stay silent in the circumstances.

"And that I let you act as you wish in my ville. But I will not, and cannot, accept anything that endangers my people. I will not chill him, as that is not my right."

The relief on Simms's face was palpable, but short-lived as Xander holstered the Luger and held out his hand. Grant shuffled forward and handed him a spiked ball on a short chain. It was like an old-fashioned mace, the kind J.B. had seen in old predark books, but it wasn't that old. Xander had obviously seen similar illustrations and had this made. The chain was like a shorter set of links from the same mold as the chain around Chino's neck, with a leather-bound wooden handle at one end. On the far end, a roughly spherical metal ball had been studded with nails, the heads facing out.

Xander began to swing the ball, the momentum growing faster and making the chain fly taut. Simms eyed it, shook his head and tried to take a step back. The barrel of the AK-47 behind him halted his progress. Xander stepped forward and the arc of the ball was broken by the contact it made with Simms's face, ripping into his cheek and temple. The ball itself was small, so it wouldn't render him unconscious with its weight; rather, it would allow the nail heads to do the damage, tearing his flesh and excoriating to the bone. A spray of blood spumed from the trader's cheek as the blow knocked him sideways and down onto one knee. Only fear of what was to follow prevented him from falling to the asphalt, leaving him totally defenseless.

J.B. thought it odd that the trader's convoy team didn't try to save him. The sight of the sec men moving among the crowd, immediately recognizable in their uniforms and matching blasters, reminded him that the sec would crush any response immediately. Xander had said the trader wouldn't be chilled. Why should they risk their own chilling when they knew he would live?

On the ribbon, the baron waited until Simms had recovered from the blow, shaking his head to clear his senses. As he tried to rise, the mace arced through the air once more, catching him on the upswing, throwing him in the opposite direction and splitting the other side of his face.

Simms was now concussed, but still managed to drag himself to his feet, swaying. The concussion got to him and he vomited on the asphalt, the spasms in his stomach forcing him to double over once more. As he did so, coughing, Xander swung the mace again, and the nails ripped the man's shirt, raising great bloody weals on his back. He fell sideways and once again the baron swung the mace, this time slashing the nails into his side. Simms was coughing, his long hair covered in blood and vomit, too choked to scream.

Xander stepped back calmly, handing the mace to Grant.

"You tried to take from me, and now I will take something that is precious to you," Xander intoned, taking a knife from Grant. J.B. could see that the blade had been carefully polished and honed. It looked like Toledo steel, and was attached to an ornately carved handle unlike anything the Armorer had ever seen.

Without another word, Xander took hold of Simms by his hair, wrapping the long strands around his hand and using this to pull the trader so that he was forced to move into an upright position. With the hair pulled tight, Xander slashed with the blade at the man's hairline, splitting the skin so that blood poured down Simms's forehead and into his eyes. The intense pain cut through his concussion and he screamed in a high-pitched, frantic tone, waving his arms uselessly as the skin of his scalp parted from his skull. As Xander cut further in, so the pressure of the baron's pull and the weight of the trader's unsupported body caused the skin to tear as much as it was cut. Blood flowed over him. The ragged scalp tore into a point, the skin and flesh coming away in the baron's hand.

Xander threw the bloodied scalp onto the asphalt, the hair falling beside its owner like a chilled animal. The baron gestured to his sec men and two of them moved from the edge of the crowd and took hold of the semi-conscious Simms. One of the sec men snapped his fingers and J.B. was surprised to see a driver get out of the silent wag. He looked like a convoy driver and was obviously nervous as he stared around. The sec man gestured impatiently and the driver reached into his wag, producing a length of rope.

Xander watched as impassively as his audience while the sec men lashed the trader to the front of the wag. When this was done, Xander turned to the driver.

"Now go, and don't stop until you're a long way away from here."

The terrified driver needed no second telling and he scuttled into the wag, fired the engine and screeched off, the almost comatose trader battered by the sudden acceleration as the wag roared out of Duma in a cloud of dust and exhaust.

Xander waited until it was out of sight, the engine noise barely audible, before turning to the crowd. "The rest of Simms's party I want out by nightfall. We know who you are, so don't fuck us about. The rest of you can now go about your business."

Like it was that easy. J.B. returned to the armory with his shadow in tow, to find that Olly was in the blaster room, cleaning a rack of Uzis.

"Y'all right, Olly?" J.B. asked quietly. The youth

ignored him at first, concentrating on his cleaning. Finally, as the Armorer was standing in the doorway waiting for a reply, Olly looked up and nodded sharply. His eyes met J.B.'s and the Armorer could see that he just wanted to be alone.

"I'll check the grens, see if there are any other batches. Mebbe reinventory them," he muttered.

Budd didn't make an appearance until the late afternoon, then he did little except berate his son for associating with the likes of Chino. The old man was in a permanent bad mood and was now taking it out on his son as well as everyone else. It made working hard, and when the time came for them to eat in the evening, J.B. found that he had achieved little during the day. The atmosphere in the kitchen was no better: Budd was bad tempered; Olly was still brooding; and Liza moaned at them both while the confused sec men on duty looked on. Only J.B. and Esquivel had any idea of the whole situation and neither was inclined to explain.

"I need to get out," J.B. said to his shadow after they left the kitchen. "Just away from here for a while."

It didn't take much to persuade him, and they soon hit the main part of the ville. Esquivel led J.B. to the bar they visited the night before.

"Not another strip act," the Armorer complained. "Besides which, I want to drink, not fight."

"Two points." Esquivel grinned, counting them off on his fingers for emphasis. "One, Icepick won't have another act for a few days, as it'll take him that long to pay for the damages from last night. Two, there won't be a very big crowd without the show, so it'll be quiet.

Three, I figure someone you'll want to see might drop by to say hello."

"That's three points."

"So I lied a little."

They entered the bar, which was deserted by the standards of the previous evening, but still had several customers sitting around drinking, accompanied by gaudies. Icepick had cleaned up the majority of the mess, but the bar still had the air of a place in need of repair. The giant barman greetcd them with a nod and placed two glasses of liquor in front of them.

"Guess you're becoming a regular, dude." Esquivel smiled as he downed his measure.

They stood and drank for some time, talking about nothing, both avoiding the subject of Olly and Budd. Neither wanted to get into a deep discussion. They were saved from any further fencing when Ella-Mae walked into the bar.

"Figured that's what she meant," Esquivel murmured to J.B. "I'm gonna make myself gone, but not a word to anyone, or I'll end up feeling the rough edge of Xander."

"Thanks," J.B. murmured back. "But you don't have to put yourself at risk."

"I figure you'd do the same for me," he whispered as Ella-Mae approached. "But watch your back."

J.B. was about to ask him about this last, cryptic comment, but the sec man was gone.

"Hey, fancy seeing you here," Ella-Mae said playfully.

"Yeah, just fancy." J.B. replied, ordering her a drink. Was it his imagination, or did Icepick glare at him as he set the glass down for Ella-Mae.

They talked and drank. Most of what she told him was what he already knew: how her talents as a mechanic had kept her away from having to sell herself as a gaudy. How she'd seen her mother drink herself into oblivion because she hated selling herself. How much trouble she had from men who couldn't understand that she wasn't for sale. Suddenly something clicked and J.B. realized what Esquivel had meant by his last comment. Looking around, J.B. could see that he was getting stares—not from convoy members who were drinking themselves senseless at inflated jack prices, but from ville dwellers who were drinking in the bar.

There was nothing J.B. could tell her about himself. The realization that her talking to him, wanting to be with him, was causing friction with the locals made him aware that they should get the hell out as soon as possible. She caught him looking around from the corner of his eye.

"Am I that boring?" she asked, a grin playing around her lips.

"It's not you I'm worried about," he replied.

"Then mebbe we should go where there's no one else to worry about," she said, moving toward the door. J.B. followed, scanning the bar's customers for any potential trouble. There were hostile glares, but no one rose to follow. Nonetheless, as he followed her through the streets, J.B. said very little other than to answer her questions in a perfunctory manner. He was triple red for any trouble that may be following on his tail.

"I think we're alone now," she said softly as he followed her into her shack and she closed the door behind him. He stayed her with a gesture, then checked through the window. Satisfied, he turned back to her.

"Yeah, now I'll agree."

She moved toward J.B. and put her hands behind his head, pulling him to her until their mouths touched. She was clumsy and hesitant.

"It's been a hell of a long time. I'm out of practice, babe," she said before trying again.

"You're getting the hang of it," he said softly when she paused. There was something at the back of his head, something that this was triggering. But the thought was gone when she stepped back and took off her shirt, revealing full, pendulous breasts and a waist taut and muscled from her work.

"There are a few more things you might be able to help me to remember," she said softly.

First there had been the barfight and now this.

It was going to be another long night.

Chapter Eleven

The rising sun had never been such a welcome sight. As the inhabitants of Nagasaki slept, so the companions emerged into the encroaching day, blinking from the light and the lack of sleep. Despite moving to the ranch house, none of the five companions had dared to risk sleep, fighting back their prickling eyes and wandering minds.

All five had emerged into the ramshackle streets of the shantytown hoping that whatever passed for fresh air in the stinking ville would restore some kind of awareness and edge to their clouded minds.

"What kind of hell is this?" Doc exclaimed wearily. "I remember some paintings that depicted hell. They were a little like last night."

"I dunno what you're talking about, but I'll agree with you anyway." Krysty sighed. "Gaia knows what that mad son of a bitch has got in store for us next."

"Who knows? I just get the idea that all this is normal to them. Which does make me wonder," Mildred pondered, "why we got a little bit of protection there. Do other outlanders get the same?"

"Buckley hasn't said anything about other outlanders coming into the ville, so mebbe they don't find many," Ryan replied. "Can't imagine many making it across the dust bowl."

"Then what's in the barn?" Jak questioned quietly, indicating the reinforced and moated building that loomed ominously to the rear of the ville.

"I figure we should have a recce around there as soon as we can," Mildred whispered. Her tone suggested that although it was an imperative, a part of her was worried about what they might find contained within its walls.

Ryan nodded. "As for what Buckley wants now, he wants us to fight for him. I've been thinking about this convoy raid and I figure that we're gonna be leading the charge. First in, first to buy the farm."

"That's a reassuring thought," Krysty murmured. "What are our chances of getting out of here?"

"With Doc still hurt and me not a hundred percent? With no wag unless we can get one of their fucking mules to haul ass? With no idea of where we are exactly and where to head? With no supplies? With no sleep?" Ryan counted off on his fingers as he spoke.

"Yeah, okay, you've made your point," Krysty conceded.

"The way I see it is that we just sit tight, see what Buckley's exact plans are and then try to find a hole in there to wriggle out from under."

Doc sighed and spoke slowly, "As plans go, it is not the most detailed that I have ever heard wrought, but in the circumstances it is all that one could concede."

"I think he means yes," Krysty said, managing a wry smile, "but I'm not totally sure. So what do we do for now?"

Ryan looked around. There were signs of life stirring in the town, and the chief had emerged from his ranch house.

"We keep triple frosty, act stupe and see what the fucker tells us," he whispered as Buckley came over to them.

"Hey, y'all ready for some action today? I'm figgering that we plan our raid. See with y'all as fighters, I's had this real great idea about getting some real good stuff—things that'll keep us in food and jack for a long time to come. And it's all 'cause y'all with us. So come eat and we'll talk about it."

Beckoning them to follow, he returned to the ranch house, limping and shuffling as fast as he could. It was obvious that some inspiration had really fired him up. The question was, what would that mean for the companions?

Inside the filthy hovel, there was more food on the table. It looked like the same slop as the night before, just heated once more on an open fire. The gnawing in their guts drove them to stomach some of the greasy, tepid mush, but it was almost as hard as trying to make out what Buckley was saying between his cleft palate and the mouthfuls of food that he spit over the table as he spoke. His guards were also there, having mysteriously reappeared after the night before, and Krysty noticed that their attention was focused on her—wondering if Buckley's plans for her had borne fruit.

"See, I's been doing some thinking and I's sure that we can pull this off with y'all on our side. See, what I was gonna be proposing is that we's all trap this convoy that's coming on the way through, take the shit they's carrying and bring a few back alive for good luck. But hell, I's thinking that with y'all around, we's can take it one step further."

"What do you mean?" Ryan prompted when Buckley seemed to pause for them to congratulate him. The one-eyed man wanted to be sure of what Buckley meant. If it was what he suspected, then they were in big trouble.

But instead of answering, Buckley went off at a tangent, emphasizing his points by bringing his fist down hard on the table, making the stew slop across the already greasy surface.

"Duma people's scum, always has been and always will be. They's thinking that they's so much better'n us and they's always getting all the trading and all the jack that's around. Every time we've tried to be at one with them they's pushed us away. They's call us dirty and inbreeds and muties and they's want nothing to do with us. And all that shit when they ain't even knowin' the right way to do things. They don't realize that we's the only one's knows the truth about what happened and why the world's like it is. We's was taught from an early age what this is all about. But do they listen, do they learn from us about the places of Nagasaki and Hiroshima and the cleansing powers of the nuke?"

He stood up and began to stride about the room, dragging his game leg as he ranted. The companions were unwilling to interrupt him. To start, he may turn hostile if his train of thought were broken, decide he didn't want them around—he seemed unstable enough to chill them as soon as look at them. On the other hand, in the middle of this ranting he might reveal something that could be of use.

"See, we's should be running these lands. We's the chosen ones, as we's was taught from when we's was young. That's why we were out here, waiting for the nukecaust. That's why we survived it. That's why we prospered."

The companions exchanged glances. This squalor was his idea of a community that was prospering?

"And why others have fallen by the wayside. Hell, it was why we's was saved. And then these fuckers come and take what's rightfully ours and we's have to rely on snatching something back when we can, like dogs in the night. Well, fuck 'em, my friends, fuck 'em all. I's was communing with the spirits of the past last night and it came to me."

"I thought you said he was jerking off to those photographs," Mildred managed to murmur to Krysty.

Now that he was in full rant, the short, fat man was striding the room as though he were a colossus.

"Y'all been sent to me and to us by destiny. We's been waiting a long time to take our rightful place, but now we can do it. We can do it because of y'all."

"Chief, you'll have to make it clearer than that," Ryan said gently. "Think of it like this—we're not the chosen and we don't have your insight. We're not guided by the spirits and we need you to tell us exactly what you mean."

"That, my friend, was beautifully phrased," Doc said softly.

"Words—all means we in line for chilling." Jak reminded him in an undertone.

Buckley ignored these asides, if indeed he heard them above the sounds of glory that were clamoring in his head now that his grand plan was clear to him. If only it had been clear to the companions, although each had his or her own idea about where the rant was going.

"Hell, I's woulda thought it was real clear," Buckley said with a look of surprise on his face. It would have been comical if the situation were not so serious. "We's gonna take a wag and get ourselves onto the end of that convoy, not attack it. It's gonna take us right into the cold heart of Duma and we's gonna get us some serious action. We's couldn't do it on our own, but with y'all along for the ride...."

Ryan frowned. In the midst of the rambling, there was one fact that he'd managed to isolate. "What wag?" he asked, holding up a hand to stay Buckley in his ranting.

"Didn't I say anything about that?" A sudden look of confusion, mixed with cunning, crossed Buckley's face. He continued. "We's gets things sometimes. Y'all ain't the only ones who get to be wandering across the wastelands."

"Hurry up, please, it's time," Doc murmured distractedly.

"And sometimes we's gets to pick up those as is doing the wandering. Mebbe they can be a problem and mebbe not. Mebbe they want fit in and mebbe not." He shrugged, becoming deliberately evasive. "Sometimes they move on and we's get to keep some of the things they arrived with."

Ryan fixed him with a glare. "I haven't often heard of a solitary wag making its way across country."

Buckley shrugged. "Mebbe it's not the first time we's been after a convoy, then."

"I kinda guessed that. So what happened to the crew?"

"Oh, we's didn't chill them. Hell no, we looked after 'em good and they had some fun."

A shudder ran through the assembled companions as they recalled Nagasaki's idea of fun.

"Where are they now?" Ryan asked.

"They's in the barn, being looked after okay, oh yes, they is," Buckley asserted, a little too swiftly for Ryan's liking. But the one-eyed man let it slide. There were other things to be assessed.

"Okay, we're in," he told the chief. "But we need to talk about who handles what—remember I'm still carrying wounds and Doc's in a worse way. When do you plan on going?"

"'Fore the sun goes down tomorrow. Hear that the convoy should run by us about then," Buckley affirmed.

It was a shock. Ryan had been counting on more than a day and a half in which to make plans. But if it was all they had, then they would have to work fast. It left them with another night to get through and not long to recce the ville properly without being tumbled.

"Okay, we're in with you, but we need to talk among ourselves, get our own plans sorted. The injuries we're carrying will change the way we do things," Ryan told Buckley, hoping that the chief would buy the excuse for their need to be left alone.

Buckley's faith in their fighting skills and his belief that they had been sent by fate left him in no position to do anything other than concede. He had his two-man guard show them to the room where they had first stayed on their arrival. Once the door was closed and Jak had checked that the guards had returned to Buckley, Ryan turned to them.

"Fireblast, this is stupe, really stupe. Buckley hates this ville Duma and is willing to sacrifice everyone involved to make some stupe point by making a raid inside it. Outside we could go along with, but going into a ville, hitting a convoy and trying to get out again? Shit, the man really is a fucking stupe."

"Given that Buckley is holding all the aces, I fail to see how we can avoid this," Doc mused. "In fact, it may perhaps be better to go along with this and be chilled swiftly and relatively painlessly. I cannot see a better fate awaiting us here. After all, where, I dread to think, are the missing convoy members who manned the captured wag?"

"He said in that barn," Mildred spit. "What they do to them in there I wouldn't like to think."

"People not so stupe as we think," Jak interjected. "Look like no guards, but barn difficult to get in and out…and always someone hanging around end of ville."

"A low, native cunning rather than an intelligence," Doc mused. "Perhaps all the more dangerous because of that. But I fail to see why we are not, also, being held in that barn. No matter what Buckley thinks sent us to him."

"The way I see it, Buckley figures we're his only hope of pulling off this raid and getting away with it. We've seen his people. A shitload of them against the five of us, on territory they know, and they can get us cornered. And mebbe if they can isolate and overrun a wag, then they can pull it off. Sure they can keep this place safe, but then who the fuck would want to come here? No, the truth of it is that he needs us as much as we need him. Hell, the only reason we're still alive after last night is because they don't dare go against him."

"Yeah, the looks we were getting from some of

them…" Krysty shuddered. "We were just meat to them, something to play with."

"And that's what we'll be when this raid is over with," Mildred said coldly.

"Exactly. So we need to cover as many of the bases as possible between now and tomorrow," Ryan added.

Given time, they were able to work out a plan of action that would, if nothing else, leave them prepared for the next day. All they had to do was wait for night-fall before it could be put into operation.

But first, they were to learn that Buckley had a little surprise of his own in store for them. They had been resting up in the cramped, shuttered room, glad of the peace after the necessity of staying awake all night, when they could hear an already familiar shuffling gait come toward them from the corridor beyond the flimsy wooden door. Buckley flung open the door so that it slammed against the wall, raising a cloud of plaster dust.

"Hey, you people, how's y'all doing? Hope y'all resting up good, 'cause we's got a lot of work tomorrow to get ready for the raid and we's planning to have some fun and get ready for it. I's had a real good idea about tomorrow and I's thinking that y'all gonna like it. See, I'm figgering that if ole Doc here is still really in a bad way, it don't make no sense for him to go on the raid. So I's thinking that he can stay here, and ole red here can stay with him and make sure he's okay," Buckley added, indicating Krysty. "The way I sees it, we's gotta keep this simple, otherwise we's all gonna get confused about what's going on. We pack the wag full of my people, with One-eye, and Whitey, hell, y'all the best fighters in my book, right? And meantimes, we got a couple of y'all back here to help clean up when y'all get back. Figure y'all be glad to see each other then and everyone's happy."

"What about the rest of the plan?" Ryan questioned, playing for time, trying to think of a way in which he could argue the chief around so that the companions weren't split up by the raid.

"What rest of the plan? We's tag on, we's go in, we's kick ass, we's come out. What more of a plan do you think there's gotta be, Ryan boy?" Buckley grinned his hideous leer and shrugged. "Seems kinda obvious to me. Listen, y'all get some rest, 'cause tonight we party."

With which Buckley turned and left the room, pulling the door shut behind him and leaving the companions stunned. Not only did there seem no way in which they could avoid the separation—thus ruining any chance of making a run for it when they were outside of Nagasaki—but there was no coherent plan apart from the vaguest kind of hit and run.

"Shit, this is really making it hard," Mildred muttered, the first to break the silence.

"Must get to barn, find out what wag team have say," Jak said urgently.

Ryan nodded. "If the whole ville's going to be occupied, then there may be a chance for one of us to slip in there. But we're going to have to be careful— not just of getting caught, but of keeping out of harm's way when these fuckers go wild."

"I suspect we may be safer than we think in that respect," Doc mused. "Consider how Buckley stepped in last night. He doesn't want these half-wits to ruin his plan with their base desires. He knows how much he will need us, one way or the other. I think he may be even more stringent with them come this nightfall."

"I hope so," Krysty whispered. "But what do we do if their blood runs so hot that they forget what he wants...or if even he forgets what he wants?"

"Keep backs covered," Jak muttered in a low voice. "Use their shit to cover tracks," he added pointedly.

There was little else to say. Until they knew the extent of what the dwellers of Nagasaki had in mind for their pre-raid celebrations, there was no way they could plan the recce on the barn. And to go there, try to find out something—anything—from those who were within was an imperative.

They rested, trying to get some sleep, preserve some energy for the night ahead. Outside, they could hear the ville go about its business, then begin to wind down as the light faded, replaced by the erratic glow of tallow and oil lamps. There was little else to do except rest and the minutes stretched into hours, seemed to stretch into days, as they waited for the distinctive sound of Boss Buckley, coming to fetch them.

It added no little foreboding to the atmosphere. Partly because of the way that, despite outward calm, they were coiled inside, and partly because of the stretched tension rope of waiting. When they eventually heard the shuffling gait of the chief, accompanied by his two unspeaking sec men. Not that they were silent. The sec men's giggles and muted laughter could be heard behind the door, responding to something that Buckley was saying, rendered inaudible by the walls and the lack of necessity for him to temper his accent.

They exchanged glances. They were ready. The question was, what were they ready for?

Buckley threw the door open, his ugly face split by a hideous leer that represented the highest of spirits.

"Hey, hey, hey," he boomed, "y'all ready to party? We's gonna celebrate tomorrow, what we're gonna come home with and whipping those Duma asses…" He beckoned them to join him and the companions filed out of the room, noting as they did that the two sec men hung back to cover the rear of the line as it left the room. Jak was last one out, and he looked at the remade Lee Enfield .303 that one sec guard held, and the homemade rifle that the other was cradling. Both men looked at ease, but Jak could see the tension in their arms, visible to his trained eye beneath the folds of their ragged clothing. One move out of line, one word from Buckley, and they would bring the blasters up into firing position.

Buckley may be acting like he trusted the companions, but he was leaving no room for error.

Outside the ranch house, the inhabitants of the shantytown were already getting into full swing. There was a gut-wrenchingly awful smell that overpowered the usual sewage and body odors. As they left the building, they could see that the center of the ville was lit by a giant fire that popped and crackled, giving off dense clouds of smoke as well as an intense heat and a brilliant light.

The light was bad. If one of them was to slip away and try to infiltrate the barn, then they needed the semidarkness they had experienced the night before.

Standing in front of the fire, Ryan could see that it was made of all the detritus that could be found in the ville. There were pieces of brush, carcasses of chilled animals, old split and burst tires...anything the inhabitants could find that would burn. The plastics and rubber crackled, causing the odd jet of blue or purple flame to spurt among the red and orange, the cause of the fumes, smoke and stench. From experience and from some old predark books and magazines he had seen, the one-eyed man knew that some of these old plastics gave off poisonous fumes. This would certainly give them cover if it made the inbreds drowsy or sick, but how could he and the rest of the companions avoid being affected?

Mildred appeared at his side. "Have you seen this circus? Shit, if we get through tonight I'd be glad to walk into Duma on foot and with no weapons."

"What do you know about smoke from old shit like plastics?" Ryan asked, ignoring her words and cutting to the heart of the matter, pointing out the sparks of differently colored flame.

Mildred stared at the fire and then gave Ryan her opinion. Whatever they did, the companions should keep as far from the immediate area of the fire as possible, so that the fumes hopefully wouldn't overpower them.

The two parted to spread the word and Ryan was suddenly aware of what Mildred had meant with her first words.

Compared to the previous nights revels, this was a whole new league.

In the light of the fire, which illuminated the center of the ville almost as brightly as if it were day, the ville dwellers were going crazy. There were several barrels of brew, which many of them were dipping their heads into, drinking deep, then emerging for air. There were also some smaller containers, which seemed to contain powders that ville dwellers were either dipping their fingers into and eating, or snorting from. It may have been a kind of jolt or it may have been something looted from the redoubt medical bay or it may have been something they mixed from plants and herbs through knowledge passed down and still just about understood. Whatever it was, it seemed to countermand the effects of the brew. Where the one made them high and energetic, the other seemed to bring them down, like they were strung out on the purest jolt.

In between the two, they were determined to enjoy themselves. Most of them were naked or almost naked, and they ran around laughing and screaming wildly, grabbing at one another. Men and women, women and women, men and men—all were touching each other, licking and stroking. It was a huge chain of rutting humanity, paying no attention to the sex of their partner, or which part of their body they were penetrating.

There was also some fighting. Drunk, stoned, not getting what they wanted or else being hurt by someone else's brutal sexuality, some were turning on each other and lashing out. But these fights in themselves did nothing but stimulate the sexual excitement and ended up in more coupling.

In the middle of it all, Buckley stood, now naked. The woman Ryan recognized as Mags—partly by the scars that still covered her from her fights—was on her knees in front of him.

Ryan turned away. He cast frantic glances over the center of the ville. It seemed that everyone was gathered within the warmth and light of the huge fire. The fumes caught at the back of his throat, leaving a sickly sweet aftertaste that turned his guts.

If it was going to knock them out, make them less aware of what was going on, then all was well and good.

Catching sight of his people, he could see that Mildred, Krysty and Doc were banded together on the far side of the fire trying to keep a distance from the fumes without becoming too conspicuous. Together, they were able to look as though they were on the verge of joining in the orgy whilst at the same time using their numbers to beat away anyone who came near. They were also farthest from the barn. Unless Jak was already on his way, it was up to Ryan.

The one-eyed man turned, and was about to strike out for the barn, imposing and silent in the darkness beyond the edge of the fire's light, when he saw Jak coming toward him. The albino teen glided through the rutting and fighting crowd like a wraith. It was almost as if the dwellers around couldn't see him as he slipped between them, fending off any clutching hands or body contact with the deftest of swerves. He could have cut them down at any moment, but he wanted to remain anonymous for the now.

"Ryan, no guards. Everyone fuck and fight," Jak murmured as he drew close. "Clear to barn."

"You've recced it?" Ryan asked.

Jak gave the briefest of nods. "Moat got spiked trap, nothing else. Mebbe sec usually guard it. Mebbe no one even in there now."

"Buckley made like there was."

"Yeah. Was," Jak interjected.

Ryan shrugged. "There's only one way to find out. If it's all clear, then I'll try and get in. These fuckers are too busy with each other to notice, but tell the others I'm going in…and cover for me if you have to."

"No problem. Go now—these all out cold before long," Jak said with something as close to disdain as his toneless voice had ever come.

As Ryan moved toward the darkened area around the barn, he looked back to see Jak melt into the crowd, threading his way through to the remaining companions. It was all in Ryan's hands now.

Ryan made his way through the crowd, pushing away advances and hands that groped at him. One woman—tall and thin, with a twisted leer where her mouth should have been and flat, empty breasts that dangled down to her navel—grabbed at him and tried to kiss him, one hand reaching for his crotch. Ryan yelled and pushed her back, cuffing her to the ground. The hungry look on her face showed him that, rather than dissuading her, he had done nothing but excite her.

He glanced toward the barn and the encompassing darkness. It was only thirty yards away, but it may as well have been thirty miles as the woman scrambled to her feet and lunged at him again. He was being watched by others who were excited by the sexual fight that was developing. There was no way he could head to the barn right now. Not in front of them.

The woman came at him again, laughing and snorting, drooling at the thought of what she could do to the muscular warrior. Ryan put his weight on his back foot, ready to counter the momentum of her lunge—for she threw herself onto him from close range, almost driving him back onto the muddy ground. If he had fallen, that would have been the end of his attempt to reach the barn.

Instead he was able to close in on her. He took one of her pendulous nipples in one hand and twisted hard. She yelped in pain, but instead of driving her back it only served to inflame her. He felt hot breath on his neck—but from behind. A man was behind him, arms clutching at him—he could tell the sex of his new attacker as he could feel the man's erection in the small of his back. Lifting a combat-booted foot, he brought it down hard on the man's uncovered shin, causing him to stumble back, yelling in anger and pain.

One down, one to go. Swiveling, Ryan took the woman off balance, flinging her into the man who had been behind him and who was still hopping in pain. She cannoned into the man and they went down in a heap.

Ryan used the moment to slip away from them, checking for any other watchers before moving into the cover of darkness.

Still keeping triple red, in case a stray sec guard had wandered into the area since Jak's recce, he moved swiftly across the land between the shantytown and the moated barn. Here, there was darkness and silence, the activity of the revelers falling away to nothing. It took a few seconds for his eye to fully adjust to the gloom.

Coming up to the front of the barn, he was struck by how silent it was. If there were any captives within, they had been subdued to silence by their ordeals. And the prospect of escape wasn't enough to entice them on this night. What if he managed to broach the moat, get inside the barn, only to find it empty?

Come to that, what exactly did he hope to discover? What could any prisoners tell him that would help in the coming day?

This wasn't the time for doubts. Swiftly and silently Ryan moved around the circumference of the moat. It took him a few minutes and when he had arrived back at the front, he was in some ways no wiser. As Jak had told him, the dry moat, dug to a depth of about ten feet, was baited with spiked metal mantraps that ran all the way around. The barn itself had only the one set of doors and the original wooden structure had been augmented over the years by concrete, stone buttresses and sheets of metal plundered—by the looks of them—from a variety of sources. The double doors were closed from the outside by a long metal bar that ran horizontally across the middle. There was a moveable wooden slat bridge to cross the divide, which was sitting on the ville side of the moat.

Would there be any alarms? Ryan doubted it. He could see no obvious wires or traps around this sole entry and the fact remained that the power to run an alarm system was something that Nagasaki failed to have. The barring of the door and the moat would be enough, especially as any attempt to break into the barn would have to be from this one spot.

Looking over his shoulder at the now distant revelers, Ryan took the wooden slat bridge and maneuvered it so that it swiveled over across the divide. It was made of a heavy wood to take great weight, and his tendons and muscles strained and popped as he heaved it around. It was at least a two-person task, but he had no option.

As it settled on the small strip of dirt in front of the door, Ryan heaved a sigh of relief. His arms and thighs ached and he let them drop for a second, breathing deeply to allow oxygen back into his bloodstream. He walked slowly across the wooden bridge, testing its strength and security with each step. It stayed firm.

Ryan was now acutely aware of his exposed position should any of the Nagasaki revelers stray from the fire. He looked over his shoulder, scanning the immediate area. All was quiet. He took the bar in both hands, testing its weight before gently lifting it, not wanting to scrape the metal of the bar against either the wood of the doors, or the metal of the retaining brackets, making any kind of noise that could attract attention to his activity.

His aching muscles protested, but he held the bar firm, gently lifting it so that he was able to clear the danger area and lower it to the ground.

Not knowing what to expect, he took hold of the doors and eased them open. As he did so, two things hit him. The first was a dim light that seemed all the brighter for piercing complete darkness. The inside of the barn was illuminated by a low tallow light that flickered and could undoubtedly be seen from the center of the settlement. Ryan pushed the door closed again, so that he blocked the light. He would have to be careful how he entered, cutting the escape of that light to a minimum.

And he would also have to take a few deep breaths before entering, allowing him to breathe only shallowly once inside. For the other thing to hit him had been the stench that escaped as soon as the doors were opened.

A combination of charnel house and sewer, it made Ryan fear for what may be within.

But there was only the one way to find that out. Taking one quick glance behind him to check that it was safe, he pulled the door open a crack and slipped himself through the crack, hurriedly closing the door again.

Inside, he despaired of finding anything or anyone that could tell him anything of any use. In fact, he despaired of finding anyone alive. For the stench hit him like a physical object and was the result of the carnage within.

The barn was lit by three tallow lamps that were suspended from brackets hammered into support struts around the central section of the floor. There was an upper level that disappeared into gloom, but it was the filth around the center that took his attention.

The straw scattered as a floor covering was old, sodden with urine and covered in feces. It was also covered in the remains of bowls of slop stew, and stains that could only be blood. There were also human remains: body parts, intestines. Hands and feet were visible in the mess, some almost mummified, some seemingly quite fresh. Hanging from nails up into the roof, attached to the stanchions that held the tallow lights but above and beyond their feeble beams, he could see round objects that were virtually indistinguishable, but…could they be severed heads?

The barn was used as a slaughter and trophy house. Whoever came in through the heavy doors stood no chance of ever getting out alive. The whole exercise had been pointless. With a sigh, trying to ignore the sickened churning of his stomach, Ryan turned to leave.

It was then that he heard the rustling, far off into the

darkened depths of the barn. Rats? No, it was too loud, too full a sound to be something that small. Aware that he could not use a blaster for fear of alerting anyone to his presence, Ryan slipped the panga from the sheath on his thigh, the blade gleaming dully in the fallow light.

Scanning the edge of the darkness with his good eye, he could see no signs of movement.

"C'mon, if you're there, then attack me. If not, then I want to talk to you."

"Why?"

Ryan was startled. It wasn't just that his hidden companion had spoken, but it was the sound of the voice. Cracked, weary, almost hushed by strain. In just one word, the speaker had expressed pain and suffering that had driven him almost beyond endurance. It was a genuine question. Why the hell should he come out of hiding and face a man with a deadly weapon, especially when it sounded as though he had no strength left to do more than crawl.

"Why haven't you come for me?" the voice continued.

"Because I didn't know you were there," Ryan replied simply. "Because I assumed this was just a slaughterhouse."

"It is," the voice said quietly, seemingly unable to speak at anything other than the one pitch. "It's just that they do it slowly. Have to have their fun first," it continued, pitch rising hysterically—or as much as it could manage—on the word *fun*.

"Listen, I don't have much time," Ryan said urgently, taking a gamble. It was true. He had little time—for himself, for his people and for the poor speaker who sounded as though he may be on the verge of madness. "I'll level with you. We were captured by these freaks, too. The only reason we aren't in here is because they want us to help them mount a raid with a stolen wag. Then, they say, we'll be let free. I'd trust Buckley as far as I could throw the fat fucker, but we've gone along because we're outnumbered. What we need is information."

He stopped, as he could hear a small, choking sound from the pool of darkness that held the speaker. It was either a sob or a laugh or perhaps even both. He waited until it had subsided and then was about to continue when the voice broke the darkness.

"You think that's gonna help you? Listen, if I was you I'd just run like hell. Or hope you get chilled in the raid so that they don't bring you back here. Do you have any idea what they do to us when they get us in here?"

"I think I might," Ryan said slowly, surveying the carnage around.

"They're the lucky ones," the voice said bitterly. "I wish I was with them right now. I figure it won't be long, but…"

"I've seen what they do to each other, I can make a guess," Ryan said gently.

"No…no, you can't," the voice said with an unexpected venom. "You couldn't even begin to imagine it unless you'd had to go through it. What they do to each other is just playing compared to what they do here. Any men they catch have to have sex with their women, and any women get raped by their men. And if they have men and women they catch, then we have to have sex with each other. They want kids, see, otherwise the ville will die. Tell me something, how many kids do you see out there?"

Ryan furrowed his brow. It was a good point. He couldn't recall seeing any during their enforced stay. "None," he answered simply.

"Exactly. You ask me, these inbreeds can't have kids anymore and they use any outlanders they can get to try and have kids. And if they don't get results, then they get bored and that's when they start to get vicious. They play these games, see, how much any of us can take. How we act when we're getting hurt or when anyone else is getting hurt. They ripped Malone's guts out in front of us—he tried to hold them as they fell out of his belly, tried to grab them as they spilled over his hands. It was like trying to catch a whole load of eels that wouldn't stay still. And I never realized that they'd make so much steam as they came out."

The hidden voice was getting lost in his memories, his tone changing and becoming more distant. Now that Ryan was pretty sure of the fate that awaited the companions after the raid—assuming they got out in one piece—he needed to get some more details. But it was going to be hard to interrupt the hidden voice, who was now lost in a reverie of awful imaginings.

"Stacey was the next. They all raped her but she wouldn't get pregnant. I figure those bastards are all sterile. So they cut off her hands and feet, burned the wounds so she stopped bleeding, then raped her again. Then they cut off her head and used it to throw at us.

We had to catch it, or else we got cut or lost something of our own. Crazy bastards, laughing as they watched."

The horrors that the voice had witnessed went through Ryan's head. In his mind's eye he could see them and it made him wince in sympathy for what the man had seen. The wonder of it was that he wasn't totally mad already. But despite this, Ryan had other priorities and he had to press the man, change the direction of his thoughts.

"Listen, show yourself to me. Come into the light and I'll try and help you get the hell out of here. They're too busy to think about you today or tomorrow. You tell me what I need to save our hides and I'll try and help you save yours. No promises—you'll be on your own. But at least you'll have a chance."

There was a long pause. Ryan scanned the darkness in the direction he had first heard the shuffling that preceded the voice. There was nothing. Taking a chance, he resheathed the panga, which had previously been dangling in his palm. This gesture seemed to have an effect, as he heard shuffling again and the source of the voice moved into the light. He was emaciated, with sores and open wounds across his body. His shirt was in ribbons and his combat fatigues were ripped and torn. He had no boots on his feet and Ryan could see some of the toenails were missing. One of the man's eyes was cloudy, but the other was clear as he fixed it on Ryan.

"I'm Ryan Cawdor. Me and four others were trekking across the wasteland when they found us. Who are you?"

The man nodded an acknowledgement. "I'm Cyrus

Gill and I was a driver for Trader Simms until the wag blew a tire when we were on our way to Duma. Simms, the stupe bastard, couldn't wait to get to Duma 'cause he had some grens to sell to the baron for big jack, so he left us. Then they came out of nowhere, like rats, and took us."

"It's your wag we'll be using. We're supposed to join a convoy and go into the ville on the back of it—will it be your convoy?"

Gill shook his head. "Too soon. Simms is probably still screwing gaudies and snorting jolt on his profits. But there's always a lot of convoys. It's a big stop in these parts. These crazy fuckers taking you right into the ville and not ripping off the convoy outside? Man, you ain't ever coming back," he said with a sad and grim laugh.

"Why? What's it like in Duma?"

Despite the situation, a wry grin cracked Gill's features. "Listen, it's the richest ville for hundreds of miles. Xander's got it all wrapped up. Half what he pays the convoys for their trade he takes back from jolt, booze and gaudies. Man's smart and all smart barons have a good sec, right? The place is guarded and wired all around. If you start firing off in there, they'll have you outnumbered fifty to one and chilled before you can even say your name. You want my advice, Ryan Cawdor? Don't go—though it'd be buying the farm quicker and with less pain than living in here," he added, indicating the barn around him.

"Buckley ain't as stupe as mebbe you think—he's keeping two of our people back with him, kind of a fail-safe, I guess," Ryan said quickly. "How we get the hell out of here I'll have to work out triple quick. But you… you up to making a run for it?"

"Do bears shit in the woods, boy?" Gill snapped back. "I dunno how far I'll get, but if you can guarantee me no sec to mow me down, then I'll run like I never have. I'd rather buy the farm out there than rot in here and play their next game."

Ryan gestured and Gill shuffled closer. He was limping and was obviously weak, but seemed to have no serious impairments.

"Why did they leave you till last?" Ryan asked out of curiosity—and perhaps a touch of suspicion.

"Lucky, I guess," Gill replied bitterly.

Ryan looked around the barn. "You'll need boots…" His eye caught a pair hidden under the filthy straw. He reached down and picked them up, then nearly dropped them in surprise when he realized that they still had severed feet in them, the blood congealed and dried on the leather.

Biting down the bile, the one-eyed man reached into each boot and pulled out the rotting flesh and bone, dropping it on the floor of the barn. He handed the boots over to Gill, who kept his face impassive. Who could tell what had to be going through his mind? He pushed his feet into the boots and winced.

"Must've been Stacey's. She did have little feet." He grimaced without a trace of humor.

"How many of you were there, for fuck's sake?" Ryan asked, looking at the carnage around.

"Only five. The rest of this shit was here when we got here. Guess they're not the world's best housekeepers," Gill managed with a sickly grin.

Ryan ignored the gallows humor. "C'mon, we'd better get going," he said shortly, unwilling to hang around the barn any longer than necessary.

Moving the door as little as possible to allow them to squeeze through, Ryan then closed the doors firmly, and carefully put the bar back into place. He looked around to see if there was any movement toward the barn from the center of the ville. The dwellers were still too occupied to notice.

The two men made their way carefully back over the wooden bridge, and Ryan heaved it back into place, so that it would seem to the casual observer that no one had been over the moat that night. He looked up to see Gill staring into the center of the ville with undisguised hatred in his face.

"Fuckers," he spit, "enjoying themselves when they reduced us to meat."

"Don't knock it right now," Ryan whispered. "They're giving you the chance to get out by doing that."

Without another word, he led the limping Gill around the moat and toward the back end of Nagasaki, away from the center of the ville. It was quiet there and dark, with the only signs of life being the slack-jawed, sloe-eyed animals that passed for livestock, watching the two men pass by with only the briefest of interest. They reached the edge of the ville without any interruption and paused at the edge of the farthest building.

"You're on your own now," Ryan said simply.

Gill stopped and looked at the one-eyed man. "I dunno why you bothered to do what you just did, but I'm glad."

Without another word and without looking back, Gill limped off into the wasteland beyond the ville until he was swallowed up by the darkness. Even when he was no longer visible and the sound of his shuffling feet was lost in the all-encompassing night, Ryan still stood and watched. Why had he helped him? Because he'd learned something about Duma and the idiocy of Buckley's plan? Perhaps, but he already knew enough to realize that the chief was a moron and the plan was tantamount to jumping into a firefight headfirst. All Gill had done was confirm that.

So why had Ryan helped him? Perhaps because, if he had been in Gill's position, the one-eyed man would have wanted to take his chances in the wastelands rather than die ignominiously at the hands of the Nagasaki dwellers. There was no dignity in buying the farm. It was messy, painful and it meant that you kissed your ass—and this life—goodbye. But it was better to face it on your own terms.

Yeah, mebbe that's all it was: having the choice of how to go.

Ryan turned and walked back through the ville, careful not to be seen by any stray passersby. He needn't have worried; they were all too concerned with enjoying themselves, celebrating the great victory that they hadn't even begun the fight for as of yet.

As unobtrusively as possible, Ryan slipped back into the circle around the fire. The fun was beginning to wind down as more of the ville dwellers were either sleeping or passed out in the dirt. A few still indulged in rutting and fighting, but even this was halfhearted as the alcohol and the chemicals and herbs claimed them.

Jak spirited his way between those left standing. He didn't ask any questions, just fixed Ryan with an impassive stare.

"Tell you when we get some privacy," he whispered. "But it doesn't look good."

"Didn't figure it would."

Following Jak, Ryan went over to where the others were waiting. There was no sign of Buckley or his two sec men.

"Interesting time, lover?" Krysty posed.

"Kinda—what about you?" Ryan countered.

"Great, just great."

As Ryan looked out beyond the glow of the fire and the billowing smoke that still obscured a great tract of sky, he could see that beyond was beginning to lighten as dawn tried to break through the chem clouds over the wasteland.

"Better try and get some rest before these bastards revive and want to start for the convoy," he murmured. "Figure we'll be safe now—they're all too tired to do anything."

"Then perhaps this would be a good time to escape," Doc pondered. "After all, you were able to slip away."

"Yeah, but I was on my own, Doc," Ryan countered. "Jak, what d'you reckon?"

The albino shook his head. "Buckley not that stupe. Back of the ville is okay, but if we want to take the wag then we got trouble. Five guards mounted on it and the road out."

"Yeah, and if we go by foot then you aren't gonna get far, Doc. Not yet, at any rate," Ryan added.

"Mayhap you are correct, Ryan. But perhaps that

means you should leave me here," Doc said solemnly. "After all, if not for me, we would not have been taken."

"We don't do that and you know it," Ryan said softly. "We stand and fall together. If at least three of us have the wag tomorrow, then at least we stand a chance of getting a ride out. See what happens."

They walked through fallen bodies back to the ranch house and the relative safety of the room. Once secured in there, Ryan told them all he had seen in the barn and all he had gathered from Gill. And his reluctance to escape became a little more clear when he added, "Thing is, if we did just run away these sick fucks would still be around to do this to other people. I don't like that idea too much. I'd like us to wait until we're in a position to grind these fuckers into their own shit and mud."

The others exchanged glances. Doc spoke for them all. "Put like that, sir, I can find no argument in my heart. We bide our time, then strike at the foulness and rip it out of the body of this land."

There was nothing more to be said. Time now only to rest, to wait for the time when Buckley would load up the stolen wag and mount his attack. Time only to wait for the moment when they could turn the tables on the chief and his pesthole ville and wipe them out. Time now only for the chief to sleep in a deceptive peace, not knowing what they would attempt to make of his grand plans.

It was going to be a long day's journey to the fall of night.

Chapter Twelve

Gill walked all day. From the moment the sun appeared on the horizon, through its rise to the apex of the day, until it began to slowly descend, bringing—if not relief—a drop in the harsh temperature. Sweat prickled his skin and dried out, leaving salt trails that stung in his open wounds. He had nothing left to sweat out and was almost delirious. He felt sure he would buy the farm, but was glad. At least he would be alone, not ripped to pieces and used as meat by those inbred half-mutie, half-mad scum who had held him captive. He had no idea which direction he was headed. The heat and dust made it all seem the same and even looking at the sun didn't help. Rather than give him a point for location, it merely blinded eyes used to the gloom of the barn.

Gill fell over. If it was once, it was a dozen times. At each fall, he stubbornly picked himself up and continued, determined to chill on his feet if he was going to…when he saw the blacktop extending in front of him, stretching as far as he could see in either direction. He thought it was an illusion—just as he thought the wags coming toward him and the motorbike rider with the M-4000 who sped toward him were also an illusion.

The biker skidded to a halt only a few feet from

where he stood, swaying. Gill raised his hand, tried to speak to his hallucination. But no words escaped his parched throat and dry mouth; then collapsed on the asphalt.

"HE'S WAKING UP," were the first words Gill heard. He opened his eyes, aware of a sickening lurch in his guts. Then, as he steadied, he realized that the lurch wasn't inside him, but was caused by the movement of the wag in which he was now lying. Faces loomed over him in the gloom of the wag's interior and he could smell that familiar odor of gasoline, sweat and old goods that every convoy member recognizes as home.

One of the faces was female: lined and old, but still with some kind of caring in it. She took a damp piece of cloth and cleaned his forehead.

"Where the fuck did you spring from, stranger?" she asked. He tried to answer, but his throat was almost closed with lack of water. She was able to interpret his strangled yelp as a plea for water and lifted a canteen to his lips. He drank heavily, his throat so sore that the cooling liquid actually hurt on the way down.

He began to speak. It was barely more than a whisper and at first his words tumbled over themselves in his haste, but eventually he managed to croak what had bought him to this point.

"What a shit stupe plan," the woman breathed, then turned and relayed the story in a louder voice to everyone else in the wag.

"Better tell Malloy," the driver said over his shoulder. "Riders haven't raised any alarm, but mebbe he'll want to do something about this 'afore times."

"Can't think how the fuckers think they're not gonna get noticed," another voice—one he couldn't see—said from the gloom.

"Sounds of it, these inbreeds are completely fucked in the head." The woman shrugged. "Figures that stupes like that think they can get away with anything. Are you trying to get Malloy's attention, Leroy?"

"What d'you want me to do, wave my black ass out the window and stop him in shock?" the driver replied laconically. "You know how hard it can be."

Using the wag's horn, he tapped rapidly SOS in Morse, attracting the attention of one of the bikers who rode shotgun to the convoy. As the biker closed, the driver yelled out of the open window to tell the trader to pull over. The rider sped to the front of the convoy and delivered the message. Following the lead of the front wag, the entire convoy came over to the side of the blacktop, grinding to a halt.

The back of the wag opened and Gill watched as the woman slipped out the back. She ran forward to relay Gill's tale to the trader, who then came back to question the man himself.

Gill was tired and could still barely speak, but he outlined what he knew once more. The trader left the wag and Gill could no longer tell what was going on.

Outside, Malloy ordered one of his bikers to go ahead to Duma and warn the sec guard what was going to happen. Malloy had no intention of risking his own men in a firefight with the rogue wagon. Let Xander's men do that. They were much better equipped for such a circumstance.

"It's a shit stupe plan they've got," he told the biker,

"But if it means all we've got to do to avoid a firefight is pretend not to notice them, then that's fine with me. We'll take them right into whatever kind of a trap Xander wants. Hell, the tight-assed bastard may even up the jack on this load if he feels grateful." A wry smile cracked the trader's lips. "Naw, nothing short of warning him about the next nukecaust would make him that grateful—even then it'd have to be a cold day in hell."

With a short, barking laugh, the trader sent the biker on ahead. Pausing before returning to his own wag, Malloy quickly walked back to the wag where Gill lay asleep. Waking him roughly, the trader told him what he'd done. Gill grunted and fell back into sleep. Right at that moment, he truly didn't give a shit. Malloy shrugged, called him an asshole and returned to his lead wag, indicating that the convoy should take off again.

But when, he wondered, would the idiot war party make an appearance?

THE COMPANIONS WAITED until it was dark. No one came for them. Outside they could hear the wag being prepared and Buckley ordering his minions about their duties. Ryan hoped that with the amount of work that was being expended on the preparation for the raid, no one would want to go to the barn and the surviving captive would be ignored.

It seemed that luck would hold. By late afternoon, there had been no enraged Buckley, no furor surrounding a sudden discovery. The companions prepared by cleaning their blasters and checking their diminishing stocks of ammo. Without J.B., supplies were quickly running low.

At least, Ryan, Jak and Mildred prepared themselves. For Doc and Krysty there was only the knowledge that they would have to stay behind, the unspoken hostages to the success of the mission. And beyond that? Only time would tell.

Hours dragged until at last Buckley and his two-man guard came to fetch them. He threw the door open as usual, slamming it into the wall.

"Hey, hey, hey—y'all ready to get rolling?"

It was a rhetorical question and they followed him out into the center of Nagasaki. The wag was waiting, with a crew of five standing by. Two of them were recognizable as the woman Mags and the man she had fought a few nights before. The other three were indeterminate: one of the thin men, a fat man and a fat woman. They could have been any of the ville dwellers.

"Are you coming with us?" Ryan asked Buckley.

"Hell, yeah," the chief cackled. "Me and the boys wouldn't miss this one for anything—right, boys?" The two permanent guards to Buckley nodded eagerly.

At a gesture from Buckley, three ville dwellers moved forward and came between the companions, separating Doc and Krysty from the others.

"Subtle. Oh, but so very subtle," Doc murmured, keeping his sarcasm as low as he could manage.

"Now then, I's a thinking that y'all could make yourselves useful around here while we's gone. Make way for all the good things we's be bringing back for y'all."

"In other words, you wish us to mop out storehouses and clean ordure from the surrounding area. To be skivvies to your glorious society," Doc intoned, sure that this level of sarcasm would fly straight over Buckley's head—and the heads of the assembled ville dwellers.

Buckley's blank expression only confirmed this view. "Hell, yeah—whatever the fuck y'all just said," he mumbled.

At his direction, the ville war party climbed into the wag, followed by Ryan, Mildred and Jak. As the door of the wag closed on those in the front, Ryan was aware of the stench emanating from the Nagasaki fighters. It was going to be a long, hard ride. Before they even got the chance to fight, he would have to work at keeping his stomach.

"C'mon, Ryan boy," Buckley urged. "Fire her up."

Ryan looked at the chief in amazement. "You mean you don't know how to drive one of these?"

Buckley shook his head and leered good-humoredly. "Think that was one of the reasons we needed y'all, Ryan."

Shaking his head in disbelief, the one-eyed man fired up the wag's engine and steered the vehicle on the track that led out of Nagasaki. The wag's suspension hadn't fared well with the rough terrain leading to the ville, and as it bumped and groaned across the wastelands, Mildred and Jak—seated in the rear of the vehicle— wondered what the hell they were doing there, and if they'd survive the journey in one piece.

The ville dwellers were excited, chattering and fin- gering their weapons with impatience, spirits high.

"What's the plan, then?" Ryan questioned. "Do we wait for the convoy or do we track them for some distance? And how the fuck do you propose that we tag on the end without them spotting we're there?" he continued, failing to keep the frustration from his voice.

Buckley shrugged. "Hell, like I knows. We's just see what happens, yeah?"

DOC AND KRYSTY HAD BEEN put to work cleaning out an area of the old ranch house to store the imagined riches that would be looted in the raid. Both worked carefully, keeping a close eye on each other in mutual defense. There was something about the way in which their appointed guardians were staring at them that suggested they would be in serious trouble if the rogue wag didn't return home in good time.

As darkness began to fall—this being Buckley's only weapon in avoiding detection as they attached themselves to the convoy—so both sets of the companions pondered their fate. Doc and Krysty wondered if they could keep their alleged protectors at bay until the others returned; Mildred, Jak and Ryan wondered if they could get out of this debacle in one piece and get back to Doc and Krysty.

Ryan's reveries was broken as the old blacktop came into view, running across the expanse of wasteland ahead of them.

"Slow down there, Ryan boy," Buckley said excitedly. "There they are."

Ryan's eye followed the line of Buckley's pointing finger. Coming toward them, likely to cross their path in ten minutes, was the convoy. There were five wags and seven outriders on bikes.

If Ryan had stopped to think—hadn't had Buckley

breathing excitedly down his neck, urging him both to hurry and also to take care in virtually the same breath—he would have wondered at that. Why an uneven number of bikers?

The convoy passed. Although it was dark, the land was flat and without any camouflaging features, and Ryan was sure that the stationary wag stood out against the flat horizon. Nonetheless, the convoy proceeded without any indication that it had noticed the wag waiting to move smoothly into position at the rear of the procession.

Ryan slid the wag into gear, drove it onto the blacktop and slipped in at the rear of the convoy, marveling at the apparent stupidity of the trader in charge, trying to ignore the delighted whoops of the chief.

At the front of the convoy, Malloy rode next to his driver. He had stared at the wag standing on the shoulder of the road with barely concealed amusement as they passed, then followed its progress in his side mirror as his wag drew farther away. The darkness, broken only by the headlights of the wags and bikes behind, prevented him from seeing the point at which the rogue wag slipped into place. However, a series of signals from the headlights of the vehicles behind told him that it had taken up position.

Malloy shook his head in amazement and looked at the road ahead, the lights of Duma visible ahead, standing out like a beacon in the wastes.

"Shit crazy fuckers. Let Xander deal with them."

THE BIKER SENT AHEAD by Malloy had told his story three times before eventually getting to relay it directly to Baron Xander. He had endured ridicule and disdain from the sec guards on the first sct of barriers, then more barracking from a second set of guards and a face-to-face with Sec Chief Hammick before being told to wait in the chief's office.

Grant was in the med lab when Hammick walked in.

"Don't see you around this way often," Grant said with a raised eyebrow.

"Yeah, well, got a weird one, and I wanted to run it by you first," Hammick replied, rubbing his chin. Grant had trained him when he first joined the sec guard, and although Grant had long since been seconded to med, Hammick still thought of him as the more experienced of the two. Besides which, Grant was close to Xander, and Hammick didn't relish the idea of going to the baron with something as plain strange as this.

Grant listened while Hammick outlined the biker's story, barely able to keep a smirk from his face. "Well," he said finally, "I always thought those inbreeds would keep themselves to themselves. All these years they've been no bother. But I guess the insanity in their tiny gene pool has finally got to them."

"Yeah, but it's not them that I'm really worried about," Hammick replied. "It's who they've got with them."

"What—a bunch of captives who have to fight or be chilled? What's to worry about?"

Hammick stared at Grant. "Weren't you listening? A one-eyed man? When we've got—"

"Xander doesn't have to know every detail," Grant interrupted. "Do we know this man?"

"Who?"

"The biker with the story," Grant snapped, exasperated. "Is he known to us?"

"Oh yeah, he's one of Malloy's all right. And a wild one last time he was here," Hammick added with a grin.

"Good," Grant said decisively. "Then we have something we can use to persuade him that there are a few—shall we say—unimportant points to his story. Wouldn't you agree? After all, we can't have Xander sidetracked by a legend and soft-pedalling at the expense of our reputation for coming down hard."

Hammick thought about this. "You're right. Come and talk to this rider for me, Grant."

"It'll be a pleasure," Grant concurred.

And so, when the outrider from Malloy's convoy got to retell his story for the fourth time, standing in front of an amused Xander, there were certain elements that he omitted.

Xander waved him away when he had finished and Hammick handed him over to a sec guard on the door.

"Take him away and get him out of his tiny little mind until this is all over," he murmured to the sec guard, knowing that the biker would be the last to object to such a course of action.

Walking back to where Grant was conferring with Xander, he caught the end of their conversation.

"I think we should allow them in as far as the wag station, and then surround them."

"Why let them get that far?" Xander countered. "Our first post could knock them out, with no danger to surrounding buildings. Think how much jack they could take to rebuild."

"I understand your point, Baron, but I would argue

thus. With a wider expanse of land in which to make good an escape and with only the outer post forces against them, they could elude complete destruction. How would this seem to Malloy? One show of weakness and word will soon spread. This could be the first crack in what has otherwise been an impeccable reputation."

"But what if these outlanders they have with them increase their efficiency and firepower? How would that look?"

Grant gave Hammick the briefest of glances before continuing. "You heard the messenger, Baron. These outlanders are probably wounded, tired and being forced against their will. I can't see that they would be much of a threat, can you? This way, we draw them into a safe, enclosed space and then wipe them out in front of Malloy and his crew. Thus we negate the threat from the inbreeds and also hammer home a message to any who would seek to come up against us."

Hammick looked from one to the other while Xander pondered that. Making the biker leave out any reference to a one-eyed man made it that much easier for Grant to persuade Xander that his tactical plan was the best. But as sec chief, Hammick would feel the baron's wrath if things went wrong. He hoped to hell that Grant was making the right call.

Finally, Xander looked up, his eyes going from Hammick to Grant, and he nodded. "Okay, let's do it your way. Alert the sec force and get the armory onto this."

J.B. AND OLLY HAD FINISHED priming the blaster section of the armory when the call came. J.B. was explaining the action of a Weatherby rifle to the younger man, out-lining optimum use, when Esquivel found them.

"Yo, J.B., dude, there's something big going down. This is where we get to see some action." With which he gestured for the two men to follow.

J.B. raised an inquisitory eyebrow at Olly; the Armorer had been enjoying himself, having not seen a Weatherby—as far as he could recall—for many years. Olly responded immediately.

"Xander likes us to reequip the sec depending on what the task is, and he also likes us to be on hand when there's a firefight—kind of like we should be there in case something fucks up with the ordnance, kind of that any armorer worth his jack should be able to hold his own in a firefight." The young man tapered off, but J.B. knew what was unspoken: if he really was the J. B. Dix that Xander spoke of, then he should be a good fighter.

Weird thing was, he really didn't know what he was like in combat, but he guessed he was about to find out.

The two men hurried down to the lobby of the armory building. As they did so, J.B. queried, "All three of us going?"

Olly shook his head. "Not dad. Xander thinks he's too old now. And mebbe he's right—Dad makes a lot of noise about it, but I figure he's slowing up a bit."

"Mebbe that's why he's not happy about me coming in," J.B. mused, broaching the unspoken subject. A sharp look from Olly prompted him to continue. "Listen, he knows this armory better than any man. No matter what Xander says, you or me couldn't do the job without his advice."

"Mebbe you should tell him that," Olly murmured in an undertone as they arrived in the packed lobby.

"If he gives me a chance to say more than two words, I will," J.B. replied.

The lobby was already filling up with uniformed sec. A force of about twenty was being deployed in the action. Some of them J.B. recognized, but others were strangers to him. He saw Esquivel work his way through, the sec man detailed to him being looser of limb and gait than any of the others.

"What's happening, Es?" Olly asked.

"Some weird shit thing, far as I can make out. Something and nothing, but Xander's turning it into a show of strength. Guess that thing with Simms rattled him."

Olly looked blank, but J.B. understood. He murmured, "Any baron who gets screwed over has to clamp down hard, show anyone else with ideas that they're on a one-way ticket to the farm. First opportunity they get."

"Heads up, guys—it's my boss," Esquivel muttered, indicating Hammick as he came through the main doors.

A hush fell over the assembled throng and for the next ten minutes the sec chief proceeded to outline what the outrider sent in by Malloy had told him and what Grant and Xander had decided as a course of action; except that he sold the course of action as his own and said nothing about a one-eyed man in the opposition wag.

The notion that they would let the convoy, with the rogue wag in tow, into the ville caused a ripple of bemusement. But when Hammick told them it was a chance to make a show of authority to let the traders know who they could rely upon, Olly looked across at J.B. with a wry grin and a slow nod. The lad was learning some important lessons, ones that would mean a lot if he did eventually become armorer of Duma.

J.B.'s attention strayed for a second as he realized that thinking in such terms meant that he had the notion to move on, though how he could escape from a shelter that may turn into a prison was something he'd have to consider when there was time.

Right now, there was none. Hammick snapped positional tactics and orders at groups of the uniformed men and told J.B. and Olly the kinds of extra ordnance he wanted doled out. The AK-47s the sec carried as standard were fine for everyday use and show, but in order to neutralize this threat with prejudice he wanted them equipped with SMGs and grens, as well as several of the M-16/M-203 combos that J.B. had noted earlier in one of the blaster racks.

The gren launcher section of the combo needed handling with care, and from what Olly had told him, they were rarely used. There could be some interesting—not to mention dangerous—fireworks if the heavy-duty blasters were put in the hands of sec men who had little or no training in how to use them. He exchanged a questioning glance with Olly, who shrugged.

Nothing for it but to hope that these guys had been trained. Not so reassuring when you were in the firing line, though. As Hammick outlined the plan of attack, once they had cornered the wag and isolated it from the rest of the convoy, it became clear that J.B. and Olly would be almost in the front line, providing ordnance support and fighting.

Dismissing his men to get equipped and into position—current reports gave them half an hour until arrival, as an outlying sec post had sighted the convoy—Hammick left them in charge of Olly and J.B.

Making sure that the SMGs and M-16/M-203s went out with full checks and good supplies of ammo kept J.B. busy, while Olly dealt with the distribution of grens both for hand use, and also for use with the combo. It wasn't until they were on their way to the wag park being used for ambush that J.B. had a chance to question Olly and Esquivel about the rogue wag.

"No one knows that much about this bunch of in-breeds, just that they've been out there since the nuke-caust and they've never really bothered us before. They like to keep themselves to themselves, if you know what I'm saying," Olly told him.

"Nasty fuckers, though," Esquivel added. "You hang out with trade crews, you get to hear shit. They've been scavenging for years, mebbe trying to snatch the odd wag here and there. Sometimes they succeed. No one ever sees those crews again… I don't even want to think about it."

"So why are they still there?" J.B. asked.

Esquivel shrugged. "Are they a threat to Xander if they do that? No, they're only a threat to the traders, and even then only if the traders' own sec are shit. They don't come near us, we don't waste time and jack on running them down. Except now they have—"

"Thing is," Olly interjected, "why are they doing this now, when they've had all that time and never tried anything like it?"

"That, my friend, is a very good question. One that

Xander would do well to ask of Hammick," Esquivel said softly. "But somehow, I don't think he has."

"So we'd better watch ourselves," J.B. said to the young armorer. "They don't sound like they'd get this brave unless they had some new trick in their own armory."

It became difficult to continue the conversation, as they arrived at the wag park and took up positions. Any words overheard that criticized the baron could cause them problems. The time for addressing these issues would be later.

Now they could only wait for the convoy to arrive.

BOSS BUCKLEY CACKLED with glee as the convoy swept unopposed through the roadblocks leading into Duma.

"Shit, if I's a'ever thought that they was this stupe, we's had ourselves a little raid like this years ago."

The crew in front and back of the wag yelped and cheered, agreeing with the chief. Only Mildred and Jak were dissenting voices, notable in their grim-faced silence. In front, eye glued to the wags ahead, Ryan could do little but concur with the silence of his fellows. This was too easy. The convoy had swept through without any routine checks. That couldn't be right, not if Duma was anything like the way it was represented.

"Keep it frosty," the one-eyed man advised Buckley. "We don't want to get caught off guard."

"The hell we will." Buckley cackled, his face lit by the menacing leer that passed for a grin. "We's home free, Ryan boy. All we have to do is come out blasting."

In the chief's insane world, the Duma sec were unsuspecting idiots who would fail to respond when the small war party came out firing, allowing them to take what they wanted and drive out unopposed.

Somehow, Ryan didn't think it would go that way. It was too easy. The convoy had swept along the blacktop, past the sec checkpoints, and was now approaching a designated area, marked out by wire fencing and strong lights. There was one on each side of the road, which bisected the ville. The one on the right was full of wags. The one on the left was virtually empty and those few wags that were parked in there were around the edges.

Ryan felt a familiar tightening in the pit of his stomach, his guts knotting and telling him that something was wrong here. He glanced over his shoulder at Jak and Mildred. They couldn't see the wag park from the rear, but both looked tense. As Ryan's ice-blue orb met Jak's glittering red eyes, an unspoken understanding passed between them.

It was a setup. Mebbe the sentries had known, recognizing the wag as not belonging to a convoy they knew well. Certainly, the convoy itself had to have realized it had an extra wag, but how could they... Of course, the outriders. Onc could have gone on ahead.

All this went through Ryan's head in a moment, but ultimately, it didn't matter. All that mattered was that they were being drawn into a trap and of the war party, there were only three of them that understood that. It was up to them to not only get themselves out of it, but also the Nagasaki dwellers. Otherwise there would be little chance of recovering Krysty and Doc.

The convoy rolled into the wag park, the vehicles peeling off to take up positions that were more redolent of attack than of simply stopping. Watching the wags stop, encircling the rogue vehicle, made even Buckley wake up to the fact that something was wrong.

"What the fuck—" he began, bewildered.

Ryan cut him short. "Shut up and listen. They're on to us. If we're going to get out with one piece, you listen to me and do what I say. Okay? Fireblast, man, answer me!"

But Buckley was lost, fear creeping over his face as he looked out of the windshield. The other Nagasaki dwellers had picked up on his uncertainty, and were either gibbering or lost in their own silent fears.

Ryan shifted in his seat to face Mildred and Jak. "They know we're here. They've got us surrounded. We're going to have to blast our way out."

"Y'know, sometimes I think the rocking chair and the back porch aren't bad things to aspire to," Mildred said quietly, almost to herself. Ryan gave her a puzzled look. "Skip it," she said shaking her head. "It doesn't matter—mebbe I'll explain some time—if we get out in one piece. Just tell us what the plan is, boss man."

SILENCE. NOTHING HAPPENING. The sec forces had taken up position around the perimeter of the wag park, using strategically placed wags for cover. Keeping silent, they had waited for Malloy's convoy to enter the park and circle before peeling off to take up its own defensive positions, leaving the rogue wag isolated.

Olly was waiting with J.B. and Esquivel, watching from behind one wag. The tension wrote lines into his young face, the corners of his eyes barely twitching as the waiting began to tell.

"Easy," J.B. said softly. "Wait until they make the first move."

"Why don't we hit them straight away? We've got the firepower," the young armorer replied.

"Yeah, and we don't know how well protected that wag is. Better for them to give us the initiative by exposing themselves."

"What worries me," Esquivel said slowly, "is they might be thinking the same way."

"They don't sound like they've got the smarts," J.B. mused.

Esquivel grinned, but without humor. "That depends who the hell they've got with them, doesn't it?"

"WAY I SEE IT, they've got us surrounded. We've got two options. One, try to reverse the wag and hit the bastard road before they have a chance to open fire and hope the move shocks them enough to slow them up in responding. Or two, me, Jak and Mildred go out and lay down suppressing fire for your people to go and take one of their wags before we all hightail it out of here. Are you listening to me?"

Ryan shook the chief by the shoulder. Buckley looked at him, fear written in his face, obscuring all sense. The Nagasaki people—Buckley in particular—talked a good firefight, but obviously only when they had superior numbers and a territorial advantage.

Looking around, Ryan could see that virtually all the others in the wag were terrified. The only exception was the woman Mags; it seemed as though nothing could scare her. Her fat, flat face was expressionless, but she nodded as his eye caught hers.

"With you—want get out in one piece," she said, barely intelligible through her palate deformity. But there was no doubting her courage, whether born of bravery or stupidity. With Jak and Mildred, that made four of them. As for the others...

"Looks like we're on our own here," Mildred said.

"Best way," Jak affirmed, believing that only his friends could truly be trusted.

HAMMICK GAZED ACROSS the line of wags until his eyes came back to the wag where Olly, J.B. and Esquivel were waiting. A full circle, waiting. The tension stretched his nerves. He rose above the roof of the wag, looking for any sign of movement from the vehicle in the center of the park. Hammick knew that he could trust his men to hold the line, but Malloy's men? The line of convoy wags had discharged a number of riders with blasters, all looking twitchy and ready to fire. They were potential loose cannons.

He wanted the rogue wag to make the first move. But could he trust Malloy's ability to hold his men?

IT HAPPENED WITH a suddenness that made it almost anticlimactic.

The rogue wag's doors sprung open and four figures emerged, firing as they dropped to the ground. Mags had an Uzi that she used to spray a blistering volley of rounds at the wags clustered on her side. The sec men at the rear were covered, but Malloy's men were careless and some of them bought the farm, not quick enough to duck and cover. Likewise, Ryan snapped off shots from the Steyr as he dropped and rolled. At the rear, Mildred and Jak had their own blasters, as well as handblasters they had taken from the gibbering and scared Nagasaki war party. In addition to Jak's .357 Magnum Colt Python and Mildred's ZKR, they had between them a 9 mm Browning and a Walther PPK. Jak carried the latter, as the blaster jammed on him, he realized that the ville dwellers didn't put much effort into blaster maintenance.

Malloy's men went wild, seeing their own taken out, and fired wildly at the rogue wag, some leaving cover, whooping with excitement, driven by rage.

Hammick swore loudly. The convoy fighters were now in the way of his own men. Blasterfire could take them out. Only one thing to do.

"Blow that motherfucking wag off the face of the earth," he yelled, gesturing to the sec men with the M-16/M-203 combos.

Rising above the tops of the wags, the sec men fired the grens from the racks beneath the blasters. The grens landed wide, the explosions shattering the air, clots of mud and earth thrown up in a cloud that mixed with the gren smoke to form an obstructive blanket over the area.

"Dark night, what the fuck is he doing?" J.B. groaned. "How the hell are we supposed to see what's going on?"

"Attack! Move forward," Hammick screamed over the chatter of blasterfire.

"This is a bastard mess, dude," Esquivel murmured as he, J.B. and Olly moved out from behind their cover. J.B. racked the M-4000 to hit the center of the park with the load of barbed metal fléchettes.

"Watch your backs, keep calm and look out for any of these stupes firing wildly," J.B. yelled, directing that mostly at Olly, who looked as though his nerves were about to snap.

UNDER THE CLOUD of smoke that covered them, Ryan sought out Jak and Mildred. The gren explosions had thrown them away from the cover of the wag, and now both were firing into the melee, hidden by the smoke and dust, hoping that they wouldn't get hit.

"Get back in the wag," Ryan yelled. "We're gonna have to hit the gas and hope—"

But as he turned, he saw that wouldn't be so simple. The explosions had galvanized the Nagasaki dwellers into action, and they had poured out of the wag, firing wildly. Two of them were immediately hit, falling to the ground. Buckley had a wild gleam about him as he turned to face Ryan.

"Y'all know how to have fun, Ryan boy. Let's grab us a wag and get the hell out with some jack."

Ryan felt an almost overwhelming desire to chill the chief on the spot. "You're two men down, they're using grens and we don't have that kind of firepower. We need to use all we've got to get out."

Buckley looked angry, like a child who had had a toy taken from him. "Shit, just as we's starting to have fun."

Ryan turned to locate his people again, despairing of ever getting out of this farcical situation. He gestured to Mildred and Jak to get back to the wag and tried to round up the Nagasaki raiders while providing covering fire with the Steyr. Fortunately, the cover from the gren smoke and debris was enough to make the sec force fire wild.

Mags had dragged one of the Nagasaki crew back to the wag and Ryan ran over to help her pull back the other. Both were still alive and the fat woman acknowledged his help with a grunt. Strange. He wouldn't have expected any of the inbreds to act like she had, especially after what he had seen her do before.

But there wasn't time for that train of thought. He ducked instinctively as a high-caliber rifle shell thwacked into the side of the wag, missing him by inches.

"Fireblast, we need to get out of here," he breathed.

J.B. HAD BEEN UNABLE to use the M-4000. There was too much confusion, too much chance of those counted as being on his side getting injured. He flung the blaster over his shoulder and unslung the Uzi with practiced ease.

"Can't even use these without risking our own," Esquivel yelled. "Hammick's really fucked this. Xander won't be happy."

But J.B. didn't hear him. He was frozen as he caught sight of a figure by the enemy wag. Then another. A slight albino teen in a camo jacket, moving low and fast, almost obscured by the smoke and dust. And a black woman whose shape seemed so familiar he could almost taste memory coming back. But it was a third figure that took his attention.

"Looks like the smart one, and I've got him," Olly muttered triumphantly, raising the Weatherby that he opted to bring with him, drawing a bead on the fighter as he moved.

A tall, muscular man with curly black hair, clutching a Steyr… Yelling, the man turned, and J.B. could see an eye patch, a scar puckering down the man's cheek, visible even from that distance.

More than visible. The Armorer's head spun as something clicked and he felt as though he stood on the lip of an abyss.

"No," he yelled, thrusting out a hand and knocking the blaster aside as Olly squeezed on the trigger, sending the shot just wide.

The young man looked at J.B., astounded, waited for an explanation—one that the Armorer tried to frame, but found no words would come. Instead, he felt as though the ground slipped from under him and he was turned upside down.

With the nausea of falling came blessed darkness.

Chapter Thirteen

Ryan slammed the wag into gear and tried to reverse out of the enclosed compound that was now more of a battle zone than a wag park. He, Mags, Mildred and Jak had managed to gather all the Nagasaki raiders together, although the two who had been hit looked as though they might not make it back before buying the farm. Buckley was furious and kept up a tirade against the sec force of Duma as the one-eyed man tried to pilot the wag to relative safety.

The sides of the wag were pitted with the scars of blasterfire, and the glass had been shot out in the brief firefight. Ryan had punched through the shattered windshield to give him a better view of the area, regardless of the smoke and dust that made his eye water.

All around, the convoy crew was coming out from behind their cover to try to get a better shot at the wag. They were all poor fighters, and Ryan was thankful for that. The Duma sec force was unwilling to injure any of the trading crew and that meant that they were unable to deploy the heavy-duty grens and blasters that would otherwise have brought the wag to a halt.

Straining every muscle in his arms and shoulders as he wrestled with the wag's steering, Ryan drove it backward and put it into a skid, bringing it around to face the still-open entrance to the park. Not that it mattered; he would have tried to drive straight through it in any case. At least the lack of resistance would gain them a few vital seconds more than they would otherwise have had.

Slamming the gears from reverse into first, Ryan hit the accelerator, ignoring the convoy crew members who stepped in front of the wag, raising their blasters to fire. He kept his foot down. They'd either dive out of the way or find a stupe way to get chilled. The screams of two were lost in the noise of blasterfire and the squealing engine as they were caught beneath the front wheels. He wrestled with the wheel, holding the wag as their bodies caused the steering to lurch. Another one yelled as the offside wing caught him on the hip and ribs, shattering the bone.

Mildred, Mags and Jak laid down covering fire as the wag left the yard, knowing that there was little chance of hitting anyone, but hoping to deflect incoming fire.

Ryan turned the wag and headed back toward the sec posts that marked the fenced perimeter of Duma. It wasn't over yet, by a long way. They had to crash the sec post and hope that they weren't followed.

"Anything behind?" he yelled over his shoulder, ignoring the continued rumblings of the chief at his side, the cries of the injured and the wailing of the frightened.

"No follow," Jak yelled back simply, keeping an eye on the fast-receding wag park. Whatever was going on there, pursuit was the last thing on anyone's mind.

"WHAT THE FUCK happened to him?" Hammick yelled, coming upon Esquivel and Olly, who were leaning over the unconscious J.B.

"I dunno, boss, I dunno. Just figure we should get him out of here," Esquivel said, gesturing Olly to help lift him and leaving the sec chief with no time to object. Besides which, he had other, more pressing concerns. With the wag gone, the sec team was beginning to blame the convoy crew for the fiasco and fights were breaking out. The whole situation had deteriorated. Hammick knew that his first task was to quell this before any of the convoy crew were chilled; only then could he think about explaining what went wrong to Xander.

Esquivel and Olly took hold of J.B. and carried him back out of the wag park and through the streets to the armory. As they did, Ella-Mae appeared from the crowd.

"How bad is it?" she asked, trying to keep her voice neutral.

"You mean the whole shooting match?" Esquivel asked.

She shot him a look that could chill. "Don't Es, I'm being serious."

"Hell, he ain't hit," Olly said, confusion still large in his tones. "I was going to fire on one of the outlanders, then he yelled at me, hit me and passed out."

Esquivel shrugged as Ella-Mae gave him a look both questioning and confused. "Don't ask me, babe— there's some really weird shit going down and I figure he'll tell us when he comes around. Thing now is to get him out of harm's way, 'cause that was one big fuckup and there's gonna be a whole lot of shit flying around."

RYAN GUNNED THE ENGINE and stamped on the accelerator as the rogue wag sped toward the sec post. The blacktop was barred and the surrounding area was fenced in as far as he could see. The only forces at the post were the sec men manning it. The question was, what kind of ordnance did they have? He didn't dare look behind, but knew from the lack of comment that they weren't being followed—or if an attempt was being made, the chaos back in the wag park had delayed its start. So if they could get past the sec post, they could lose themselves in the dark night of the wastelands.

"Fire on these fuckers as we get near and pass—don't let them get a clean shot," Ryan yelled over the roar of the wag engine.

Jak, Mildred and Mags began to fire steadily at the sec post from the glassless windows of the wag, joined by a few of the Nagasaki dwellers who had begun to recover their nerve. Fire from the sec men at the post peppered the wag and the road around. Heavy SMG and rifle fire, but not enough to halt them unless it took out a tire and sent the wag into a skid.

The wag ate up the distance between the ville and the sec post at an ever increasing speed, the covering fire driving the sec men deep into the recessed post, making their fire less accurate.

"Grens," Jak snapped, taking one and handing another to Mildred, who was covering the other side of the wag. They pulled the pins, held the spoons until the time was right and lobbed the grens from the shot-out windows so that they landed near the sec dugouts. Mildred's throw bounced once and landed inside the post, leaving the sec guard scrambling to climb out when it detonated, the metal load spreading out with a razorlike intensity, slicing flesh and bone to ribbons. The sec guard didn't even know what had hit him.

On the other side, Jak's gren bounced and hit the earth wall of the post, rolling to one side. The blast and shrapnel load was deflected enough to prevent the sec guard being chilled, but he was still injured by flying metal and the concussion of the blast, dazed with bleeding ears as he slumped back to the dirt floor of the post.

The barrier between the posts was a long metal bar, spiked, at windshield height to the wag. Still keeping a firm hold on the wheel, Ryan ducked as they came into it, yelling for the others to do the same. The wag hit the barrier with a shuddering jolt, the wheels veering to the left as the hinged end of the barrier gave with more resistance than the free-standing side. There was a crunch of metal on metal, shards of glass still left in the frame of the windshield being dislodged and raining down on Ryan and Buckley as they hunched below the level of the open windshield.

Ryan wrestled with the steering, keeping the wag on the blacktop with a squeal of tires. The weight of the barrier pulled it out of its tenuous hold on the frame, the indentation made by the impact not deep enough to keep the metal barrier attached to the wag. It fell onto the road, pushed to one side by the front of the wag, the weight making the steering tear at Ryan's already straining forearms. He hoped that it wouldn't fall under the wheels. There was no telling what the barbed metal would do to the underneath of the wag, ripping holes in fuel and brake cables as well as ripping tire rubber to shreds.

The wag groaned, bucked and rode the impact of the

barrier, but there was no telltale pull from tire damage, no indication that anything else was damaged. He would have to hope for the best.

Ryan kept the wag going straight down the blacktop, killing the lights and trusting his own senses. He didn't want the taillights to be seen, as they would surely be visible from a vast distance when there was nothing except the blackness around to highlight them.

"What the fuck was all that?" Buckley asked, bewildered. The chief didn't seem to have taken in quite what had happened and his people were still obviously shocked. But Jak and Mildred had kept triple frosty when it counted. Ryan called over his shoulder. "Anything?"

"Empty," Jak said simply.

"Like the grave, boss man," Mildred added. "Doesn't look like they've got it together to follow us."

"Let's get the hell back to Nagasaki the quickest way," Ryan yelled.

He kept on the blacktop for another twenty or so minutes, eating up the asphalt with his foot down. His only worry was that the wag would run out of fuel, but he figured there was little he could do about that right now, so it was best left to fate. As the sky began to lighten, he turned off the blacktop, killing the speed so that the battered wag's suspension could cope with the sudden switch from a relatively smooth road surface to the hard-packed earth and loose dirt of the uneven wasteland. Leaving a cloud of dust billowing up behind it, the wag headed across the wastes toward the hidden shantytown of Nagasaki.

Each of the three companions in the wag thought the

same thing, though their thoughts were phrased differently. They had escaped potential disaster in Duma, but were returning with nothing in the way of supplies or jack. Moreover, it was obvious that they had been expected. If the sec in Duma knew where they were from, then they would be hunted down. So even if Buckley let them go despite their failure, then they would still have to face the wrath of Duma along with their captors.

It was more than a rock and a hard place. Either way, they would have to fight when they were exhausted.

But first they had to get back Doc and Krysty.

RARELY HAD NAGASAKI SEEN such activity. The people were so convinced that their chief's master plan would bring them food and jack that they had set to with a vengeance, clearing out old buildings and cleaning them. This was far from easy, as the shantytown was encrusted in generations of filth. But they were determined to preserve the food and goods that the road would bring them.

Krysty and Doc were set to work with the others, despite the still fragile nature of Doc's health as his wounds healed. It was hard work and they had to keep one eye on the ville dwellers, some of whom eyed them through the night as though they could be useful meat for enjoyment now that the chief was away.

But despite that, things didn't really sour until one of the taller, facially deformed dwellers came running into the center of the ville. He gabbled out to anyone who would listen something about the barn. Krysty and Doc strained to understand him through the quickness of speech and the distortion of his cleft palate. It was impossible to make out all of the story, but that didn't matter. They already knew what he had discovered— that the last surviving captive in the barn had been set free. And from the way that the ville dwellers were eyeing them, it was obvious that they thought the out-landers had something to do with it.

"I fear, my dear, that this could get a little difficult," Doc murmured.

"I wouldn't often say you had a gift for understate-ment, but this time…" she replied, trailing off as the ville dwellers closed on them.

Before she or Doc had a chance to make a serious move toward defending themselves, they were over-whelmed by the mass of inbreds, who wrestled them to the ground. Hands and fingers gouged and poked, and for every hand they fought off, others pulled at them. They were stripped of their weapons and their hands and feet trussed.

"Chill the fuckers," yelled one dweller, a call taken up by the others with alacrity.

"No," boomed one of the fat, wart-encrusted women, standing over them. "Take them to the barn. Wait until the chief comes back and then we can have some fun with all the fuckers in one go."

THE PALE LIGHT of early morning had begun to spread tentatively across the wastelands as Ryan drove the wag into the hollow that sheltered the shantytown of Nagasaki. The wag was spluttering, almost out of fuel, or else suffering blockages in the fuel feed caused by the traumas of the past few hours. The two Nagasaki dwellers had bought the farm and Buckley was now depressed, realizing that the mission had been for naught.

Ryan cursed to himself as the wag drifted the last few hundred yards into the center of the ville. From the way that the dwellers clustered around, and from the fact that Krysty and Doc were nowhere to be seen, he knew there was trouble. Looking over his shoulder, his eye met with Jak's and Mildred's gaze. They were thinking the same thing.

In his self-pity at how things had gone wrong, Buckley seemed not to notice that anything was amiss.

Ryan killed the engine and before he had a chance to move, the door was wrenched open and hands reached in for him, pulling at him, not giving him the chance to reach for his panga, or the Sig Sauer. He was hauled out into a mass of humanity, stinking and angry. In the back of the wag, Mildred and Jak were subjected to the same thing. Jak was able to palm one of his razor-honed knives from its hiding place in the heavily patched camo jacket, but despite a few thrusts that drew blood and caused one or two hands to be withdrawn, they were too swiftly replaced by others, which beat at him until the knife was dropped and his hands were pinned.

Buckley hauled himself out of the wag, suddenly galvanized by what was happening.

"Whoa, there. I know y'all are unhappy we's come back with nothing, but y'all can't just blame—"

"Why you come back with nothing?" yelled a voice from the crowd.

"'Cause they was ready for us—don't know how.

Only got out 'cause of Ryan's way with the wag," Buckley blustered.

A mutter went through the crowd. Voices yelled at the chief, too quickly and too close together for him to make out what they said. But then one cut through the others. "'Course they's know you's coming—one-eye there and his fuckers emptied the barn."

What little color there was drained from Buckley's face. "What? What y'all say?" he yelled, his authority now restored by his anger. "Let the fuckers go, but take their blasters and blades first," he commanded.

The companions felt hands move over them while they were constrained, removing their blasters. Ryan felt the panga unsheathed from his thigh, and Jak was stripped of his camo jacket. Then—and only then—were they released to stand.

Buckley stood in front of them, quivering with rage. "Y'all let the prisoner go and he's gone told the cold-heart fuckers in Duma to be ready for us," he said, as though this guess were confirmed fact.

"I released him," Ryan confirmed, figuring it was pointless to lie at this stage. "But he couldn't have let the sec in Duma know. He went in a different direction and he was going off to take the last train west. He was chilling on his feet and wanted to buy the farm alone. I figured that wasn't too much to ask."

"You figured…you figured, did you?" Buckley gritted before spitting in Ryan's face. Ryan lunged for the chief, but the butt of an old Lee-Enfield long blaster caught him in the kidney, the sudden shock making him gasp and drop to his knees. Buckley took the opportunity to swing his boot so that it caught Ryan in the chest. It could have been worse. Had the chief put the whole of his not-inconsiderable weight behind the kick, and had it connected with Ryan's jaw, it may very well have dislocated it. As it was, the one-eyed man still went down heavily, coughing up bile.

"So you thought you'd spoil our fun by letting our prisoner go, did you?" Buckley screamed. "And you gets us in an ambush, two's chilled and no jack or supplies at the end of it? You think we's gonna let y'all go for that? Fuck no. But I's a fair man, you knows that. We's have a little trial for you and then you get punished. And we's make you suffer. If'n we ain't got no food, at least we's can have ourselves some fun with y'all. And who knows, Ryan boy, mebbe y'all gonna be real good if'n we's cook you. Gotta eat something, right?"

Buckley looked around his people. The thought of torturing the companions after a summary trial had cheered them all up and there were even a few who were cackling in anticipation. The three companions, by contrast, met his gaze with grim stares.

"Where the fuck's the red girl and the old man?" Buckley asked peevishly, realizing for the first time that Doc and Krysty were missing.

"They's already in the barn. Put them there soon as we realized what had happened," the wart-covered woman who had earlier taken control yelled as she stepped forward.

Buckley looked at her and grinned. "Y'all got brains, I'll tell y'all that. Barn's the right place for them. Put these fuckers there and we'll deal with them when we's dealt with our chilled. Get that sorted and let these fuckers think about what's gonna happen to them. Now get they's out of my sight," he shouted with a dismissive gesture, turning away and heading for the ranch house.

The companions found themselves lifted by the throng of irate Nagasaki dwellers and swept along toward the barn, the bridge pulled rapidly into place. The door was disbarred and they were flung into the gloomy and stinking building, the door slammed shut behind them.

Ryan, Jak and Mildred were covered in cuts and contusions, and they dragged themselves to their feet, looking around. For Ryan, it was too familiar and he thought of the condition Gill had been in when he found him. They wouldn't even get that far, it seemed.

Doc and Krysty shuffled out of the darkness, the redhead supporting the older man, who was breathing heavily. His jaw was puffy where he had been struck and one of his eyes was closed by a bruise. Krysty was also cut and covered in blood from scratches.

"My dear Ryan, welcome back. So nice to see you again," Doc husked with as much irony as he could muster.

Chapter Fourteen

J.B. could hear voices…distant, as though they were at the end of a tunnel, but voices all the same. He tried to speak, but all that came out was an incoherent scream. He could hear the voices telling him to take it easy and it made him want to hit whoever said it with a gren. It was important he speak, but he couldn't.

With an immense force of will, the Armorer dragged himself out of the dark tunnel and forced his eyes open. Everything was blurry, indistinct. He realized he wasn't wearing his spectacles and swore heavily, groping for them. One of the three figures looming over him passed them to him, and despite having to narrow his eyes against the light, violent as it was after the tunnel of unconsciousness, everything came into focus.

J.B. was lying on his bed in the armory, with Olly, Esquivel and Ella-Mae standing over him. The first two had been in the wag park with him, but how Ella-Mae got to be there… Shit, it all started to come back to him. He'd seen Mildred, he was sure of it. And Jak. The reason he was sure was because he'd got a good look at Ryan and just stopped Olly from putting a hole through him with the Weatherby.

J.B. knew who they were. He knew where he had been for the past few years. He was kind of hazy, but he could even remember something to do with dogs and a cave-in getting him here in the first place. Dark night, he thought. Ryan had been leading the raid on the ville. That put J.B. in a quandary: should he let on what he knew or should he try to play dumb for the moment?

"Dude, say something," Esquivel said, waving his hand in front of J.B.'s face. "You're with us, but not at the same time. Care to share what the fuck went on out there?"

J.B. looked at the sec man, still undecided. It was Olly who tilted the balance. The young man said, "C'mon, J.B., something went on and it had to do with that guy I was gonna take out. He only had one eye."

"Shit, you've remembered," Ella-Mae breathed. "It's all come back to you."

J.B. nodded. "Too quickly, I guess. But that's why I couldn't let you try and chill him—I couldn't let Ryan get shot."

Esquivel whistled. "The famous Ryan Cawdor turns up near you after all and he's blowing fuck out of our people. Xander is not gonna like this."

Olly bit hard on his lip, showing all too clearly the thoughts that were racing through his mind. "How did he come to be involved with those mutie inbred fuckers? And why was he doing something so stupe as driving into a trap? And why—"

J.B. cut him short with a raised hand. "Not that simple, Olly. Ryan wasn't on his own." He went onto explain about seeing Mildred and Jak, and also that he hadn't caught sight of Krysty or Doc, giving them the barest detail on each to save time, but also to make them see that the six had traveled together so long that strong bonds had been forged.

Esquivel whistled. "So if they were two down, then what are the odds they're safely tucked up back in the pesthole those scum come from?"

"Exactly," J.B. said, levering himself off the bed and pausing as the room spun before his balance was properly restored. "I need to see Xander about this."

"He's gonna be real mad and out for blood. He won't be happy until they're all chilled, J.B. Tonight won't make him look good—word'll spread real fast and that was the one thing he really didn't want." Olly shook his had ruefully. "I don't reckon it'll matter who they are. He'll want to go in and wipe them off the face of the desert."

"But that's the point," J.B. snapped. "Those inbreeds may be shit fighters usually, but with Ryan and the others working with them, there's no way it'll be easy for your people, especially if Hammick fucks up again."

"So what do you suggest, dude?" Esquivel asked softly.

J.B. stopped. It was true. He hadn't thought of an alternative course of action. "I dunno," he said softly. "But I guess I'll think of that when it comes to it."

He pushed past them and swept out of the room, intent on heading for Xander's palace. Esquivel hurried after him and Olly was about to follow when he noticed that Ella-Mae was holding back.

"What is it?" the dreadlocked youth asked her, puzzled.

She shook her head, smiling sadly. "You see the look on his face when he talked about them? We've lost him. Not matter what happens, we've lost him."

Down in main section of the armory, Budd was detailing sec men to strip and distribute weapons from the storage rooms while he kept record of what was released. He looked up as he heard the Armorer descending the staircase.

"What the hell happened to you out there?" he asked, barely able to keep the smug satisfaction out of his voice. "The great J. B. Dix lose his nerve?"

J.B. glared at him. "Another time," he said, brushing past the old man. Esquivel, close on J.B.'s heels, kissed his teeth at Budd. This was no time for petty scores.

Budd ignored them, devoting his attention to his son, who was now chasing after the Armorer and his sec shadow, Ella-Mae at his heels.

"Hey, son. Heard you did well out there before you were screwed over. Mebbe this'll show that you're the one to—"

He was cut short by his angry son. "Dad, this is about more than just you and me and J.B.," Olly snapped. "He doesn't want your job and he doesn't want mine. He doesn't even want to be here...and neither do I," he added, brushing his father aside to follow the Armorer.

Ella-Mae, following, could only think of the look on J.B.'s face when he mentioned seeing Mildred. One way or another, a lot of lives were going to change this night.

XANDER STRODE THE FLOOR of his ornate throne room, anger boiling within him, the seething silence broken only by the halting attempts of Hammick to explain why the action had gone wrong. It should have been simple, he knew that, But no one had figured on the convoy crew wanting to join in the action and getting in the way. And surely Xander could see that Hammick couldn't risk chilling any of them. What would the baron have said if he had to give a trader compensation to stop word spreading? Come to that, surely he knew that word would spread anyway?

Hammick, halting and stumbling through his report, going back over details to try to justify himself, looked to Grant for help or any indication of sympathy. But the healer and sec adviser sat at the throne's right hand, looking impassive. He hadn't intended to scheme and leave Hammick high and dry, but at the same time he was too old and had lasted too long under Xander and his father to step in and take some of the storm that was about to break.

As Hammick paused once more in his halting address, Xander stopped pacing the floor and swiftly and savagely moved across to the sec chief, catching him across the face with a backhand blow that stunned him. Xander wore several heavy silver jeweled rings; these scored Hammick's cheek, drawing blood that he touched delicately as he tried to rise to his feet.

He was stopped by the cold metal barrel of Xander's Luger pressed against his forehead.

"Tell me why I shouldn't just do it now," the baron said softly. "You're an incompetent fool and my reputation will suffer. To chill you as the one who should take the blame won't save that, but it will show that I'm strong and that I won't tolerate failure or fuckup."

Hammick heard the hammer click back on the Luger, felt the pressure of the cold metal increase on his forehead. He closed his eyes and waited for oblivion, sure that his bladder had released with fear.

Instead, he heard Grant's measured tones.

"Why don't you let him take a sec force after them? Wipe them out in their own filth, see to them once and for all?"

"And what if he fucks that one up, as well?" Xander demanded angrily.

"If he does, then who's to know, out there? We claim a victory, you deal with him as you see fit and then we send out someone who can do the job. At least this gives him a chance to redeem himself."

"Why should he have a chance?" Xander demanded once more. Hammick was wondering about that himself. Terrified beyond the ability to think rationally, he hoped Grant would supply an answer that he could not—literally—for the life of him.

Hammick could hear Grant's measured breathing before the man spoke. "Because if he succeeds, he will know how close he came to buying the farm. He will know how closely he walks in the shadow of being chilled. I have found that there is nothing like such knowledge to focus the mind and enable a man to fulfill his tasks with a maximum of diligence and efficiency."

That was a good answer—a triple-good answer— thought Hammick, his muscles starting to spasm from the awkward, half-prone position he had been forced to adopt. He could only hope that the baron would also think it a triple-good answer.

The barrel of the blaster didn't move, but Hammick heard the baron begin to laugh. Softly at first, but with a genuine amusement and understanding.

"Yeah… Yeah, I like that. I like it a lot. It's a very good point." Xander took the Luger away from Hammick's head, thumbed the safety, and reholstered it. The sec chief risked opening his eyes to find himself looking into the face of the baron. "You can stand up now, you stupe bastard," Xander said softly. And as the sec chief did so, he continued. "That's what I want you to do. We'll mount a raid and we'll wipe out those ugly fuckers."

"I'll get the armory right on it, sir," Hammick said, trying hard not to sound too grateful and pathetic for being spared.

"I think you'll find I've already instituted a plan," Grant said softly. When Xander gave him a quizzical look, he added, "Regardless of what you did to Hammick, it was something that I felt would have to be our next move."

"I shall have to watch for the day when your next move is to dispose of me," the baron murmured with a deceptive mildness.

Hammick sighed to himself. As the two men exchanged looks, they had—thankfully—forgotten about him.

But before the exchanges between Grant and Xander could move into potentially dangerous territory, the door to the throne room was flung open, and J.B. strode in, followed by Esquivel.

"What do you mean by bursting in without appointment or announcement," Xander yelled, his baronial pride further dented by this intrusion.

"Sorry, chief," Esquivel addressed to Hammick, "but he's got something kinda important."

"It's okay, Es. No one apologizes for me," J.B. said shortly.

Addressing Xander, he continued. "I've got my memory back—"

"Very interesting, I'm sure, but we are in the middle of a battle here," Grant interjected mildly. "There are things that are, to be frank, more important than—"

He was cut short by an impatient gesture from the Armorer, who interrupted. "This is important. I've remembered how I came to be here and when I last saw Ryan Cawdor. In fact, I don't even have to remember, as I saw him only an hour or so ago."

The announcement dropped like a bombshell. Grant had guessed that Cawdor would be involved in the raid from the earlier information; Hammick had seen a one-eyed man during the battle and had drawn the obvious conclusion; but Xander had no knowledge at all that Ryan was associated with the raid. Whereas the other two fought to show surprise, there was no mistaking Xander's astonishment. As his jaw dropped, J.B. explained about the moment when it had come flooding back, seeing Ryan in the middle of the firefight.

"But why would someone like Cawdor be involved with inbred filth like that?" Xander asked, genuine bemusement in his voice.

J.B. explained about seeing Mildred and Jak, and how that meant that two of the companions were missing. He added, "It's true that they could have bought the farm in the same accident that landed me here, but somehow I doubt it. I figure they're being held as leverage to make Ryan, Jak and Mildred do what these bastards want."

"That's certainly feasible," Xander said softly. "But it doesn't alter the fact that we need to go after this scum and wipe them out. And if that means—"

"Wait. Before you say anything else, hear me out," J.B. said quickly. "Ryan and the others are only fighting for those bastards because they have to. If I'm with your people when you go in and they see me, they will join us and turn the tables on their captors."

"Fine words, but you are, after all, assuming that Cawdor and his people aren't fighting against us out of choice," Grant said.

J.B.'s eyes flashed. "If they've got Doc and Krysty as prisoners, then Ryan would fight for them. No other reason. And why not? What do you mean to him?"

"What do we mean to you?" Grant countered.

"Not as much as Ryan, Jak, Mildred, Doc and Krysty," J.B. said heatedly, and cursed himself as it came out of his mouth. If Xander thought he would sell out Duma for them, then he wouldn't trust him on the raid. Would the baron see that it was more—so much more—than simply a matter of ville loyalty?

"If we mean nothing to you, then I fail to see how you can be trusted on this mission," Grant snapped immediately.

He addressed the baron. "We can't let this man endanger the mission. We have a point to prove."

"Grant's right."

J.B. turned in surprise. Olly was standing in the doorway, Ella-Mae at his elbow. They had followed close behind the Armorer and his sec shadow and had listened to the explanations and arguments within the chamber. Now Olly had decided to step forward.

"You of all people know he can't be trusted," Hammick blustered. "It was your shot on the one-eyed man that he deflected."

As soon as he said it, he realized what a mistake he'd made. He wasn't supposed to know about Ryan's involvement. In fact, by omission he'd only just denied all knowledge. By implication, if he knew, then Grant, too, had to have known. He shot the lame man a glance. Grant was furious, but only the slight tic at the corner of an eye on his otherwise impassive visage gave him away. Xander looked at both of them.

"I think there is more to know, here," he said slowly.

"Baron, that isn't important right now," Olly said impatiently. "What's important is this—I believe J.B., and I figure you should. You were going to put him in charge of Duma's ordnance. If you would trust him with that, why not trust him now? What's changed?"

"His loyalty to old friends means he cannot be trusted—"

"I'm sorry, but that's so wrong," Olly interrupted again. "He's not fighting for us or for those inbreds but to help his fellow travelers. But they're not on anyone's side except their own." He shook his head. It had seemed so clear when he started, but now he found himself getting lost in a morass of "buts."

He drew a breath and started again. "Look, if J.B. goes, I'll go, too. I'd trust him with my life and mebbe he'll have to trust me with his. If he tries to stop our forces carrying out their task, then I'll chill him myself. Except I know it won't come to that."

Olly's impassioned plea took everyone by surprise. Xander looked at the young man in a new light. He hadn't considered that Budd's son was up to the task of handling the Duma armory, but he could see that the lad had depths he had never suspected. Grant and Hammick didn't know what to make of this at all. Covering their own backs was going to be hard enough after Hammick's slip of the tongue, without matters becoming more complicated.

Esquivel grinned. J.B. had only known the young man a few days, yet already he had drawn him out of himself, made a man out of what had been a boy, living in Budd's shadow. The old armorer would be as pissed as hell when he heard about this. Somehow, that only added to Esquivel's pleasure.

Ella-Mae could understand why Olly felt the way he did. Like him, she had only known J.B. for a few days, yet in that time he had affected her more, touched her on a deeper level, than anyone she had ever known. And even though she was sure that he would soon be gone, one way or another, she knew that she and Olly would never be the same again.

J.B. watched the young man with a growing sense of respect and friendship. Being placed by Xander in the armory above Olly, to Budd's obvious disgust, J.B. had expected the young man to be hostile. To have his character judged thus was perhaps just what he needed to swing things his way.

The moment seemed to stretch into an infinity as J.B. waited for the baron to make his decision. Finally, Xander nodded slowly. "Okay, I'm going to trust you. Not just because of what Olly says, not just because of what I know about you and not just because I have to trust someone if I can't trust this stupe," he added, indicating Hammick. "But because you're J. B. Dix and you didn't have to tell me any of this shit. You could have joined up with Ryan Cawdor during the firefight, you could have just looked at your position here and kept your mouth shut. But you didn't, and that counts for something. Shit, something has to count for something," he muttered, looking at Grant and Hammick. "Go and prepare and leave me to these bastards," he said, dismissing them with a wave and turning to the sec chief and the lame man.

Without a backward glance, J.B. left the throne room, followed by Olly. Esquivel lingered, taking a good look at his boss, the baron and Grant. He wondered just what games had been going on. After all, he had to live with whatever happened after this. From the expression on the baron's grim and stony visage, things were going to be changing.

"Es, time for us to go," Ella-Mae whispered in his ear, pulling at the sleeve of his camo shirt.

"Yeah, guess so," he muttered reluctantly as they left, closing the door on what had become a tableau, none of the three men prepared to make the first move on their fate.

Ella-Mae and the sec man hurried after Olly and J.B., to find that both had made their way directly to the armory. When they met up with them, the two men had taken over the handling of the inventory from Budd. The old man stood to one side, with a look that told anyone who cared to glance his way that his time had passed. Whichever of the two men returned alive from the battle would be the new armorer. Budd's authority had disappeared.

Olly had taken over the blaster room and was handing out SMGs and rifles to the assembled sec force. There was little doubt that Xander took this raid seriously. As Esquivel did a quick head count, he figured that a quarter of the ville's sec force was clustered in the hallway, receiving new blasters and ammo, while Olly checked off the list with ease, passing comments and advice to the individuals as they collected their weapons.

Esquivel looked around for J.B. He was supposed to be the Armorer's shadow and he'd lost sight of him— not that he could see J.B. needing a shadow now. His credentials for Xander had been well and truly established. Nonetheless, Esquivel had formed a liking for the wiry man with the glasses and the ever-present fedora. If J.B. was going on this raid, then he wanted to be in on it with him.

Almost as though she could read his thoughts, Ella-Mae asked, "Where's J.B., Es? Shouldn't you be with him?"

"I dunno, babe. If Olly's doing the blasters, then our man's gonna be handling the grens, right?"

"Guess so. You gonna go on this raid with him, Es?"

The man grinned. "It's a dirty job, but someone's gotta do it, Ella-Mae. I'm supposed to shadow him, right?"

"You haven't always stuck to that task," she said with a smirk.

"Hey, dude's entitled to his privacy," Esquivel returned with humor. But his voice dropped into a serious tone as he continued. "Yeah, I'll go with him. Wouldn't be right to duck out on him now, even though I figure

Xander's not suspicious anymore. Besides, when was the last time I did anything other than fight in Icepick's bar and smash fuck out of it?"

This last drew a smile from her, but didn't deflect from her next question. "Can I come along, too?"

Esquivel looked askance. "What d'you mean, babe? You're a mechanic. By rights, you should be going over the wags we'll be using right now, not hanging around here. When was the last time you had combat experience?"

"Not that simple, Es, not that simple." She hesitated before continuing, mindful of the activity around her. But even so, it seemed at that moment as though the two of them were alone, sec men moving around them without even noticing they were there. She ran her fingers through her long curls before starting again. "I have to come along," she began, "I might not see J.B. again—"

"Hey, being chilled is a risk we all take, but—"

"No," she interrupted. "It's not about that. There was something about him that changed when his memory came back. And that's good for him, but mebbe not for me. His place is with them and he may not come back here after the firefight. And I…I dunno, I just want to see him go."

"Even if it means you might buy the farm yourself?" Esquivel asked gently. "Shit, you got it bad, girl."

"Yeah, real stupe—the untouchable iron maiden ends up being like a kid over one guy. It's like those old vids that trader brought through a few years back, y'know?"

Esquivel looked up the staircase as a procession of sec men filed down. Had to be nearly half the sec force moving through the armory building, getting ordnance for the attack. The sec man could see faces that hadn't figured in his initial count and realized the scale of the action. He couldn't let Ella-Mae in on this, yet short of knocking her out, what could he do?

"Listen, babe," he said finally. "We'll get ourselves equipped, go see J.B. and see what he says. If he says no, I'll deck you myself if I have to."

"I'd like to see you try," she retorted.

They fought their way up the stairs, past the stream of sec men coming down, and around toward the gren and plas ex room. As they approached, they could hear J.B.'s voice as he kitted out each man and explained the use of each gren to him before moving onto the next. It was the voice of a man who knew his job back to front. He was so engrossed in his task that he didn't even notice them enter the room, so attentive was he upon the sec man he was equipping.

"Dude, we need to talk to you," Esquivel said, interrupting the Armorer at his task.

"Not now—work to do," J.B. snapped back. Then he caught sight of Ella-Mae. "No, now isn't the time," he reiterated.

"We want to come with you," she blurted.

"'We'?" J.B. questioned.

"Yeah, she wants to come with us," Esquivel explained. "Me? It's my job, dude. Still supposed to be your bodyguard and still supposed to be a sec man, right? But Ella-Mae wants in. I've tried to tell her no, but she won't listen to me, dude."

"Dark night, I can't stop and talk about this now."

The Armorer sighed. "Wait over there and let me finish what I'm supposed to do."

Esquivel led Ella-Mae into a corner of the room while J.B. finished equipping the sec force taking part in the raid. Most of them had already received grens before going down to be equipped with blasters by Olly, so it didn't take long for J.B. to work through the rest of them. When he was finished, he went over to where Esquivel and Ella-Mae were waiting.

"You can't come. You don't have the combat experience," he said simply.

"Bullshit. How do you know that?" she countered heatedly.

"Because you're an ace mechanic. No baron is going to put someone with those skills in the front line."

She was exasperated. He was right, but she wouldn't let it rest. "What does that have to do with it?"

"Everything," he said. "You go into battle not knowing what you're doing and you're a danger to everyone you fight with. Hauling your ass out of trouble could buy the farm for me or Es or anyone whose own back isn't covered while they're covering yours."

"And you wouldn't want me to be chilled?"

"Of course not. Look, I know why you want to come, but things are real fucked up now that I can remember everything. If we get Ryan and the others out of there in one piece while we chill the scum who are holding them, then we're coming back here. They'll need some R&R and Xander'll treat them like legends. That suits everyone. So if it's not my turn to buy the farm, I'll be back and we can talk then."

"If you're sure," she whispered.

"Sure? You don't have a choice, lady," J.B. snapped, suddenly catching her with a left hook out of nowhere that caught her on the jaw and laid her out.

Esquivel looked at him in amazement.

"What?" J.B. snapped. "You think we've got time for arguing?"

Esquivel held up his hands. "Hey, none of my business, dude. I just know how pissed she'll be when she wakes up."

"Worry about that later," J.B. muttered while he finished checking his own inventory in his canvas bags. He racked the M-4000, checked the Uzi and sheathed his Tekna. He was ready. "Come on, Es, time to get your shit together if we're going to do this."

Galvanized into action, the sec man moved rapidly, taking grens from storage and attaching them to the clips on his uniform. He still had the regulation issue AK-47 slung on his shoulder.

"Need to lose that," J.B. said as he filled in the grens on the armory records. "And we'll get Budd and Liza to look after her," he added, indicating the blissfully unconscious Ella-Mae.

Without a backward glance—for now there wasn't the time to waste on such things—J.B. left the gren room and led Esquivel down to the blaster store on the ground floor of the building.

Olly was fitting out the last of the sec men and the armory was almost deserted. The majority of the men, now fully equipped, had made their way to the wag park where their transport to the ville of Nagasaki would be waiting.

"Yo, Olly, fit me out," Esquivel said, handing over

his AK-47. The young man took it without a word and gave the sec man an H&K MP-5 and an M-60 with a bipod attachment. He ran through each weapon's capabilities and operation at breakneck speed, trusting the sec man to comprehend what he said, and then handed over a relevant amount of ammo for each blaster.

"What about you, J.B.?" Olly asked.

J.B. patted the M-4000 lovingly. "I'm set. Let's go."

Olly stuck to the Weatherby and augmented it with an Uzi. He also had several cases of ammo to be loaded into one of the wags, which he deputed to Esquivel and J.B. as well as taking some himself.

"You want to go and say goodbye to your old man?" J.B. asked as they were about to leave.

"I dunno if he'll want to listen," Olly replied ruefully.

"Go anyway, dude. He knows you've got a chance of not coming back," Esquivel said.

Olly nodded briefly and set out for the back of the house, where he had seen his father slink off earlier.

"One more thing," J.B. called after him. "Get him or Liza to look out for Ella-Mae when she comes to." Olly shot him a puzzled look.

"Too long to explain," J.B. said by way of explanation.

The young man disappeared into the back of the armory and was back within a couple of minutes. His drawn face spoke of the encounter with his father, but he said nothing of it, merely muttering, "Let's do it," as he passed them in the hall.

When they hit the wag park where the war party was massing, ready to depart, the scale of the action hit them. The park that had been used as a trap a few hours before had been cleared, the convoy led by Malloy now relocated to the park on the far side of the blacktop. The blood and debris had been haphazardly swept aside, the vehicles used as cover moved out and replaced by a series of armored wags painted a uniform dull brown color to blend with the land when in transit.

There were eight wags, each capable of taking up to ten men. If half the sec force for the ville was being used, as Esquivel had estimated, they were short of transport for twenty men, as around a hundred soldiers had been equipped.

"They're either gonna leave some of us behind or it's gonna be a tight squeeze in there," he murmured. "And I'll tell you guys. I don't reckon that'll be good for the fighting forces, to arrive cramped up and stiff, unable to move."

J.B. shrugged. "Mebbe some'll think of it, or else we'll have to suggest it."

"You think Hammick's gonna listen to you?" Esquivel asked.

"Es, from what I saw, I'd be surprised if Hammick's in charge anymore," J.B. countered.

Olly looked from one to the other. "Then who the hell is gonna lead the charge?"

Neither man answered. It wasn't an unreasonable question, but one that posed more questions than there were answers.

As the three fighters entered the wag park, all was still in the prebattle confusion that arose from men trying to find their positions with no guide. Esquivel stopped several of his compatriots and asked what was happening, but was met each time with a shrug of confusion and the repeated answer that his guess was as good as anyone's.

The three men stood in the center of the park, waiting for something to happen. It looked as though the war party wouldn't even get out of the park, let alone reach Nagasaki. J.B. looked up at the sky. The ambient light from the ville made it hard to tell, but the sky seemed to be lightening in that manner of predawn. The rogue wag had been gone for some time and had a good start on them. Although this didn't matter to Xander and his sec force, it did to J.B. He knew that every minute wasted put his friends at greater risk.

"Fuck this, we've got to make something happen," he said to Olly and Esquivel, before gesturing to the young man. "Let's go," he beckoned. Together, they mounted onto the roof of one of the war wags. Following an indication, Olly fired a single shot from the Weatherby into the air. The report of the rifle cut through the milling confusion of the sec force around, drawing their attention to the two men standing on the wag.

"There anyone in charge here?" J.B. asked. When he was met with a general murmur of dissent and ignorance, he held up his hands to quell the crowd. "Then there needs to be. Me and Olly will do it if you'll have us. Esquivel will work with us. We need to get some strategy together for the attack."

"What about Hammick?—he's boss," came a shout from the crowd.

"Yeah, what about him?" Olly retorted. "He's not here, is he? And we need to move."

He trailed off as he saw Xander enter the compound on his own. The baron cut through the crowd and mounted the wag until he stood next to them.

"Hammick has been relieved of his post," he announced. "There'll be a new sec chief appointed when you return triumphant from this mission. In the meantime, I'm going to brief you. And then you will be led by these two, as they so rightly suggested," he added with a sweep of his arm to indicate Olly and J.B.

A ripple of surprise swept through the sec force, but the baron quelled it with a cry. "Listen to me— Hammick was responsible for the fuckup earlier. No way he's chilling more of my people—you—with his stupe ideas. Instead, I want you to travel to that pesthole ville and use the wags to encircle it, moving in at a synchronized time. You hit at the same time, circling them to stop them running and blast the fuck out of them. Wag drivers, here now."

The baron jumped down from the wag, joined by Olly and J.B., with Esquivel sidling up to them. As the wag drivers gathered around, Xander gave them their intended positions and the attack time, making them synchronize their wrist chrons. The order of attack for the individual sec teams in each wag was detailed, with the drivers holding responsibility for passing orders to their crews.

At J.B. and Olly's prompting, he then stood down twenty of the fighters assembled to avoid wag overcrowding. As the baron allotted wag teams, J.B. could see that he knew more about his sec force than the Armorer had thought. The baron knew each man's strengths and selected his wag teams accordingly.

Within half an hour, as the sun was creeping up over the horizon, they were ready to depart. With a last word of farewell for his men, Xander left them to file into the wags, with J.B., Olly and Esquivel in the lead wag.

The convoy fired up and filed out of the wag park, turning onto the blacktop and heading for the sec post that had been shattered by the departing rogue wag. A work party had already started reconstructing the emplacements and the barrier. Although J.B. wouldn't recognize them, two of the workers were the men who had discovered him only a few days before: Sim and Hafler. They stopped to watch the convoy roll across the blacktop and toward the horizon before going back to their work.

As the wag train reached the point where they turned off the blacktop and headed into the wasteland in search of the ville, the sun threw its first rays of morning across the land.

The nights had been pivotal points in the last week of his life. Now J.B. felt he would face his fate—and that of his companions both new and old—in the glare of daylight.

Chapter Fifteen

There was nothing that the companions could do except wait for Buckley's next move, wait for a chance to escape, wait for their end. A quick recce of the barn had revealed nothing in the way of a possible escape. The tallow lamps, sputtering as they were dismounted and moved by Ryan and Jak, cast a dim light that reflected nothing but a mounting sense of despair.

Before, Ryan had only seen the dimly illuminated central area of the barn. That had been bad enough, showing little but filth, rotting meat and the results of Nagasaki torture methods. That much Doc and Krysty had also discovered. They had only been in the barn a short while before the others were cast in with them and had not yet had the chance to explore its farthest reaches.

It was a slim hope knowing of the mantraps that had been set in the dry moat surrounding the building, but if it were possible to find a weakness in the structure of the barn, some way in which they could effect an escape, they could at least cause some confusion amongst the ranks of Buckley's people. Anything would be a plus, anything that gave them an edge, especially as they were now stripped of their weapons.

Taking the tallow lamps from their brackets on the

stanchions that held up the barn roof, Ryan and Jak
ventured into the darkness. Beyond the area in the
center, the stench of decay and death got worse, causing
both men to breathe shallowly, swallowing down the
urge to vomit as they balanced taking in breath with
keeping out the smell. The flickering lights illuminated
a scene of barely describable horror. The floors were
stained with years of blood and gore, bones sticking up
from the muddy mixture in the recesses where the
slightly sloping floor had gathered years of waste in a
miniature cesspool. Some of the bones were just that,
whereas others were still recognizable as once belonging to human beings, scraps of rag or mummified flesh
clinging to the calcified remains.

There was evidence of some of the tortures that the
captives in the barn had been subjected to over the
years: hooks and nails covered with rusty dried blood;
wicked-looking blades that were imbedded in the wood
of the barn, carrying scraps of material and what could
have been dried flesh; pits of ash and tar that were the
remains of some kind of fire, along with long irons that
were charred and covered in a crust of some sort at one
end.

The residents of Nagasaki took their pleasures seriously.

But along with all this and the ever-present smell of
decay, old blood, feces and fear that permeated the barn,
there was the security. This was a place of no escape.
The walls, inside as well as out, were reinforced and
there was only the one method of entry and exit.

The edges of the barn were so dark and full of stench
that the air seemed almost fresh by comparison when

Jak and Ryan returned to the central area and reported their findings to the three who had remained there.

"Of course," Doc ruminated when he had heard all that had to be said, "if there is only the one method of entry, then it should in theory be as easy for us to keep them out as it is for them to keep us in."

"What good is that?" Jak asked. "No food, no water. Why want stay?"

Doc shrugged. "Survival instinct, perhaps. A little longer before we are chilled, a little longer to savor the sweetness of life."

"Not so sweet in here, you old fool," Mildred muttered darkly. "You mean a little longer to contemplate our fate."

Doc nodded. "Perhaps…but a little more time bought means a little longer for something to happen."

"Like what?" Mildred countered.

Doc shrugged. "It strikes me that human nature does not, in essence, change, no matter what happens to it over the years. You dared to impinge on the universe of the baron of—where was it again? Ah, yes, Duma. Well, to return to my point, if you impose on him, would he not wish to impose on you in return?"

"You really think he'll bother to raid this pesthole?" Ryan queried. "Why wouldn't he have done it before?"

"Because he had no need. These people are inbred cretins, incapable of causing his ville any serious damage. But with us, they have struck at his heart. And it strikes me that any baron would not like that in the slightest. So what would he do? Why, he would mount an attack of his own, to eradicate the menace."

Krysty shook her head. "Sit it out here in the hope

that your speculation comes true? We can't afford to do that. It'd be a slow chilling and I'd rather go quickly."

"Not much of a choice, is it?" Mildred sighed. "We hang on and hope for a miracle, keeping them out but ourselves prisoner, or…or what? How can we put up any kind of a fight without weapons? They outnumber us so heavily that we need something to even that up."

"Yeah, and we got it," Ryan affirmed. "We're smarter than them. We must be able to think of something."

Even as he spoke, Ryan's mind was racing. He looked around the barn, thinking of all the things he and Jak had seen in there and what they could use. As he caught Jak's eye, he could see that the albino hunter had also been pondering this. A rare grin flashed across Jak's bone-white, scarred visage.

"Yeah, mebbe could do it," he said.

It didn't matter that they had no idea whether or not there really was an attack coming. That was nothing more than an excuse. The only thing that really mattered was that they could now fight back. If they were going to buy the farm, there was no way they would go quietly into that dark night.

DAYLIGHT HAD SPREAD across the land by the time that the lead wag in the Duma war party drew to a halt. The other wags pulled up behind and the drivers dismounted, meeting in the middle of the small circle formed by the stationary vehicles. J.B., Olly and Esquivel joined them.

"Why have we stopped?" Olly asked as the three men approached.

The driver of the lead wag scratched his armpit and

then used the same index finger to point off to the northeast.

"Shit hole they call home is about half hour's drive away, just out of sight. It's recessed into a small valley. We won't see it until we're on it, but their sec can see us coming from a few miles away. So we all figured this is where we'd stop and get our tactics right."

J.B. agreed, trusting the men that Xander had taken into his confidence when relaying tactics. "You been told which wags take which position or you got to sort that now?"

The lead driver shrugged, this time scratching his ass. "Xander gave us the tactics and told us who went where, but I figure we're the men on the ground and as long as we keep to the battle plan and know what we're doing, a little adjusting ain't a bad thing."

"So how well any of you guys know this place?" Esquivel asked. "You been around these parts before?"

"Tell you the truth, Es, we all keep well clear of the sick fucks and weirdos who live down there. There have been some scouting parties, see what the fuck they're up to, but really…" He shrugged.

"What about basic layout, distances, any weak spots or strong points?" J.B. pressed.

One of the other drivers spoke. He was lean and rangy and his tanned arms were cut with white scar tissue. He looked and sounded like a long-serving sec man and J.B. immediately trusted his words. Anyone still fighting with that number of scars had courage and willpower…and a fierce determination to stay alive.

"Seen that place fairly close the once. Valley forms a circle about two miles around. Most of the buildings are clustered in the center, but they got one big 'un that's set apart. Mebbe the armory, mebbe where their baron lives. Looks more like a jail, though, with a trench all the way around. That could be a fucker to crack. Otherwise, they ain't got much guard 'cause they ain't got much to guard, if you see what I mean. Figure that we need to get some real heavy blasters around the back for that barn. Not many shacks behind it, but that could be the fucker," he reiterated. "Only the one road in—more like a dirt track. No sec posts. But no track around the back or sides. Rough terrain but no hidden posts."

"That we know about," J.B. emphasized. "Okay, listen up. I know I ain't got any authority as you got your orders from Xander direct, but I do want to say one thing. I know how to blast the fuck out of things like that barn, so I want to take that back end of the ville. Me and Olly will ride the wag that does that. Any problems?"

The drivers looked at one another, concurring. The lead wag driver spoke for them. "That's fine by us. We'll move out from here into a pinwheel that circles the shit hole. Attack starts when our chrons make twelve-fifteen. That give everyone enough time to get into position?" It was a question that he directed at the others. They nodded. "Okay, let's do it," he said.

As the drivers turned toward their wags, J.B. halted them. "Wait—one more thing. You know we're supposed to haul out the people that I travel with. The one-eyed man, the red-haired woman, the black woman, the old guy and the albino." He stated this slowly, wanting to impress the descriptions on them.

The lean, rangy driver looked at him askance. "Look,

man, that might be what you want, but it ain't our problem. Xander didn't say shit about that. He just wants the whole shit heap wiped off the face of the desert. If you want to save them, you're gonna have to get to them before the rest of us, 'cause we won't have the time to stop and ask questions."

With that, the drivers returned to their wags, leaving J.B., Olly and Esquivel standing alone in the center of the circle.

"The coldheart bastard makes noises about wanting to save Ryan and all the stories he's heard, then he doesn't tell these fuckers," J.B. gritted. "What kind of a lying, two-faced fuck is he?"

"The kind who's kept a tight rein on Duma for a long time, dude," Esquivel said softly. "I told you there was something corrupt about the ville, didn't I? Never trust that bastard. The only thing we can do is make sure that we get to your people before any of the others here."

"You make it sound so easy," J.B. said with a hollow laugh.

"Mebbe it will be," Olly countered. "Think about it—they're all gonna have their hands full with the inbreeds. They're not actually looking for your friends. But we will be."

"Yeah, mebbe you're right," J.B. agreed. "Best thing we can do is get the attack going and blast our way through the back of the ville, see what we can find."

"Dude, that ain't gonna be a problem." Esquivel smiled at his friends. "C'mon, let's go."

IT TOOK THE COMPANIONS some time to gather together items that they could use to defend themselves and secure the barn as a fortress. They were hampered by the fact that too much activity in the vicinity of the tallow lamps caused them to flicker dangerously close to extinction. Taking them to the rear and farthest sides of the barn, using them to illuminate the darkest corners, meant that any work had to be done slowly and carefully, close to the lamps but without knocking the flame so that it went out.

Even though the barn was cold, the temperature kept low by the thickness of the reinforced walls, they sweated as they tried to work loose the old blades that were stuck into the wooden stanchions and wallboards. They were deeply embedded, but Ryan and Mildred, who had set to this task, found that once they had managed to pry one loose, they could use the point to gouge the wood around the next, in order to hasten its exit.

While they did that, Doc and Krysty rummaged among the detritus on the floor of the barn, searching for any old bowls or receptacles they could use to gather the tar and ashes that were gathered in circles around the floor. Using the flame from the tallow lamps on a small sample of the material as they scraped it into the bowls, they could see that it was highly inflammable, burning and hissing brightly with a blue-tinged flame, sending up a cloud of noxious smoke. They extinguished it quickly, in case it start to smoke the barn out and defeat its own purpose.

Jak spent his time moving around the barn in the darkness. He was less reliant than the others on the light of the tallow lamps, as his albino eyes adjusted far better to the shadows. He moved swiftly and with a great sense of purpose. In essence, his task was simple: where Mildred and Ryan were taking time to remove blades from the walls, Jak was picking at the many nails that extruded from the wood. He gathered a selection of them that he carried into the center of the barn. He then took the branding irons that they had found and used the nails to scratch the dried crust of blood, soot and melted flesh from the ends of the irons. The nails were bent and rusty, but the ends were still sharp; with diligence and patience he worked at both the nails and the branding irons, using each to hone the point of the other until they had a degree of sharpness to them. They couldn't replace the knives taken from him before they had been imprisoned, but they would suffice as a deadly enough weapon if used at close range.

They worked as fast as they could under the circumstances. They didn't know how long they had. Would there be an attack from the sec force of Duma? If so, when would it be? And if not, how long before the Nagasaki people, led by an enraged Buckley, came to bring them to trial and take their revenge?

Finally, they were ready. The bowls were placed on the floor on either side of the door, with fuses made from lengths of hemp rope found around the floors and tied to stanchions. Each companion had a blade or a sharpened branding iron, with clusters of nails hidden about their person.

Now all that remained was to wait.

Half an hour passed before they heard the wooden slatted bridge being hefted into place across the moat and the bar removed from the outer side of the doors.

Ryan looked across at his people and nodded: time

to be triple red, triple frosty. He was behind a stanchion on the left of the doors, with Doc just to his rear, hidden behind a hastily constructed bale of hay. Across the empty center of the barn, Krysty and Mildred were also using stanchions and hay to shelter. Doc and Mildred each had one end of a fuse and a tallow lamp with which to light it when cued. Ryan glanced up. Somewhere above them, hidden in the shadows, Jak was perched on a crosspiece where the stanchion supported the barn ceiling. He had clambered up and was waiting to jump from above on the enemy beneath.

The doors began to open, a shaft of blinding light coming through the growing gap. Ryan judged the time as best he could, before muttering "Now," the cue for Doc and Mildred to light their fuses.

As the doors swung open, and Ryan's ice-blue orb became accustomed to the increased brightness, he could see that Buckley and his two personal sec men were standing on the threshold, with a group of ville dwellers behind them. In fact, there seemed to be so many that it was a wonder that the bridge remained intact.

The fuses burned rapidly toward the bowls. Krysty had coated both of the hemp ropes with the mixture to expedite their burning.

Buckley and his henchmen were almost comically puzzled by the sudden smell and light of the burning fuses. Realization dawned almost too late as the fuses were burned up to the rims of the bowls. With a yell, the boss gestured his people back, turning and pushing as he did so, trying to fight through them and away from the imminent explosions.

Despite their drooling, cretinous appearance, the two sec men who were his personal guard were loyal and quicker thinking than they appeared. Risking their own safety, they each grabbed a door and pulled it toward them, hoping to reduce the angle for the explosion to catch the crowd outside.

It was the one flaw in the plan that the companions had implemented, and one about which they could do nothing. They had hoped that they could catch the Nagasaki people off guard, that the ville dwellers would be too slow to react.

Instead, it backfired, exploding almost literally in their faces. The bowls of tar and ashes ignited in a flash of brilliant light, almost blinding in the enclosed, darkened barn, soon to be replaced by plumes of thick, choking black smoke that were kept within the confines of the barn by the closing doors. The loud hissing of the tar and ashes made it difficult for any of the companions to tell for a moment what was happening as the thick, oily smoke began to clog their lungs.

The doors were almost totally shut now. If the Nagasaki dwellers managed to shut them completely, then it would mean that they could let the companions either buy the farm from the smoke, or at least be reduced to unconsciousness. There was little circulating air to drive the smoke around the cavernous barn, so if they retreated, they would have fresher air for the time it took for the smoke to drift back. But by the same token, they would be reduced to huddling at the rear of the barn, at the farthest point from the exit, at the mercy of whatever Buckley decided.

The smoke bombs had been a gamble that had failed.

If they were to be faced with the option of going down fighting or waiting meekly for the end, then there was only one option.

Choking back on the acrid smoke that filled his mouths and lungs with its foul taste, Ryan yelled for the others to join him. He could feel, rather than see, Doc at his shoulder. Mildred and Krysty appeared through the clouds and Jak descended from the ceiling on the hemp rope. He was in a better condition than the others, as the heavy smoke had been slow to rise and he had been able to breathe cleaner air for longer.

Ryan gestured to the doors and the companions rushed them, pulling against the people on the other side, desperation to escape the smoke driving them on. All strategy was out the window now. To get out and fight was the only aim.

The people on the other side of the double doors were taken by surprise at the suddenness and ferocity of the attack, their grip on the doors easily lost. The companions wrenched them open, the light from outside nowhere near as fierce as it might have been if not for the flare of the smoke bombs. The movement of the doors brought a sudden rush of air into the barn, driving the clouds of smoke back and bringing in cleaner air, making it easier for them to breathe.

The Nagasaki dwellers were in confusion. Some were still on the bridge, others had retreated to the far side. Most were facing away from the attack, expecting the doors to be closed and barred. Few were ready to face the onslaught of five people fighting for their lives.

Ryan was in the vanguard, with Jak at his side. Both

men were carrying sharpened branding irons, leaving the blades to those who were less practiced and needed the greater maneuverability of the blades. Ryan drove the point of his branding iron through the eye of one of Buckley's personal guard, the man's slack jaw falling even lower with shock and pain as the point drove through into his brain. Screwing the iron as he drove it in, Ryan reversed the screw and pulled. The iron was slow in coming out, and he assisted it by raising a foot and kicking the inbred sec man backward, so that he almost fell off the iron. No sooner was it free than Ryan had to reverse it, using the blunt end as a club to drive away an onrushing fat man, who was yelling incomprehensibly and waving a rusty-looking sword made of an old blade lashed to a homemade handle. Driving the club end upward, Ryan caught him under the chin. The fat man grunted and staggered backward, falling into the moat and screaming as he hit one of the mantraps.

By the time he yelled, Ryan's attention was already taken up in fighting off two more inbreds. To his side, Jak was a blur of arms, the branding iron whirling in a circle as the sharpened and blunt ends wreaked havoc among the ville dwellers.

Behind them as they tried to make progress across the bridge, Doc, Krysty and Mildred followed, using their blades to hack and slash at anyone who came near, hampered by the fact that they hadn't been able to get the old metal too finely honed. The chips and nicks taken out of the blades made them stick in clothing and flesh, all the harder to disengage for the next thrust and parry.

They were moving slowly across the bridge with no

idea of where they were headed. At the back of his mind, Ryan knew that the stolen wag had to be somewhere around the ville. If they could get to that, they might be able to get out of Nagasaki. But how much fuel would it have and where would they go?

Now he was aware that some of the people on the bridge weren't directly attacking him or the others. While their attention was taken by a head-on attack, others were slipping by so that they could approach from the rear. The Nagasaki dwellers had taken several casualties who had been chilled, and more who had been cut, bludgeoned and injured, yet pain seemed to mean little to them. They were used to it as a part of their everyday lives; it was no obstacle to them in a fight.

The companions became aware of the fact that they were now surrounded on all sides and fighting became harder as they were given less room in which to wield their weapons. Blows broke through their defenses; their adversaries were hacking at them with blades, catching them painful blows with blunt ends of blasters that numbed nerve endings, making them stumble and fall.

The Nagasaki dwellers weren't going to chill them; not yet. They were softening them up for the main event and none would care to consider what that might be.

They had one last weapon, each of them. The nails they had secreted about them. As one, they refrained from using them, hoping that they wouldn't be searched before their final ordeal. They could do nothing with the nails now: better to wait, hope and keep them in reserve for if the chance came to use them.

One by one they went down under a hail of blows that was enough to render them senseless, but not to chill them. There was more yet to come.

THE TERRAIN AROUND THE EDGE of Nagasaki was rough, making it hard on the suspension of the wags as they got into position. J.B.'s wag was one of those with the farthest distance to go as it had to scout 180 degrees until it was directly in line with the only track leading in and out of the ville.

The journey was hot and cramped as the sun rose high in the sky, heating the crowded wag. The jolting progress of the wag threw the crew against the walls and roof of the vehicle, causing them all to curse, putting them all in a foul mood.

It wasn't the best preparation for a firefight that J.B. had ever had, especially one in which he had to snatch his erstwhile companions from whatever fate had in store for them while protecting them from both sides. He looked around the wag at the other riders: Esquivel looked serene, shutting out everything around him in order to focus and concentrate on the fight ahead. J.B. had no doubts about Esquivel—he was a born fighter. Olly, on the other hand, had no shortage of courage— but had never been in a firefight like this before; the strain etched lines on his forehead and around the corners of his grim-set mouth. He shot J.B. a look and managed a brief nod of acknowledgment.

The young armorer might snap in the heat of battle. Much as it pained him to admit it, J.B. couldn't rely on him like he knew he could on Esquivel.

As for the other fighters in the wag, all the sec men

were dressed in their regulation uniform. They wore shades, which masked their eyes. They could be relaxed, or they could all be about to foul themselves in fear. There was no way of knowing.

The wag slowed to a halt and the driver cut the engine. He turned to J.B. "We're here," he said completely unnecessarily. He gestured out through the windshield. "Want to take a quick recce?" He looked at his wrist chron. "We've got eight minutes until the attack begins. Mebbe you could get a look at the land, see if you can work out where your people are. Mebbe we can't stop to hunt them out, but at least you could get yourself a notion."

J.B. nodded his thanks. It was a gesture he appreciated. The sec force had their job to do for Xander and he was part of that; but he had his own agenda that wasn't entirely incompatible.

Keeping an eye on his wrist chron, J.B. exited the wag and made his way toward the ridge that led down into the valley where Nagasaki lay. As he neared the edge, he dropped onto his haunches, and then his belly.

Hearing noises him, he turned to find Esquivel and Olly beside him.

"Think you're the only one wants to know where he's going, dude?"

"You don't have to do this," J.B. said simply.

"Yeah, but mebbe we want to," Olly replied.

"Anyway, you forgot these," Esquivel continued in the same friendly tone, handing J.B. a pair of binoculars. When the Armorer gave him a puzzled glance, Esquivel continued. "I knew the driver had them, and the stupe bastard wouldn't think of giving them to anyone unless he was told."

"I owe you one, Es," J.B. commented as he trained them on the ville below and ahead of them.

"'Course you do, skip—you might have to haul my golden-brown ass out of trouble down there," the sec man replied with a slow smile.

J.B. reckoned the distance from the ridge to the center of the ville to be less than a mile or so—enough for them to get across quickly, but also enough for plenty of people to be chilled in the time it took. The outer edges of the ville seemed deserted and it looked as though there had been a fire in the barn structure, as a pall of thick, black smoke hung over it, partly obscuring what lay beyond.

As J.B. penetrated the veil of smoke, he nearly choked on the sight that met him—it seemed that the entire ville was concentrated in one sector, a clearing just beyond the barn and in front of an old predark ranch house that seemed to be the centerpoint of Nagasaki. The crowd was restless and seemed to be listening to a fat man who marched up and down in front of them. Even without hearing him, J.B. could see that he was ranting and raving about something.

That something would be the five people hanging from a crossbeam that had been hastily erected. They all hung with their arms pulled up above their heads, tied by the wrists. The beam was one height, so Jak was dangling with his feet off the ground, while Ryan could keep his toes on the earth. The others were at points between. They were being kept alive for now.

J.B. checked his chron. Two minutes to the attack. The good thing was that they were still alive and that they were all in the same place. The bad thing was that it would make it all the easier for the Nagasaki inbreeds to chill them as soon as the attack began.

He filled in details for Esquivel and Olly as they returned to the wag, which was already firing up. They were no sooner back inside that the driver released the brake, and the wag squealed forward, leaving a cloud of dust in its wake.

It was twelve-fifteen.

THE BRANDING IRON HIT Mildred in the ribs. It was almost a playful blow, designed to hurt but not to cause any great damage. It didn't have to be hard; there was no way that she could avoid it, as her arms strung above her held her torso taut, gravity pulling her down.

She winced, tried to make no sound, but a small grunt escaped her as the air was driven from her lungs.

"Hey, y'all think I's could play a little tune on y'all if'n I's hit y'all like that?" Buckley cackled as he walked up and down the line of companions, striking at random to see what kind of noise each would make. Ryan and Jak stayed firm, swallowing the involuntary noise of pain and escaping air. Doc tried to hold his tongue, but his already weakened body wouldn't allow for his willpower and a groan was forced from him. Krysty muffled her cry, the blow for her being sharper, under the breast and specifically targeted to cause maximum pain with minimum damage. Buckley had a personal score to settle with her. On top of everything else, he hadn't forgotten that she hadn't screwed him when he wanted.

Buckley strutted up and down in front of the line. After overpowering the companions, the Nagasaki dwellers had hastily erected the framework to which the companions were now tied, stringing them up before they had a chance to recover consciousness. Each of the companions had been roused by the pain of their upper arms and shoulders, muscles and tendons straining to pop as they were stretched at an unnatural angle.

"Hope y'all are real comfortable," Buckley said as he reached the end of the line again, "as we's got a little something to talk to y'all about."

"Just get on with it, asshole," Ryan muttered.

Buckley glared at him, then walked up and spit in Ryan's eye. "Y'all show some respect, and mebbe y'all won't buy the farm too slow. But then again," he continued, stepping back, "mebbe y'all will, just for the fun of it."

The people gathered around the frame were yelling and screaming incomprehensibly, a sea of faces distorted by rage and lust, drooling and grinning at the thought of what they were about to do. Buckley held up his hands for silence and gradually they subsided.

"Now I's a fair man, as y'all know, and I's say we give these shit heaps a fair trial." The noise rose again as the crowd either agreed or disagreed, it was impossible to know which. Buckley quieted them again before continuing. "Question is, did these fuckers sell us out by telling the Duma scum we's was coming? Hard to know how, 'cept for one thing…who let our little prisoner go? Was it any of y'all?"

The crowd howled. Once they had discovered that the prisoner in the barn was gone, it had been obvious to them that one of the companions had released him.

Buckley held up his hands to silence them. "Yeah,

yeah, I know. It don't need no other saying than that. They's let the prisoner go, they's screwed up our raid and got some of us chilled. They's guilty as charged. I say the penalty for such an offense is capital. They's buy the farm by being pounded on and having their guts spilled on the ground, their bowels laid out in front of 'em. Nice 'n' slow. But first we'll have ourselves some fun, right?"

The crowd roared its approval. Doc muttered to himself, recognizing the language Buckley was using as some obscene paraphrasing of legal terms that had been prevalent in predark times. To hear such words again, even in such a bizarre context, was strange. But then again, it was strange that it would seem his life was finally to end as the plaything of a bunch of drooling cretins.

Buckley cackled wildly and took a step toward them, pulling out a metal pipe with which to begin the beatings. With a roar of approval the mob picked up cudgels, sticks and blades. And then the torture began.

"OUT, OUT, OUT—GET AN M-203 on that, now!" J.B. yelled as the wag ground to a halt. It had swept easily down the valley and into the rear of the ville, careening into shacks and sending them flying into splinters of wood and glass, carving a path through the Spartan back of Nagasaki. There was no opposition as everyone was gathered in the square by the ranch house, only a few mules and goats remained.

"What if there's anyone in there?" Esquivel yelled above the noise.

"It ain't who I'm after and fuck the rest of this scum," J.B. returned.

The sec man shrugged. Their orders were to level the ville, and the only people he would look to rescue were those his friend was looking for. He stepped aside as a heavyset sec man carrying an M-16/M-203 combo dismounted and took up a firing stance on one knee, loading a gren into the bottom rack of the blaster.

"Make it two, take the bastard out quick. Fire, then cover," J.B. added, slapping another sec man with a combo on the back, directing him to join his comrade.

The two men exchanged glances and synchronized their firing. The two grens left the launcher, carving a path through the air before shattering into the reinforced rear of the barn, exploding on impact. The force of the blast rent the air and ripped the wooden structure apart, shards of the metal sheeting used to reinforce the walls flying in all directions, joined by sharp splinters the size of a man's forearm. The sec men, J.B., and the rest of the wag crew hit the ground, feeling the force of the blast wash over them, the debris hit the ground, the earth rumble.

Looking up, the Armorer could see that barn had almost disintegrated, the front and back ripped apart by the blast, remnants of the side walls still standing. The wood, covered in pitch, was burning steadily, adding to the pall of smoke from both the blast and the earlier fire. Now, with this obstacle removed, and the knowledge that it had contained no threat, the men felt ready to move on.

The way for the wag would be indirect because of the moat around the area where the barn had—until recently—stood. J.B. gestured to the sec men, dividing them into two parties.

"Take the track each side, keep frosty, triple red. They all look like they're in the center, but don't be taken by surprise. And watch for your own. It's gonna get hard to see who's who in there."

The wag crew did as ordered and J.B. set off with one-half, joined by Olly and Esquivel. They took the track to the left of the barn, leaving the wag driver to guard his vehicle, moving on the double, blasters ready for action.

Around the edges of the ville, it was eerily deserted, contrasting with the sounds of a firefight up ahead. The other wags had been able to penetrate to the heart of the ville and had discharged their crews, who were now engaging with the Nagasaki dwellers. The air was filled with the sound of automatic and SMG blasterfire, mingling with the screams of the injured and chilled.

"Man, I'll be glad to see some action," Esquivel murmured. "This shit is making me jumpy."

"Well keep your finger away from the bastard trigger while you're right behind me," J.B. threw back at him.

As far as he could tell, the sec detail on the other side of the old barn was also making unhindered progress. There was no blasterfire that he could pinpoint from that area, but the smoking wreck of the barn made it impossible to see across the gap.

The track was leading round to the front of the shattered building and the square that lay beyond. J.B., taking the front, held up a hand to halt his crew.

"Take it easy, guys—we're entering the battle zone," he yelled, unable to completely take in the sight that confronted him. J.B. had seen many a firefight in his time, but nothing quite like this.

ON CUE, THE WAGS HAD ROARED in from their positions
on the ridge of the valley, speeding down and into the
ville. The wag taking the only track in had the quickest
route and had squealed to a halt at the head of the
square. The mob of gaping, slack-jawed inbreds was
still focused on the five prisoners they had strung up in
front of them, unable in their bloodlust to comprehend
quite what was happening.

So they were easy meat for the first wave of blasterfire as the wag discharged its crew, who came out firing.

At the same time, the other wags slid down the sides
of the valley and careered into the shacks, sending
pieces of glass and wood in all directions. The wag
drivers kept their engines gunning and blasted through
any obstructions. The only buildings that were too
sturdy to be mowed down were the ranch house and the
original outbuildings that were being used by some of
the Nagasaki dwellers as housing. These the wags
skirted, taking the dirt paths around them and carving
a way through the shacks on either side.

Their arrival, therefore, was staggered by a matter of
minutes. This worked to their advantage as each crew
discharged from a wag had clear shots at the backs of
the ville dwellers, who were disorganized and unprepared for the attack.

But the sec men from Duma made two mistakes.
First, they broke ranks and started to close in on the
crowd, putting themselves in the line of their compatriots' fire. Secondly, they underestimated the threshold
the inbreds had for pain and stubbornness. Fired up by
beating their captives, and used to lives of pain and
injury, the Nagasaki dwellers were almost immune to

the blasterfire that rained in on them. Unless it hit hard enough to chill them straight away, they were able to remain upright and to fight back.

The sec men moving among them now made it impossible for the sec force on the margins to fire at will on the inbreds. They had to pick their shots with greater care and accuracy, and this gave the ville dwellers a chance to regroup and counterattack.

The companions were only dimly aware of what was going on when the attack first hit. In their shared universe of pain, the only thing they knew was the pain had suddenly ceased, that fewer blows were landing, that fewer blades were cutting and that there was an increase in the noise and activity around them. None was in any state to take in what exactly was happening.

It was when the blasterfire stared to chatter around them that the companions realized something major was happening. The problem was how to avoid being hit when you were trussed and hanging in one spot, unable to take cover of any kind.

Doc was almost totally out of the picture, nearly unconscious. But the other four were able to rouse themselves by effort of will. Muscles refused to respond and movement was sluggish, but as they opened their eyes they were all able to take in what was happening around them, and to recognize the sec men moving among the crowd by their uniforms.

Not that it was doing the sec men much good. Buckley yelled incomprehensibly, his guttural voice cutting through the noise. The chief's rallying call had an immediate effect. His people carried blasters as well as blades and it took them a matter of moments to move into a position where they could fight back. Ignoring the blasterfire that rippled all around them, they swarmed over the oncoming sec force, engaging them in hand-to-hand combat as well as exchanging blasterfire.

The Duma sec force was unprepared for that and as they attempted to use their longblasters at close range, the Nagasaki fighters brought their blades into play, slashing at their opponents, and using their handblasters to fire into the bodies of the oncoming sec men.

Suddenly, what seemed like a simple operation was becoming something they were in danger of losing.

"Dark night, what a bastard mess," J.B. breathed as he took in the scene. He also scanned the crowd for the frame from which the companions were hanging. It was nowhere to be seen.

A blast of SMG fire had splintered the cross-piece of the frame, causing it to give way under the combined weight of the companions. Severing toward one end, it had crashed down, pitching Doc and Krysty—the two nearest the break—to the ground. The others also fell, their wrists sliding down the pole until they were tangled in a heap.

Ryan and Jak were the most alert, but the albino could hardly move his arms from the strain on his shoulders. Although he could feel some circulation come back, he was still too stiff to move. Ryan, whose feet had touched the ground, had been luckier, and his shoulders were still relatively mobile. He passed his wrists over any obstruction until his hands were free, albeit tied. Ignoring the carnage around him—if he was hit, there was nothing he could do about it—he concentrated on the task in hand. As he had hit the dirt, he had felt the sharpened nails beneath him, trampled into the dust. They had fallen from their concealed hiding place in each companion's clothes as they were strung up.

Ryan scrabbled in the dust with nerveless, bloodless fingers, trying to get a grip on at least one of the nails. He managed to keep hold of a few, and worked at the rope tying his wrists, working the sharpened nails between the hemp strands. Mildred could see what he was doing and joined him, grabbing at the scattered nails to begin on her own wrists, ignoring the pain as the movement of one hand caused the rope to bite harder into the wrist of the other. Krysty was also able to begin, but Doc was too far gone to notice what was happening and Jak was still struggling to move his painfully locked arms and shoulders.

Over at the edge of the clearing, now a heaving mass of hand-to-hand combat, J.B. looked frantically for any sign of his friends.

"Dude, they may have put them in there," Esquivel said, indicating the ranch house. "You and Olly go and scout it out."

"What about you?" J.B. asked.

The sec man looked at the carnage before him and at the wag crew behind. "I figure it's about time some of these stupes found out what combat is really about. I'm gonna try and get them organized and haul some stupe asses outta there," he said grimly, indicating the mass before them.

J.B. nodded. "We'll recce the house, then join you."

While Olly and J.B. sprinted toward the ranch house, Esquivel turned to his troops and ordered them into formation. His plan was simple. The wag crew would work around the perimeter of the mass, picking off Nagasaki fighters and dragging Duma sec from the periphery before relaying the same orders to them. Slowly, they would tighten the noose around the remaining Nagasaki fighters, drawing them into a circle where they could all be wiped out. It would be a slow, stubborn action, but it was the only controlled way that the sec man could think of to try and get his people on top of the situation.

The ranch house was eerily quiet when Olly and J.B. gained access. The thick walls cut down on the sound from outside, making the conflict seem a thousand miles away.

"Fuck, what kind of shit do these fuckers live in," Olly exclaimed, wrinkling his nose at the stench and filth.

"Their own," J.B. muttered shortly. "I'll take down here—you take the upper level. Be careful. I think they're all outside, but we don't know."

Olly took the stairs, the Weatherby unslung and ready to fire at anything that got in his way. He was quick, but cautious. J.B. allowed himself a brief smile at the way the young man had adapted to battle.

Taking the downstairs room, he could see that all of them were empty. He came to the locked room where the archive of the ville's history lined the walls. Kicking down the door and throwing himself back against the wall to one side, expecting an attack, he found nothing. Cautiously, he entered the room and stopped dead when he saw the walls covered with photographs of rad victims.

"Explains a lot," he said out loud, although his mind raced at the thought that his friends had been in the hands of these perverted scum. He was about to leave the room when he heard a shout from Olly.

"J.B., here," the young man yelled.

J.B. left the room and raced to the stairs, taking them two at a time. Olly's tone had been free of danger and caution; rather, he had been excited about a find.

The Armorer stopped dead as he entered the room. There was a collection of blasters and blades and a med satchel in one corner, and beside them a patched and metal-covered camo jacket and a bearskin coat that he recognized all too well.

"But—" he began.

Olly cut him short, starting to gather the ordnance to stash it on his person. He handed the satchel, coat and jacket to J.B. "I know it ain't them, but at least we got their weapons. And at least we know where they are."

J.B. looked out of the window. Down there, without any weapons....

"C'mon, man, let's get to it," Olly said, clapping him on the shoulder. His belief was infectious.

Shrugging, J.B. joined Olly.

Below, Esquivel's tactic was beginning to take effect. There had been Duma casualties in combat, but the sec force was gradually separating from the Nagasaki fighters, driving them back into a tighter and tighter circle.

The only problem was that the companions were in the center. Ryan and Krysty had freed themselves, and while Mildred cut loose Doc and helped Jak, who was still having trouble with his shoulders, the two of them were working at keeping the Nagasaki fighters at bay. They had nothing except their bare hands and a few nails to use, but they were holding on. Mildred and Jak had helped Doc onto his feet, although the old man was raving and had no idea where he was.

Both Ryan and Krysty had guessed the Duma tactics, and knew this left them in the middle of a hail of fire. How the hell could they get out?

J.B. and Olly were thinking much the same thing as they raced from the ranch house, searching for Esquivel. The sec man had assumed control and under his guidance the sec force had the upper hand. He was about to give the order to open rapid fire on the knot of Nagasaki fighters, satisfied with their position, when Buckley's voice boomed out, staying both Esquivel and J.B., as well as quietening the mob.

"Y'all wouldn't want to chill those who helped y'all, would you?"

Esquivel stayed the firing, and gestured to J.B. to stay silent. "Explain yourself," he rapped out.

"You knows like we's does that y'all found out on our raid 'cause you was told by snakes among us—outlanders."

"So?"

"So I's got 'em here and I's a fair man. Y'all let us go and we'll hand 'em over. Y'all take 'em and go, leave us in peace. We's let you go. Honest." Buckley was now raving, desperately trying to save his own skin if not those of his people.

"Why should I believe you?" Esquivel asked calmly.

"'Cause we's got everything to lose, y'all got nothing," Buckley shrugged.

"What makes you think I even want them?" Esquivel returned, ignoring the look he knew J.B. was giving him.

"Mebbe y'all don't, but I's got nothing else to offer," Buckley replied.

There was a moment's tense silence before Esquivel assented. "Send them out," he said.

The companions found themselves manhandled by the remains of the Nagasaki fighters, sly punches peppering them as they were shoved through the crowd and, one by one, thrown out in front of the Duma sec force, sprawling dazed and confused over the corpses that littered the blood-soaked earth.

Ryan looked up and caught sight of the Armorer. "J.B.?" he whispered, unable to believe what he saw.

Esquivel raised his arm and as he was about to bring it down, Buckley—knowing that he had been betrayed—yelled, "Y'all said you'd let us go."

"I lied." Esquivel shrugged, then lowered his arm.

A hail of blasterfire rained on the Nagasaki crowd as they struggled to flee. They fought against one another, each trying to run in a different direction. But there was nowhere to run.

The echoing noise of the blasterfire, and J.B. running, crouched low, toward him, was the last thing Ryan registered before he blacked out once more.

Chapter Sixteen

"Let's level this pesthole," Esquivel murmured with a look of extreme distaste as he surveyed the pile of corpses in front of him. "Let's burn everything so there's no trace of it ever having been here to blight the land."

"Noble words for someone who's just chilled an entire ville," Olly remarked mildly.

Esquivel turned on him. "Don't think I enjoyed it and don't think it was easy, dude. Don't ever think it's easy. But think about that poor stupe bastard that Malloy ran into. Think about them—" he gestured toward the companions, now being carried by J.B. and a group of sec men toward one of the wags "—and think about how many other poor fuckers have ended up like that. Or worse."

Olly shook his head. "Yeah, I guess—"

"We just do what we have to," Esquivel said dismissively before turning his attention to the men gathered around the corpses.

While the young armorer turned and made his way over to J.B., Esquivel had directed the sec force to hunt down all the tallow candles and oil that they could find, as well as the grens and plas ex that was in the Nagasaki armory. Paltry as it was, it would be enough for the task. Pillaging the armory and the corpses for any blasters that may be of use when stripped and cleaned, Esquivel had the pile of extinct flesh covered in oil and mined with grens.

Then, taking the time to ensure his men did the job properly, Esquivel sent them out along the narrow tracks that ran through the shantytown, pouring oil and tallow on the dirt and the wrecked shacks, distributing fused plas ex along the way and using some of the ville's own grens to mine areas where there were still shacks standing after the wag invasion.

The sec men worked until the entire area was a maze of oil, plas ex and grens. The ranch house was mined and the fuses set.

"This needs a finishing touch—just to cleanse the earth," Esquivel muttered. He ran over to the wag where J.B. and Olly were with the companions. Krysty and Jak were semiconscious but unaware of their surroundings. Ryan and Mildred were still out cold. Doc was conscious now, raving. The old man seemed to believe he was back in his youth, about to take a brougham ride with his beloved Emily.

Esquivel could read the concern on J.B.'s face, but still felt it necessary to pull him away. They exchanged a few words and the Armorer handed over two small canisters from his canvas bag.

Esquivel allowed himself a small grin. This would clean up the place more than a little. He bellowed orders for the sec force to withdraw to the ridge overlooking the shallow valley. Returning to their wags, they began to retreat.

They had five minutes to get clear, ample time if they moved on the double. Esquivel joined J.B. and Olly with the companions in the wag that took the dirt track leading in and out of the ville. The sec men who had traveled in it were allotted to other wags. It would mean an extra man per wag and an uncomfortable journey home, but the companions needed some space for their ride to Duma.

For the Duma sec team, it was a job well done. Which was just about to be finished. The wag retreated to the ridge and came to a halt. Esquivel studied his wrist chron, counting off the remaining minutes. When the five minutes elapsed, it would be half-past one. The mission would be initiated and completed in only an hour and a quarter. Hammick would be pleased at the efficiency—if he was still around when they got back. Esquivel knew he had overstepped the mark by taking charge, but there was nothing else that could have been done in the circumstances.

He wondered how Xander would feel about that. Then he looked at J.B. and Olly, tending to the five captives they had rescued, and figured that getting the legendary one-eyed man out of trouble would keep him out of jail.

The second hand ticked around again.

"If they ain't out now, they never will be," Esquivel murmured to himself as he dismounted from the wag. He walked to the edge of the ridge. The valley formed a shallow pan and the ville lay in the center. It was too far for him to throw the canisters, so he improvised a slingshot from the sleeve of his shirt, which he ripped off without a thought.

"Hope I still got the eye for it," he murmured, remembering a childhood spent chilling small mammals for food.

He loaded up the first canister and let it fly. It took a high, looping trajectory into the air, landing on the edge of the ville. It landed with a thump, nothing happening.

"Nukeshit, this was supposed to be easy," he muttered.

"Would be if you got it right," the Armorer said laconically, appearing at Esquivel's elbow. He was holding Olly's Weatherby. The blaster was a good long-range hunting rifle, and Esquivel understood immediately what J.B. intended. With the briefest of nods he wound up for another throw, launching the canister high into the air, looping out over the ville.

J.B. sighted the Weatherby and fired once. The canister exploded into a ball of liquid fire that spread out over a vast distance, falling to earth and raining flame on the wreckage beneath.

The flames ignited the oil beneath, spreading trails of fire across the ville. The fuses on the plas ex and grens caught and chains of explosions gouged the earth where the ville of Nagasaki once stood. The canister on the edge of the ville exploded as the fires reached it, gouts of liquid fire flying up into the air and coming down to ignite scrub and brush around.

The fires and explosions leveled what was left of the ranch house and the barn, eradicating all trace of the shacks, a pall of thick, dark smoke marking the point where the corpses burned.

"Always knew that napalm would be useful," J.B. remarked as he and Esquivel stood watching the destruction. They only realized how long they had been standing there when the other wags, moving from their positions around the ridge to form up a convoy for the trip back to Duma, hove into view.

"C'mon, man, let's get home," Esquivel said, clapping J.B. on the shoulder before stopping to shake his head. "Man, that's first time I've ever called it that."

IT TOOK SEVERAL DAYS for the companions to be restored to a reasonable state of health. The cuts inflicted by the Nagasaki dwellers had become infected and Doc was still suffering from shock and trauma from the blaster wounds that had been inflicted in the redoubt. Jak's left shoulder had been badly dislocated and for the first two days they were in Duma it kept popping out again, much to his frustration.

But rest, a warm environment and food and water contributed much to their recovery. The main shock was in seeing J.B. again. They had all resigned themselves to his demise and it took Doc a while to trust his own senses. After his injuries and trauma, he feared that he was hallucinating when he saw his old friend.

For his part, J.B. saw them only briefly over the period. It put him in a difficult position. For most of the time he had been in Duma he had been a man without a past and his life as he knew it had been based around settling into this ville and becoming a part of it. There were a lot of things about Duma that he didn't like, and despite the manner in which he had been greeted by the baron—because of his past, the one he knew nothing of—he found that he didn't trust Xander at all. For all its wealth, Duma was a harsh place, where everyone walked a tightrope every day of their lives.

At the same time, the memories that had come flooding back to him when he saw Ryan didn't, in some ways, seem real. They felt like stories that had been told to him. He felt that he had to accept them as his past, yet he didn't really believe them. Being in the same room as the five people he had spent so long traveling with seemed bizarre: they were people who risked their lives for each other so many times, yet he didn't feel he was one of them. But he was…

On the surface, J.B. went about his business in the armory, and fended off Xander's questions. The baron still trusted Grant, albeit with qualification after the debacle of the ambush, and the healer advised that they be allowed to rest before the baron questioned them. J.B. had his own ideas on why that should be and knew that it may prove dangerous if Xander persuaded them to stay.

Meanwhile, Budd had accepted him and working in the armory was better than before. Olly was keen to learn and Esquivel was no longer his permanent shadow. But all that did was give him no one he could really talk to…except maybe for Ella-Mae.

The mechanic hadn't forgiven him for laying her out before the raid on Nagasaki, and had been steering clear of him. But he tracked her down and tried to explain the position he now found himself in.

"And you trust me?" she queried, ordering another glass of Icepick's potent spirit.

"Have to trust someone," J.B. replied.

"That'll have to do, I guess. I'm surprised it's me, though. Why not Es?"

"I haven't seen much of him since he was taken off my back." J.B. shrugged.

Ella-Mae smiled. "Nah, he's too busy right now. Word has it that he's gonna replace Hammick."

"He never said anything about it," J.B. mused.

"He wouldn't. Es knows when it's time to keep his mouth shut. Word is that he did a good job cleaning out that shithole inbred ville. But he's not Grant's man and Hammick was. Grant and Xander have always been like this," she elaborated, crossing her fingers for emphasis, "mostly because of Xander's father trusting him. But now Es has made a reputation and your friend Ryan—who Xander's been banging on about for quite a while—is in the frame, then life could be hard for Grant. And he still has friends, if you know what I mean."

She paused, then took J.B.'s hand and made him look directly at her. "Look, you know how I feel, but that's not the reason I'm gonna say this. I reckon you should get the hell out of here. If it turns out Xander wants the one-eyed man to head up sec, then Es won't be too bothered, but Grant will. And that could mean some kind of war you'll end up in. Face it, you don't like this place and the last thing you want is a stupe battle when there are real ones to face."

"Anyone would think you want to get rid of me," J.B. said quietly.

"You know that ain't it, babe, but mebbe it would be best for everyone."

J.B. shrugged. "Can't say it hadn't occurred to me. But how can we do it without Xander raising hell?"

"Leave that to me. I haven't lived here all my life and kept living without learning something."

XANDER FINALLY GOT TO SEE the companions on the fourth day after the attack. He pumped them for all they knew about Trader and all that had happened to Ryan and J.B. since their days in War Wag One. Ryan was puzzled by Xander's curiosity and it was only after the baron explained why J.B. had been unable to tell him anything that the companions started to see why J.B. had seemed so strange when he had seen them.

Ryan fed the baron the stories he wanted to hear.

"I heard something a while back," Xander said, "some people have claimed to have seen Trader. He doesn't operate in the same way anymore—it's like he's on some kind of quest, I guess—but I wouldn't be surprised if he was still around."

Then, before Ryan had a chance to assimilate this information, Xander sprung something else on him.

"I've already got J.B. working in the armory and I've got a vacancy for a chief of sec. There's a good man who could do it, but if I had you, Ryan Cawdor, the man who traveled shotgun with the legendary Trader… To have both you and J.B. on the team would make me invincible. In fact, it's just what I need. Think about it."

Xander rose to leave. There was something about the way he said it that suggested it was a nonnegotiable request. That could be a big problem—as could be other people in the ville. Ryan didn't know who the other man in the running might be, but he sure as hell noticed the looks they all got from the limping healer as he left with the baron.

J.B. WAS WORKING IN THE BLASTER store at the armory, cleaning out the M-16/M-203 combos that been used in the raid, when Ella-Mae walked in.

"How did you just get past the sec like that—" J.B.

began, but stopped when he noticed that Grant was limping behind her. With the shadowy presence of the ex-sec man, anything was possible.

"Grant's got something to say," Ella-Mae began, "about what we were talking about the other night."

"It's safe to talk," J.B. told them. "Olly and Budd are going through the ordnance we pulled in from that shit hole a few days back. That'll keep 'em busy."

Grant nodded with satisfaction and walked over to J.B. "I won't screw with you. You know I was never happy with you here and you must have realized I'd be less than happy with the rest of you hanging around."

"Xander wants Ryan to replace Hammick, right?" When Grant assented, J.B. continued. "That doesn't suit you. But what about Es? He'll be the replacement."

"Not perfect, but at least I know him…and he won't have the baron's ear," Grant explained.

"So you'd like to see us go—" J.B. looked at Ella-Mae "—and you know we want to go, right?"

Grant agreed. "Be ready tonight. Best to move quickly, before whispers spread or people change their minds."

Without another word, the healer turned and limped away, leaving Ella-Mae alone with the Armorer.

"It's quick," he said simply.

"Mebbe it's better that way." She shrugged, looking J.B. in the eye. "Be at the healing room at eleven. Duma's never quiet, but if we move, then we can slip past the sec rota changeover."

"I didn't know you knew that much about it," J.B. murmured.

"It's Grant's plan. I wouldn't trust him at any other time, but he wants you gone without fuss. He wouldn't dare fuck with you because of Xander. So I guess we can trust him now."

She left the room without waiting for a reply, leaving him wondering about the word *we*.

J.B. SAID LITTLE DURING the evening meal, and made an excuse to go to his room. He packed quickly and let his bag out the window, allowing it to drop to the soft earth beneath. A noise in the doorway made him turn. Olly was standing in the doorway, watching.

"What's going on?" he asked simply.

"I'm leaving tonight. We all are. It's got to be this way." His hand crept toward the sheathed Tekna. He didn't want to use force, but if Olly got in the way, he'd have little option.

Olly noticed the move. "You really think that's necessary? I'm gonna miss you, but I wouldn't stop you going. You don't belong here and you don't want to. I won't say anything."

J.B. nodded. "I'm glad. For whatever it might matter, you'll be as good an armorer here as I ever would have been. And although I think a lot of this ville is dangerous, there are a few good people—"

"I know who they are," Olly interrupted. "Now go."

He stood aside in the doorway. J.B. looked back when he was at the bottom of the stairs. Olly was watching him. J.B. touched the brim of his fedora, then left without looking back.

Retrieving his bag, he made his way to the healing room, where he found Ella-Mae and Grant waiting. The healer had sent the sec guard away and there were no other staff.

"Won't Xander get suspicious that we escaped when you'd sent everyone away?" J.B. asked.

"I can handle him—I have been since he was a boy." Grant shrugged. "Have I bought the farm yet?"

They went into the room where the companions were staying. Although they were glad to see J.B., they were wary of what was going on. Quickly, the Armorer explained the situation. Given Ryan's reading of Grant's reaction the day before, things made perfect sense.

"Heavens, a reunion would be emotional enough, without this added circumstance," Doc mused.

"Talk later, move now," Jak rapped at the old man.

"Pithy and succinct—and, as always, quite correct," Doc countered.

Their ordnance restored by Grant, the companions—now including J.B.—followed Grant and Ella-Mae to the rear of the building, where a wag was waiting. Somehow, J.B. wasn't surprised to see Esquivel at the wheel.

"Should you be risking your neck right now?" J.B. asked.

"Shit, dude, every day's a risk of my neck." Esquivel grinned at his friend. "Besides, if I do this, then Grant thinks he has something on me, which means he'll be easy about me taking the sec chief post. You have to think everything around three thousand times to make sense here, right? Think I'm getting used to it."

The companions mounted the wag and Ella-Mae went to follow.

"Where d'you think you're going?" J.B. asked, bewildered.

"See you away safe. Don't hit me again," she answered.

J.B. caught Mildred's quizzical eye, but said nothing.

Esquivel fired up the wag and left Grant standing, impassive, watching them go.

"Where are we actually headed?" Doc asked as they hit the blacktop that bisected the ville.

"Gonna ask you that myself, dude," Esquivel replied. "Wherever you want, you got—within reason."

J.B. knew the direction they needed to go in order to get back to the redoubt. With the secret of the lost base gone with the community of Nagasaki, all they had to do was make sure that they were left within a few hours' walk and not followed. He instructed the sec man, who seemed bemused at driving off-road and seemingly into the middle of the desert, but trusted the man he had come to think of as a friend.

Getting past the sec posts was easy. With Esquivel at the wheel and with the changeover in sec guard at the outlying post, it took just a few words to get them past and into the desert beyond.

They traveled for the most part in silence—the companions unwilling to give too much away in front of strangers; Esquivel concentrated on the road ahead; Ella-Mae didn't know what to say. It was a relief when J.B. directed Esquivel to turn off the road and head across the wasteland.

They had been driving for three hours when J.B. halted the wag. He stepped out, looked at the clear sky and took his bearing by the stars.

It was the right place.

"Everyone out," he said simply.

"Where the fuck are we?" Esquivel said as he and Ella-Mae joined the companions. "Dude, this is nowhere."

J.B. smiled. "Yeah, but even nowhere leads somewhere. You'll just have to trust me that we're not wandering blind…not that you're going to know. This is as far as you go."

Esquivel grabbed J.B. before he had a chance to object and, despite the sec man's wiry frame, he engaged J.B. in an embrace that the Armorer thought would pop his ribs. "Dude, you go and have a blast."

"I will. You, too," J.B. replied, knowing that he would probably never see this man again, and yet— despite the shared history he had with the others, but because of the memory loss—he was probably the closest friend he'd ever known.

Ella-Mae found it hard to say goodbye. She couldn't look at the Armorer as she spoke. "You stay out of shit, yeah? 'Cause me and him won't be there to bail you out," she said, gesturing to Esquivel.

"But especially you," J.B. said gently. "Now go."

The companions watched while Esquivel and Ella-Mae got into the wag. The sec man turned it around and headed back toward the road. He didn't wait to follow or see where they headed. He just drove.

The rear lights vanished into the dark, the black shape of the wag absorbed by the larger darkness of the wasteland.

When it had finally disappeared, they turned to head toward the redoubt. They had a few more hours of darkness, then the searing sun would rise again. There was little of anything left in the redoubt, but mebbe they could rest and shower before using the mat-trans.

As they marched, J.B. at point, Mildred broke rank to walk by him.

"So what was with the woman, John? Something I should know about?" she teased.

"No, Millie. Just a passing friend. I'll tell you the whole story sometime soon."

JAMES AXLER

Sunspot

The land around the Rio Grande reaches the breaking point in a bitter war with an old enemy whose secret stockpile of twenty-first-century nerve gas is poised to unleash infinite madness once more upon a ravaged earth. Can Ryan save the ville from the potential destruction?

__Available in December wherever books are sold.__

AleX Archer
WARRIOR SPIRIT

A priceless artifact could restore a family's honor—
or destroy everything in its wake.

Annja must trek through fog-enshrouded
mountains in Japan to find the varjra, a mystically
endowed relic that can
aid the forces of good
or evil. Encountering the
vicious Yakuza and ninja,
who are dangerously
close to uncovering the
relic first, puts everything
at risk, including Annja.

**Available
November
wherever you
buy books.**

GRA9